Return to Sullivans Island

DOROTHEA BENTON FRANK

Return to Sullivans Island

**Doubleday Large Print
Home Library Edition**

wm

WILLIAM MORROW

An Imprint of HarperCollins*Publishers*

**This Large Print Book carries the
Seal of Approval of N.A.V.H.**

For everyone on Sullivans Island,
past, present, and future

CONTENTS

1

Beth

Maggiepie2@marthagene.net
Susan, I'm arriving exactly a week before Beth and can't wait to see you. Itching to get in my kitchen and cook! Please stock up and kick the bugs out of my bed! Maggie xx

Susanthepen@writenow.org
Maggie, Your kitchen? Which 50% do you mean? Change your own sheets. Susan

Maggiepie2@marthagene.net
Somebody needs estrogen! C u soon! xx

Her plane circled the Lowcountry. Acres upon acres of live oaks stood beneath them, guardians festooned in sheets of breezy Spanish moss. They passed over the powerful waters of the Wando, Cooper, and Ashley Rivers and hundreds of tiny rippling tributaries that sluiced their way in tendrils toward the Atlantic Ocean. It was so beautiful. The shimmering blue water seemed to be scattered with shards of crystals and diamonds. Beth's heart tightened. Every last passenger stared out through their windows at the landscape below. Whether you were away from the Lowcountry for a week or for years, it was impossible to remember how gorgeous it was. It never changed and everyone depended on that. Seeing it again was like seeing it for the first time—hypnotic.

The small jet finally touched down on the steaming tarmac at Charleston's airport, and after a few braking lurches it rolled to a stop at the terminal. When the flight attendant opened the cabin door humidity poured in, blanketing the cabin in a great whoosh like an invisible gas. The air was heavy, weighted by the stench of jet fuel diluted with salt.

"Hold on, baby."

Beth's miniature Yorkshire terrier Lola seemed to understand everything she said. If she spoke to her in Swahili she would look at her with those licorice eyes of hers, raise her eyebrows, and smile. Yes, her dog smiled, but not just then. Lola whimpered and began to squirm. Beth stretched her finger through the netting of her dog's carrier to console her with a tiny massage. All five pounds of Lola settled against her as they slowly made their way with the restless passengers across the muggy Jetway and into the sorrowful, weak air-conditioning of the terminal. She hoped Lola wasn't going to start wheezing. Could a mother love a child more than Beth Hayes loved her dog? She doubted it.

The climate had changed over the years. Global warming was obvious, and in Charleston the weather was practically tropical. Beth had decided that it was too uncomfortable to consider anything except escape into the jungle or a total surrender to the ruling party.

Beth had chosen surrender, and was there to begin serving her one-year sentence in the Lowcountry, house-sitting the family's grande dame on Sullivans Island. The Island Gamble. The family's château stood in defiance of her age and history and she reigned over them like Elizabeth

I, the Virgin Queen. Beth could not envision England's history without Elizabeth I any more than she could dream of Sullivans Island without that particular house as center stage for the disjointed hauntings of her sleeping hours. All of her dreams were acted out on Sullivans Island and at the Island Gamble. In the rooms. On the porch. In the yard looking back. Always, always there.

They used the term *château* loosely, even jokingly, but during the days and nights of their lives the Island Gamble was where any and everything of significance for generations had been told around her tables or had been revealed in the confessional of her front porch. Lives were dissected and discussed deep into the night until aunts, uncles, and especially children, exhausted from the heat and laughter, nodded off in their rockers or hammocks. Their aspirations, broken hearts, and victories were all recorded for posterity in the family's collective memory, the details rearranged and embellished as time went on to make for better storytelling. The house knew everything about them, and being there made them believe that they were safe from the outside world. In their case, telling family tales was what they seemed to do best. They would laugh and say that if there had been an Olympic event for working a jaw, the walls of the Island Gamble would have buckled from the burden of gold medals. Truly, the family was a very sentimental lot, and their point of view was that the ability to poke fun at their own foibles was what saved them from despair on many a day.

That's how it was. The aging, sometimes shaking ramparts of the Hamilton fortress were stockpiled with invisible weapons of *Remember when . . . We never . . .* and *We always . . .* as though they existed in their own great saline bubble, with a sacred family crest to live up to.

Sometimes the family wore Beth out with what she saw as excessive self-importance and righteousness. One day her aunts, uncles, and cousins would all be the stuffings of novels, even memoirs perhaps, if she could find the courage to put it all on paper. But not just yet. Today Beth was on another mission. The Dutiful Daughter was back.

Beth gathered her luggage, walked Lola

on the grassy median outside, and found a place in the short taxi line. Part of her was excited and the other part was simply miserable. She loved Sullivans Island because it was her personal time warp. Even though it was 2009, when you were there you could almost believe that Eisenhower was still in office, even though that was well before her time. But in her heart she felt the island really belonged to her mother's generation and those before her. The last four years had prepared her to live her own life, independent of her tribe. Isn't that why she went to college a thousand miles away in the first place? Further, this *assignment,* decided upon with the cavalier flick of her mother's and aunt's royal wrists, blocked her from pursuing her own dream but enabled her mother to live hers. It wasn't a fair trade but she wasn't exactly given an option. If asked, she would say dryly, "My mom and my Aunt Maggie could benefit from even one session of sensitivity training. Seriously."

She climbed in the next available rattletrap and soon she was on her way. At least she had Lola to console her.

"Could you turn up the air-conditioning,

please?" she asked. Beth's upper lip was covered in little beads of moisture and the roots of her hair were damp.

"Sure," the driver said. "Today's a hot one, 'eah?"

"Yep. It sure is."

The old van complained with each pothole and strained against the slightest rise in the road. Its ancient driver, an old man whose white hair was as thick and coarse as a broom, was crouched over the steering wheel. The intensity of his focus on the road was nerve-racking. He drove like a lumbering walrus in the middle lane as hundreds of cars zoomed by them. She actually considered offering to drive, thinking she preferred death by her own hand.

Memorabilia was strung across the old man's dashboard, photographs attached with bits of curling tape and lopsided magnets from Niagara Falls and, in Beth's opinion, other painfully boring vacation spots. Judging from their faded condition, the people in those pictures, his children she guessed, were grown and had been gone from his home for a long time. His taxi license read *Mr. George Brown*. He sighed loudly and cleared his throat as the van's transmission struggled and jerked with each changing gear. She wondered if they would ever reach the causeway. Mr. Brown did not know that he was delivering her, her little dog, two large suitcases and a duffel bag bulging with university memories, soggy farewells, and a poor attitude to one very bittersweet destination.

"You want to take 526 or the new bridge?"

"Whatever you think," she said.

She had told her mother, Susan, that she would take a cab from the airport to the beach. She was in no hurry to see anyone. Besides, she had just seen her mother and family at graduation a month ago, so the usual sense of urgency she felt to be with her, the excitement of those initial moments of grabbing each other's eyes, had been satisfied. She was home before the longing could begin again. As all mothers do, Susan frequently drove her daughter to the edge of what she could endure, but the truth was Beth loved her mother no matter what and more than anyone in the world.

Like most mothers and daughters, their

relationship was naturally complicated by simply living, and lately by the many small acts of letting each other go. But theirs was different in that it was scarred by the pain of tragic loss. To be completely honest, the loss was epic to Beth but she felt it was less so to her mother. That single fact marked the beginning of a worrisome divide between them. Beth was not exactly sure of all the reasons why she felt so burdened, but she sometimes staggered under the weight of the sea of emptiness she carried. She felt like her mother had tossed aside her share and left her to flounder for herself. It wasn't fair or noble.

Then there was the matter of expectations, ones Beth would never meet much less surmount. It was impossible to be the oldest girl in the next generation of Hamiltons/Hayeses and ever expect raving accolades from the lips of her elders. She might have looked for some measure of satisfaction from them but she would never expect a parade in her honor. There was no excessive flattery to be found.

Her aunts and uncles owned the past and they still thought the future was theirs as well. Beth begged to differ. She felt they were wrong about so many things that she was embarrassed for them, one more reason she had planned to continue to build her life elsewhere.

The distance between Beth's college and Sullivans Island had allowed the rest of her relatives to revel in their shared hallucinations of perfect family. College had spared her four years of their self-congratulations and she thanked everything holy that she had not been there. If she had been on that porch or around that table peeling shrimp with them, she would have said that what they actually were was very far from perfect. They would not have valued her observations. In college, she had developed a tongue.

It didn't matter now. She was not going to be the one to point out that their conservative ideas had never advanced their family's name one inch. She was going to try to be the good daughter, the responsible niece, the one who came and did her duty. Why? Because even though they all practically bored her to death, Beth loved them with a fierce passion she doubted she could ever duplicate in another relationship. But that's how they were, the Hamiltons and the Hayeses, bonded by loyalty and an unseen force.

Beth suspected what everyone else already knew. That unseen force, that Lowcountry Force, the Goddess of the Island Gamble, if you like, was waiting for her. That's why surrender was the only choice. She guessed that any other course could be met with some strange but actual version of Universal Mockery until she gave in and became a willing player in the game. Welcome back to the chessboard! Get in position! Let's see, that would make Beth a pawn.

But, she thought, in spite of everything, it would be very interesting to see how the year would unfold. A year was a long time. Her intention was to avoid any and all controversy and every kind of chaos.

Beth laughed to herself realizing she had almost no real hand in the whole scenario anyway. She knew better. With the beckoning curl of their fingers, Aunt Maggie and her mother, Susan Hamilton Hayes, had coaxed her to the edge of their ancestral frying pan and she was crawling in like a lean slice of bacon. It wouldn't take long to cook her.

The taxi crossed over the Cooper River on the new bridge, and the next thing she knew, they were cruising down Coleman Boulevard, Mr. Brown's van straining to meet thirty miles an hour.

Stylistically, that is, if you wanted to impress anyone, his vehicle, that great hulking Chariot of Smoke and Fire, was not the optimal way to arrive in your hometown. Not that anyone beyond the gene pool was expecting her. But Beth thought it would have been awesome to be driving in some hot convertible wearing oversized sunglasses listening to some new music, something she knew all the words to so that she could sing at the top of her lungs. It would have been very, very awesome, she thought, if someone in another convertible, someone of the opposite sex who resembled a movie star perhaps, like Robert Pattinson, turned his head, and the question of her true identity stopped him dead and all he could do was grin and follow her home, promising to rescue her from her dreary existence. Starting now.

Lasting forever. Why not? A girl could dream, right?

But she wasn't of that ilk—the rescued damsel type. She was, well, sort of the pathetically serious one, the one sporting the inexpensive copy of Tina Fey's eyeglasses, without the benefit of her jawline or innate sense of style. Not to mention Tina Fey was really smart and funny while Beth was smart, her humor was dry, and sometimes she was marginally dour. Okay, so she knew her eyeglasses were an infinitesimal attempt at stardom chic, but it was a start.

Beth left Charleston four years ago dressed like a Lowcountry princess-in-training and somehow fell into the student life, adopting a Beacon Hill slash Jack Kerouac kind of look that wasn't exactly Lilly Pulitzer. Lately, people knitted their eyebrows together at the sight of her and, completely unsolicited, they offered her rubber bands to restrain her hair. She was the first one chosen as a lab partner and the last one invited on the conga line. Oh sure, she drank her share of beer in college and once she actually got completely toasted on tequila shots and had to spend two days in bed drinking Maalox and nibbling little bites of bananas dipped in peanut butter. But that was the exception, not the rule. Perhaps she had overdone the brainiac study thing in college and didn't look like a Carolina girl on her way to the Windjammer to shag all night—and that's a dance, not a sexual act—and, well, so what? Beth was still a smart cookie who simply had yet to latch on to a lasting personal style.

Beth knew very early on that if she wanted to go to graduate school she was going to need a scholarship. So when all her girlfriends were out raising hell, dressed in bedsheets and acting like boozerellas, she was in her dorm memorizing biology spellings and studying finance. Unlike her friends and roommates who all seemed happy to have predestined futures, she viewed college as a ticket out of a life on that great southern hamster wheel. One generation hopped off and went to heaven and the next one hopped on, picking up where the others left off, running like idiots in Ray-Bans and Top-Siders until they dropped dead too. Not that she really had anything super serious against her family or that life, it was just that she wanted to see the world and think about things, be somebody different, do something great, like write the Great American Novel or at least have her blog picked up for publication before she was thirty. Was that too much to hope for? She was thinking now that maybe it was. At least, so far. Because if she was so Albert Einstein smart and destined for such global literary greatness, what was she doing with a deferred scholarship, sweating like a pig in the back of a clanking van, headed for a funky old haunted house on a sandbar? She already knew the answer, but to reinforce her own commitment, she would breathe the words again. She was Beth Hayes, the Obedient One.

They crossed the Ben Sawyer Bridge and for the billionth time she wondered who Ben Sawyer was. It would have made sense if the bridge was named for Edgar Allan Poe, who actually lived on Sullivans Island for a while. But Ben Sawyer? She had never heard of any Sawyers on Sullivans Island. Like her mother always said, who were his people? But there you had one more small but significant enigma of Sullivans Island, a land washed in mystery and populated with the kind of characters Tennessee Williams would have loved to have known.

They were on the island then, and Beth was straining her neck to read the leash laws that were posted on the huge sign on the right. She didn't want Lola to get busted by the dog police for dropping her carte de visite in the wrong spot.

She rubbed her eyes. What was this? Oz? Perhaps it was the time of day but the houses seemed brighter, more well-defined, and the palmettos and oleanders seemed greener, their branches and the edges of their fronds were sharper. The sky seemed to be a more vibrant shade of blue than she could recall. She took a deep breath and even with the van's air-conditioning running full blast she could still smell plough mud, which was an acquired taste and danger-ously addictive. In her dreams she actually smelled plough mud.

Despite the economy, there was gentri-fication everywhere, but the kind that pleased her. Most of the old migrant worker cottages that flanked the road onto the island had been resurrected and trans-formed into million-dollar futures with colorful lush window boxes of fuchsia geraniums, hot pink petunias, and bushy asparagus ferns to prove it. It was amazing, she thought, what you could accomplish with the combination of elbow grease, a little money, and a clear vision.

They came to the corner and she noticed that the gas station was under new ownership, gouging its customers an extra twenty cents per gallon for the privilege of convenience. That would never change no matter who owned it. The patrons of Dunleavy's Pub, noisy families and happy dogs, spilled out onto the sidewalk picnic tables, laughing, talking, and having lunch. Her stomach began to growl when she thought about their quesadillas. Judging from the parking lot, Durst Family Medicine appeared to be doing a brisk business. Probably legions of poison ivy and sunburn victims, she thought. People were walking to the beach pulling wagons loaded with gear, toddlers, and ice water in their coolers, and Beth thought she might like a walk on the beach that day to introduce Lola to the ocean.

The dependable rolling panorama of robust life gave her some relief. For as much as Beth embraced the twenty-first century, like all true Charlestonians, she hated change of almost any kind. Commercial development made her suspicious and she generally ignored its creeping advance, hoping it might go away. If she had lived there full-time she would have fought it with all her might. They could build all the Starbucks and Sonics in the world on Mount Pleasant and the adjoining island of Isle of Palms, but something deep inside of her depended on the peninsula of Charleston and the entire length and breadth of Sullivans Island to remain the same. So far it was reasonably so.

They turned right on Middle Street, the Champs-Élysée of the island, and began to head toward her house. In the time it might take to swallow a pill, she would be back, perched on the threshold of her childhood. Her stomach began to flutter.

Memories flooded her mind—all of them together, cousins, aunts, uncles, all of them. She could see herself and the others as children, running around in their pajamas, spinning like helicopters in the silver dusk, fall down dizzy, chasing lightning bugs, scooping them into mayonnaise jars with holes punched in the top. The holes were made by her Uncle Grant's ice pick, which they were forbidden to touch.

"Don't you children even think about laying a hand on that thing," he would say in a very stern voice to his boys. Then he would turn to Beth with a wink and she knew he wasn't so very mean as all that.

Summers! Searching the thicket for wild blackberries in the full sun of the day, filling coffee cans with them, and later, sunburned and freckled, how they feasted on hot sugary blackberry dumplings that her Aunt Maggie whipped up in her copper pots. There were literally hundreds of days when her boys, Mickey and Bucky, and Beth caught crabs down by the rocks with Uncle Grant. They used chicken necks for bait, tied up in knots on weighted ends of cord. They caught blue crabs by the score, shrieking as they moved them ever so carefully from the line to the net to the basket, trying not to get pinched—the Revenge of the Ill-Fated Crab. They shrieked again with excitement when one escaped the basket in the kitchen or on the porch, clicking its claws as it hurried sideways, looking for salvation. There was no salvation for those guys, no ma'am. They wound up steamed and dumped right from the colander on newspapers that were spread over the porch table, cracked apart and dipped in cocktail sauce. It made her laugh to remember. She realized then that she had not been crabbing in years. And she remembered how she had completely embraced her closely knit family when she was young and how important they had been to her.

"Maybe I should take up crabbing again, Lola. Do you want to come and help?"

"What's that?" Mr. Brown said.

"Nothing. I was just talking to my dog."

"No reason why not."

They passed the hill fort then and Beth sighed with relief as it had not changed one lick, except for the children's park built in front of it that had sprung up some years ago. In her mind's eye, she could see herself, her cousins, and a gang of island kids sliding down it on flattened cardboard boxes and catching the devil from the town fathers for trespassing and sledding on the patchy grass. They had been very young, not quite ten, when Mickey had his first brush with the law.

"What do you think you're doing, son?"

Mickey looked up into the face of the chief of police and everyone thought he was going to wet his pants right there in front of the whole world.

"Um, nothing?"

"You children get on out of here now, before I have to lock you all up! You hear me?"

Beth giggled to remember how they had abandoned their cardboard and run in every direction to escape incarceration.

She remembered flying kites on the beach in the winter and all those stories they told and retold . . . you see, as long as things looked about the same and they told and retold the same stories, the past was still alive. They could all stay young and live forever. In that moment, that was what she wanted—for her life to be as it had been before her father died and to live forever in that corner of her childhood world.

"Turn left here?" Mr. Brown said, snapping her out of her daydream.

"Yes, left here and then right to that driveway on the left. Yes. Left here."

"Welcome home," Mr. Brown said, and

put the car in park, leaving the engine to continue its rumbling. "Always good to be home, ain't it?"

She simply said, "Yeah, it is." What she wanted to say was something else entirely. She wanted to say, You don't know how complicated this is. I might be swallowed alive in the next year. Get me out of here. But she didn't.

She only said, "Yeah, it is."

Beth leaned forward in her seat to size up the Island Gamble. She thought she had known exactly what to expect. The house would loom large, spooky, and scare the daylights out of her with its enormity. But it didn't. She was ship-shape. Her shutters were straight, her white clapboards glistened from a recent paint job, and her silver tin roof mirrored the enormous clouds overhead like the compact mirror of a dowager. The Island Gamble seemed sweet, grandmotherly, and nostalgic, as safe a haven as one could ever want. At the sight of it she became emotional and suddenly she wanted to cry. There was her mother's old Volvo wagon and her Aunt Maggie's car too. They were there, waiting for her.

She got out and liberated Lola from her crate, hooking her leash to her collar. She paid Mr. Brown and he deposited her luggage at the foot of the steps, meaning she would have the pleasure of hauling it all up the steps and into the house and then up another two flights to the second floor.

"Thanks," she said, and gave him five dollars instead of the ten she would have given him if he had taken her bags inside.

Mr. Brown shrugged his shoulders, got back into his van, put it in reverse, and backed out of her life.

Lola was nosing around, sniffing the lantana and the pittosporum, when a screen door slammed against its frame. *Thwack!* Beth looked up to see her mother and Aunt Maggie hurrying down the steps to greet her.

"He-ey!" Aunt Maggie called out in a singsong. "Come on and give your auntie a kiss, you bad girl!"

"I'm not bad," she said, and smiled.

"Yes she is!" Mom said. "Come here, Lola baby!"

"What about kissing your daughter?" she said.

"After I scratch my granddog," she said,

gave Beth a slap on her bottom, and scooped up Lola from the grass. "Look at my precious widdle baby!" Lola proceeded to wash Susan's face, one slurp at a time. "Come see, Maggie! Our Lola's got your nose and my chin!"

"Well, look at that! Would y'all look at this little bit of a fur ball? Hey, darlin'." Aunt Maggie allowed Lola to lick her hand, much like you might kiss the pope's ring, and then she turned her attention to Beth, narrowing her famous blue eyes. "All right now, missy. Want to tell your aunt what in the world you did to your hair?"

"I merely enhanced the red."

"I'll say! Whew! Well, hon, it's just hair, isn't it?" She sighed so large Beth caught the fragrance of her toothpaste.

Aunt Maggie, the self-proclaimed matriarch of the family, did not like Beth's hair. Apparently. Beth did not give a rip what she thought. She was there to do them a favor, not to get a makeover. She was immediately annoyed but hiding it pretty well. She deemed it unwise to arrive and start bickering right away.

"Don't you pick on my child," her mom said to Maggie, and gave Beth a dramatic hug, fingering her ringlets. "I happen to love red hair!"

Beth took Lola back from her. As usual, her mother had read her mind.

"Let me help you with the bags, kiddo," Aunt Maggie said, groaning under the weight of her duffel bag. "Lawsamercy, chile! What you got in here? Bricks?"

"Books," she said, "and more books. Sorry. This one's worse."

Everyone took a bag and they grumbled their way up the stairs, across the small back porch, and into the kitchen.

"Where do y'all want me to sleep?"

"Take your old room for now, but when we leave you can rotate bedrooms if you want," Aunt Maggie said. "You must be starving. I made lunch, so why don't you go wash airplane and dog off your hands and we can eat?"

Airplane and dog? She was almost twenty-three years old. Did she *really* need someone to tell her to wash her hands?

"Sure," she said, kicked off her flip-flops, and took two of her bags up the steps to her old room that had never really been hers.

The bedroom where Beth had spent

many nights housed her parents' four-poster bed, which had come into their hands when her grandparents went to their great reward. When her mother and stepfather sold the house on Queen Street and moved in with her Aunt Maggie and Uncle Grant just as they were moving to California, her mother had sold most of their belongings in an undistinguished yard sale and brought only the most important pieces of furniture and some other things with her. Those things that mattered to her and those she thought mattered to Beth, and yes, that was another issue Beth had with her. How could someone else decide what was important to you?

The big mirror was the first artifact to arrive, followed by an old grandfather clock that chimed when it was in the mood. But the mirror was the thing. The Mirror, the curious and well-used doorway for those no longer of the flesh, was firmly installed in her Aunt Maggie's living room the week before her mother married Simon Rifkin. So her mother's exodus back to the island had actually begun before Beth realized what was going on. Maggie had always wanted the mirror back, saying it was original to the house. She had whined about that thing like it was made out of the skin of her children. But that's how Beth's Aunt Maggie was—acquisitive to the tenth power. Her mom didn't mind returning it, saying she didn't need the deceased walking around her house at all hours anyway. This made her mom happy and Aunt Maggie happy and Beth, well, not so much if she had recognized its departure as a sign of the times.

So, in addition to house arrest, Beth would have the company of every dead person the family had ever known, if you believed in that stuff, which she did, because she knew it to be so from firsthand experience.

This was the moment of Beth's return, and moving into the house required considerable energy. After twisting her spine in every conceivable direction, Beth finally managed to get her luggage upstairs and opened her bags. She took Lola's dishes and a Ziploc bag of her food downstairs—after she washed her hands—and placed it on the kitchen floor in a spot that was out of the way. Lola began to drink, lapping the water in such an anxious way that everyone remarked she was just adorable.

Maggie had produced a spread of tuna salad sandwiches with no crusts, pickles, celery, and olives, iced tea, and sliced watermelon. This was the hallmark hot-weather lunch of their childhood.

"This looks great," Beth said, determined to be pleasant.

"Good, honey, why don't we say grace?" Maggie said, and sat in her usual spot at the head of the table. She snapped her linen napkin in the air and pulled it across her lap, bowing her head, mumbling some words in a voice she never used except for serious prayer and holiday toasts.

"Amen," they all said.

"My sister can make tuna salad like nobody's business," Susan said, taking three sandwich wedges, a load of pickles, celery, and olives. She passed the platter to Beth. "Saltshaker?"

"Hungry?" Maggie said, pushing the salt toward Susan, and winked at Beth.

Beth took three wedges and more pickles, celery, and olives to support her mother's healthy appetite and passed the platter to her aunt.

"Don't we have any potato chips?" Beth said. She couldn't stop her inner devil from having a word.

It was well known within the family that Maggie thought everyone should act like an anorexic at meals. In her mind, it was unladylike to fill your plate, even if you had been stranded out in the ocean for ten days, eating nothing but raw seagull, and just came home from the hospital blistered and starving, barely recovered from life-threatening dehydration.

"No, darlin'. Sorry. I don't keep that kind of thing in this house."

Maggie scanned everyone's plates, corrected her posture, and gingerly took two wedges for herself, two slices of Mrs. Fanning's Bread 'n Butter pickles, and one small stick of celery. Then she smiled her smug little smile of superiority, the one that had irked Beth all her life.

It was sweltering. Beth was wearing a long, lightweight, pink scarf made of cotton gauze, twisted and double-looped around her neck, but now the room seemed warmer and even more humid, despite the ocean breeze and the ceiling fan, but mostly because of her Aunt Maggie's opinions. So she unwound it, pulled it off, and horrified them with her cleavage.

Maggie inhaled with a great gasp. Maggie and Susan were markedly less endowed.

Her mother giggled and said, "She got those from Tom's side of the family, I guess."

"Gee-za-ree, honey! What's happened to you?" Beth thought her aunt's eyes were going to burst forth and join the olives. "You know, this is Sullivans Island and you just can't go around like that!"

"Like what?" Susan said.

"Like, like . . . you know! With your tatas almost showing!"

"My what? Did you say my tatas?" Beth started to laugh but stopped when she saw how serious her aunt was. "Um, Aunt Maggie, this is how everyone dresses these days. Little tanks layered up, long scarves, tight jeans . . . it's how we dress. It's okay. Really. I can show you on Facebook."

Beth looked around. Her mother's face was confused. She had always trusted Beth's sense of propriety in matters of clothes and so forth. It wasn't as though she had come home tattooed all up and down her arms. Or with twenty little rings pierced through her lips and nose. But Beth decided her mother had bowed to Aunt Maggie's judgment too. They should see what goes on in the world, Beth thought. And even though Beth thought Maggie could be an old-fashioned, out-of-touch, world-class prude, her face and neck got hot. She was pretty sure her skin matched her hair.

"I'm sure you're right, Beth honey," Maggie said. "I just don't want people to get the wrong impression of you, that's all."

"What? Did Sullivans Island suddenly become some kind of Islamic fundamentalist country or something?"

"No, sweetheart," Maggie said, and Beth loathed Maggie calling her *sweetheart* like you cannot imagine. "But you know, ahem"—Maggie cleared her throat, and Susan and Beth hated that gesture of hers because it was always the precursor to her reminding you that you were a big stupid idiot—"your Uncle Grant always says that the bait you use determines the kind of fish you catch, right? That's all."

Now Beth's anger was on the rise.

"Well, I didn't come here to fish. I put my life on hold and came here to watch this house so you two can go do your thing. How about instead of insulting me someone says thank you, Beth, for giving up a year of your life?"

There was complete silence at the table then. The only sound was the clicking of the ceiling fan, which seemed to grow louder by the second. Beth had been rude and knew she had better quickly make amends.

"Look, Aunt Maggie, I'm sorry, but here's how it is. My hair is a little crazy, I know it, but it's only color, for Pete's sake. And humidity doesn't help. And my top? I dress like everyone else my age. Believe me! You all are like a lot older than me, and maybe, just maybe, a little conservative? No one in Boston ever looked at me funny. Well, not anyone I knew anyway. I swear. Anyway, thanks for lunch. I'm gonna go unpack now and walk Lola on the beach."

She left the table and put her plate in the dishwasher. Silence.

"Awesome tuna salad, Aunt Maggie. I'll see y'all in about half an hour?"

"Just a minute, miss," Mom said. "Sit down."

Whenever Susan said *Just a minute, miss,* Beth knew the ice on which she was skating had grown thin. So she sat and Lola settled back down at her feet.

"Your Aunt Maggie and I thought long and hard about who to ask to watch the house, and you were the only candidate who made sense to us. Above all your cousins and everyone we could think of, you are the most responsible and you have good common sense."

"Your momma is right," Maggie said.

"And, we are a family, which means we come to each other in our hour of need. I won't have you coming in here with a chip on your shoulder like you are so put upon to do this for me and for your aunt. It isn't nice. So let's drop the martyr attitude right now. I mean, I have done everything for you I ever possibly could, so let's be fair. It's one year, not the rest of your life."

"Fine. Look, I know all this and I appreciate how you feel, but I don't feel like getting pecked to death the minute I get here either. I mean, I'm almost twenty-three, right? Can I please have some respect as an adult?"

"If you want us to treat you like an adult, then perhaps—"

"Hold on, Maggie," Susan said, and it was a good thing she did or Beth might have grabbed a sharp object and done her worst. "Beth's right, you know. She is. Maybe we were a little harsh?"

Maggie sighed as only their mother, according to legend, had ever been able to do, and looked from her sister's face to Beth's.

"I'm sorry, Beth. I don't know what's the matter with me. I am so glad you're here. I am. And I know everything's going to be fine. You go on and unpack and walk that precious dog of yours. She is housebroken, isn't she?"

"Yes. She's housebroken." Beth accidentally made a guttural sound, picked up Lola, and left the room.

The fact was that Lola was not entirely housebroken and there would be hell to pay if Maggie's rugs got ruined. Beth made a mental note to double up on Lola's outside schedule, wondering again how she got suckered into this.

Upstairs, Beth dropped Lola on the bed and Lola settled down to watch her. She hung up her clothes, arranged her ten pairs of flip-flops and four pairs of shoes on the racks in the closet, stacked her books on the floor, and made a pile of laundry to wash later on. It was remarkable to her that she could unpack almost four years of her life in under an hour.

"Want to go see the Atlantic Ocean?" she said to Lola.

Lola lifted her tiny head from the bed and then plopped down again, staring at Beth through the fringes of her long eyebrows. Lola, having had enough action for one day, was bone tired from her trip and needed a long nap.

"Okay," she said, "you rest right there, don't move, and I'll be right back."

It was just like having a baby, Beth thought, but a very hairy one that would never give her any sass. She changed into a T-shirt with a high neck to calm her aunt's nerves.

Downstairs she found them in the kitchen, lunch cleared away and everything tidy as could be. They had moved on to the next item on their agenda. Maggie was painting Eiffel Towers on plastic wine-glasses, but Eiffel Towers that appeared to be dancing.

"Isn't it unbelievable that you went from writing that 'Geechee Girl Remembers' column to teaching in Paris?"

"I'll say!"

They stopped talking when Beth came in.

"All unpacked? Do you need anything?" Maggie said.

"No, everything is fine. Lola is zonked out. What are y'all doing?"

"Planning your momma's bon voyage soirée. Want to help?"

"Sure," she said, and sat at the table. "What can I do?"

"Here," Maggie said, "stamp these napkins. Ink pad is in there."

She handed Beth a small shopping bag with several packages of white paper cocktail napkins, an Eiffel Tower stamp, and a flat tin of black ink on a blotter pad. She opened everything, lined it up in front of her, and stared at it.

"Now what?" she asked. "When's the party?"

"Next Saturday. Okay, let's try one on an

angle and one straight, in the corner there, and then we can decide which one we like best. What do you think?"

"Sure," she said, and stamped two napkins, holding them up for judgment. "And the verdict is?"

"On an angle," Mom said.

"I agree," Maggie said.

"On an angle it is then," Beth said, and proceeded to stamp away, thinking this was the most ridiculous job in the world. "So, who's coming to the party?"

"Our whole clan," Susan said. "Kids too."

"Excuse my groan," Beth said.

"Who makes you groan, darlin'?" Maggie said. "Doesn't this look so good?" She held out a wineglass for us to observe her creation, and what could you say? She was right.

Beth had to give the devil her due. Maggie was one of those people who could duplicate the colors inside an abalone shell in bedroom paint and it would make you feel like a goddess when you woke up in the morning. She could spot a piece of driftwood on the beach, bring it home, redesign the living room around it, and have it featured in *Charleston Magazine*. She was the family wizard in all things artistic and culinary, while Beth and her mother were, well, not.

"Looks amazing," Beth said, and continued to stretch her creative muscle by stamping napkins. "Uncle Henry's boys are a pain in the neck. They're coming too?"

"Yep. But it's Uncle Henry who's the colossal pain in the neck of all times," Susan said, "not to mention our sister-in-law Teensy, right, Maggie?"

"It is poor taste to speak badly of one's own family," Maggie said. "And Henry is our patriarch, so he says."

Beth giggled to herself. "Who doesn't talk about their relatives?"

"You're both right, of course," Susan said, looking at them in false innocence. "I just think it's a shame Henry can't think of anything to talk about besides his wallet."

"And too bad that Teensy can't find clothes to fit her size zero cadaver," Maggie said. "But maybe if she didn't spend so much time in the loo—"

"She wouldn't be so skinny," Susan said, finishing Maggie's sentence.

"Yeah, and it's a pity Uncle Henry's charming boys got kicked out of Sewanee for plagiarizing term papers from the Internet," Beth said. "If they hadn't been caught with that case of liquor and all those files, they'd still be in college."

"Now, now," Aunt Maggie said, "let's be charitable. Phil's going to finish up at Athens this fall and Blake is going to be a sophomore at Georgia State. They've learned their lessons."

Beth and Susan just looked at each other and shook their heads.

"Yeah, sure," Beth said. "And what about the rest of Uncle Timmy's crew?"

"Uncle Timmy and his slightly less exciting family will be here Friday morning," Susan said. "Crazy or not, I can't wait to see every last one of them. I mean it, y'all."

"Me too, but you have to say that Aunt Mary Jo is a little bit of a mouse," Beth said. "At least their daughters are somewhere in the range of normal. Boring but normal."

"Hush now," Maggie said. "They cannot wait to see you! They told me so three times. Timmy said his girls said the only way they were coming was if you were here."

"See?" Susan said, smiling like they had all just won the state lottery.

"See what?" Beth said. "If they are all staying here, this place is gonna be a crazy house! Where's everyone gonna sleep? Do we have help to clean up and all?"

"What for?" Maggie said with her quiet smile. "We don't need help. Why, we're all healthy and you're all young . . . If everyone pitches in, it won't be a burden to anyone."

Beth began to stamp napkins with a vengeance. She had been brought home in shackles to watch a house that would be watching her and to cook and clean for a bunch of ingrates. Her cheeks and neck were scarlet and she knew it.

"Have you heard from the twins?" Susan asked Maggie.

"Sophie's coming for sure. I think. But Allison? Who knows about Miss Hoity-Toity? She's too important to return phone calls," Maggie said.

"She's a pain in the A," Susan said.

"Aunt Sophie's coming?" Beth perked up then because Aunt Sophie was her favorite and she rarely saw her.

"As far as I know," Maggie said. "She's got a new cell number if you want it."

"Definitely," Beth said.

"Yeah, so big house party next weekend and then I'm off to Paris," Susan said. "Incredible."

"It's what you always wanted," Maggie said. "Remember when you used to say you were going to run away to Paris and live in a garret and smoke French cigarettes?"

"I was thirteen."

"Well, now you're postmenopausal and isn't Simon good to let you go?"

"Thanks for reminding me not to pack tampons—"

"Hush! Your! Mouth!" Maggie said in horror. "We're in the *kitchen*!"

"Whatever. You think the milk will go sour? Anyway, I did not need his permission. Like he asked me if he could go to California for a year to work with Grant?"

"Like he could do anything about it anyway?" Beth said, trying to catch her breath from laughing so hard. "When my mom wants something that badly, I wouldn't want to tangle with her!"

"Seriously, Maggie, I didn't need my husband's permission. That's ridiculous!"

"Well, I'll keep an eye on him," Maggie said. "All those cute young nurses! Woo hoo!"

"Oh, thanks a lot," Susan said.

Maggie took some measure of delight in making her sister insecure, but Susan knew it and after all these years, she had learned to take it in stride.

Beth had finished all the napkins and suddenly couldn't hold her eyes open.

"I'm going to catch a nap for a few minutes," Beth said.

"You go on, darlin'," Maggie said. "Thanks for all your help."

Susan followed her to the foot of the steps and then gave her a hug.

"I'm glad you're home, baby," she said. "I always miss you."

"Me too, Momma. Call me if I sleep more than an hour, okay?"

"Sure," she said, and kissed her on her forehead.

Beth climbed the stairs envisioning the laughing faces of her relatives. Her mind had time-traveled to the next week and she could already feel them there. She became giddy thinking of the endless teasing that would go on, the advice that would be freely dispensed from their generation to hers. She knew how it would be. Their voices would be a continuous hum like a swarm of honeybees around a hive. White breezes from the Atlantic would drench the rooms in something sweet and delicious. Thousands of memories would be whispered to them from inside the weathered boards of pine. And they would move around one another like tiny planets in their own elliptically shaped orbits, revolving and revolving.

She was so tired. Her legs seemed to weigh a thousand pounds. She reached her room and could barely open the door. Beth did not remember having turned down her bed or that she had put Lola in her crate, where she snored in tiny puffs. But there were the facts. She could not recall lowering the blinds and positioning the slats just so, so that the air could sweep in and around the room cooling everything off, with the rising tide playing its age-old lullaby. It was all a welcome mystery, typical of the things that happened there. She pulled off her jeans, dropped them to the floor, and slipped between the crisp white sheets. Pale fragrances of mint and jasmine escaped from the pillows, lulling her into dreams of what? She did not know. Someone was there; she could feel them, there in the room with her. A faint presence. She was too tired to open her eyes or to ask who it was. It did not matter. She did not care. She smiled to herself knowing she had already been sized up, the rules of engagement were being laid forth, and the games were about to begin.

2

Bon Voyage

By friday, the house was loud, bulging with bodies, excited voices, and there wasn't a vacant bed or chair. Beth's aunts Sophie and Allison had yet to arrive but all the others were in various stages of getting settled. Everyone wanted to spend the weekend in the bedrooms of their childhood, but that was, of course, impossible.

On the flip of a quarter, Uncle Henry and Aunt Paula, affectionately known as Teensy, were enthroned in Uncle Henry's old room, which did not measure up to Teensy's highfalutin standards at all.

"There are mosquitoes in here, Henry.

Do you hear me? Nasty!" she complained in her often-imitated shrill juvenile voice from behind their closed door.

"Shut your damn mouth," Beth heard her Uncle Henry say. "The whole world will hear you."

But they were staying there anyway because everyone knew that Uncle Henry was tighter than a mole's ear and wouldn't waste money on a hotel if he didn't have to, which was probably one reason why he had so much money in the bank. As a boy, he had shared that room with Uncle Timmy. Uncle Timmy and Aunt Mary Jo had decided to sleep in the twins' old room, downstairs with two of their four kids in the next bedroom, on creaking rollaway beds that were older than Beth. Maggie and Grant were staying in her grandmother's old room, and her mother and Simon were staying across the hall.

The rest of the clan was sleeping down the island in Mary Ellen Way's rambling eight-bedroom house on the marsh, which she occasionally loaned to friends or friends of friends. Maggie and Grant's oldest son Mickey, who was now called Mike because he was twenty-six after all, knew about Mary Ellen Way's house because he had dated her niece and, after winning the campaign for the uncles, including Henry, to foot the bill for some groceries and so forth, he invited all the boys to stay there and organized everything. Beth thought this was an excellent idea as there was only one bathroom on the second floor of their house and two tiny ones downstairs. It didn't matter how large the capacity of the hot-water heater was, no residential system was going to deliver hot showers to that many people. Anyway, the most important detail is that Beth had too many cousins to know and all of them were lazy cows when it came to pitching in to help.

Coming to that same realization, as she tripped over running shoes and tote bags that were thoughtlessly tossed and dropped everywhere, that her nieces and nephews were a bunch of slugs, Maggie snapped out of her delirium and engaged the services of a woman named Cecily Singleton to help with meals on Friday and Saturday. Cecily was the granddaughter of Livvie Singleton, who, according to family lore, had single-handedly saved the whole family from implosion back in the sixties when Beth's mother was a girl. So, between the second house and an extra pair of helping hands, Beth began to think they might survive the house party after all.

Friday afternoon, almost everyone had disappeared to walk the beach or to browse the new Whole Foods for exotic breads and olives. Beth's hair was restrained in a ponytail, her breasts were almost concealed, and she was tying on an apron (with an Eiffel Tower hand-painted on the front) to help with Friday night's fish fry, which would take place in two hours' time. She looked out the kitchen window and there came the person whom she rightly assumed was Cecily, straight up the back steps. She rapped on the screen door, but before Beth could answer it she walked right into the kitchen like she owned the place.

"Humph," she said, looking Beth up and down with a huge grin, dropping her tote bag on the table with a thud. "Nice apron."

"Humph yourself," she said. "I'm Beth."

"If you say so." Cecily arched an eyebrow at her. "Where's our Miss Maggie?"

Beth arched an eyebrow back at her and said, "Out on the front porch with her hot glue gun, building a last minute four-foot-tall Eiffel Tower out of shells she personally collected from the beach. With her own hands. Without wrecking her manicure."

Cecily held herself still for the entire span of two seconds and then they both burst out laughing.

"Oh Lord! That woman is so crazy!" Cecily said between hoots. "You got an apron for me?"

"You're telling me?" Beth said, reached for a tissue to blot her eyes, and tossed her an apron that matched her own.

"But it's a good crazy, I guess. Thanks."

"Yeah, I think so too." She blew her nose and looked at her again. "So you're Livvie Singleton's granddaughter, huh?"

Cecily was tall and lean with high cheek-bones and a smile so bright that it seemed to flash light all over the room. Her hair was pulled back in a low knot and she was dressed in white linen trousers and a jade green cotton knit shirt. Beth liked her right away because Cecily was smart and for some inexplicable reason she seemed like an old friend.

"That's my claim to fame," she said.

"That's a very big pair of shoes to fill. It's great to meet you."

"Same here," she said, and they shook hands.

"So, how do you know my Aunt Maggie?"

She reached in her bag and pulled out a business card, handing it to her. It read:

Get it Together
For all your Organizing Needs
Cecily Singleton 843-555-1212

"Cool," Beth said. "This explains a lot. Except that it reads like you do more office work."

"Honey, at twenty-five dollars an hour, I do office work, cater, garden—you name it, I can do it, and if I can't, I call my men who can. In this recession? Wouldn't you?"

"Yeah, most definitely."

"I've got over thirty houses and condos I take care of. It's a great business," Cecily said.

"Wow!" Beth said.

"And, your mother and Miss Maggie hired me to see about you while they're gone."

"Oh really?" Well, *that* was annoying.

When was somebody going to tell Beth she had a babysitter? "To do what?"

"Pay all the bills, balance the household accounts, take care of all the hanging baskets and window boxes, make sure the yard gets cut and I guess to generally just see about things—you know, call someone if something breaks? Like the plumber?"

Admittedly, none of those jobs held any appeal for Beth, and although she was glad to have them taken care of by someone else, she was still mildly torqued. When were they going to treat her like an adult?

"Oh. So, if we need a plumber, I have to call you first?"

"No, you call the plumber. I'll give you the list of household contacts." She looked at her, understanding why she was miffed. "Beth? You don't want to do all that stuff, do you? Please. Anyway, aren't you gonna get yourself a job or something? Hand me a cutting board, okay? I need to start chopping onions."

Beth pulled the old wooden board from under the cabinet where all the cookie sheets and trays were lined up like warped soldiers.

"I can do it," she said. "What do we need onions for?"

"You ever have a decent meal that didn't have onions in it?"

"Guess not," she said, and didn't bring up cereal or peanut butter and jelly sandwiches, the two headliner onionless dishes from her student budget.

"We're making onion rings and hush puppies. As long as we're going to stink up the house frying fish, we may as well go all the way. Why don't you put together the salad?"

"Fine," she said. "Okay, so, tell me about Livvie. There must be at least *one* story I haven't heard."

Cecily cut her eyes in Beth's direction in the first of what would become countless glances to note unspoken inside jokes and mutual understandings.

"She was something else, 'eah? I'll tell you about her but first you have to tell me why your hair is so blazing red. It ain't natural!"

"Ah yes. The hair. It was, alas, a poor decision," Beth said in a dramatic whisper, coming clean with how she felt about it for the first time. "But don't say I admitted it, okay?"

"Not me!" Cecily said, chopping the ends off an onion. "So, let's see now. My grandmother Livvie? Well, she was the most magical woman I ever knew, that's all. She could charm the birds right down from the trees. In fact, I used to watch her do it."

"Seriously?" Beth looked in the refrigerator and found six bags of prewashed lettuce stuffed together on a shelf.

"Yep. When I was a little girl I used to follow her everywhere. I can remember playing hide-and-seek with her in the rows of corn in her vegetable garden. Anyway, when she got tired of me chasing her around we'd sit on the front steps of her house with a glass of iced tea. All these little birds, wrens, I think, they would just glide down from the big oak and land around her feet. She would reach in her apron pocket and come out with a handful of seed or bread crumbs. Those little stinkers would hop right on her hand and take some. She would pet their heads and then they would fly off so another bird could come say hello."

"Shut up! You're lying, right?"

"Excuse me?" Cecily's smile turned to ice. "Who you calling a liar? You must think you're talking to a white girl."

Apparently, there were some limits to Cecily's humor and good nature.

"No, no! Sorry. It's just a figure of speech. I mean, you're fooling with me, right?"

"Not one bit."

"Okay. You mean to say that untamed birds ate from her hands? Just like they were pets?"

"Only if she wanted them to."

"Holy crap. Francis of Assisi, no less."

"Amen. You'd better wash those tomatoes. Who knows where they've been?"

"Right."

She was taking orders from Cecily the same way her mother said she took them from Livvie! History repeats itself, she thought.

They went on telling stories until they found a solid ease with each other. One thing was for sure. Cecily didn't take to sloppy language. And Beth realized she should have known better than to assume that level of familiarity with someone she had just met. This was the South, not

Boston, and Beth was borderline impolite. Besides, Beth thought, Cecily was probably thirty-five. Maybe older.

"So, you just graduated from college, is that right?"

"Yeah. I was supposed to be on my way to graduate school but I got hijacked into doing this."

"I see. Humph. Well, what did you major in?"

"English lit. I want to be a writer."

"Sweet. But you're stuck here."

"You got it. I'll just have a life starting like a year from now." Beth made a mental note to stop saying *sweet* because using the same terminology as someone Cecily's age was just as pathetic as singing along to music in the grocery store.

"Lemme ask you something. You can tell me it's none of my business if you want to, but why can't you write while you're here?"

"Well, I can, but it's not the same thing as studying with serious academics. I mean, I'll probably make some attempt to keep up with my journals and I still have my blog."

"A blog. I see. Well, to my way of thinking,

all blogs do is put all your thoughts out there for anyone to steal for their book or their magazine article. You're just giving it away."

"Maybe."

"Ain't no maybe about it."

Beth knew Cecily was right, of course, but everyone blogged—everyone with too much time on their hands, that is. And there wasn't any real reason why she couldn't write while she was in lockup except that it just wasn't how she had envisioned beginning her career. She wanted to submit her first manuscript with *Graduate of the Iowa Writers' Workshop* on her résumé. Stubborn. She knew it. Muleheaded and stubborn. But she also knew that platinum credentials would give her an edge in the world of letters and all things literary.

She threw the lettuce in the bowl, chopped cucumbers and tomatoes with a fury, and soon the oversized salad bowl was filled with enough roughage to stimulate the collective digestive system of Charleston County.

When the whole family had returned to the house and began pouring cocktails for one another, Beth brought Cecily a glass of wine. That is, after she had the requisite chat with every one of her relatives for a minute or two.

"I really shouldn't because I have to work," Cecily said.

"Oh, come on! Let's toast to something!" Beth held her glass up in the air. "To meeting you and to the summer!"

"Cheers!" Cecily said, and then burst out laughing.

"What's so funny?"

"Nothing."

Beth looked at her with her most suspicious face and said, "Come on. What's up?"

"Okay," she said, pointing to a platter on the table. "Did *you* make ham salad? Because *I* didn't make ham salad."

"What the . . . ? Where did that come from?"

"Ham salad. My grandmother's specialty, besides her world-famous egg salad, of course."

"Which my Aunt Maggie makes too . . . um, wait! Are you saying what I think you're saying? That these things just appeared out of thin air? Come on! Gimme a break!"

"All I'm saying is that I didn't make any ham salad. Shoot, if she wants to come round 'eah scaring the liver out of people, the least she could do is fry the fish!"

Beth assumed she meant Livvie and she cleared her throat. Loudly and deliberately. "They're all out on the porch. I'm gonna go get us a whole bottle of wine!"

"Will you take that platter with you and pass them around?"

Beth gave Cecily a thumbs-up, picked up the mysterious sandwiches and a handful of cocktail napkins, the ones she had stamped, thinking for a split second that her artistic efforts might go unused if she hadn't seen them.

"Weird," she said, and went out to the front porch wondering what kind of nonsense this was. Nonsense or not, Beth had goose bumps the size of jelly beans.

She left the aroma of fresh fish and onions and entered another world when she reached the ocean side of the house. The French doors and windows were opened wide and the breezy air smelled like rosemary and Confederate jasmine, which at that time of year was blooming in great tangled masses on fences and trees all over the island. It was the most beautiful window of time for a summer evening on Sullivans Island, after the heat of the day was broken and right before sunset. Perhaps a brief shower had come and gone, judging from the heavy dew on the lawn. I must have missed it, she thought, remembering that it was not unusual for rain to fall in the front yard and nowhere else.

She looked out toward the sunset. The radiant western sky was streaked with impossible colors, and the sun, blinding white in late afternoon, had become a massive fireball. It was so gorgeous she wondered how she had stayed away so long. Perhaps I should place a story here, she thought.

"Sandwich?" Beth said to Aunt Teensy and Uncle Henry.

"Thanks, sugar," Teensy said, and took a nibble. "Ooh la la! Heavenly!"

You have no idea, Beth thought, but maybe not. "Uncle Henry?"

"He can have the rest of mine," she said.

"Right," Beth said, looking her square in the eyeballs, sending her a subliminal message that they all knew she was the Vom Queen. Gross. "Momma? Want a sandwich?"

"Sure. Mmmm! Ham salad? Did Cecily make this?"

"Nope." She wondered if she had been on the receiving end of this kind of thing before. "They just appeared on the freaking table. Crusts off, the whole nine yards."

"Don't say *freaking,* darling. It implies you really meant to use the F word."

"I did."

Susan took a bite and then stared at her with the most peculiar expression, as what Beth had said finally dawned on her.

"What?"

"There's only ever been one person who could make ham salad like this."

"Yeah, and she ain't exactly dead, despite the facts."

"Livvie. Some pretty strange things happen in this house, don't they?"

"You're telling me? At least I won't get lonely while you're gone."

"You're not frightened to be here on your own, are you? Oh, honey, I hadn't even thought about that."

"Right. No, don't worry; I'll call an exorcist if I have to."

"Very funny. Just send Simon the bill."

Maggie came over to inspect the platter. "Oh, good! I was so sure Cecily would forget all about this!" She took a bite and looked at the surprise on their faces. "What? I whipped up two quarts of this mess earlier today and cut up the bread too! Why in the world are y'all looking at me so funny? Have one, they're pretty fabulous if I say so myself."

"Here," Beth said, handing the platter to her mother, "I gotta go strangle somebody."

She took a bottle of wine from the bar and marched back to the kitchen, where Cecily was waiting, laughing so hard there were tears streaming down her cheeks.

"I'm going to have to kill you," Beth said.

"Oh my! You should have seen your face! Oh! Goodness!"

"You must think I'm a gullible dumbass," she said, although she was having a hard time staying angry with Cecily whooping like a crazy person.

"Oh, Beth, I'm sorry. I am. I just couldn't resist. But that doesn't mean this 'eah house *ain't* haunted, and you know it too, don't you?"

"Yep. I know it. Oh, just forget it," she said, wondering how she could get her back.

Beth refilled their glasses and thought about the confounding truth of what she had just said. After all, years ago she had certainly seen Livvie in the mirror all through her childhood like many others had. And some unseen hand had most definitely turned down her bed the day that she arrived. They did hear things go bump in the night, all the time in fact, and the family's possessions moved around from one shelf or table to another on a regular basis while the clock chimed when it wasn't even wound. The bed in the room where her grandmother used to sleep was perpetually unmade no matter how many times they pulled up the covers, and a man who fit the description of her grandfather was frequently seen in the yard by neighbors, shaking his fist at the house. What in the world did these things mean? It would be an interesting topic for discussion when everyone got sick of talking about themselves. Which could take eons, she thought.

"How's that flounder coming? Anything

I can do to help?" Maggie appeared in the doorway to the kitchen. "Y'all getting acquainted?"

"I've got her number all right," Beth said, smiled at Maggie, and hooked her thumb in Cecily's direction.

"Now, just what do you mean by that?" Maggie said. "Come on, the buffet's all set up, so let's get that fish on the fire. We're all about to swoon from hunger." She began slitting the sides of brown paper bags and laying them on the table to drain grease from the fish. "Instant recycling!"

At the very least, they had to admire her endless ingenuity.

Eventually supper was ready and Maggie called everyone to the meal. There were nineteen of them if you included Lola, who was being passed around like a beanbag, loving all the attention, yelping only occasionally.

They held hands while Grant, who had flown in from California for the occasion with Maggie and Simon Rifkin, Beth's stepfather of the uninvolved sort, led them in a short prayer.

Just as they were serving themselves from the steaming platters of fish, onion rings, hush puppies, covered dishes of grits swimming in butter, and a huge bowl of salad, the back door slammed. Her aunts Sophie and Allison Hamilton, exercise and fitness gurus to the southeastern United States, popped into the living room from the kitchen like two matching corks.

"Hello, hello!" they called out.

In Charleston visitors normally announced themselves with *Hey, anybody home?* But Beth guessed that in Miami, where the twins lived, they said things like *Hello, hello!* And probably *Ciao, ciao!*

At first glance, she couldn't tell them apart. Identical twins were a curious phenomenon. Her aunts may have had the same DNA, but their personalities were polar opposites. Sophie was gregarious and generous, but Allison was sort of a haughty, humorless wretch. None of the family could say with certainty who was who until they began to speak, and that was how they knew the difference between them. They made their way around the room, offering more *Hello hellos* and dispensing polite hugs, back pats, and air kisses directed at cheeks.

While everyone was piling food onto

their plates and looking for a place to sit, Henry offered them goblets of wine, which they both declined. They didn't drink a drop of alcohol, which Henry said to anyone who would listen made them highly suspicious characters in his book. But to be frank, Henry was suspicious of social interaction with any nonimbibing human.

It was all *Don't you look wonderful!* And *Aren't you excited about Paris, Susan?* And *Look at these boys! Aren't they darling? And your girls, Timmy! My my!*

Until Allison got to Beth.

She said, "Whatever on this earth has happened to you? The last time I saw you, you were just a little bitty bug. It was your daddy's funeral, wasn't it? That filthy rotten son of a bitch. Horrible man. Yes, it was the funeral. But you surely didn't have all this and this! My word, honey!" Her accusing hand demonstrated she meant to remark on, yes, Beth's breasts and, yes, her hair. It was as though her body was a dartboard and anyone who wanted to could just lob a shot her way.

"I really wish she hadn't called him that," she said under her breath, feeling nauseated.

"You shouldn't call Tom a sumbitch, Allison," Grant said, having caught what Beth mumbled. "It's bad juju to speak ill of the dead."

Grant was next to Beth and she was trying hard not to look at him so he wouldn't see how upset she was.

"Oh, screw you, Grant," Allison said, and pulled her hair up into a ponytail, holding it with one hand. "Like you all don't do it all the time? Why is it so sticky here? I don't remember it being this sticky."

"It's the real beach, Al," Henry said, and rolled his eyes. "There's no humidity in Coral Gables?"

"Oh, fine. Well, I was just saying that the last time I saw Beth she was only a little girl and now she's all grown up. I mean, look at her!"

Every eye turned to Beth and she wanted to disappear. She felt like she must have been purple with embarrassment. God, she thought, I really, really hate her guts right now.

"What do you mean, Allison?" Maggie said. "That's all y'all gonna eat? I think Beth's grown into a perfectly magnificent young woman, don't you, Sophie? Come on and let's fix y'all a decent plate."

Maggie had temporarily redeemed herself to Beth, but Beth didn't know if she would ever feel all right about her Aunt Allison.

"I do. Don't mind your Aunt Allison," Sophie said. "The filter between her brain and her mouth appears to be malfunctioning." Sophie popped a hush puppy into her mouth and watched while Maggie loaded her plate with meager portions—*lady servings,* she would call them.

"It's okay," Beth said.

But it wasn't okay. Beth didn't care so much what Allison thought about her, but she really, truly, seriously, and deeply minded that she unapologetically referred to her father as a *filthy rotten son of a bitch.* How many times had she asked them not to say terrible things about her father?

"I'll get my own food, thanks," Allison said to Maggie. "So what are the sleeping arrangements?" She scooped salad into a small mound on her plate and took a sliver of fish.

"Aunt Sophie can sleep with me," Beth

said, knowing it was the last available portion of a mattress. She was attempting to get back in the conversation without her anger showing.

"Fun! It will be like old times!" Sophie said.

"We weren't sure you were even coming, Allison," Maggie said with a theatrical sigh, leaning against the table. "You never returned any of my calls."

Was there a reprimanding tone in Maggie's voice? Yes ma'am. Maybe she was sticking it to Allison on my behalf, Beth thought. Although she knew Maggie enjoyed giving Allison a little grief just on general principles.

"Oh, I see. Well, fine then," Allison said, equally dramatically, sitting on a corner of the sofa eating her salad with her fingers. "I don't have to stay here at all then, do I?"

"Actually, you and Aunt Sophie can have my bed and I'll sleep down the island," Beth said. "No problem."

"Excuse me? You think I'm sleeping with my sister in the same bed? I don't think so. What are we? Twelve years old?"

What a bitch, Beth thought. Allison was

worse than ever. It wasn't like her bed was crawling with cooties or something.

"Now, see here," Henry said in his most authoritative voice.

"See here *what,* Henry? Oh! Are you warming up a little lecture for the occasion?"

Allison was on a roll.

The chatter stopped and everyone watched as Allison stood and locked her jaw, working up steam for one of her notorious snits, shifting her weight from foot to foot and crossing her arms so tightly that her fingertips left white marks wherever they gripped her upper arms.

Timmy cleared his throat and said, "Now, Allison, there's no reason for anyone to get hysterical. I'm sure—"

"Shut up, Timmy. Freud's dead, you know, and I'm hardly hysterical."

Zing!

"I don't think I really heard her tell my husband to shut up, did I?" Mary Jo said, piping up, evidence of a spine no one knew she had. "That's not nice."

"Let's not be like this, Allison," Maggie said, ignoring Mary Jo. "I'm sure we can figure something out. The boys have another house down the island and I'm sure they can make room. Mickey? Y'all got an extra bed down at Mary Ellen's?"

"Um, I'm Mike now, Mom. Sure, Aunt Allison can even have my bed. No big deal. There's plenty of room."

"Thanks, honey. That's real sweet of you. Know what, Maggie? You are just as condescending as you were twenty years ago. It doesn't matter. I have to be in Columbia tomorrow anyway to review the vitamin clinical trials with Geoffrey. I'll just drive up there tonight and then no one's inconvenienced."

Beth was standing there taking it all in. Allison struggled to say she was leaving as calmly as she could, but anyone could see she was about to blow a major, major gasket. How could the family treat their most famous relative so casually? Did they forget to roll out the red carpet for the Second Coming? Uncle Henry had money but her aunts Allison and Sophie were famous in capital letters, at least in this neck of the woods. For once, Beth agreed with Maggie—Aunt Allison was an egomaniacal pain in the butt. But it was just as true that her Aunt Maggie did egg her on.

"You just do what you want to do, Allison. You know what's best for you," Maggie said in the most patronizing voice she had in her repertoire. "I don't."

"There you have it!" Allison said a little too loudly. "It was good to see y'all even if it was so very, very brief. You coming, Sophie?"

"Oh dear. Oh shoot. No, I think I'm gonna stick around, Al. I'll meet you in Columbia Monday if that's okay with you," Sophie said.

"Oh? And just how are you going to get there if I'm taking the car?"

It was a stupid question, Beth thought. There were any number of ways Sophie could get to Columbia, including hitching a ride with Uncle Timmy since he was headed to Charlotte early Sunday with his clan.

"Don't worry about me. I'll work it out," Sophie said, and gave her twin a pat on the arm. "Anybody want a glass of cold water? I'm going to get myself one."

"I'll take a beer if you're buying," Timmy said.

"Sure. Come on, Al. I'll walk you out to the car," Sophie said.

Sophie Hamilton was the Smoother, but then she had dedicated her years to ironing the wrinkles out of Allison's life.

As they left the room, you could feel the party spirit fizzle because of Allison's hissy fit. Beth slipped away and back into the kitchen. She had lost her appetite anyway. Too much angst. Cecily was leaning against the sink, picking at her plate of food. Beth looked out the window and watched Allison's animated rant and Sophie reaching out to calm her at least five times.

"My entire family is crazy," she said. "My aunt needs a slap across her Botox face and ten milligrams of something to chill her out."

"I ain't saying *nothing*," Cecily said.

"You don't have to," she said. "I think this crowd needs dessert. Something to sweeten them up. What have we got?"

The microwave pinged and Cecily put her plate down to retrieve whatever was in there.

"One step ahead of you." She showed Beth the Pyrex dish of peach cobbler.

It smelled delicious. Despite the fact that she was still furious with her Aunt Allison, Beth's mouth was actually watering.

Cecily said, "See if there's any vanilla ice cream in that freezer, okay?"

"Fine," she said. There was a large un-opened tub of chocolate but no vanilla. "How's this?"

"Works for me," Cecily said. "Don't you want to be out there with all of them? Hey, what's wrong?"

"Believe me. I'll spend enough time with them."

By the time Sophie came back into the house they had plated dessert for every-one, Beth's face was still grim, and Cecily was certain something had happened.

"Want a hand with that?" Sophie said. "My sister is a nut job sometimes, but she means well."

"Whatever. It's okay," Beth said, think-ing, No, she doesn't mean well, she's as mean as a snake. "Who's Geoffrey?"

"Allison's boyfriend. Believe it or not, she has one."

Beth wanted to say, Yes, that was ex-tremely unbelievable, but for the sake of the evening, she said nothing more. They carried out the pie and ice cream and when everyone was served, Sophie settled herself in a rocking chair next to Timmy, who flipped off the cap of his bottle of beer with his bare hands.

That's impressive, Beth thought, seeing there was no place for her to sit. And no one seemed to notice that she was just standing there. She went back to the kitchen, with the intention to help Cecily straighten up the kitchen. Before she got there Cecily stopped her in the hall.

"Okay, I can feel you seething. You gonna tell me what happened or do I have to squeeze it out of you?"

"Oh, shoot. It's nothing. My Aunt Allison is only the most insensitive woman on the planet, that's all."

"And why?"

"She referred to my father, who just died a few years ago, as a filthy rotten son of a bitch."

"Oh no. Not nice."

"Not nice at all. In front of everyone. I mean, even if he was one, it's not for her to say. And he wasn't."

"Come on. There's a story here, right?

I'm like the Sphinx. You can tell me anything and it stays right here."

"Thanks, I'm okay," she said, and then
choked up. "Look, my father was everything to me . . ." And Beth's tears began to
flow.

"Oh, honey, I'm so sorry," Cecily said.

"And no one understands."

"Well, I do. Come on now, let's get you
a tissue and we can talk about it."

"I don't want to talk about it. They'll know
we talked and then it will be a big discussion and everyone will have something to
say. I just . . . I just want to get through tonight. She's gone. I'm okay."

"We can talk when they're all gone."

"Thanks but I'm all right. Really."

They pushed open the swinging door to
the kitchen and in front of them was the
second shock of the evening. The kitchen
was immaculate. Every hair on Beth's body
stood up and a chill ran through her from
the top of her head down to her toes.

"This is impossible," Beth said. "Wait!
You did this!"

"Humph." Cecily examined the sink.
"Ain't been done by my hand. No ma'am."

Her eyes were wide in honest astonishment.

Beth opened the refrigerator and there were all the waiting leftovers wrapped neatly in waxed paper, something she hadn't used in her entire life. For some reason, the room smelled like lemons.

"Oh my God! What do you think about this?" Beth said. "Livvie? For real this time?"

"For real. Guess she didn't want to miss the party, 'eah? But looky here! We still have glasses and the dessert dishes to wash," Cecily said in a shaking voice. She opened the garbage can, which was full. "She never did like to take out the trash."

"I'll do it," Beth said, and pulled the bag out after tying the top corners tightly together. "Holy crap." She still had the shivers.

"Holy crap is right. I'll go get the rest of the dishes," she said. "And see if anyone wants coffee."

"Okay," she said.

Brave as Beth considered herself to be, she was spooked and she wasn't too sure she wanted to stay in the kitchen by herself for longer than two seconds. So she scooped up the heavy bag and raced down the back steps as quickly as she could to the larger garbage can, praying the bag wouldn't spring a leak on the way. Dinner parties were too much work, she decided. And this one was bordering on science fiction. And a little hand-to-hand combat.

"I gotta go walk my dog," she said to Cecily, glad to see her back in the kitchen.

"Well, I'm almost ready to go," Cecily said, and turned on the dishwasher. "Hey, I'm so glad I got to meet you! And thanks for all your help."

"Sure. Me too. See you when?"

"Tomorrow afternoon. You gonna tell them about the cleanup?"

"What's the point of that? Aunt Maggie and my mom will probably know anyway when they see the waxed paper, and the rest of them would just say we're nuts or something."

"You're right. And Beth? Just hang on, honey. Time cures a lot of things."

"Yeah, I know. And some people are just stupid. And mean."

"That is for true!"

Beth put Lola on her leash and after saying good night to every member of the family, she took her over the dunes to the beach. As it turned out, Lola was quite taken with the beach, which was fortunate because Beth loved to walk.

It was beautiful and clear and the flickering stars overhead were millions upon millions of tiny lights against the vast deep sky, as if she needed anything else to make her feel small. Beth had a case of the blues and she couldn't shake them. It wasn't about being stuck on the island for a year. It was what her Aunt Allison said that had triggered an entire emotional episode. Her eyes began to burn with frustration and tears for the second time. It wasn't that she didn't like her stepfather. He was a nice enough guy and her mother was crazy about him. Well, as crazy as people their age got over one another. They probably even had sex once in a while, which she tried not to think about because it was completely disgusting to even consider what people their age looked like naked.

Beth was remembering the period of time when she thought her parents were going to get back together. That was the ground zero of her pain. Her father, Tom, was deathly ill from prostate cancer but ambulatory and struggling to maintain a good face. He had broken up with his girl-friend and was spending more time with Beth and Susan. It was Christmas 1999 when he appeared on their doorstep. He had brought a new computer for her mother, which was thoughtful as money was pretty scarce all around. He gave Beth a gener-ous allowance for a shopping spree, which was just completely stunning because she bought her clothes with babysitting money, which was to say not much and not often.

Beth gave them—him really—an album of photographs that she had worked on for months. Every picture was chosen for the sole purpose of making them remember how happy they had been when they were all living together as a family. She thought, no, she *knew* that when her parents looked at those pictures they would fall in love again, and whatever time her father had left, he would be spending it with them. And she had thought, hoped, and prayed that their love for each other would some-how cure him.

It didn't work out at all. Her plan that was so carefully thought through, all those novenas and trying to cut a deal with God, it had all failed miserably and completely. Oh, he loved the album; they both did. They even got all choked up when they went through it. But the album, the petitions to God, and what she wanted most was not enough to reunite them. Her efforts were not powerful enough to change anything. In fact, her father went back to his ridiculous girlfriend, betraying her mother and abandoning Beth one more time. He actually preferred that life to having one with them. Did either one of her parents or any of her relatives ever think about how that made her feel?

He was in remission, he announced, and shortly afterward he moved to California with Karen. Things were all right for a while but then he got sick again and died in no time at all. Gone forever. Just like that. Her mother, who organized the whole funeral because Karen didn't have the brains or the wherewithal to do it, appeared to recover in record time and then she turned around and married Simon. They were living happily ever after. Good for them, Beth thought, because I am surely not.

When the discussion of families would come up, Beth would say to her roommates,

"What good is a commitment to a marriage if one person doesn't honor it and the other one doesn't seem to care? It's all so stupid. The whole marriage thing is a bunch of hyped-up bull."

One thing was certain, or at least she thought so. She was never going to let herself get sucked into a delusional world of white picket fences and minivans that depended on someone else's honesty. Her mother had jumped off the cliff head-first, not once but twice. Beth didn't know how Susan coped with all that fantasy because in her mind there was nothing more dangerous than what her mother called love.

She'd had her share of boyfriends. But none of them had ever amounted to a serious relationship because she was so very guarded. Besides, Beth or the object of her affection always seemed to be headed somewhere else—college in another state, summer jobs, internships, or just studying until all hours. These things were surely obstacles between Beth and love, but mainly it was her thick wall of self-protection. She told herself that she probably had not met the right guy yet.

Besides that, it just seemed to her that people her age were all hooking up without a relationship and that was just too weird to her. Not that Beth Hayes didn't have an appreciation for some acceptable degree of shallowness, but she had seen the damage an *anything goes* kind of attitude could do, and she couldn't see any reason to change. Read: If her mother found out she had turned into a slut, she'd murder her in cold blood and her Aunt Maggie would turn her bones into a lamp. Nice thought.

She had walked the whole way to the water tower around Station 25 and she knew it was getting late. When the tide was low and the breeze was so nice it would be so easy to keep ambling along until she ran out of island. But soon, thinking her mother might start to worry that she had been raped, murdered, and thrown to the sharks, she turned around and began to walk back toward the house. Lola was whining. She knew her little dog was exhausted from all the excitement of the night and picked her up.

"Momma can carry you, baby. It's okay."

When she got close enough to see the

house, there were the silhouettes of her Aunt Sophie and her mother, on the porch rocking back and forth in the moonlight. Their laughter echoed across the dunes. It warmed Beth to see them so obviously enjoying themselves. This was what was good about families, she thought.

She walked across the yard and her mother stood up to greet her.

"Hey, baby! You were gone so long we were about to call the Coast Guard."

"Yeah, well, your granddog likes to stop and inspect everything." She climbed up the steps and gave her a hug. "What are y'all talking about?"

"We are solving the problems of the world, my beautiful niece. That's all," Sophie said. "Come sit here."

She sat in the rocker next to her aunt and Sophie reached over and patted the back of her hand.

"I should really put Lola in her crate," Beth said. "She's had it."

"Give her to me," Susan said. "I'm going to bed anyway. I've had it too."

Beth gave Lola a nuzzle and handed her over. "Night, baby. Thanks, Momma. See you in the morning."

Susan said *Love y'all,* blew them kisses, and closed the screen door carefully so that she wouldn't wake the others. The house was quiet then. Sophie and Beth rocked for a few minutes, back and forth in silence.

"So what did I miss while I was out there?" Beth said.

"Well, we sliced up my twin pretty good."

"Yeah, that's the dangerous part about leaving early. People get vicious and talk about you. Especially if you deserve it."

"That's every family, sweetheart. Anyway, Allison has me worried lately."

"Why's that? Not that she doesn't seem even more bitchy than ever. Excuse me."

"Right? No, I agree with you. She's practically insufferable."

"So what's new?"

"Well, when we started our business, the workout studios were one thing, then it was infomercials selling DVDs and that's still a good source of revenue for both of us. But now that we're getting into these herbal supplements, Allison is popping more pills of unknown and unapproved substance than I think is healthy for her. Her boyfriend, Geoffrey with a *G,* thank you, is her new guru. I mean, she's the company guinea pig and it's obviously taking its toll on her. She's got mood swings like the one you saw tonight, and—"

"Maybe it's stress."

"Yeah, no doubt. But she's become insanely ambitious, and once we launch Vita-Supp, she's talking about taking our whole business public. Don't tell that to anyone, though, okay?"

"Who am I gonna tell? Lola?"

"Still. Anyway, she told me she wants to be a billionaire. A billionaire. Who in their right mind thinks we can make a billion dollars doing this?"

"Geesch. Pretty crazy."

Sophie said, "Well, that's the thing. She might actually be crazy. But enough of that. Tell me how *you* are."

"Reasonably miserable in my boring pathetic existence wondering why I actually deferred my scholarship to babysit this crazy house for a year."

"Well, that's obvious. This house needs a sitter because if some responsible person wasn't here the haints might take over."

They both giggled about that. Whatever haints occupied the Island Gamble were, in the family's opinion, reasonably harmless and just something else to talk about late at night on the porch.

"Seriously, right?"

"You're awfully good to do this, Beth. Your mother is half out of her mind with excitement over going to Paris."

"I know, I know. That's why I'm doing it. But you know what?"

"What?"

"I worry that this is a slippery slope. I could wind up with frosted hair wearing little sundresses covered in tiny flowers if I don't watch myself. Not that there's anything wrong with that, but I don't want to be that girl. I'm pretty sure I don't want this life."

"Gotcha. You want to be yourself, is that right? An individual with your own mind? Your own taste in things?"

"Exactly."

"So what do you think it's like to have an identical twin?"

"Weird, but I'm just guessing."

"Weird like you can't imagine. We even have freckles in the same spots."

"Really?"

"Really. So you want to know what I

did? I got a tattoo. Even Allison doesn't know. So if you tell, I'll have to kill you."

"How cool are you? Let me see it!"

Sophie stood up and pulled down the waistband of her skirt. There, in the darkness of the porch, Beth could make out a tattoo of a butterfly on her left hip.

"Branded! When did you do this?"

"Like ten years ago. I was pretty sick of being exactly—and I mean *exactly*—like someone else."

"Wow."

"Yep. There you have it. I feel your pain. So, is the other reason for your unhappiness that you're not headed to graduate school?"

"Yeah. I'm itching to try and write a novel."

"About what?"

"I don't really know yet. I mean, I've got some ideas."

"Well, honey, I love you more than anyone except your momma so I'm gonna give you a tip."

"Shoot."

"There's plenty of plot right here, so start taking notes."

"Maybe."

"And get a job to keep yourself busy."

"You're right about that. Otherwise I'm going to lose my mind."

"Well, whatever you do, don't complain about your awful lot in life. You won't get a lot of sympathy from anyone that you have an all-expenses-paid vacation on this island for a year. Besides, this family has enough malcontents."

"Boy, is that ever the truth!"

"Listen, Beth. If I had a daughter, I'd want her to be just like you. If you ever need anything, not just this year, but ever, you come to me. Come on, let's close up the house. It's late."

Beth thought she would sleep like a stone that night and start taking notes tomorrow. Maybe look for a job when they all left. They went inside, closing and locking the door behind them. Next, they went to the kitchen to make sure everything was put away. There was Teensy wearing a silk nightshirt of all things, sitting at the table, pressing a cold cloth on the back of her neck.

"It's too hot and humid to sleep," she said, "I don't know why this house doesn't have central air-conditioning. It's miserable up there! You could die for a breath of air!"

"Oh, let me get you a glass of ice water, Teensy," Sophie said, checking the knobs on the stove to assure herself they were all in the off position. "It's only two nights, for heaven's sake," she mumbled.

"I'm at a delicate stage of life," she said with a pout.

Sophie and Beth rolled their eyes at each other.

Beth said, "I'll bet it's hot in our room too."

"Yes, but there are bugs in my room," Teensy said. "Big disgusting cockroaches. Henry has already killed two. Heaven knows how many more are lurking about."

"My hero," Sophie said in a cartoon voice. "They're palmetto bugs."

"They're the state bird," Beth said, checking the lock on the back door and then the stove. Again. "Or maybe that's the mosquito?"

Even Teensy had to smile, but she still went on like a whiny sissy.

"You all are used to this. I'm not," she said in a last attempt to defend her case.

"Used to this? Come on, Teensy, let's

call it a night," Sophie said. "In less than forty-eight hours you can go back to Atlanta, where apparently they don't have summer. Or bugs."

Teensy got up, smoothed out her night-shirt, which in her defense did have a streak of perspiration down the back, but Beth thought, Who wears silk in the summer? Morons, that's who. She poured them all a glass of water. They went upstairs together and said good night to one another.

Sophie was in the bathroom. Beth checked on Lola and crawled into bed. She could hear her aunt humming as she brushed her teeth. She thought about Aunt Teensy and how pampered and spoiled she was to complain so much. It wasn't all that hot. And then her thoughts drifted to her Aunt Allison, her temper and her wild ambition—greed really—and she vowed never to become like either one of them. But at least I wasn't the only one being used for target practice, she thought, and that was a small consolation.

Her Aunt Sophie was so wonderful. She understood everything. And the more she thought about meeting Cecily, the better she felt. They would be friends and that was nice to think about. But this was no vacation. She was determined to make the year mean something.

The tide had turned and there was a gorgeous breeze in the room. The next thing Beth knew she was dreaming that Confederate jasmine covered the entire house and she was laughing, chasing Lola down the empty beach right before dawn.

3

Family Jewels

With the exception of Allison, who blew out of town so hard she initiated small-craft warnings, everyone else seemed to be relaxed and having a good time reminiscing about the past and big-timing one another about the present. But Allison had served her purpose. It always heightened the family's mood when there was one relative to throw in the fire along with some mesquite chips. The general consensus was that success had gone to her head and perhaps she really was slightly insane.

It was Saturday night, many pigs had sacrificed their ribs for the occasion, and a classic southern barbecue was in full swing—pork, burgers, coleslaw, potato salad, cornbread, and, of course, plenty of cold beer and sweet tea. Despite the fact that the adults were all counting carbohydrates, watching their cholesterol, blood pressure, and just generally trying to stick to one diet or another, the mountainous platters of food would disappear all the same. People would give themselves special dispensations for the occasion or they would be goaded into tasting, *Just a little, it's so good* . . .

The porch was overflowing with relatives and many of Susan's lifelong friends and colleagues who had come to wish her well. Timmy was tending the grill, where he and Henry were bickering like twelve-year-old brothers over whether it was better to turn the baby back ribs over and over, basting them each time, or to turn them only once or twice and baste them at the end when they were fully cooked.

"It depends on who's cleaning the grill," Beth heard her mother say. "That gooey sauce sticks to the grilling rack like plaque in your arteries."

"Ew," Beth said, walking over to them

with a platter of pigs in blankets and a dish of mustard. "Anybody want some of America's favorite hors d'oeuvres? Watch out, they're really hot."

"And only marginally fattening," Susan said with a wink. "Where's Maggie?"

Beth smiled to herself because her mother wouldn't fully enjoy bingeing on a handful of carbs and fat in front of her skinny older sister; that much was for sure. In addition, having Sophie there with her hard body gave them all another reason to suck in their abs and correct their posture.

"Don't worry. Eat all you want. She's in the kitchen with Cecily cutting ribbons from lemon and lime skins and tying them into bows to garnish a big platter of shrimp."

Beth said this with a straight face because as absurd as it was, it was the truth. Beth's Aunt Maggie was a fool for her paring knife and the kit of garnishing tools she bought on the Home Shopping Network. Susan arched her eyebrow at Beth, that famous arch Beth had practiced in the bathroom mirror and had nearly perfected, and jammed a pig in a blanket in her mouth as fast as possible.

"Really," she said, implying that she agreed with Beth on Maggie's compulsive nature. "Well, there are worse afflictions than a little OCD in the cooking department. Can I have another one of those?"

"Sure. Uncle Henry? Y'all want one?"

Each of her uncles put four on a napkin, slathered them with mustard, and let them rest on the side of the grill. They said *Thanks, kid* and went back to their argument.

Timmy said, "Tell you what, bubba. I'll cook a rack on this side of the grill my way and you smother and suffocate yours over there, destroying their natural integrity—"

"What's integrity got to do with pork? You're as crazy as a low-flying loon."

Susan put her hand on Beth's elbow to lead her away.

"Numskulls," she whispered. "Let's go see what your cousins are doing."

They spotted Mike, the cousin formerly known as Mickey, over by the bar with some adults and he waved to them. Beth stuck the platter into their circle and the pigs in blankets disappeared as though they had been devoured by a school of piranhas.

"So, Mike? What's up with you?"

"I'll go get some more," Susan said, taking the empty serving dish from Beth. "Be right back."

"Aunt Susan?" Mike said. "See if they've got any of those sausage balls left too? I love those things."

"You know it! I'll be back in a flash."

Susan smiled at all of them and Beth wondered if she would ever look at anyone like her mother did. Susan's eyes were brimming with maternal affection and it occurred to Beth that those kinds of looks were as natural to her mother as taking a breath. Beth was miles away from that stage of life. She could not even imagine seeing the world through eyes glazed over with happiness, much less happiness born from serving others.

They watched Susan disappear into the crowd and reappear as she climbed the steps to the front porch. Beth and her clan had made hundreds of trips up and down those steps all day long, bringing out tables, chairs, candles, hurricanes, and Eiffel Towers to serve as centerpieces so the tablecloths wouldn't blow away if the breezes turned to wind. She had helped to string Christmas lights between the palmettos to light the yard and jammed tiki torches filled with citronella oil into the soft ground near the dunes to ward off bugs. It had been like a cardio workout all that day and Beth was already hoping for a short night.

"Your mom is the best," Mike said.

"Yeah, she is. Thanks. I'm real proud of her."

"Yeah, so you graduated. Congratulations."

"Thanks. Now I get to spend a year here losing my mind, going completely insane, doing nothing, withering in total obscurity."

"Obscurity? That's a pretty big word for someone your age, isn't it?"

"You must've missed the memo. I graduated from college? And where's my gift, you cheapskate?"

Mike was waving his three-year advantage over Beth's just to irritate her. Boys were all the same, she thought. Everything was a big, fat, stupid competition.

"Right. Sorry. Well, a year in obscurity sounds good to me. I'm still Uncle Henry's personal slave in Atlanta working hundred-hour weeks. I could come and hang out, you know, so you don't go nuts or some-thing."

She gave that a moment's consideration and then brightened up.

"Yeah, that would be really, really good actually. No doubt I will want some com-pany. Plus, we can go downtown, check out the bars, you know, have some fun?"

Beth was thinking that sooner rather than later she was going to need to go over the causeway, and get some kind of a life going. She had not had the time or the de-sire to dig up her old friends from high school and see what they were doing. Half of them were probably married because in the South it seemed that people married young, as though a marital partner would make the transition into adulthood easier emotionally and financially.

"Oh? You have a fake ID?"

"Hello? I'm twenty-three, hello."

"You look like you're sixteen."

"Yeah, right. You need an eye doctor. And why are you still gelling your hair? It's like so nineties."

Beth snickered and Mike looked up at the sky.

"It's wet, moron. I just took a shower."

"And the world is a better place for it, Mr. Hamilton."

"Let's get a beer and go torture Bucky."

"Sounds good."

Bucky and especially Mike were Beth's favorite cousins because they had practically grown up together. Her Uncle Henry came home to Sullivans Island with his family once a year and her Uncle Timmy came only for important occasions. Timmy's daughters, who were decked out in pink and green sundresses with pink pedicures and white headbands and whom she had not seen in ages, were avoiding her. Beth sucked her teeth when she saw them, feeling a thousand years older than them, and realized her Aunt Maggie was exaggerating to say they were dying to see her. They could not have cared less.

In addition, Timmy's sons, the biblically named Mark and Luke, were friendlier with the other boys, especially when it came to family outings that usually excluded the fair sex like dove hunting in the woods and gigging for flounder at midnight. Those other cousins, Phillip and Blake, even though they had reached the ages of twenty and eighteen, were just as annoying as they had been since the day they were born. Still, Beth marveled at the way they all came together, her aunts and uncles and their herd of offspring.

The desire to remain close and in touch with one another was propelled by the lone but stalwart efforts of Maggie. Beth wondered who among her generation would emerge as the matriarch or patriarch and work to keep their traditions alive? Or would they all drift apart and never see one another except for weddings and funerals when their parents went to that great house party in the sky? Would it be worth the energy when the family now lived in four different states? Beth did not know the answer to any of these questions and shrugged them off thinking that in time they would see.

Mike reached into the cooler and pulled out two bottles of beer, twisted off the caps, and handed one to her. He gave his cousin an assessment from head to toe and decided to contain his opinions, remembering she was his cousin. There were remarkable changes in Beth. Maybe it would be fun to come back to the island

and hang out with her, go to the bars and see how she handled men.

"There's Bucky by the grill," he said. "Hey, Bucky! You want a beer?"

"Yeah, thanks!" he called back.

Grabbing one more, Mike and Beth moved across the yard to where he stood. Bucky, who was twenty-four, was in constant competition with his older brother. When Mike announced he was going to business school, Bucky decided he was going to medical school. When Mike got into Carolina, Bucky began the application process to attend Duke. It was plain old sibling rivalry and one-upmanship that had been going on since Bucky came home from the hospital on day three of his life and they looked each other in the eye. Beth, as an only child, thought their jealousy was ridiculous. She would have done anything to have had a sister or a brother.

"So," Beth said, "what's going on?"

"Well," Bucky said, "I was thinking about taking the golf cart out for a spin. Want to come?"

"Dude, there's the sundown law for golf carts. And a huge fine." Mike said.

"If we get caught. Which we won't."

"Right," Mike said.

"Come on, what's the big deal? If the cops stop us, we just tell them we're from out of town and we didn't know. I'm taking Blake and Phillip. They're like catatonic from boredom."

"Yeah, and Uncle Grant will kick your ass if you get caught," Beth said.

"Nice mouth, Red. Just stay on the backstreets, okay?" Mike said.

"Whatever," Bucky said, and walked away to find his cousins.

Beth and Mike watched him go and thought Bucky was taking a dumb risk for something that wasn't worth it. Couldn't they just go play Frisbee or Halo? And sure enough, barely an hour later on the edge of night, here came Sullivans Island's finest.

Henry and Grant heard the squad car pulling into the yard and went around the house to see what was going on. There were Bucky, Blake, and Phillip sitting in the backseat looking extremely uncomfortable, staring at their feet.

"Evening," Henry said, and recognized the police officer as someone he had known slightly in high school. "Wait, don't I know you? Did you go to Bishop England? Maybe, Wando?"

His name tag read *Dan Howard, Chief of Police.*

"Yeah, Bishop England, Class of '79," Chief Howard said. "Wait a second, I know you. Henry Hamilton! Didn't you grow up here in this house? Is that your boy I picked up?"

"Yeah, that's me. Two of them are mine. The other one is my nephew. What did they do?"

"Well, we've got a golf cart curfew violation that carries a hefty fine, and the more serious charge for all of them is open container and that the two younger boys are underage."

"Great," Grant said.

As Mike and Beth came around the corner, they could tell that Uncle Grant was furious just by his posture. His feet were spread and dug in, his arms were crossed across his chest, and his jaw was tight. Their Uncle Henry, on the other hand, was standing there smiling with his hands in his pockets. Henry was a cool customer under duress.

"Holy moly," Beth said under her breath. "Right?"

"What happened, Uncle Henry?" Mike said, nodding to Beth, using his most manly voice.

Henry did not respond to Mike, who did not press the issue, knowing the facts would emerge quickly enough. Beth had the good sense to remain silent for once in her brief but opinionated life, making mental notes to be used later.

Chief Howard was writing up tickets, tearing them off the pad, and handing them one by one to Grant, who looked at each one and passed them to Henry.

"Sorry, Henry, but I have to do this. We got regulations to follow like every other town."

"Understood. But there is still plenty of light. Perhaps the golf cart violation could get some consideration?"

Chief Howard looked up at the sky. Henry was right. It was almost nine o'clock and the sky was still light although the sun had set. Howard decided that they were both right. He took the golf cart ticket back from Henry and tore it in two. Thus Henry and Grant saved themselves five hundred dollars that they would have taken out of the boys' hides.

"In memory of Father Kelly and for old times' sake. I assume I can release these young men into your custody?"

"Thank you. Father Kelly was a saint. Yeah, I'll take these marauding hoodlums off your hands."

"The underage consumption of alcohol will have to be dealt with in Family Court downtown. Our court meets on Tuesday night."

"Great," Grant said. "We go back to California tomorrow morning."

Henry said, "And we're going back to Atlanta. Can we just plead guilty and pay the fine?"

"Probably, but I'd call Judge Steinert. He can tell you what to do."

"Kids," Grant said. "Steinert?"

"You're telling me?" Chief Howard said. "I've got four with two more on the way. Can you imagine? Anyway, Steve Steinert is a really good guy." Chief Howard opened the back door of his car to release the boys. "All right, gentlemen. Let's go."

When they were out, Chief Howard slammed the door and went around to the driver's side of the car.

"Good night, Chief. And thank you," Henry said.

"Yes," Grant said. "Thank you very much."

Chief Howard saluted Henry and Grant in that friendly but official way in which manly men acknowledged one another's departure.

Bucky, Phillip, and Blake stood around waiting for Henry or Grant to kill them.

Henry's cool demeanor evaporated. Through gritted teeth he said to Phillip and Blake, "Let's go inside for a minute. I want to have a word with both of you."

Beth and Mike would have sworn on a Bible that there was a trace of steam around Henry's head. Phillip and Blake looked terrified as they followed their father up the back steps. Henry had more than a little of his father's well-known temper.

Then Grant, who seemed to be struggling to restore even breathing, turned to Bucky, drawing back, inhaling deeply.

"So what do you have to say for yourself?"

"I'm a dumbass."

"Yeah, we could start with that. You know, here's what disturbs me, son." He pointed his finger into Bucky's chest, which was something Grant rarely did. "You're the older one, right? The role model? You got your two cousins in some very hot water when it wasn't necessary. Why did you do it? Explain this to me because I don't get it."

"We were bored, I guess. You know how it is. It didn't seem like such a big deal, Dad. I mean, it was just beer."

"Just beer. And probably a five-hundred-dollar fine. Pretty expensive beer, don't you think?"

"I guess." Bucky was staring at the ground. "It's not like half the world doesn't ride around the island with something in a cup."

Mike and Beth looked at each other as if to say, Why is he digging himself this hole? But Grant was leading the questioning around to impose his own measure of justice.

"Perhaps they do, but you got caught. Didn't you? You had a can of beer, logo showing for anyone to see, a blatant violation of the law, and you knew it, right?"

"Yeah. I guess."

"Did you say *yeah*?"

"Yes sir."

Beth and Mike looked at each other because every person on earth knew that saying *yeah* in this situation was basically suicidal. Besides they could both see Grant's temple twitch, which was his renowned telltale clue of extreme frustration.

"That's better. So, just how do you propose to make things right?"

"Pay the fine? Not let it happen again?"

"That's a start. You may have five hundred dollars in the bank, but do you think your cousins do?"

"They probably have like a zillion dollars in the bank."

"Is that the point?"

"No sir. It's not. Should I offer to pay their fines too?"

"There you go. I like it when I see you take responsibility for your actions, son. Now let's go back and rejoin the party without announcing this idiotic episode to everyone, okay? This is your aunt's party, not yours."

Until that moment Grant and Bucky had

not noticed that Beth and Mike were still planted there like cornstalks with, well, ears.

"Way to go, dude," Mike said to Bucky as he and Beth followed him back to the party. Beth skipped ahead and looped her arm over Bucky's shoulder in a gesture of solidarity.

"That's Dr. Dude to you, asshole. I just got hosed for like, I don't know, probably a thousand? Shit."

"Boys, boys . . . potty mouth!" Beth said. "Let's go find Blake and Phillip to see if they need to go to the ER. Big Henry was seriously pissed."

But Bucky and Mike broke away from Beth when they saw the boys on the porch and Beth decided to let them get the low-down on their own. After all, they had all the time in the world to discuss it. This story was already page one million and seventeen in the family's history book. She spotted her mother.

"Okay," Susan said, walking toward her, "what happened?"

"Boys are stupid," Beth said. "Always pushing the limits."

"You know it, sugar. Golf cart?"

"Yeah, and a few other details like open container, underage—"

"Nice."

"Uncle Grant is making Bucky pay the fines for all of them."

"You don't learn anything if it doesn't hurt a little."

"Mom! That's pretty cold!"

Susan looked at Beth and fell in love with her daughter for the trillionth time.

"Maybe. But it's true. Speaking of money, we have to talk about the nasty stuff."

"Yeah, I know. I'm totally broke. How am I supposed to live? I mean, you know, like what if I have to go to the doctor or what if your hunk-of-junk car breaks down?"

"That car is a classic and it has four brand-new tires, all in your honor. But if something happens, put it on your credit card and call Simon. He'll pay you back right away. Anyway, I am putting three hundred a month in your checking account to cover food and gas and stuff like that, but I strongly recommend you get a job."

"A job. Right. Doing what?"

She had toyed with the idea, even spoken about it, but what was she going to do for gainful employment in Charleston with a degree in English literature? Teach? She didn't even like children! She realized she was going to starve. Beth felt a panic coming on. Three hundred a month. It was a lot of money for house-sitting for her own family, she supposed, but she could see herself spending it all on food alone.

"So, whatever you don't spend is yours to keep! How's that? What's wrong, honey?"

"I don't know, it's just, well, what am I going to do?"

"Did you eat yet? I want you to get something before it's all gone. The food's fabulous."

"Don't change the subject, Mom. I'll eat later. What am I going to do?"

"Why don't you check out the restaurants? You could wait tables? Tend bar?"

"That would be better than nothing, I suppose."

"Well, excuse me but you can earn a pretty penny bartending on this island. People drink like fish."

It was true enough that the sultry island breezes seemed to put people in the mood to overindulge, and she thought maybe that could lead to overtipping. The commute would certainly be easy. Suddenly that three hundred dollars a month stipend seemed generous. Then Beth felt guilty about complaining. Here was her mother leaving for the dream of her life and she was moaning like a spoiled child.

"Don't worry, Mom. I'll work it out. I'll just be gathering a plot for my first novel or something."

Susan looked at Beth's face, searching for any signs of insecurity and, seeing none, she relaxed.

"That's my girl," she said. "Try to look at this time as some kind of reward for busting your butt for the last four years. Relax! Enjoy it! Believe me, in the blink of an eye you'll be an old goat like me!"

"I wish you wouldn't say that you're old, Mom. You seem like you're my age."

"Sweetheart, that's very nice, but we need to face the facts here." Susan stopped then, thinking that the year away from Beth was going to break her heart. She would miss her something terrible. "Hey, do you promise to email and text me every day? Promise me you'll be inconsolable, longing for me like mad?"

"Yes ma'am. I will miss you every minute of every day and I will email and text you like crazy. Don't worry so much, okay? I'm an adult and I can handle this. I swear."

"Don't swear, honey, unless you're taking high office. It's common."

"Oh, Mom."

Susan put her empty goblet down on a table and pulled Beth into a long hug. Then she pushed a stray tendril away from Beth's face. Tears began to bubble over Susan's eyelids.

"Momma! Don't cry! Come on now! Everything is fine."

Susan wiped her face with the back of her hands and began to stutter.

"I know, I know, it's just, oh my, well, what if something happened to you? I just couldn't stand it, that's all. I love you so much, you just don't know, more than, well, anyone. Just please promise me you'll be careful? Lock the doors at night? Check the stove? Look under the beds? Don't let anyone smoke in the house? All that stuff?"

Maggie had spotted them and made her way over, waving a napkin, offering it to Susan.

"Girl? Dry your eyes and come try the

shrimp! I swanny, those little boogers were swimming this afternoon. They're so sweet!"

Susan blew her nose and Maggie leaned into Beth for a whisper that Susan definitely heard.

"Tell your momma to compose herself. Her estrogen is obviously running low again." Then Maggie walked away.

Beth giggled and said, "She's got like radar or something. I mean, how does she know what's happening with everyone at once?"

"She's the omniscient goddess. I'm used to it. Sometimes it's just awful."

Beth put her arm around her mother and gave her a squeeze. "Well, the witch is right. We're having a party here, not a wake. Let's go do tequila shots together or something like that, you know, have a mother-daughter bonding experience?"

Susan laughed then and gave Beth a kiss on the cheek.

"Bad idea, but I do love you, you know?"

"And I love you too! You're my favorite person in the entire universe and all I want to do is make you proud of me."

"I am so proud of you I could just burst. Do you know that?"

"Yes ma'am. I do." Even Beth, who was not prone to weak moments of sentimental emotion, felt like crying for the second time in forty-eight hours, something she rarely did.

Later that night, after everyone had said goodbye, after Cecily, Beth, Maggie, and Susan had restored order to the house, Cecily said good night and left. Maggie and Grant, Susan and Simon, Timmy, Henry, and Sophie and Beth all gathered on the porch for a postmortem discussion of the evening. They occupied the length of it in rockers and most of them had their feet up on the banisters. Then there was the late arrival of Mary Jo and Teensy, who had taken Mary Jo's girls to the other house and had stopped to buy milk, but whose hands had not been sullied by a sponge or a paper towel all night, which had infuriated Maggie, annoyed Susan, and amused Beth.

"This house has more rockers than a Cracker Barrel," Teensy said.

Despite the population you could hear

Maggie and Susan suck their teeth, making a sound like *snnkk*.

"Meanwhile, every one of them is being put to good use," Timmy said.

"Good thing this porch can't talk," Henry said.

"You can say that again," Maggie said.

"What happened here?" Grant said. "Anything I should know about?"

"Maggie wore the lips off of Lucius Pettigrew," Susan said.

Maggie burst out laughing. "Susan! Hush your mouth! Oh my! Luscious Lucius! I haven't thought about him in a million years."

"Lucius Pettigrew? What kind of a sissy name is that?" Grant said.

"Maybe he's bald," Henry said. "I heard he was a bazillionaire."

"Screw him," Grant said.

"Life is so unfair," Teensy said.

"Lucky you never got caught by the Invisible Sheriff," Henry said.

Beth said, "Who's the Invisible Sheriff? Another ghost like the Gray Man on Pawleys Island?"

"Henry? Don't go packing my child's head with all that old bullshit," Susan said.

"Do you eat with that same mouth, sweetheart?" Simon said.

"Listen, Dr. Heartbreaker, you'd better behave yourself in California or I'll send the Invisible Sheriff to get you, okay?" Susan pointed her finger at Simon and he threw his arms up in surrender.

"For Pete's sake!" Beth said. "Will somebody tell me the flipping story?"

"All right, all right, but honey, don't say *flipping.* It sounds like you really mean to use—"

"The F word. I would, except that you and Aunt Maggie would beat the stuffings out of me."

"You are correct," Maggie said. "We don't use that kind of language in our family."

"Okay, girls!" Henry said. "Here's the skinny. When we were really little, little kids, way before Sophie and Allison were born, this island was still pretty untamed. I mean, we had roads, but mostly they were paved with oyster shells. Dogs ran around, people had chickens, and there was this wild horse who just sort of roamed the beach and the streets. Somebody must have fed him, I don't remember who."

"Momma always said it was Pell Pozaro," Timmy said.

"Maybe," Henry said. "Anyway, our parents would tell us to stop our foolishness or the Invisible Sheriff would come get us and lock us up in the pokey. And brother, we'd stop. We'd see that horse coming and we would take off, running like all forty."

"Oh," Beth said, "that's it? What's *all forty*?"

"Forty-Mule Team Borax," Maggie said. "Maybe it was actually twenty?"

"That's the whole story," Timmy said. "Hey! Y'all remember Marvin Struthers?"

"I remember the time he pulled my big head out of the ventilation duct on the Thompson Battery," Henry said.

"During a hurricane, no less," Maggie said.

"What?" Beth said.

"Yeah," Timmy said, "your Uncle Henry was quite the hellion in his day."

"I could have died. I can still taste the motor oil. Blechh!"

"Why do I get the feeling that y'all have a secret history?" Beth said.

"Would you want the whole world to know your brothers were like animals?"

Sophie said. "Although they're so much older than me, they're like from another generation." She gave Henry a good-natured punch in the arm.

"Stop, you big Amazon!" Henry said. "You could hurt somebody!"

"Yeah, right. The boys were terrible, Beth, right, Maggie?" Susan said. "Remember the bicycle wars?"

"Oh Lord, not that story again," Timmy said.

"Come on, tell me!" Beth said, thinking this was definitely the best part of the night.

"Well, when I was a lad—" Henry said in a deep baritone.

"*A lad? A lad?* How was it growing up in Victorian England? You pompous ass," Timmy said, laughing. "Look, Beth, here's how it was."

"Shut up," Henry said.

"No, you shut up. I'm talking to my niece! Okay. When we were kids, it was a big deal to have a bicycle. Nobody had a lot of money back then and getting up enough cash for all of us to have our own bikes probably put our parents on a short list for the poor house. But the old man understood what it meant to us and so somehow, he managed to give us all bikes."

"Why do you always bring up the nice things about that son of a bitch?" Henry said.

"Because I spent twenty years in therapy to earn the right to forgive him. Move on, Henry. Hatred is a cancer, you know."

"Oh, up yours, Freud. It is my childlike hatred of that masochistic bastard that springboarded me to all I am today."

"I'm gagging over here," Susan said.

"Me too," Timmy said. "Anyway, Beth, in those days, the island was divided into territories. All us Catholic kids owned this end of the island. If any of the Protestant kids came down here on their bikes, we would chase them off. We had guards on every corner and our war plans were very elaborate, given our resources."

"We would engage after supper and before dark," Henry said.

"Did you have actual fights? Like hitting each other?"

"Uh, yeah. We kicked their bony little asses all the time," Henry said, and flexed his muscles.

"That's absolutely true," Timmy said, and high-fived Henry.

Maggie said, "So why don't one of you big muchachos tell your niece what happened when you went into their territory?"

"That? Well, basically, they kicked ours," Henry said.

"Yep. They killed us all the time."

"Sounds stupid to me," Beth said. "My mother would've put me on restriction for a year if I did anything like that."

"Sure would have," Susan said.

"As well she should have," Maggie said. "Ladies of this family do not involve themselves in street fights."

The Christmas lights twinkled in the landscape, the last remaining evidence that something festive had taken place that evening. The dunes stood in their snowy mounds, festooned with goldenrod and clumps of beach grass that waved in the breeze. The ocean murmured as the incoming tide gently lapped against the shore. And the beams from the lighthouse washed everything before them in steady intervals of gossamer light. They rocked quietly until Simon spoke.

"What a great party, Maggie. Thanks for everything. You sure gave Susan one helluva bon voyage."

"Amazing weekend," Susan said.

"Yes, it was lovely," Teensy said, drawling on *luuuvley*.

"Shucks, 'twern't nothing," Maggie said in her best hillbilly accent, slipping it a little to Teensy.

"Right," Henry said, and laughed. "Just your basic royal wedding. No big deal."

Timmy and Grant said a few things about the antics of their sons and Susan threw in, "They're just boys."

Exhaustion was hiding in the shadows, preparing to claim them for the night as the older members of the family fell silent again.

"Somebody's gonna be smelling croissants and chocolate in two days," Beth said. "You getting excited? I know I'm getting excited for you. Ooh la la!"

Everyone was keenly aware that Beth felt great distress over having her feet nailed to the floor for the forthcoming year. But when she expressed her support and indeed delight for her mother's adventure, you could hear a collective sigh of relief.

Even in the dark, Beth could feel their unanimous approval and it felt really good. She felt like an adult then. Did the converse hold true? At that moment the world came together for Beth. She had been disagreeable, even belligerent, she had been a burden at times and a renegade too many others. She had fought battles unworthy of the effort they took, and so many times had looked at the world only through her eyes. But not that night. This was what acting as a family felt like and it was a wonderful thing. Now she understood the old saying *We all rise together.* And she had a better handle on her aunts and uncles than ever before.

One by one, they left the porch, thanking Maggie and Susan for all of their hospitality, until only Susan and Beth remained.

"Great jumping jelly beans!" Susan said with a sigh. "In the blink of an eye, I'm going to be speaking really lousy French and dealing with students."

Beth giggled at her mother's exclamation, which was so lame it was funny. But Susan had always used juvenile expressions for as long as Beth could remember.

"You'll be brilliant, Mom. Don't give it a second of stress."

"I'm not so sure. Anyway, I taped my email address to the refrigerator with all the emergency contact numbers, you know, in case something happens."

"Good thinking, after all, Sullivans Island is known for being a wild and crazy town."

"Listen, miss, things have changed around here. This ain't the sleepy island we knew ten years ago."

"Yeah, sure. But I did see that Bert's was closed and that whole scene at Poe's is pretty insane. What happened to Bert's? They made the best burgers."

"They sure did. That's the end of an era for sure. I guess it depends on who's talking. One story is that the people who own the building were raising the rent so high that the people who ran Bert's couldn't afford it. The other story is that the reason they couldn't afford the increase in rent is due to the smoking ban. The smoking ban killed their business."

"Who smokes? Like two people? That's ridiculous."

"Yeah, I'm with you. As a former smoker,

I'm sympathetic, but if I didn't want to be around smoke I would just go somewhere else. So maybe they did lose some customers. But truth be told, I've been in there when it was rocking and rolling and I don't remember anyone smoking at all. Mostly they went outside, at least I think so. Must be the rent hike."

"Must be."

"So? You okay, Doodle?"

Beth smiled all over. For all of her insistence that she was fully matured, she adored being called by the childhood nickname only her mother used. "Sure. What do you mean?"

"I mean, are you okay with me leaving and you staying here?"

"Yes ma'am, I am. And I'll tell you why. Reason number one: I've been in school since I got out of diapers and this is the first real break I've ever had. It's probably healthy to take a sabbatical, right? I intend to use the year to get in really great shape and to think my thoughts about everything. And the other reason is that this is something you have wanted to do since like forever. The idea that I can help my mom on something this big is, well, huge. So don't worry about a thing. I'll have it all under control. Me and Cecily, that is."

"Cecily and I," Susan said, gently correcting her grammar. "She's a good egg. A little spooky, but then she's got Livvie's blood in her veins."

"She doesn't scare me. I already love her to pieces."

Susan smiled at that, thinking that inside of the few days since her pseudo-Bostonian daughter had returned with blazing red hair and a blazing attitude to match, she was softened all around her urban edges and had fallen back into using expressions like *love her to pieces*.

Susan reached over to hold Beth's hand.

"That's good, Doodle, just watch yourself, okay?"

"Please. Don't worry about me. I can handle this. No problemo."

4

Alone at Last

Sunday morning the grand exodus began. Moody, moaning teenagers were told to gather their belongings, dozens of pancakes and Krispy Kreme donuts were consumed, cars were packed, and the splinter tribes of the Hamilton clan slowly prepared to return to their various corners of the globe. For some annoying matriarchal reason Maggie felt compelled to give a loud and public lecture to Beth on house rules, which of course incited convulsions of snickers among the younger generation.

"Now, be sure to check the stove twice before you go to bed."

"Twice?"

"Yes. Twice. I always do and so does your mother."

"Um, okay." Beth cut her eyes to Mike and Bucky, who made such faces at Beth that she had to bite the insides of her cheeks to keep from bursting out laughing.

"Keep the screen doors locked at all times, because you don't want people just walking into the house and sticking a knife between your ribs."

"Right," Beth said, and gave the ceiling a sweeping glance, causing her to wonder if cobwebs were part of her job description or Cecily's.

"Remember the sanitation engineer comes on Tuesdays and Fridays, and he comes early so it's best to put the cans by the curb the night before. Be extra sure they are closed tightly or the raccoons will have a party."

"Raccoons?" Sanitation engineer?

"Yes, raccoons. They're everywhere. Speaking of parties, please don't have any wild parties, but if you want to have a few friends over, that's fine, but please don't let boys stay over, if you know what I mean, because people talk on this island . . ."

"What boys?" Beth said with a trace of self-defense in her voice. "Mike and Bucky?"

"Oh, for the holy love of Mary!" Susan said. "Will you please stop?"

"I know, I know. It's just that this house has been in our family—"

Grant, who was refilling his coffee mug, took Maggie by the arm and led her from the room.

"Come, my darling Maggie, we have to go, and let's not treat Beth like an imbecile."

"Sorry, Beth," Maggie said. "Grant? I didn't mean—"

"She drives me out of my blooming mind," Susan said, shaking her head. "Have you seen my handbag? I'm so unorganized this morning."

Before Simon made his exit with Maggie and Grant, he kissed Susan on her mouth and down her neck with such slurping noises that everyone responded with a collective "Ew!"

"Just remember who you belong to," he said to her. "Keep your bloomers on, you hear me?"

"Oh, Simon!" Susan said, with such a gooey look in her eyes that Beth blushed.

Beth was glad then that her room had not been next to theirs as she was absolutely positively certain that some rambunctious doing of the wild thing was responsible for the glow of her mother's complexion that morning. She tried not to dwell on it and refocused her thoughts on other things, such as you could watch the entire Macy's parade on Thanksgiving in less time than it was taking this gang to move along.

Timmy and his family departed without much fanfare, but with much backslapping and many hugs.

"Beth, here's my cell number and Mary Jo's. If you need a single thing, pick up the phone and call me, okay?"

"Thanks, Uncle Timmy. Y'all have a safe trip!"

"I put all our sheets and towels in the laundry room," Aunt Mary Jo said. "And I started the sheets—"

"Oh! I suppose I should have done that too!" Aunt Teensy squeaked with a theatrical Betty Boop sigh that was so disingenuous Beth sighed back.

Beth said, "That's okay. I'll take care of it." Aunt Teensy had not shown well over the weekend and was running a close second to Allison.

Susan's departure was teary and emotional. She gave Beth one more hug, memorizing her face as though she might be seeing her for the last time in her life. But in her next breath, Susan gave Beth a modified Maggie message with fewer instructions and a more foreboding warning.

"Just be careful, Beth. I know you think—and I do too—that Sullivans Island is the safest place there is, or ever was, and you might be right, but that doesn't mean terrible things don't happen here too or that they couldn't. Or might."

"Oh, Momma. For somebody who makes their living with words, that was about the most jumbled-up—"

"I know, I know, but you know what I mean, right? Henry? Did we pick up my red canvas tote bag? I think it's on the floor next to my bed."

"It's already in the car," Henry said. "Let's move it, sister."

"I'm so excited I feel like I'm gonna throw up."

"Gross, Mom."

Susan was a bundle of nerves and Beth

knew that the sooner her mother got on her way the happier she would be. She was driving to Atlanta with Henry and his family and flying to Paris that night.

"Love you, Mom! Just go have a ball and quit worrying!" Beth was standing by the kitchen door with Lola tucked in her arms. She had been carrying her all morning because with all the people shuffling about, she worried that Lola might get stepped on and squashed like a grape.

"Love you too, sweetheart, and your precious dog. Okay, that's it. If I forgot anything, I'll just buy it over there. They have stores in Paris, right?"

"Um, I think so."

Henry blew the horn of his car with two short toots. Susan hugged Beth's neck one truly last time, ruffled her granddog's tiny head, inhaled and exhaled with enough gusto to shift the curtains, and hurried down the back steps.

"Whew! I thought they'd never get her to leave!" Sophie said. "If I was going to Paris for a year, I'd already be there!"

"For real," Beth said.

Only Beth and Sophie remained. Sophie was lollygagging about, unenthusiastic about getting on the road in her rental car to drive to Columbia to meet her twin.

"I could stay here for a month," Sophie said. "The breeze on that front porch is nothing but a drug."

"Yeah, it is. I'd better go pick up all the newspapers before they blow over to Morris Island. I wish you would stay. Hey, how come you didn't go with Uncle Timmy?"

"And be the seventh fanny in a hot SUV? Nah. I'm way too spoiled for that. Anyway, it would take him an hour just to find Allison and I knew he was antsy to get going. That reminds me, I need to MapQuest the directions. You got a laptop?"

"Yep, in my room. I can do it for you."

"That would be great. Come on, I'll give you a hand with the porch."

The front porch, which had been straightened up over and over throughout the course of the weekend, was littered with newspapers, sandy flip-flops, coffee mugs, and a half dozen or so beach towels still damp from morning swims, hung haphazardly over the rails to dry.

"Gee whiz," Beth said, "what a bunch of pigs. Ding-dong. The maid's here."

"I hear you. I'll knock the sand out of

these because otherwise it ruins the washer. Or, maybe I should wait until they're dry. What do you think?"

"Leave 'em till they're dry. If I total the washer and dryer, Aunt Maggie will get on a plane, come back here, and kill me."

"Yeah, with her ESP, she probably already knows." Sophie giggled. "Listen to me, Maggie was Born to Mother. When I was a kid, Maggie was all over us, wiping our faces every two minutes like a crew from *60 Minutes* was dropping by to document what a bunch of filthy little Geechee brats we were."

"I figure Aunt Maggie can't help herself, that's why I never get too upset with her. Here, Aunt Sophie, hand me those mugs and I'll throw them in the dishwasher. And I always think it would have been more fun to be my mother's sister than her daughter because then I wouldn't be an only child. You know?"

Sophie was lining up the rocking chairs.

"And all I ever wanted was to be an only child! This porch could use a broom. How come we always want what we don't have?"

"Good question. Forget the broom. Pray for a stiff wind or I'll do it later."

After Beth printed out the driving directions to Sophie's destination in Columbia, Sophie brought her things to the kitchen, preparing, at last, to leave.

"Do you need anything for the road?"

Sophie opened the refrigerator and peered in at all the leftovers, wrapped in waxed paper and plastic bags.

"Maybe a bottle of water. What in the world are you going to do with all this food?"

"Dump it. When you leave I'm going on starvation. That's the only diet that works."

Sophie reached in her canvas tote bag and pulled out a handful of DVDs.

"Actually, it really doesn't. Here you go! Stretch and workout with your aunties! But kiddo, you don't need to lose any weight. You look gorgeous. However, exercise is good for your brains, you know."

"Yeah. Metabolism. Endorphins. Tone. Fat-burning machine. I know, I know."

"Ah! I see you've read the literature! And I bought this for you yesterday at Staples."

Sophie handed her a shopping bag.

"What's this?"

"It's a journal, a dozen number two pencils, and a pencil sharpener."

"Oh, that's so sweet! Thanks, Aunt Sophie!" She hugged her aunt and gave her a kiss on the cheek. "You always think of everything!"

"I wish that was true! But you fill those up with all your thoughts and all the things that happen to you. Before you know it you'll have enough material for a book. Anyway, sweetheart, I'd better get going. My crazy twin is probably marinating in a putrid mood."

"Oh, I hate for you to leave! I never get to see you."

"Are we pouting?"

"Yes. We're pouting."

"Tell you what. I've got some time at the end of September. Why don't I fly in and take my favorite niece shopping for clothes or something, I don't know, get our hair done? We can spend some time together and really get caught up."

"I think your niece would love that. This hair has to go."

"It's a little wild. Interesting but wild."

Sophie smiled at Beth. She wished then

that she had married someone and had a girl like Beth to call her own. But that didn't seem to be what the universe had planned for her.

"Okay, sweetheart, I'll call you, okay?"

"Okay. Don't worry. I'll be fine."

"Right now I wish there were two of you so I could take one with me."

"Hmmm. Is that a twin thing? What if you put me in your pocket and I turned out to be like Aunt Allison?" Beth giggled and Sophie gasped in mock horror.

"Hush! You'd better keep that sharp tongue in your mouth!"

"I'm only kidding!"

"I know, baby. Keep yourself busy. Start writing that book."

"Right! I'll get right on that. Have a safe trip, okay?"

"And remember, if you need—"

"A thing? I'll call you first!"

Beth stood at the top of the steps and watched until her aunt had backed out of the yard in her rental car and disappeared down the street. Earlier that day she couldn't wait until everyone was gone and suddenly she felt herself slipping into loneliness, that awful pall of sadness that plagued her from time to time. Those feelings were sometimes so hopeless that she frightened herself. But she knew there was a kind of manic quality to her personality, and at the first signs of despair, she would do certain things to shake it off. Sometimes she would eat. For years she bit her fingernails. Later on as she learned more about the world and herself, she knew that by merely placing herself in the sun for an hour or so, she would feel a considerable improvement. And having Lola's company had helped immensely.

She decided to take Lola for a walk to see what was going on in the neighborhood.

She hooked Lola's leash to her collar and set out toward the western end of the island. Lola trotted along beside her, seemingly happy to finally be alone with Beth. She passed Stella Maris Church and kept to the left, continuing on Middle Street until she reached the old Hagerty property. What was this? It appeared that the five acres the Hagerty family had owned forever were being subdivided. What would become of their Fallout Shelter where she had played spin the bottle as a young girl just learning about the mysteries between the sexes, or the dilapidated train car that for some unknown reason had been sort of set up as an ersatz museum before she was born. That train car had seen a lot of beer cans and bongs in her teenage years. The stories about how they got it on the island in the first place were always a great topic of discussion among the boys she knew.

"In the middle of the night, they closed down the causeway to traffic and brought it over on a flatbed—"

"No way! It wouldn't clear the bridge—"

"Y'all are crazy. They brought it on a barge and unloaded it right here!"

"Who cares?" the girls would say.

Beth looked around, swatting mosquitoes on her ankles and behind her knees, and on a disgruntled turn of her heel she walked toward the old house and looked over the harbor toward Fort Sumter. It was beautiful and awe-inspiring to think about the history of it, but Beth also realized she had been alone for a total of perhaps forty-five minutes and she was already bored out of her skull.

"Let's go home, Lola, and figure out our lives."

Later, when the washing machine was loaded with more sheets and humming away, Beth was sitting at the kitchen table putting together a résumé. There was a rap on the door. Beth looked up to see Cecily standing there in oversized sunglasses.

"Hey! I called the house but there was no answer."

"Come on in," Beth said. "You look like Hollywood in those glasses!"

"I know it, right? And you'd better start wearing them or you're gonna have cataracts by Christmas with those pale eyes of yours. Humph. So? Everyone gone?"

Cecily removed her sunglasses, wiped them with a soft cloth, and put them in their case. The fact that she cleaned them and put them in a case instead of just tossing them in her handbag greatly impressed Beth, who had never used an eyeglass case in her life.

"You're probably right. Yep, they're all gone. Sure is quiet around here."

"Well, I brought you some tomatoes from Johns Island and I thought you might need some help with cleaning up."

"Thanks!" Beth put her nose in the brown paper bag and inhaled the perfume. "Man.

Wow. Know what? I had forgotten about Johns Island tomatoes. How could I forget about something so powerful?"

"Honey? They are God's gift to the Low-country, 'eah?"

"Yes ma'am. They sure are! It's all in the dirt. At least that's what Momma always said. Want a sandwich?"

"No, girl. Those are for you. I've got a pile of them at my own house."

"Well, sit down. Stay for a few minutes. I don't need any help really. I'm just doing sheets and then I'm gonna do a load of towels. Even I can manage that."

"Okay. Maybe I'll have a glass of water."

"Bottle's in the fridge."

"Thanks. It's terrible outside. Humid? Whew! Terrible." Cecily helped herself to a glass from the cabinet and filled it with water and ice. "Must be a million degrees out there."

"Truly. I just walked Lola down to the end of the island and she's probably gonna sleep for the rest of the day."

"Can't blame her. So, what are you doing?" Cecily looked at Beth's laptop screen.

"Résumé. Gotta get a job and fast or else I'm gonna lose it."

"Humph. This island's the kind of place you long for, but it's not so fabulous for solitary confinement."

"For real. Mom thinks I should bartend at one of the restaurants or be a hostess or something. Meet some people? Get a social life going? But who knows if they even need help? Like a zillion people are out of work these days."

Cecily pulled a newspaper from her bag and dropped in on the table.

"Want ads. Give them a look." Cecily snapped her fingers. "Atlanticville is open now. Want to go over there for brunch? Check it out? They have great eggs Benedict and wicked Bloodys."

"Great idea! Give me two minutes to do something to the way I look." Beth coiled her hair up into a rubber band, put Lola in her crate with a treat, grabbed her purse, and they were out the door.

Cecily went down the steps and then called back to Beth from the yard.

"Hey, did you lock the door?"

"Twice, okay? No, wait, that's the stove."

In just a few minutes they were parked under a palmetto tree and climbing the steps to the second floor of the old island cottage that was home to Atlanticville Restaurant. Bright oils of local landscapes by Caryn Smith hung against the fabric-covered walls in the main dining room, lending an unexpected sophistication. But the floor of the old windowed porch that ran the length of the side of the house was noticeably sloped and hence it seemed a more casual environment, with built-in banquettes lining the walls. It reminded you that the cottage, like all island structures, was built on beach sand and subject to settling this way or that because of the regular occurrence of tiny earthquakes that took place just offshore. Or perhaps the floors were intentionally slanted, allowing for runoff from torrential downpours in the days when the porch walls were defined by screens instead of windows. And of course, there was a large open-air front porch with café tables if you had a sadistic urge for suffocating humidity along with your omelet, which Beth and Cecily did not.

They were greeted by the manager, who looked like he should be in the movies breaking hearts on the big screen instead of saying, "Hey, how're y'all doing today? Two? Inside or out?"

"Inside, if it's possible," Beth said, and thought she wouldn't mind working for him one single little bit and blurted out, "I can bartend, you know."

"Good to know," he said with a huge smile. "Follow me."

"Very slick," Cecily said. "What's the matter with you?"

"I don't know. That sounded a little desperate, didn't it?"

Cecily cocked her head to one side and looked at Beth.

"Hopeless," she whispered.

"Yeah," Beth said.

He led them to a table, handed them menus, and said, "I hope y'all enjoy your lunch." He looked again at Beth and said, "Do I know you?"

"Maybe. My family grew up over here, well, not me, but my mother's family. I just come here a lot, when I was a kid I did, that is. Now, well actually, I'm house-sitting for a year. They're the Hamiltons?"

"Oh yeah! You've got those Hamilton eyes way back there behind those glasses. I think I know your aunt. I'd know that color blue anywhere! I'm Drew Harris. Well, it's nice to meet you . . ."

"Beth. Beth Hayes." Beth shook his hand and said, "This is Cecily Singleton. Old family friend."

Drew nodded to Cecily and shook her hand as well. "How're you?"

There were six or eight people at the entrance podium waiting for tables so Drew excused himself. Cecily and Beth looked over their menus.

"What are you in the mood for?" Beth said.

"Eggs Benedict and a Bloody Mary? Isn't that why we came here? Are you *with* us, Miss Hayes? Excuse me? Are you blushing?"

"I'm just looking over the menu; that's all. Do you think it would be disgusting if I got a corn dog on the side?"

"Yes. I do."

"Okay then. I'll just have what you're having."

Of all the peculiar things in the world for which one could have an Achilles' heel, Beth had an emotional weakness for corn dogs on a stick. She seldom if ever saw them on menus in Boston, even on children's menus. There was something about the crunch of the sweet fried cornbread contrasted with the mouthwatering tenderness of the nitrate-laced meat that reminded her of the best moments of her childhood. Her father bought them for her at the state fair, and more than cotton candy, they were the ultimate indulgence. Her mouth began to water as she remembered the taste. He would lean down to hand it to her with the stick wrapped in a napkin and warn her to take little bites as it was still sizzling hot.

Beth was shaken from her daydream when a strikingly handsome and very fit young man appeared at their table. He was dressed in a crisp black shirt and black trousers. Alan was his name, he said. He filled their water glasses and put a breadbasket of steaming biscuits on the table along with a slab of honey butter on a ceramic tile. Cecily cleared her throat.

Then, just as their hormones began to recover from the onslaught of biscuits and buns, another man named Robert arrived, who was a dead ringer for a young Cary Grant.

"Can I get y'all a drink to start?" His voice had an interesting raspy quality.

"Bloody Mary," Cecily and Beth blurted

simultaneously, which was better than blurting *Bloody hell!*

Cecily wondered if they were male models doing this job for a lark.

"That was easy," he said. "I'll get those drinks right out for you."

"Man," Cecily said, "did you look at those guys?"

"Stupid," Beth said aloud without realizing it.

"What's stupid?"

"What? Oh, nothing. The corn dog."

"If you want a corn dog, just get it."

"No, that's not it."

"Dieting?"

"What? Do I look like I need to diet?"

"No! Of course not! But women are always on a diet, aren't we?"

Beth relaxed then, thinking it was nice that Cecily referred to her as a woman.

"Sort of, I guess. Listen, this is going to sound really melodramatic or something, but here's the thing. You know my father died a few years ago?"

"Yes." Cecily knew Beth was not entirely well adjusted to his death. Despite what had happened Friday night, Beth did not remember that Cecily already knew it. "My father passed when I was not quite sixteen. Leukemia. I thought my momma was gonna go with him. She's still not over it."

"Well, my mother got over it in about two seconds."

"Oh, come on now."

"I swear. Anyway, my dad used to buy me corn dogs when I was a kid. So, I saw it on the menu and thought of him. That's all."

"Beth? Listen to me. People grieve and mourn in their own way. I swear to you on a stack of Bibles that your momma was as sorry as she could be to lose the father of her only child. Word of honor." Cecily held her hand up as though she was taking an oath. "And I am just as sure she worried the same amount about how you were handling it too. Don't you think?"

"Oh yeah, I think she did, at first anyway. But when she married Simon, I went off to school and she went off her rocker, like the old people say."

Cecily giggled, the drinks arrived, and they clinked the edges of their glasses as if in a toast.

"What are we drinking to?" Beth said.

"To rounding the bend," Cecily said.

"And just what does that mean?"

"Well, you said something about what the old people say and it made me think of what my grandmother said all the time . . ."

"Livvie?"

"Who else, hmmm? The elders had all these sayings. So, if I was being hard-headed or sassy, she'd say to my mother, Give that chile some time and she'll come on roun' the bend. Anyway, you ought to get contact lenses. Use what you got."

Beth was startled by her non sequitur. Did she look so pathetic that everyone around her thought she needed emergency attention? Clearly no one liked her hair. But she thought for a moment about contact lenses.

"What you thinking, Beth? Man, this is a spicy Bloody! Whew!" Cecily drained her glass of water. "Whew!"

Alan reappeared and refilled her glass. Cecily cleared her throat again.

"Too hot for you?" he said, smiling. "Can I bring you a mimosa instead?"

"Maybe some iced tea?" Cecily said, seeing no wedding band and wondering how old he was and how inappropriate would it be to encourage Beth to flirt with him? "How about you, Beth?"

"I'll just drink my water and sip this killer slowly."

Alan smiled at Beth, and although she smiled back, she felt uneasy.

"Sounds good," he said.

"Who are these guys?" Cecily said. "They weren't here the last time I was. They are too adorable, aren't they?"

Beth was glad that Cecily did not linger on what Beth was thinking so she just went with the flow of Cecily's conversation.

"Too old for me. I'm not looking for a man right now."

"What are you hiding from, Miss Beth? You're never going to be this age again. You have perfect skin, a body that's nothing but walking sin, and some crazy eyes behind those forbidding eyeglasses."

"Forbidding?"

"Yeah, they say, *I'm a librarian from 1955, no talking! Oh, and P.S., I hate sex.*"

Beth giggled. "They do not. I happen to adore sex—crazy about it, in fact, last Halloween I dressed up as a hooker."

"I would have loved to see that!" Cecily shook her head and leaned back in her chair as Robert placed their eggs in front of them.

"Can I get y'all anything else?"

No wedding ring either, Cecily noted, and realized the small amount of vodka she had consumed made her slightly light-headed.

"I'm a cheap date," Cecily said.

"Oh?" Robert said with an expression that registered surprise and confusion.

"Oh! I just meant I've had two sips of this, nearly *died* from the spiciness, and I can already feel the alcohol. What's in this thing?"

"Don't mind her," Beth said. "But she had asked Alan for some iced tea. She could probably use that, whenever you have a chance, you know, to bring it out?"

"Oh, sorry. Alan has a mind like a sieve. I'll be right back!"

"He's gorgeous," Cecily said, loud enough for Robert to hear.

As if he doesn't already know that, Beth thought. She looked at Cecily and whispered, "Look, I might not be the expert in the men department, but I know good-looking guys are nothing but trouble." Beth took a bite of her entrée and thought, well, Cecily might be a little aggressive toward the male species but she sure knew her eggs. "This is delicious."

"You're right." Cecily raised her eyebrows, sighed, and then pouted. "Besides, he's probably involved with someone anyway."

"You mean someone besides himself?"

"Girl? What kind of an ax you got to grind about men? Somebody break your heart?"

"Nope. And they never will."

After that, they ate in relative silence for a little while. Cecily didn't want to pry into Beth's personal life. Cecily could see that Beth was becoming sullen as Beth pushed the remnant of her English muffin around in the little pool of hollandaise sauce.

"Do you want dessert? Want to share something?"

Beth shook her head.

"Okay. I'll be right back."

Cecily excused herself to go to the ladies' room and was gone for what seemed to be eternity.

Alone at the table, Beth reviewed her brief and unspectacular history with the opposite sex. Why she was so wary of intimacy? Was she hiding her looks? Why *had* she never gone to the trouble to wear contact lenses? Did that really matter? Did

anyone *really* care about something as insignificant as hair color in 2008? And what
was the real reason that there were so few
men in her past?

Beth knew the reason. Her heart was
numb. Damaged beyond repair, she
thought. She also knew that she had better figure out how she was going to support herself, not just in the short term, but
for the rest of her life. The stoic in her was
making initial preparations to be alone, as
her Aunt Sophie was. Sophie was happy,
wasn't she? Would it be the worst thing
not to have children? Or a husband? Beth
looked up to see Cecily engaged in a conversation with Robert. Robert was preening and Cecily was smiling wide like a big
hungry cat looking at a plump canary.

After they shared the bill and left a tip,
they got up to leave and almost bumped
into Drew, the manager, on the way out
the door.

"Hey, Beth? It's Beth, right?"

"Yeah. Beth Hayes."

"Well, I don't need a bartender but it
seems I could use a hostess. The one I
had just called to say she was going back

to college. Want to give it a try? Just Thursday, Friday, and Saturday nights."

"Sure, why not? Thanks."

"Come in Thursday around five? I'll show you what you have to do. Piece of cake."

"Well, look at you!" Cecily said as they got in her car. "Tough interview!"

"Woo hoo! I've got a job!"

"Have you ever worked as a hostess?"

"Nope. Have you?"

"Nope, but I imagine it's a little bit like being an air traffic controller."

"Oh, big deal. How hard can it be?"

"Well, you're about to find out." They pulled into Beth's driveway and Cecily said, "I'll see you Tuesday to pick up the bills, okay? If you need anything—"

"I'll call you. Don't worry. See you then!"

"I'll slip by tomorrow too, to water the baskets and the pots."

"I can do that, if you want."

"What? Those babies are my children. I raised them from seeds! See you tomorrow."

Beth waved goodbye to Cecily and took the steps two at a time. She unlocked the door, went straight to Lola's crate, hooked up her leash, and took her out in the front yard. Lola sniffed around and when her mission was accomplished she stood on her hind legs, leaning against Beth's shin.

"Oh, Lola! You're such a good girl!"

"Ark!" Lola said, which Beth took to mean, Pick me up!

Lola taunted Beth with lots of little jumps and chasing around in circles, and when Beth finally picked her up, she covered her face with kisses. Beth giggled with delight and her heart swelled with affection for her little dog.

It was three o'clock. She looked out over the dunes and decided it was still too hot to walk the beach. The tide was very high and would continue to rise all week until the moon went on the wane. Maybe the moon was somewhat to blame for her moodiness since her arrival on the island. It was certainly possible.

"Should we go back inside and finish my CV now that I don't need it?"

Lola burrowed into Beth's neck with another lick to her chin.

"Did I tell you that I got a job? Come on;

let's go wrap that baby up so I have a fresh résumé on file."

Beth unhooked Lola's leash, raced her back into the house, slamming the screen door behind them, and together they rushed to the kitchen, where she had left her laptop. She flipped on the ceiling fan, filled Lola's dish with cool fresh water, put it on the floor, and sat down to work.

After she added in her new address, updated her work experiences and a paragraph about her personal goals, she hit the save button. She decided to let it rest for a while, reread it, and spell-check it again before printing it. Beth knew that if there was ever one place you didn't want to have typos, it was in your résumé. She picked up the newspaper that Cecily had left behind, scanned the police blotter for a laugh, and turned to the want ads.

"Well, what do you know, Lola. This very same newspaper is looking for a freelance journalist to write feature articles! Would that be me? What do you think? Should we call them tomorrow?"

Tiny Lola had somehow pulled a huge pink bath towel from the laundry basket and had curled it around and around into a bed in the corner behind Beth. The effort and the heat had worn her out because Lola was fast asleep. Beth looked at her, remembered the beach towels on the porch and the mountain of sheets remaining to be washed, dried, folded, and put away, and her enthusiasm sank.

"I'm gonna be doing laundry for the rest of my life," she said.

But sometime past dark, as the moon began its glorious rise, the last pillowcase was matched up with its sheets and she was able to close the door on the linen closet. She tossed the leftovers and the contents of all the bathroom wastebaskets in the garbage cans outside and pulled the spreads up on all the beds. The last traces of the weekend were erased and the house was finally hers.

She was lying in the old Pawleys Island hammock on the front porch, sharing a piece of toast and peanut butter with Lola, when she heard slamming noises coming from inside the house. Beth sat straight up, swung her feet to the floor, and held Lola tight.

"What in the hell was that?"

Then, just as suddenly as the noises

had started, they stopped. She waited a few heart-pounding minutes. Slowly and quietly, Beth made her way back into the house and stopped in front of the mirror in the darkened living room. Nothing. She put Lola on the floor and Lola raced upstairs, presumably to Beth's bed. Beth passed through the dining room and then the kitchen. Nothing. She went to her deceased grandmother's bedroom and the door was locked. How could that be? She tried the knob again several more times, and eerily, the door opened easily the last time. As quickly as she opened the door she felt the wall for the switch and flipped it, flooding the room with light from the ceiling fixture. The bed was a shambles, all the dresser drawers were pulled open, and the room was freezing cold. Beth's heart was racing and she could feel her pulse in her ears. She was terrified, furious, and realized she was screaming as loud as she could.

"What is this? You call this scary? Let me tell you something, whoever you are! You get out of this house! You don't scare me one damn bit, but I'm not spending the next year cleaning up after you! So, get out! Get out right now!"

She slammed the door behind her but left the ceiling light on, thinking that maybe the bright light might somehow deter further activity for the night. And, she decided to leave things as they were until she saw Cecily again. Perhaps Cecily would have some Gullah wisdom on what to do.

"This is some major bullshit," Beth said to the thin air. "Lola? Where are you, baby? It's okay now."

Lola was indeed in the bed, huddled under a pillow.

"Come here, sweetheart. Looks like we have some company. Don't worry; it's just your dead great-grandmother. Probably. I think. Maybe. Let's go downstairs and lock up the house for the night."

Beth poured herself a glass of milk, wondering if she should sleep downstairs or upstairs, but in the end she decided that no ghost was going to dictate her life. She secured all the locks, checked the stove twice, and went to bed with Lola snuggled next to her in the same room where she had been sleeping all along.

She pulled her laptop into her bed to check her email and there was something from her mother.

Arrived Paris safely. Trip was great except for the businessman in the seat next to me who got drunk, fell asleep, and snored the whole way across the Atlantic. Typical. Faculty housing isn't exactly the Ritz but then I never lived at the Ritz anyway! How are you, baby? Hope everything is all right. Love you!

Beth wondered if she should tell her mother about the haunting and then decided against it. What could she do when she was an ocean away? Nothing, she decided. She wrote back:

Take lots of pictures and email them to me! Everything is cool! Love you too! Stop worrying! xxx

She woke in the morning amazed that she had not tossed and turned all night. In fact, she had slept more soundly than she could remember having slept in months. She hated to get up and face the day.

Even Lola was feeling lazy, stretching with her tiny fanny up in the air and yawning so wide it made Beth smile. Looking over at the alarm clock, she was surprised to see that it was almost nine.

"Come on, girl, you're a loaded bomb. Let's get you outside."

Beth quickly brushed her teeth and Lola followed her down the steps, out the front door, and into the yard. It was the beginning of another gorgeous day. It would be hot, there was no doubt of that, but Beth was getting used to the heat and pacing her day around it.

"Okay," Beth said to Lola, "let's go see if I can make a little bank as a journalist. What do you say?"

After a fast shower, a granola bar, and a short ride down the island, Beth was in for a shock. Middle Street was blocked to traffic. She stopped the car a half block away and got out to look at what was going on. A wrecking ball and a crane were taking down the building that had once housed Bert's. A crowd of old islanders were there, taking pictures and remarking to one another that this was the end of an era, the end of every good thing that had kept

Sullivans Island what it had always been—unspoiled by the outside world.

"Next thing you know we'll have traffic lights at all the intersections," an old man said.

"Yeah, and superstores," another man said. "Big parking lots . . . I just hate seeing this happen. My beautiful momma must be spinning in her grave. Thank the Lord she didn't live to see this pitiful day."

"You said it, bubba."

It wasn't that Bert's had any real architectural merit. No, the élan of the building lay in its history. Once, it had been a drugstore where a grandmother stopped in to buy her grandchild their very first ice cream cone. In those days, you could buy the latest Archie and Jughead comics or fill a prescription there. Teenagers shared banana splits spinning on the barstools and bought copious amounts of Clearasil and chewing gum. Decades went by, and when the pharmacist who owned it finally retired, it became a local haunt for a great burger and a game of pool. Friends met there. People fell in love there, slow dancing to bluegrass music on hot summer nights.

Every island native had sweet memories of Bert's for one reason or another, and knocking it down was like witnessing a sort of death.

"Excuse me," Beth said politely, "do y'all know what they plan to do with the land?"

The two old codgers, their faces lined from years of sun exposure and hard work, turned to face Beth. Their rheumy eyes were brimming with suspicions that perhaps they had outlived their usefulness, just like Bert's.

"Yeah, they just posted some drawings over there. They say it's gonna be a multi-purpose retail establishment, whatever that means."

"It means whatever they're selling, I guaran-darn-tee you, I don't need," the other man said.

"Me either. Too highfalutin for my blood. Come on, Lloyd. Let's go over to Dunleavy's and get us a beer. They're open."

Beth watched the two men walk away. They moved slowly and the shuffle of their gait was unsettling to her. She was touched by their sorrow and she knew just how they felt. Just how modern and shiny was this new place going to be, and how would it fit in the landscape that was the business district of the island? Would it make the rest of the establishments look shabby?

The population of the island didn't just go around knocking down things. They recycled. Hadn't Dunleavy's Pub once been a liquor store? Didn't Off the Hook begin its existence as a Red & White grocery store? Wasn't the old barbershop where Bill the barber would give you a flattop for twenty-five cents now a dentist's office? Even Sullivan's Restaurant had been Burmester's Drug Store. Beth knew these things. Her mother might say, Would you look at Dunleavy's? When I was a kid that was the liquor store and it smelled like booze too! Or her Aunt Maggie would reminisce that they always got their bait for crabbing at the Red & White at no charge. No, razing Bert's was extremely dubious, and Beth knew the islanders were holding their breath.

Beth looked up at the offices around Station 22 Restaurant and saw the sign for the *Island Eye News*. She walked across the street and up the stairs, feeling confident enough for a walk-in interview. It wasn't like she was interviewing with the *New York Times,* she thought.

"Hi!" she said, opening the door and facing the receptionist.

"Hi, can I help you?"

The receptionist, who was maybe a year or two older than Beth, was sizing her up from head to toe, testing the limits of her Juicy Fruit chewing gum, which Beth could smell. Suddenly Beth's confidence faded, replaced with a creeping dread. What was she doing there?

"Yeah, I was wondering if I could talk to someone about the opening you have for a freelance journalist to write feature articles? I saw the ad? In your paper?"

A female voice thundered from the other room and Beth jumped.

"Katie? Send her in here!"

"That's Barbara Farlie," Katie, the receptionist said, rolling her eyes. "She owns the paper. Go ahead in."

"Thanks. I think."

Résumé in hand, Beth took a breath and went to the next office to meet the publisher and editor in chief of the *Island Eye News.*

Barbara Farlie, who was one of those

women of an undeterminable age, stood to her full height, which Beth reckoned was in the zone of nearly six feet. She had gorgeous thick honey blonde hair, cut in layers and blown back, away from her face. Beth thought the maintenance of it must cost her five hundred dollars a week. Barbara was wearing a T-shirt with the paper's logo across the front tucked into a pair of black linen trousers. Everything about Ms. Farlie's attire said she was casual on first glance but underneath she was all business, as Beth was about to discover.

"Hi, I'm Beth Hayes," Beth said, and offered her résumé.

"I'm Barbara Farlie. So, what makes you think you're a journalist? How old are you anyway?" She sat down in her chair and stared at Beth.

"Twenty-three. I'm not a journalist, actually. I just got out of college. Boston. See? It's right there." She pointed to the place on her résumé where her educational background was printed. Beth was still standing, feeling very awkward, and wondering if this was all a big mistake.

"Sit down," Barbara said. "You're making me nervous standing there like the Leaning Tower of Pisa."

"Oh! Sorry!"

Beth dropped in the chair opposite her as fast as she could sit. She didn't know whether to put her purse on the floor next to her or if she should hold it in her lap. She decided to hold on to it as it gave her some comfort to have something to anchor her to her spot.

"You want coffee? Put your purse down. Nobody's gonna steal it."

Beth immediately put her purse on the floor and said, "No thanks. Water might be good, though."

"Katie?" she called out loud enough to rattle the walls. "Bring Beth a bottle of water, okay?"

Barbara leaned back in her chair and scanned Beth's résumé. Katie appeared and handed Beth a small bottle of Evian.

"Thanks," Beth said, and made eye contact with Katie, who gave her a reassuring smile.

Who would have thought that an interview with the publisher of a small newspaper could be so stressful? Beth's hands shook as she tried to remove the cap from the bottle. At last she broke the seal and she began to drink like she was just crawling in after a month of being lost in the desert.

"Katie?" Barbara hollered out again. "Bring reinforcements! We got ourselves a binger here!"

Seconds later, Katie handed Beth another bottle and took her empty one away. Beth was so embarrassed she wanted to run out of the office and never see these people again in her life. But Barbara Farlie had other plans.

"So, what do you want to write about?" she said.

Beth knew she had better have some ideas but she had yet to learn about pitches and things like that. But still jarred from the sight of the demolition outside, she just blurted out, "Well, have you seen the disaster outside at Bert's?"

"Yeah, what about it? That place was a dump."

"Well, seems to me that every old-timer on this island is going to be pretty pissed— I mean, upset. Don't you think so?"

"Doesn't matter what I think. I want to

know what you think. Why is that news, beyond the obvious?"

"Where are you from, Ms. Farlie?" Beth had a hunch she was dealing with someone from the other side of the causeway, perhaps even the Mason-Dixon Line.

"Michigan. I was in the army. Wrote for *Stars and Stripes* for over twenty years. Then the dust in Afghanistan began to upset my asthma and I decided I had been in the trenches long enough. So, I came here—my old aunt lives on the Isle of Palms. My kids are grown and scattered with the wind. My husband Amos kicked the bucket three years ago and left me lonely. Ah, Amos. He was a good man. Anyway, I figured this would be a good retirement job and it's got great benefits, namely, my kids come and bring my grandchildren because everyone likes the beach. But to get back to our conversation about the wrath of the old-timers?"

"Listen, I grew up here. So did my mother and grandmother and her mother before her. This island is a crazy place. We like things just as they are. I'm telling you, if they put up some glitzy new building next door and start selling ten-dollar coffee and ten-dollar muffins, people around here are gonna burn it down." Beth was surprised by her own passion.

"Really?"

"Well, not literally. But they won't support full-blown gentrification. That's for sure. Would you pay ten dollars for a cup of coffee?"

"Hell no. You know, that's an interesting position. I wonder how many islands in this state have developers coming in and trying to change things."

"I'm just guessing here, but I would say all of them?"

"You got a car? And a camera?"

"Yes."

"Okay. I'll tell you what. You bring me twelve hundred words and some good pictures of what's going on out there and on the other islands. If it's any good, I'll pay you for it if we run it. And I'll cover your expenses either way. How's that?"

Beth considered it for a minute. What did she have to lose? She could even take Lola with her, couldn't she?

"That sounds great! Thanks!" Beth stood and shook Barbara's hand soundly.

"Beth Hayes?"

"Yes ma'am?"

"Welcome to hell, honey, welcome to hell. By the way, love the flip-flops."

Barbara was smiling as she said it. Naturally, Beth smiled back, but she wondered what Barbara Farlie meant.

5

Hello Trouble

Maggiepie2@marthagene.net
Susan, Got to Paris fine? Dead in the
Seine? Want to let us know? Hmmm?
xx

Susanthepen@writenow.org
Maggie, honestly! Busy eating pommes
frites and drinking Dom with de Gaulle's
grandson and his wife. Whaddya think
I'm doing? Love Paris! Love you too!

Early that afternoon, armed with her digital
camera and a small notepad, Beth left the
house, feeling some urgency to document
the final hours of Bert's Bar. After all, this
was the end of a landmark and if she was
going to be a successful journalist, she
needed to be smack in the center of things.
Where Bert's once stood, the scene was

now all but a pile of rubble, the air swirling with dust and tiny bits of debris. Chunks of cement and ragged piping were being tossed into dump trucks by a streamlined backhoe, designed to work in small spaces. The noise was surely going to destroy the lunchtime business of the surrounding restaurants and that cash flow for the foreseeable future which would result in a litany of complaints to the Town Council and headaches for everyone.

At the scene, there were still a few people hanging around watching, but the crowd that had been there earlier in the morning had gone on about their day. Beth walked toward the site with a brisk stride of purpose. She stopped to take in the details of the drawings that were posted on the brand-new gleaming placard along with the permits. Two thick tubular columns stood on either side of the display window. The placard itself was almost six feet tall and constructed of brushed chrome, as was the frame of the window itself. Copper pyramids topped the columns to discourage perching birds and the droppings they left behind. The non-glare glass that protected the documents from the elements was etched along the frosted edges in shapes that suggested seagulls in flight.

"Seagulls," Beth said out loud. "Ew. How original. And just what the heck is all this?"

The whole thing was offensive because the obvious truth was that if the placard was an indication of the money that would go into the new construction, the future building would stand out against everything else in the realm, just as the old islanders and Beth had feared.

Beth harrumphed, snapped several photographs of it, and mumbled, "I'll bet this rocket ship has night-lights and a dehumidifier."

"Actually, it doesn't, but that's a good idea."

Beth turned to the source of the manly voice and fell right into the laughing brown eyes of Max Mitchell.

"Given the climate and all . . ." he added, putting his sunglasses on top of his head like a surfer.

Did she know him? It seemed to Beth that this was a reunion after many lifetimes of separation. Cosmic. And Max, usually calm, cool, and copasetic, was so taken by her face and the sound of her voice that he actually felt a shiver of déjà vu. But Max Mitchell shivered over women a million times a day, women of every shape and size, age and cultural orientation, married and single. He just loved them.

Then there was a virtual blast of pheromones and Beth, completely unaccustomed to anything like it, was rocked at the strength of it. What kind of kismet was this? Beth vowed to get her story and walk away as fast as possible. Max stopped himself, having sworn off female temptations until his project was further under way. He thought she was probably too young for him anyway. Or not.

This is ridiculous, they both thought, but knew they were caught in the net of fate's intentions just like a couple of fish.

An awkward silence hung between them before they finally regained their senses and introduced themselves to each other.

"Um, I'm Beth Hayes. *Island Eye News.*" She hoped she sounded professional.

"Max Mitchell. Architect. And builder."

They shook hands and by all appearances any passerby would have said the act of shaking hands was simply a cordial business gesture. But Max was astounded by how small and soft Beth's hand felt in his. For a split second, as any man would, he wondered if the rest of her was so, well, so what was she like in the sack? And Beth, whose hormones had been practically dormant most of her life, thought his hand was the most perfect hand she had ever touched, and for a brief moment she wondered what both of his hands would feel like on her face.

"This is your idea?" She gestured toward the site with her chin.

"Well, yeah, I guess so. I have several minority partners but it's mostly my own investment."

"Right." Beth struggled to maintain her composure. "Of course." Never before had she felt so off guard. This was not some frat boy, not even some law school student. This was a man. A man who was angular, tanned, and fit, with longish dark hair that skimmed his collar with curls, and who smelled like something she wanted to guzzle.

"You're with the local paper?" Max said.

"Yeah. I'm doing a piece on the changing face of coastal communities in the Carolinas." Beth blushed, knowing she had deliberately inflated the scope of her assignment to make herself sound important. "Maybe, if you have a few minutes? You'd like to comment?" She realized he was taking a lingering inventory of her breasts and blushed again.

"Sorry, I don't do interviews. Usually, that is."

"Oh. Well. Shoot. It must be like a thousand degrees today," she said, not wanting to appear pushy by asking if he would make an exception.

"It is. I just checked. Can I buy you a drink? Nonalcoholic, of course. I mean, I wasn't thinking of plying the press with alcohol to sway your opinion or anything like that. Unless you *want* a beer or something. I mean, that's fine with me."

Beth giggled. "Sure. Why not? But hey, Max?"

"Yeah?"

"Are you smirking at me?"

"Who me? Never. Never smirked at a woman in my entire life."

"Right," she said, satisfied that she had nailed him for the indiscretion of his traveling eyes. But traveling eyes or no, she liked it that he had called her a woman.

She liked it very much. It seemed that lately this was happening more and more. And despite his words to the contrary, Max Mitchell was smirking from ear to ear.

They crossed the street to Poe's Tavern. Max put his hand in the concave area of her lower back in a proprietary and a protective measure, as if the sparse oncoming traffic was a danger to her life. Beth could not recall any one of the guys she had ever dated doing anything beyond taking her hand or elbow to move her across a crowded room. This was different. It made her warm to him even more. The small gestures mattered tremendously to her because she had experienced so few.

They took a seat at the bar and ordered iced tea. They squeezed their lemon wedges into the tea and added exactly three large spoons of sugar to their glasses, stirring it around in an attempt to dissolve it. Beth considered this similarity of taste to be a positive omen of common ground.

"So, Max Mitchell, tell me something."

"Anything you want to know. My life's a completely open book."

"I'm sure. Off the record, how did a nice

guy like you get mixed up in a controversial project like this?"

"Controversial? What do you mean?" His perfectly shaped eyebrows were knitted together in genuine concern.

"For real? People here hate change. Don't you know that?"

"Change is inevitable, but don't quote me on that."

Beth giggled.

"I'm not going to quote you on anything unless you want me to. And yeah, change is inevitable. Disraeli said so, like a zillion times?"

"Disraeli? Where'd you go to school?"

"BC. Who cares? I also know that the building you propose to put right on top of Bert's grave is pretty flipping radical."

"What do you mean *flipping radical*? Is that journalismspeak for *very*?"

"Very funny. I mean, I'm just surprised you could get something so contemporary-looking past the design review board."

"You're right. It wasn't easy. But given the tax revenue it should generate—"

"Ah geez. Money. It's always about money, isn't it?" Beth had some idea of what he meant but she was only mildly knowledgeable about taxes or finance in general.

"Seems to be. The root of all evil. St. Paul said that. Or maybe it was St. Timothy."

"Some apostle. Whoever. Anyway, look around."

"I'm looking." But he was only looking at her.

"You've got a problem whether you know it or not. All these other buildings are from the thirties and forties or earlier, and if they're not, they're built to look like they are. This island has a certain style. If you come in here—where are you from anyway?"

"Atlanta."

"Cool. Well, I'm just saying don't expect our population to embrace something that looks like it belongs in a *Jetsons* episode."

"Wow. Are you always this hostile when you noninterview someone?"

He smiled at Beth and she blanched. Rude, rude. Professional journalists were not supposed to rebuke their subjects if they wanted their subjects to divulge what they needed to learn and she knew it. But was this an interview? Maybe it was.

"Oh, crap. I'm sorry. You're right. Let's start over."

Max, who seemed to possess a perpetual grin, said, "Right. Crap. Let's do that."

He was making fun of her, and as disturbing as it was on one level, she liked it on another. "Okay. So. Tell me about your project, Mr. Mitchell." She spoke in a deep and very serious voice.

"Well, Miss, Miss . . . shoot! What was your last name?"

"Hayes."

"Right! Miss Hayes, when it's completed, it will blend into the landscape very nicely. Scout's honor. And I'm going to venture a guess that every resident of this island will be thrilled we built it."

"And why's that?"

"Because this is going to be a multipurpose retail space."

"I heard that this morning. Is that like a mini mall?"

"Exactly! It will minimize the need to go off the island to buy organic groceries. You'll be able to get a healthy breakfast in a place where you can actually sit at a table, to buy things for your house and garden. You'll even be able to color your hair to match the fire engines, if that's what you're into."

"Oh please, this hair of mine. Okay, you're right. We don't have any of those luxuries here on the island but it's all just right over the causeway."

Beth wished desperately that the salon was already open for business because, at that moment, the blazing redness of her hair fed her massive insecurities.

"And gas isn't getting any cheaper, is it?"

"Actually, it is."

"Okay, granted, but there's time. Is it becoming less important?"

"For real." She looked up at him and he was staring at her again. "What's wrong?"

"Nothing. I was just wondering . . ."

"Wondering what?"

"Who are you? Who is Beth Hayes with the crazy hair and eyes like the water around the mystic Isle of Capri?"

Beth didn't quite know how to respond. No one had ever asked her a question like that. Should she paint herself as an environmentalist or an intellectual? A woman of the world? She decided then just to be herself because what did it really matter what he thought of her? This whole rush of excitement was ridiculous anyway.

"Um, I'm just me. I grew up on this island, sort of, and I went away to school and now I'm back."

"Fresh out of college?"

His smirk in full blossom was one thing, but now he had implied that she was too young to be taken seriously. So, she said to herself, you do care what he thinks! Look at you! You're a mess!

"Out of college, yes, but not so fresh. So, how old are you anyway? Like fifty?" Beth said, thinking it was a pretty clever retort.

"What? Um, I'm thirty-seven. And, not married. See?" Max remembered that his hair was getting a little thin on the sides but he thought it could be seen only in certain lights. Maybe he needed to wear more sunscreen. But to buoy his credibility, he held up his left hand.

Beth saw no evidence that a wedding band had ever been there.

"Why would I care if you're married or not?"

"Because I want to have dinner with you tonight and it wouldn't do for a woman of your stature to be running around with some Lothario, would it?"

"Heaven forbid. So, you want to have dinner? Tonight?"

Beth gulped, knowing she was at risk because if he had said, Let's go jump off the bridge around seven-thirty tonight, she would've said, Okay, that sounds like a great idea. She was a smitten schoolgirl with all her good judgment on a temporary leave of absence.

"That was my freaking thought. Seven-thirty? You make a reservation and I'll pick you up."

"Okay, that sounds like a great idea."

She scribbled her address, her cell phone number, and the telephone number at the house on her pad, tore off the scrap, and handed it to him. He gave her his card.

"In case you chicken out," he said, "you can call my cell."

"Chicken out? Really? Do you have a reputation I should know about?"

He stood up and put twenty dollars on

the bar. Then he laughed, pushed his hair back, and placed his sunglasses on his face. "No. Not at all. See you later."

With that, Max Mitchell left Beth Hayes sitting alone in her world, on a barstool at Poe's Tavern.

Beth swallowed hard, gave his back a little wave, and said to the empty space between them, "See ya!" And then she thought, Wow, he must be loaded.

When Beth got home, the first thing she did was to clean up after Lola. In her haste, she had forgotten to put Lola in her crate and now there were some political statements from her dog to discover and deal with. Lola did not appreciate being left alone. When she had the entire house to herself, she turned over wastebaskets and tore apart the contents. Needless to say, she allowed nature to take its course behind every chair in the living room and on the pale aqua bath mat in Maggie's bathroom.

"Oh no! Lola? Bad dog! You are a bad girl!"

The phone rang loudly and Beth hurried to answer it.

"Hello?"

"Hey, Beth! It's your Aunt Maggie calling from beautiful California to see if everything's going all right! How's that little dog?"

Beth stepped back and looked at the telephone receiver. Was Maggie psychic or what? She laughed with a trace of nervousness that she knew her Aunt Maggie could detect.

"Who, Lola? Lola's great! Great!"

"Well, good, darlin'. So, what's going on with you?"

"Well, I got a job freelancing for the local paper, which I'm pretty excited about. And I got another part-time job as a hostess at Atlanticville."

"Well, shugah, you didn't waste any time, did you? Whew! That's good! Maybe you'll meet a young man to, you know, have dinner with?"

Beth gulped. Had someone from Poe's Tavern called her aunt to say she'd been seen in the company of a male member of the species? This conversation was just too bizarre.

"Yeah, who knows? Stranger things have happened."

"You're telling me?"

They talked for another minute or two and then said goodbye.

"If you need anything—"

"I'll call, Aunt Maggie. Don't worry."

Beth put Lola on her leash, took her out, brought her back inside, and deposited her in her crate. There was a little puddle by the leg of a kitchen chair.

"This has to stop, Lola. You're almost three years old and you know it's wrong. What am I going to do with you?"

Lola's ears were down, flat against her cheeks, and Beth could see the guilt all over her little dog's face. She made a mewing sound to express her regret and Beth just shook her head.

"Kids," Beth said.

Beth did some rechecking to be certain that all was in order and then felt a panic rising. She had a date or was it a date? Yes, she decided, it was. What to wear? Where to go? She decided to call Cecily. If Cecily knew where the best eggs Benedict were, she might have an idea for dinner too.

"Hey! You busy?"

"No. What's up? You okay? You sound nervous."

"No, I'm good. I'm good."

"So, what's going on?"

"Where's a nice place for dinner in Charleston?"

Cecily was quiet for a moment and then she said, "Mmmm? Is somebody we all know and love going on a date?"

"Well, I don't know if you'd call it that exactly . . ."

"So, then . . . what is it?"

"Well, it's sort of business . . ."

"You mean monkey business. Uh-huh. Okay. Listen, if you want great food and an elegant atmosphere, go to Peninsula Grill. If you want, you know, something smaller and more intimate? Take him to Fulton Five."

"And where is Fulton Five?"

"Um, hmm. Right where it should be. Number 5 Fulton Street, off King, right past Saks on the right."

"Oh, right! I know that place. It's adorable. I guess I should call for a table."

"I would. It's pretty popular. So, what are you going to wear, and what about your—pardon me—hair?"

"I'm going to shave my head and wear a

push-up bra, okay? What kind of a question is that?"

"I'm just saying . . ."

"I'll find something in the closet. I'm sure I own one clean dress."

"I'm coming over."

Within the hour, Beth heard the slam of a car door and looked out of the kitchen window to see Cecily climbing the steps with a shopping bag.

"Hey! You didn't have to do this, you know." Beth held the door open for her.

"Don't you have a glass of ice water or something? You could drop dead in this heat." Cecily dropped the bag on a kitchen chair.

"You're telling me?" Beth opened the refrigerator and handed Cecily a bottle of water. "What's in the bag?"

"Accessories, because I know you and I know you ain't got nothing to wear. And you better not be wearing those skank flip-flops on a date, you hear me?"

Beth giggled and Cecily smiled, glad that Beth wasn't offended. The fact was that Beth wasn't offended in the least because she looked up to Cecily, probably in much the same way that her own mother had that kind of simpatico relationship with Livvie.

"Well, Miss Makeover, it turns out that I have a simple black linen dress and some sandals that work just fine."

"Handbag?"

"Um . . ."

Cecily reached into the bag and pulled out a red leather envelope bag and held it in the air.

"Perfect!" Beth said.

"Jewelry?"

"Uh . . ."

This went on until Cecily was satisfied that Beth would look well-turned-out that night.

"My goodness, I feel like Cinderella going to the ball!"

"You are. So? Who's Mr. Wonderful? Could it be one of those cute guys from Atlanticville? Which one? I'll bet it's Alan, right? I knew it! I just knew it!"

"Excuse me, but I would never date somebody I work with."

"You don't start until Thursday, if I remember correctly."

"Still. Anyway, I met this guy who is building this new building where Bert's was and I had to write about him for the paper—"

"What paper?"

"The *Island Eye News.* I got a freelance assignment, and so—"

"And just when did all this happen?" Cecily crossed her arms, turned her head to one side, raised her eyebrows, and sucked in her cheeks.

"Look at you, standing there like Judge Judy!" Beth giggled. "Today, actually. It all happened today. It's been kind of crazy around here."

"I'll say!" Cecily ticked off the events on her fingers. "Let's see now. Got a second job, found a man, got a date . . . shoot, girl! It's not even four o'clock!"

"Dinner's at seven-thirty. He's picking me up."

"And the man is picking her up. Dang! What's his name?"

"Max Mitchell. From Atlanta."

"Max Mitchell. Sounds like an alias. How old is he?"

"Um, thirty-seven?"

"Thirty-seven! Beth Hayes? Your momma would beat your behind!"

"It's just business!"

"Look at your face! You're as red as a blister! Don't you know it's a sin to tell a lie?"

"I ain't lying to you! I never lie. It's business and that's all it is."

"Humph. I gotta go."

"You do? Shoot! There was something else I wanted to tell you."

"What's that?"

"Last night, I was out on the porch with Lola and . . ."

Beth told her the story about the slamming noises and the mess she found in her grandmother's bedroom. Cecily listened intently with narrowed eyes.

"Honest?" Cecily said.

"Could I make this up?"

"Probably not. Humph. Well, I know about the bed because I have seen it myself. And I've seen plenty of fool things in that mirror too but I don't like noises and carrying on. That's not good."

"I haven't been in there since last night. I switched on all the lights in there and left them on too."

"Well, let's go have us a look and see what we see."

"I hate this stuff," Beth said.

"Who doesn't?"

Together they went to the bedroom and opened the door. The lights were still on and the room was still a wreck.

"Humph," Cecily said. "Must have scared you to death."

"Only half to death. Actually, it made me mad."

"Can't blame you for that either. Well, I know what to do. Let's clean this up and then I'll give this haint my grandmother's favorite kick in the sheets."

"Sounds good to me," Beth said. "I knew you'd know how to handle this."

"Yep. Thank the Lord I had the grandmother I did!"

When order was restored Cecily went to the kitchen and returned with a box of salt and a broom.

"What are you gonna do?"

"Watch me. You got any tape?"

"Yeah, sure. I'll get it."

Cecily swept the floor clean and sprinkled salt in all the corners of the room. When Beth gave her the tape, she took a piece and covered the keyhole in the door.

"I'm gonna put some salt here for good measure," Cecily said as she shook some more over the windowsills.

"I'm not gonna ask . . ."

"Old Gullah remedy for haints and hags, that's all. Just let me know if you hear anything tonight."

"Okay, thanks. Speaking of tonight, what do you think I should do with my hair?"

"Lord, that hair! Wash it and pull it back in a bun. It's too hot and humid for anything else."

"You're right."

"Anyway," Cecily said as she put the salt back in the kitchen cabinet and picked up her bag, "it looks more professional. For business and all."

There was a pause in the conversation as Cecily reinforced her opinion that Beth was maybe ten percent delusional in her grasp of the truth.

"Right! Business! Hey, thanks for all this stuff, Cecily! You're the best!"

Cecily started down the steps and turned back to face Beth. "You're right, I am."

"Can I ask you a question?"

"Sure," Cecily said.

"Do you think my Aunt Maggie is clair- voyant or something?"

Cecily looked at Beth long and hard. "Yes, but no more so than anybody else with plough mud in their veins, and mainly when it comes to this house. But, you? This ain't no business of mine, but some- body's got a date! Yes ma'am!" Cecily laughed then and it was clear by the sing- song of her high pitch that she meant to make Beth laugh too.

And Beth did laugh, for the rest of the afternoon in fact, but in between those small bursts of laughter, she wondered about Max Mitchell and what he was thinking.

By the time quarter to seven rolled around, Beth was a scatterbrained bundle of nerves, wandering from room to room, talking to herself.

"Okay, it's just dinner. No biggie. Right? Right. Okay. I'm cool. No problem."

She decided to turn on some music, but as she rifled through the huge stack of CDs, she honestly couldn't decide what to play. If she used her own music that she had upstairs, he probably wouldn't know any of it. Worse, she couldn't remember what her aunt and mother had played when she was six, which would be music from his era.

"What about the Beatles?"

The Beatles were always safe, she thought. Or the Stones. But there was no Beatles music to be found. Or anything by the Rolling Stones.

"Shoot! They took everything worth a crap with them to California!" There was, however, a *Johnny Cash Greatest Hits* and something from Pottery Barn that described itself as retro cocktail music.

"Cocktail music. Good. This is good."

After a minute or two of unsuccessful starts, she managed to get the stereo playing and she adjusted the volume. Then she realized she had not prepared anything for cocktails and felt a rise of panic.

"There's wine in the refrigerator. For goodness' sake, Beth, get it together!"

Rushing to the kitchen, she swung open the door of the refrigerator and pulled out a bottle of white wine whose stick-on price tag was still attached.

"Thirteen dollars. Okay, not too cheap. This is fine."

But for her Uncle Henry, Beth's family lacked a serious focus on things like great wine or the other trappings of an epicurean's existence. She reached for a can of generic-branded salted nuts and an unopened bag of Goldfish from the cabinet and dumped half into two small bowls. She placed two wineglasses with everything else on the counter with some funny paper cocktail napkins anchored under the nuts. Her aunt and mother loved the character Maxine and thought all the cartoons of her were a riot. Beth wasn't so sure about that as her humor ran in other directions, but she was pleased with the small offering of drinks and snacks she had pulled together. It was surely better than nothing and it seemed very appropriate to offer her dinner companion, business or not, an adult beverage before going out for the evening.

"Seven on the nose," she said to herself. "So where is he?"

Beth looked out the kitchen window. No sign of Max. Maybe he was lost. Maybe he got caught by the drawbridge. Maybe he had a flat tire or a wreck. She had his number but didn't want to call him. After all, it was only just seven. He didn't know it would take half an hour to get to downtown, did he? No, probably not. He didn't even know where they were going! She went back to the living room to check herself out in the mirror one more time, pulling at the hem of her dress and checking her teeth, even though she had brushed, flossed, and used the Water Pik, adding mouthwash to it the way her dental hygienist did. Beth decided she looked pretty good that night and not at all like a kid just out of school.

She wondered if she should light candles and just as quickly she dismissed the notion.

"Candles? I might get raped!"

Then she had a fit of giggles. She was so nervous it was difficult to swallow, much less think straight. She decided to let the ocean breezes work their magic. The heat of the day was broken and the air on the porch was thick and delicious. That's what she would do. She would tell him hello, pour him a glass of wine, take him out to the porch, and tell him a little bit about the house and its history.

"All set," she said to the thin air, as

though the house was coaching her, and reapplied her lip gloss for the umpteenth time.

She looked out the kitchen window again. Still no sign of Max. It was now seven-fifteen. Her heart sank. Was she being stood up? Did he think this was a joke? God! She was so stupid! He wasn't coming at all! She could feel the perspiration of humiliation on the roots of her hair and the back of her neck. She checked her cell phone for missed calls. Nothing. Actual tears began to well up in her eyes.

"What's the matter with me?" she whispered to herself.

Beth checked that Lola was still in her crate and then positioned herself in the doorway to the porch so she could let the breeze reset her thermostat and listen for Max at the same time. Then she became annoyed. If he was going to be late, why hadn't he called? If he had to do something else that night, he could have canceled with her, couldn't he have? She told herself that it didn't matter to her except for the inconvenience of blowing her evening, so why had he not just picked up his cell and used it?

"I mean, it's not like I want to marry this guy or something!" she said to the mirror.

Seven-twenty.

"Men!" she said, thoroughly exasperated. "I'm such a jerk."

Beth was ready to turn off the lights and lock the doors, but that would have been a worthless move because it wasn't even dark yet.

The phone rang and she rushed to answer it.

"Beth? Hey! It's your mother!"

"Mom! Hey! How are you?"

"Missing my baby girl. Hey, Aunt Maggie said you got two jobs! Congratulations!"

"Thanks! They don't pay jack, but who cares?"

"It gives your life structure and that's good."

"Oh, Mom. That's so anal."

"Please! Don't say—"

"Okay! Got it!"

"Honey? Are we in a poopy mood?"

"No. I'm fine. Really. I'm fine."

"No you're not. What's wrong?"

"Oh, I met this guy and we're supposed to be having dinner and he's like totally late and I hate dating. Don't you remember what this was like?"

"Yep, men stink but we love the smell. Remember I used to say that all the time?"

"Yeah, I should ask Aunt Maggie to do it in needlepoint for me."

"Anyway, he'll show. Don't worry. Now is there anything else . . ."

After a few more minutes and telling each other they loved each other three times, they hung up.

Beth was still furious with Max. She decided to put the wine away, turn off the music, and turn on the television to CNN. In her mind, there was no longer any reason for him to think this was anything more than an appointment. If he showed up at all, that is.

"I hate him!" she said.

Beth had misplaced the remote control, and after scouring three rooms for it, she gave up the search. She bent down to the dark shelves that housed the equipment that operated the cable box, the television, and the DVD player, trying to figure out which buttons did what. She pressed a few of them and suddenly there was an explosion of static so loud it completely startled her. She jumped, causing the cord of the floor lamp to catch her heels, tripping her, bringing the lamp to a crash landing. She felt herself careening backward to the floor with nothing to grab to save herself from the fall, biting her lip, and hitting her head in the back of her skull so hard that she thought it must've been cracked.

"Oh my God! Ow, ow, ow!"

She felt the back of her head and looked at her hand to see if there was any blood. Thankfully, there was none.

"Hello? Are you in there? Hello? Beth? You okay?"

Max Mitchell was in the house, standing over her and offering her a hand to disentangle herself from the wires and rise from her unfortunate sprawl.

"Crap!" she muttered. "I didn't hear you come in!"

"Sorry I'm late. Are you okay?"

"Oh yeah, I'm fine. Just fine. Just the klutz of the world, that's all. Thanks."

"Sorry I'm late," he began again. "Here, let me turn this off."

He pressed one button on the stereo and silence followed.

"You're a genius."

"I wish! Anyway, I was on a conference call with my partners that ran on and on and then it was that bridge . . ."

Beth, now standing, smoothed out her dress and looked at him curiously, wondering how he had the nerve to just let himself in.

"Anyway, just as I was about to knock on the door, I heard this huge crash and the frantic voice of a young lady calling out for her Maker, so I let myself in . . ."

"To rescue me?"

"Yeah, that was the plan."

"Wow," she said. "Would you like a glass of wine?"

"Sure, that would be nice. Did you know your lip is bleeding?"

"It is? Gross." Beth put the back of her hand to her lip, and sure enough, there was a streak of blood. "I'll be right back."

"Are you sure you're okay?"

"Yeah, I think my pride took the most damage here. Help yourself. The wine's in the fridge."

Beth went to the closest bathroom and examined her lip in the mirror over the basin. The wound was in the center of her lower lip but very small. She swished her mouth with water and then with mouthwash, which stung. She hoped her lip wouldn't inflate like a balloon.

When she returned to the kitchen, Max handed her the glass of wine he had poured for her.

"Damage report?" he said.

"Not bad. I just hope I don't wind up with a lip like a sock monkey."

Max laughed and said, "Hold a cube of ice on it and it won't swell."

"Oh, forget it. It could've been a lot worse. Come on; let me show you our zillion-dollar view of the deep blue sea."

"Yeah, I'd love to see that."

They stepped out onto the porch and into paradise. The Atlantic Ocean rushed before them, unrelenting eastern winds whipping the silver stacks of so many small waves to the western end of the island. It was as though the water was in a race with itself, in a panic to imprint the beach with its high watermark. The white sand raced from the dunes across the yet unwashed beach in fiery torrents, leaving ever-changing serpentines carved in its path. The sky was moving toward the deep shades of early night, changing by the minute, the horizon painted in the rich hues of mangoes and plums.

Beth looked over at Max, whose gaze was fixed on the massive power of the landscape before him. Neither of them had taken a sip of their wine. She raised her glass toward him and he did the same.

"Cheers," she said. "Here's to meeting you."

"Thanks," he said, and touched the rim of her goblet with his. "You too."

They drank and Max looked back out across the dunes at the beach.

"You grew up here?"

"Pretty much. The house has been in our family for like a hundred years or something. It's really my mother's childhood home. But when I was a kid, I was over here all the time, and now that my family is all over the place, I've got the keys."

"Wow! You're a lucky woman! I wonder what a view like this is worth in the market?"

"I don't know, but my great-grandfather bought the property for, I don't know, a thousand dollars or something. It had the eight rooms that are the central part of the house but over time they added on for new babies. You know, good Catholics? Having kids to populate the Army of the Lord?"

"Are you a good little Catholic?" Max smiled at her.

"Are you?" Beth had no intention of discussing religion or politics.

"I don't like to talk about religion," Max said, surprised that she had turned his question around.

"Me either. Do you want another splash of vino?"

"What I'd like is to spend the whole night looking at this view."

"Yeah, you don't have an ocean in Atlanta, do you?" Beth was enjoying giving him a bit of a hard time. She was ready to leave for dinner but Max seemed to want to linger. Remembering her Aunt Maggie's warning about men in the house, she knew she needed to move him along. He was thirty-seven, after all.

"No ma'am. Got the Chattahoochee and a pretty nice lake nearby, but there isn't anything to compare to a whole ocean."

"Right. Well, I'm thinking we had better get going or we'll blow our reservation.

And hey, have you had a look at Charleston Harbor?"

"Not in a while. Did they change it?"

"Yeah, right. They haven't changed a thing downtown since the seventeenth century, which is the whole point. Maybe after dinner, I'll show you around?"

Max nodded and then looked at his watch. "Wow! It's almost eight."

"We're really late! Should we call the restaurant?"

"I'll do it. Where are we going?"

Without a care about the money he was wasting by calling information instead of using a phone book, Max dialed Fulton Five restaurant on his cell. In a very authoritative voice he informed them that the Hayes party of two was en route but delayed because of a terrible automobile accident. Just as Beth was absorbing the fact that Max had just told a gratuitous lie, he smiled at her and said, "All taken care of." Okay, she said to herself, he throws money around and he tells a convenient fib. So what? Beth preferred to overlook these small shortcomings and just enjoy his company. Maybe, she thought as they drove to Charleston, he's nervous, and that would be a good sign.

Walking through twinkling lights and trellised vines in the winding courtyard of the restaurant, Max once again held his hand close to the small of her back. Should she trip or stumble he would be able to keep her from falling.

"This is very charming," he said. "Very charming."

"The food's supposed to be really delicious too," she said. Normally Beth might have said, It's supposed to be totally hardcore, or The tiramisù is seriously fabulous, but that night, acutely aware of their age difference, Beth was making a conscious effort to bridge that gap. And Max could feel that it was important to Beth to be taken seriously.

Inside the restaurant they were led to a table in the far reaches of the small dining room, right under a window to the street. The room was washed in the soft glow of candles and small chandeliers that bounced light from the brass fixtures and chartreuse walls.

"It's like a jewelry box, isn't it?" Beth said.

"I love it! It reminds me of a place I used to go in New York, down in the Village."

"Greenwich Village?"

"Yeah. This atmosphere is very authentic. Excellent choice, Miss Hayes."

"So far, Mr. Mitchell."

Without using a wine list, Max ordered a bottle of Barolo. This impressed Beth very much even though she entertained a fleeting thought that a Barolo might be related to footwear.

"You do drink red, don't you?"

"Of course," she said, laughing, thinking she was glad it wasn't footwear.

"What's so funny?" he said, smiling at her.

The waiter poured Max a small portion to taste and Max nodded his head.

"Nothing," she said. "I have this goofy sense of humor sometimes."

"Oh," he said, "you know what? I've been thinking about you all afternoon."

"Really?"

"Yeah."

They took the menus and the waiter placed a tiny dish of olives and a basket of warm bread before them. Beth picked at a piece of the bread's crust, wishing she could read his mind. It wasn't that she wanted him to be seriously interested in her as an object of intimate affection; it was that she wanted to know if he was interested. At all. Then she quickly realized she was playing a game with herself and told herself to snap out of it.

"Gosh. So, Mr. Mitchell," she said, resuming the journalist posture, "tell me. Where are you living?"

He looked up and smiled at her.

"Well, I've got a furnished condo in Mount Pleasant. For the moment, that is. It's not a place I'd brag about to you. I'm thinking I might actually buy something here and stay for a while. The whole Lowcountry thing is pretty hypnotic. Very different from Atlanta."

"I'll say. Life around water has a very different pulse beat."

"That's an interesting observation. Why do you think that is?"

"It's all about ebb and flow. The tides affect everything."

"You're probably right. Like the moon."

"Exactly." He was looking at her so

sweetly. It felt like she'd known him forever.

The waiter reappeared and recited the
specials.

"Do you know what you'd like to have?"
Max asked, staring at Beth, pleased again
to be in her company.

Beth looked up at the waiter and said,
"Do I want the papardelle all'Anatra or the
tagliatelle Bolognese?"

"I'd go with the papardelle myself. Would
you like a small salad with that?"

"Sure. Thanks."

"And you, sir?"

"I'm thinking the sea scallops."

"Salad?"

Dinner was ordered without a lot of hur-
rah, and with the wine to warm them, there
was more heat growing at their table than
there was in the kitchen. Beth continued
to ask Max trivial questions about where
he went to school (Georgia Tech), did he
play sports (tennis), and why had he never
married (unsatisfactory response).

"You really don't believe in marriage?"

Beth was amazed that someone of his
age wasn't interested in having a wife and

family. Not that Beth was in a hurry to secure a mate. Frankly, her biological alarm clock had yet to tick or tock.

"Maybe I just haven't met the right woman," he said. "Besides, women get married, have babies, and they get fat and cranky. Then they nag you to the grave. I've seen it with too many of my friends. And to be honest, who really wants to spend twenty years trying to convince their children to do the right thing all the time? I mean, it's hard enough for me to convince *myself* to do the right thing."

"Aha! A Bad Boy?" Her hands began to perspire.

"Oh, not really. I'm just too busy for love, I guess. I haven't been in one place long enough to think about marriage and commitment. Right now it's all about career."

"You seem pretty sure about that, that women get fat and cranky and turn into nags. My mom's not a nag. Never was. And my aunt? Well? She's not actually a *nag,* per se. She just wants to know that everything is as photogenic as possible."

Max chuckled at Beth's choice of words. "Photogenic? What do you mean?"

"Well, I guess the difference between

my mother and her sister is that we just live our life without photo ops and my Aunt Maggie's life is completely styled. You know what I mean?"

"Yeah. I do." Max's eyes seemed to regain some of their former light. "So, you only have one aunt?"

"Gosh no! I have three aunts and two uncles. My Uncle Henry is . . ."

Beth went down the list of all the relatives of her immediate family, their colorful personalities, and as alcohol will lead one to do, she revealed their approximate assets. Max listened, especially when she got to her celebrity twin aunts from Florida.

"Even I know who they are!" he said. "Wow! They have to be worth, I don't know, a lot."

"Yeah, they're pretty much rolling in it. Uncle Henry's not exactly broke either."

"Really?"

"Yeah, and he's in charge of my trust fund, which is kind of a pain in the neck."

"Why's that?"

"Because he's tighter than a gnat's fanny—excuse me—and he rolls over every dividend back into the account. Might be nice if I had a decent car, don't you think?"

"You poor thing, a trust-fund baby. I should have known there was a good reason why you are so much more sophisticated than other girls your age."

"Oh, sure."

Max leaned across the table, poured her more wine, and said, "No, I'm not kidding. I am really looking forward to getting to know you, Beth. Who would have thought I would meet someone so fascinating on Sullivans Island?"

6

The Mother Ship Is Calling

Susanthepen@writenow.org
Mag, Beth's met someone. Hope he's not a rape artist. See what you can find out? xx

Maggiepie2@marthagene.net
Worrywart! I'll call Cecily and nose around. xx P.S. God, I love a cause!

Susanthepen@writenow.org
Old woman! Cecily ain't telling you nothing! She's in cahoots with Beth! xx

Maggiepie2@marthagene.net
Watch me work! xx

After dinner, Beth and Max took a stroll along the sea wall of the Battery. Now and then he took her arm and crossed it over his, and she resisted leaning into his shoulder. That would have been too much, she thought, although the urge to do so was strong. But the night was like a perfectly ripened peach, the stuff of delicious memories. They stopped along the way, leaning on the railings over the dark choppy waters of the harbor. They talked about the past glories of Charleston and how important history was to every Charlestonian. Over the course of the evening, they had grown more familiar and comfortable with each other. Imps and angels seemed to have conspired, casting their spells all around them, to remind them of all that was so irresistible about summer nights and the Lowcountry. Max was at the pinnacle of his most engaging self, and naturally, Beth was thoroughly mesmerized.

When she laughed Max thought her voice sounded like wind chimes, infecting him with an overwhelming desire to seduce her. But Max would not seduce her. That was not his style. He would maneuver events so that she would come to him. He was a loner. He wondered why he was unable to really allow himself to fall in love. The truth was, he was afraid of love and he knew it. Then, when the affair ended, he could claim no responsibility for her broken heart. At least that was his fleeting thought then, in that moment.

When the night grew late and it felt as though the city had turned in for the evening, Max drove Beth home and, as a gentleman should, he walked her to her door. The ocean rolled quietly in the distance, whooshing in tiny laps and withdrawing with the most remote of sighs. The tide was dead low and the air was still. Beth stopped at the top step and turned to face him.

"Well, it's late, huh?" she said, wondering if he would try to come in on the excuse of wanting to see the ocean again. And then what would happen?

"Yeah. It's almost midnight. But I have to say, I hate for the night to end."

"Me too. Gotta work tomorrow." Why, she wondered, did she say that? Why not just yawn in his face? I'm no damn seductress, that's for sure, she thought.

"Yeah. Well, thanks for a great evening," Max said. "Dinner was delicious. Good choice."

"No, thank you! I thought dinner was great too. Really great."

"Okay, well, good night then." Max took

her hand in his and kissed her palm. No one had ever kissed the palm of her hand in her entire life. She blinked hard, wondering if he was going to kiss her on her mouth. Sadly, she had overjudged his intentions. He cleared his throat. "Take care of that lip."

"Right. I'll do that. Thanks."

"And if you need any help with that article, just let me know."

"Thanks. I'll do that."

He had not said, See you soon, or I'll call you tomorrow, and Beth resisted the bit of disappointment she felt because of it. She told herself it did not matter. She was reasonably confident that she would see him again. Inconceivable as it seemed, she thought that this was probably what the beginning of mature love might feel like. How did any sane person tell the difference between love and infatuation anyway? She'd had her share of love affairs, but the way she was feeling now was vastly different from anything she'd ever known. This felt like emotional quicksand. She was happily sinking and didn't want a rope. She wanted to pull him in with her. And she had a glimpse of them together, years

ahead in the future—in a house with children. Maybe there would be an old-
fashioned garden swing that he would
make and attach to the limb of a tall live
oak. Maybe there would be . . . who could
say? Everything was possible. It did not
seem too saccharine or that far-fetched an
idea. Even though she had always professed that marriage was not for her, she
would surely wind up with someone,
wouldn't she? Why not him? What was
happening to her resolve? But how had
she gone so off-kilter so quickly? Had she
not sworn a thousand times that she had
no intention of getting sucked into the black
hole that was marriage? Well, *so what* about
that? she thought. She was frightened but
her fears were completely eclipsed by her
deep attraction to him.

She watched as he descended the
steps. He paused at the bottom, turned,
and gave her a little wave. Cast in the
scant ambient light, standing down there
in the grass, was the most handsome man
she had ever seen. So, he didn't kiss
her after the first time they went out to dinner, so what? Smiling, she unlocked the
door, and nearly floated into the house.

"Wow," she said to no one.

Lola, who had been behind the plastic grillwork of her portable prison for five hours, began yelping in earnest, piercing Beth's bubble.

"Okay, okay!" Beth sighed and knelt, unhooking the latch. Lola bounded out, jumping into Beth's arms and licking her face with so much highly energized desperation it seemed as though Lola must have thought Beth was never coming home. "Come on, miss. Momma's gotcha."

Beth decided to take her out to the front yard without her leash, hoping Lola would stay close. She carried her down the steps and deposited her on the grass. It was dark on that side of the house. In the shadows, Beth watched as Lola sniffed around and then slipped behind a lantana bush to fertilize the pine straw.

She marveled over the fact that the island smelled exactly the same as it had when she was a small child. Salty. Wet sandy earth. Safe. Alive. She could almost feel the grass growing, rising under her feet. Stars twinkled overhead. She wondered for the hundredth time, Who was

Max Mitchell? She scooped up Lola and went inside.

"I've got a story to tell you, Lola. Your momma's feeling a little bit weak in the knees."

After she locked the screen door and the actual door of the house behind her, she passed the living room, stopping to put Lola on the floor and to turn off the lights. The large mirror had a foggy center and every hair on Beth's body stood on end.

"Oh no!"

She had seen that fog often enough to know that a visitation was imminent. She shivered and Lola began to whimper, racing toward her crate in the kitchen as fast as her little legs would carry her.

Beth could hardly breathe she was so stricken. The pointing finger came first, attached to a fist that waved back and forth. It was a warning not to do something.

"Please, no," she whispered. "Please leave me alone. God, I hate this!"

But she couldn't walk away and she couldn't stop watching. Slowly, slowly she began to make out the unsmiling face and torso of Livvie Singleton. Livvie was wearing a dark dress with a white lace collar, probably something like what she would have worn to church. To Beth these things meant Livvie was not fooling around with her but had appeared to tell her something serious.

"What are you trying to tell me? Don't get involved with Max?"

Livvie folded her hands as though satisfied that Beth understood her message. Beth felt her spirits sink and sink like so many stones thrown in a river.

"Why?" Beth said aloud. "Why? Tell me why!"

But the image of Livvie faded until it was gone, leaving Beth tormented and superstitious and her mind swirling in the scent of lemons.

"Dammit! I hate this house! Dammit!"

Fearful that she was in for an all-out assault, she decided to peek into her deceased grandmother's room to see what wonders might be found there. But when she opened the door, all was in order. Beth breathed a deep sigh of relief.

She closed the door and called out loud for the record, "This house is too much, sometimes. Too much! Make it stop! Do you hear me? I hate this!"

She swore that in the morning she was going to go down to the rectory at Stella Maris Church and make an appointment with the priest to bless the house with holy water and prayers. Not that she was completely sold on those kinds of rituals, but it couldn't hurt anything and it might actually do some good. It was nearly one o'clock in the morning and Beth was a little fed up with this world and the other.

"Lola? Come on, baby! Time for bed!"

Lola was in the very back of her crate. She opened one eye to Beth, showing zero desire to move. Beth reached in and pulled her out, putting her up on her shoulder like a baby.

"If you think I'm sleeping without you, you're a crazy dog. You need to protect your momma tonight. Okay?"

All through the night Beth could hear whispering in the halls. Or maybe it was the wind of the incoming tide. Either way, no sleep was to be found. Finally, she nodded off just as dawn was breaking and slept hard until almost ten. Still exhausted, she awoke to overcast skies, no appetite, and an email from her mother.

Two jobs—wonderful! How's it going? Did he show up?

Beth emailed her back:

Everything is great. Yep, we had a great dinner downtown. He's dreamy! Hostessing at Atlanticville—starts Thursday—should make a little moola with that. What about you? Did you start classes yet?

What she wanted to say was, Why in the world do we keep this god-awful scary house? Do you really understand what goes on around here? Why is it necessary for us to have this connection with the dead? What good did it really do anyone? It's just so weird. And useless. Because the fact of the matter was that Livvie could show up in a gold chiffon gown beaded with pearls and wag her finger at her about Max until the cows came home and Beth knew that she would still do exactly what she wanted to do.

It was around noon when Cecily appeared to pick up the bills and to water the plants. Beth, struggling to write something about Bert's and waiting for a return call from the rectory, was nursing a cup of cold tea and some measure of anxiety that Max had not called. Not that he needed to call or had promised to call, but she just wished he would so she could hear his voice. She was posturing and smiling, hoping Cecily could not tell what was on her mind. And every time she thought about Livvie's warning, she pushed it out of her head.

"So, how was your *business* dinner?" Cecily asked with a straight face, smelling secrets in the air.

"It was great, actually."

"And what did you find out about him?"

"Um, that he's a really sweet guy? I mean, really wonderful."

Cecily looked hard at Beth. Beth decided the ceiling was a far better place to focus her attention than her friend's face.

"Oh law. Girl done fall down the rabbit hole." Cecily, who recognized Beth as a friend, slipped into Lowcountryspeak when she wanted to razz Beth without offending her.

"What's that supposed to mean?"

"Means your goose is cooked. Done like dinner. Time to get you a haircut. You need one anyway if you're gonna be any kind of professional-looking hostess. Besides, it's too hot for all that hair. And you know what? Go whole hog. May's well see the eye doctor too. As long as you're traveling downtown, that is."

"I'm traveling to hell is where I'm traveling."

"Mmm, mmm. You said it, sister, not me."

Beth made an appointment to see an ophthalmologist on King Street, and at Cecily's insistence, she agreed to see a woman named Hailey at the Allure Salon.

"Where is it?"

"It's farther up King Street past the Francis Marion Hotel. Let's see if she can work you in."

Beth listened as Cecily exercised her most diplomatic powers of persuasion to secure the all-but-impossible-to-nail appointment.

Darlin'? You are an angel from heaven! Do you hear me? An angel! Thank you so much! Yes. Her name is Beth Hayes. Okay!

"Kinda hard to tell you no, huh?" Beth said.

"Humph," Cecily said. "You'll be grateful. Trust me."

"I do!" Beth said.

Now, if Beth's mother or aunt had bullied Beth to immediately change her appearance, Beth would have shown them a gnarly tooth. But because it was Cecily, Beth took it in complete stride. The truth was that Beth lacked the self-confidence to do these things for herself, and besides, she wouldn't have known whom to call in a thousand years. Cecily was eons ahead of Beth in terms of navigating the world— well, Charleston at the least. This was going to completely decimate the budget, but for the first time in her life, Beth didn't care.

Cecily went about her business, taking hanging baskets down, picking off the dead leaves, and giving them a good soak while Beth went back to the kitchen and her laptop. Her notes were a jumble of facts that made no sense to her. Why had she ever thought that writing a simple newspaper article would be so easy?

Her email pinged to alert her of an arriving

message, and sure enough, it was another one from her mother. It was short and sweet.

Check this out! Classes are wonderful! Love you!

There was a jpeg attachment with pictures of her mother under the Eiffel Tower and another of her drinking café au lait in an oversized cup at a little sidewalk table in some random bistro. She wondered if some French guy named Jacques had taken the picture, and just as quickly she decided only if Jacques was the name of her waiter. Her mother looked so completely happy and completely stress-free. Beth printed the pictures, stared at them for a few minutes, and then taped them to the refrigerator. They would remind Beth why she was there. Her mother deserved this thrill, and at the end of the day, Beth knew it would be good for her as well. Then, she wondered how in the world her mother could just pack up her stuff and leave her and Simon for a whole year? Wouldn't she have pangs of longing for her husband? But then, maybe women her age didn't have pangs anymore. But wouldn't she be missing Beth or feeling even slightly guilty that she was stuck there in a spook house that raised a ruckus all on its own? Apparently, not so far.

"What's that?" Cecily said, returning the empty watering can to the floor of the pantry closet.

"Look at my momma. Isn't she beautiful?"

"Will you look at our Miss Susan in Paris, France? My oh my. I thought I'd never see this day. She looks like she's my age." Cecily let out a long sigh. Then Beth followed suit.

"Yeah, I was just thinking the same thing."

"Well, I best be moving along. Got too much to do for a Tuesday. I need Monday back!"

Cecily looked at Beth and flicked a stray lock of her hair. Beth could hear her thinking, Well, finally! Goodbye to that nonsense!

"I'll call you when I am all done."

"Don't be late, 'eah? Hailey's one very busy lady."

"Gotcha. And, thanks."

Cecily gave her a little wave on her way down the stairs and seconds later she was gone.

"Okay, Lola," Beth said thirty minutes later as she secured her in the crate, "Momma's going to town and I'll be back soon."

Her cell phone rang and her hopes spiked as she hoped it might be Max. When she checked the caller ID, she saw it was her Aunt Maggie and she sighed in disappointment. Tempted as she was to let it go to voice mail, she answered it in as upbeat a manner as she could muster.

"Hi! How's my Surfer Barbie aunt? Are y'all having fun?"

"Hi, honey! How's everything?"

"Good, good. I'm on my way to Charleston to get my hair color recalibrated? You know? Maybe to a color found in nature?"

"Goodness! That's wonderful! Well, I'm sure you'll be mighty glad you did that. After all—"

"And, I'm getting contact lenses. Hope Mom doesn't flip a shit when she sees the bill."

"What's that, honey? It sounded like you used a bad word for poopy."

"What?" Then Beth remembered who

she was talking to. "Sorry. Potty mouth. Um, do you think Mom will mind?"

"Beth? You listen to me. There's nothing more important to a man than how you look. You remember that, okay?"

"Okay," Beth said, and gagged a little.

"And, I was always of the opinion that you should have contact lenses anyway. Maybe, just maybe, your momma didn't want you to be so attractive. Did you ever think about that?"

"No. I gotta say I never thought about that." That's sick, Beth thought.

"Well, some women want their daughters to stay little girls forever, that's all I'm saying."

Thinking that this kind of talk was definitely somehow unflattering to her mother, Beth decided it was time to bow out of the conversation. "Right, well, I gotta go or I'm gonna be late."

"Okay, just close all the windows before you go. There's supposed to be a big storm this afternoon."

"No problem. But how do you know that?"

"The Weather Channel, you silly girl. How else?"

"Oh. Okay. Don't worry."

"And Beth? It seems that my boy wants to pay you a visit this weekend. Is that okay with you?"

"Bucky and Mike?"

"Well, darlin', they're the only two I have. But we're talking about just Mickey—um, I mean Mike—and maybe a friend or two of his."

Did Beth really have a choice in the matter? Seeing that she did not, she decided that she may as well be gracious about it.

"Of course! I'd love to see him! I'll call him right away!"

After they hung up, Beth closed all the windows and doors, wondering how her aunt knew they were open. The woman had a pair of eyes on a satellite in outer space, she decided. Or maybe she was somehow supersizing the house with Google Earth. She would not have put it past her.

She drove over the bridges to Charleston and found a parking spot on Warren Place. As she walked over to King Street, the oppressive heat of the afternoon sun bore down on the top of her head, burning her scalp. As of yet, there had been no rain that day, but the heat index was spiraling out of control.

Beth squinted in the afternoon sun and wished she had sunglasses. When she saw the eye doctor, she would buy a pair. Cecily was right; she would have cataracts by Christmas if she didn't.

"I'm going for broke," she said, and pushed open the door of the Allure Salon.

Beth stepped into the rejuvenating air-conditioning and exhaled in relief. She checked in at the desk, changed into a robe, and took a seat at Hailey's station. She was flipping through an old issue of *Us* magazine, fully absorbed in an article on the Olsen twins.

"Think those girls are skinny enough?"

She looked up to see someone standing behind her with her hands on the back of her chair.

"Uh, yeah. Are you Hailey?"

"Yep. And you must be Beth Hayes. So what on earth do we have here?"

"An unnatural disaster," Beth quipped. "Do you think you could make it look like something I could have grown?"

"Uh-huh. Cecily told me this was a big job. You're friends with her, right?"

"Yeah. She's my most amazing friend."

"Well, just so you know, you can tell her that your hair doesn't scare me, okay?"

"Good."

Two hours and a rather stunning amount of money later, Beth was a new woman. And although she worried about how she was going to explain the exorbitant expense to her mother, she knew her mother would be relieved that Beth was taking some initiative to resemble other functioning members of society. She took off her glasses and stared at herself in the mirror. Her hair was back within the zone of its authentic color. Hailey had shortened the bottom by several inches and dried it with a diffuser, giving new shine and bounce to her natural ringlets.

"Wow," Beth said.

"Wow is right. Those glasses don't match your new do, you know." Hailey was smiling and meant what she said in the nicest way.

"I'm aware," Beth said with a self-conscious giggle. "But I'm on my way to fix that too." Beth thanked her and gave her a generous tip. "Guess I can't say I'm with the band anymore, huh?"

"Truly. Should've taken before pictures," Hailey said with a smile. "You take care of yourself now, okay? No more red dye."

"For real," Beth said, nodding.

• Dark clouds continued to gather as Beth hurried to the car. The predicted storm was brewing. She debated whether to go see the eye doctor or return to the beach. But she decided to keep her appointment because if she didn't do it then, she was afraid she would lose her resolve. Besides, with hair spun into corkscrews like an angel, she knew she looked like she was wearing someone else's eyeglasses and not Tina Fey's.

Before long Beth was loving her new contact lenses and, most important, the way she looked, which was surprising to her. She looked like a Hamilton for the first time since high school and it pleased her. Why had she not done this before? Just the improvements to her peripheral vision were more than worth the annoyance of the handling and care of the tiny fragile lenses. She could not wait to call Cecily. But like most females would, she wondered if the change to her appearance was enough for people to say she was actually good-looking. She would not have admitted it to anyone then or ever, but what if looking the best she could wasn't good enough for Max Mitchell? It was one thing to have a kind of funked-out demeanor. Then the more off-the-grid you looked, the cooler you were assumed to be. The worst thing in her mind would be to go mainstream and then be considered to be as homely as a mud fence.

It looked more like the dead of night than late afternoon as the storm gathered strength. Just as she turned the corner onto East Bay Street, the first crack of thunder boomed like the beginning of the Apocalypse. Next came the pounding rain, fat droplets at first and then sheets and torrents, coming down so fast Beth could hardly see the rear end of the car in front of her.

Jagged bolts of lightning ripped the skies apart. Beth worried about Lola and knew she must be terrified. As she crossed the Ravenel Bridge, fog rolled in from across the Cooper River. These were the worst driving conditions Beth had ever endured and it made her hands clammy. She drove slowly in the rush-hour traffic, inching along, mindful of the dangers. As she reached the end of the bridge, she could see dozens of cars pulled over on the shoulders of the road. Coleman Boulevard and the side streets were flooded because the sandy ground and gutters had not had the time to absorb all the water. But that was the way of Lowcountry afternoon squalls. They blew in, drove the faithful to their knees, and scared everyone else out of their wits. Then they blew out to sea, leaving the world washed clean and the skies bluer than you could ever remember seeing them before. By the time she rolled by the Boulevard Diner, she reckoned the storm was probably halfway up the coast toward Georgetown.

She had one hand on the wheel as she reached in her purse for her cell phone and saw that she had missed two calls. One was from the rectory at Stella Maris Church and the other was from her cousin Mike. She had little enthusiasm to return either one and decided to wait until she got back to the house on the island.

With its wide range of historically insignificant architecture and commercial signage, Mount Pleasant was looking a little worse for wear, she thought, until she crossed the bridge over Shem Creek. To her right, the creek was completely placid and the shrimp boats were reflected in the water in perfect mirror images. Great beauty did *not* always require great sums of money, she thought. Sometimes something as easy and undemanding as an old shrimp boat, moored to an ancient piling battered from salt and time, could stop your heart in the same way as might a great work of art. It certainly seemed so at that moment. The little pocket that was the commercial area of Shem Creek was one of the most charming spots in the entire Lowcountry and she reminded herself to have a meal in one of the dozen or so restaurants that were strung along its shores.

As she crossed the top of the Ben Sawyer Bridge, it happened again. Just as she had seen on her initial arrival to the island several weeks ago, everything seemed to glisten and shimmer.

"I'm definitely losing my brains," she said, adding, "Maybe it's the rain."

But there was no mistaking the curious phenomenon. The greens were greener, blues were bluer, and everything was sharp and in focus.

"Maybe it's my contact lenses. Great. I'm talking to myself. Great."

She passed over Middle Street, deciding to take Atlantic Avenue down the island to avoid the possibility of seeing Max. The fact that he had not called her all day had mushroomed into the Great Insult. As much as Beth intellectualized that there could be a thousand legitimate reasons why he had not dialed her number or texted her or sent her dozens of roses, inwardly she sulked. Here she was, ready for her proverbial close-up and no one was there to pass judgment or click the camera.

"Men stink," she said as she passed the back side of his construction site, straining to see if his car was parked anywhere in the vicinity. If it was, she missed it.

She arrived home, walked Lola, and debated her next steps. She returned the call to the rectory, finding it closed for the day, and left another message. Then she called Mike.

"I heard you're coming for the weekend. Is that true?"

"Yeah, if it's cool with you. And I might bring a friend and this woman I'm seeing, if that's okay?"

"Anything's cool with me, big shot, but you gotta know your mom will have a cow if she finds out you're shacking up in her house."

"Oh, please. I'm twenty-six years old. Does she think I'm a virgin?"

"Uh, yeah she does. Do what you want, but when she starts raising hell, don't blame me."

"How's she going to find out?"

"She has little bitty cameras buried in the paneling, okay? How should I know? I just know that she'll find out, that's all. Anyway, I have to work so I won't be around too much."

"You got a job? You mean, someone actually hired you?"

"Yeah, ya big jerk."

"To do what? Cut grass?"

"Like this place is crawling with career opportunities? Um, I'm hostessing at Atlanticville. I get my dinners for like next to nothing and the food is actually pretty good."

"Oooh! Some perk. Girls don't eat anyway. So maybe I'll get everyone organized and come for dinner on Saturday."

"You'll need a reservation, dude."

"Right, can you help me out with that?"

"Maybe. So who are you bringing besides some poor misguided woman?"

"A really great guy that I work with. He's Henry's heir apparent. The guy's like an unbelievable brain."

"Nice."

"You won't like him."

"Good."

They talked for a few more minutes and then hung up. Beth was actually excited that her cousin was coming. He was very good company. He was bringing someone? She concluded that he was probably bringing some random stupid girl and another guy—read: gargantuan nerd—from their Uncle Henry's investment banking firm. But at least she wouldn't be alone, not that she technically was if you included the Other Side.

"We're having company, miss!" she said to Lola, who was curled up on one end of the sofa. "Should I put Mike and his Little Miss Hot Pants in the haunted bedroom? Come on, let's figure this out."

Beth walked from room to room with Lola scampering behind her. She opened windows in the rooms that smelled musty from the rain and checked the bathrooms for toilet paper and tissues. She decided that all the company could sleep downstairs and she would keep the upstairs for herself. She would rearrange the furniture in the second bedroom upstairs to resemble an office, which would deter Mike from sleeping across the hall from her with his girlfriend and making disgusting noises all night. It would also discourage his friend from staying there. After four years of living in dorms and cramped apartments with roommates, Beth was quickly adapting to having some space and some privacy—once again, the dead notwithstanding.

She found herself digging around in the attic for a folding table that could work as a desk. There was nothing up there except dust, old luggage, and boxes of junk.

"Oh no you don't!" she said to Lola, who was sniffing around all the corners of the rafters. Beth scooped her up and quickly took her outside to the yard, where, as it happened, Lola needed to be.

When they got back inside, Beth called Cecily.

"May I just tell you how much I love your friend at the salon?" she said.

"Oh yeah?"

"Yeah. I look like, well, I don't know, better. I think."

Cecily started laughing.

"Law, girl! You are supposed to say good things about yourself! If you don't, no one else will! You want some company? Is that what this call is about?"

"Yeah. You had supper yet? And do you know where I might find a folding table?" Beth looked at her watch. It was almost seven.

"Under the house, next to the showers and the hoses. I'm starving."

"Me too."

The difference between supper and dinner might need some clarification. In the not-so-recent past, respectable Charlestonians from all walks of life paused their daily business to enjoy dinner at around one in the afternoon. Dinner was the main meal of the day and it usually included rice, which is why people say Charlestonians have important ties to the Chinese in that both cultures eat a lot of rice and worship their ancestors. Supper was much lighter fare served at the end of the day. These customs came into being as a result of climate and lifestyle. But with the advent of air-conditioning, business travel, and the wretched stresses of our times, dinner had become supper, except on Sundays, when, if a mother is extremely lucky, she can still coerce her family to gather around a table after church and before a football game. In any case, because she was still a Lowcountry girl, Beth said *supper*, which really meant *dinner,* although according to her cousin Mike, generally girls didn't eat enough to call it a meal, except for Beth, who frequently claimed that she could eat a horse.

"Why don't we go up to the Boathouse and have a Cosmo? Maybe pick on an appetizer?" Cecily said.

"Breach Inlet or downtown?"

"You think I'm going over that big bridge tonight? Honey, it's enough to get me over the causeway!"

"I'll meet you there in thirty minutes."

The waiting area at the Boathouse was

crowded and Beth edged through the crowd to where Cecily waited at the bar, sipping a cocktail and chatting with the bartender, who was clearly under her spell. When she spotted Beth, Cecily's eyes popped opened like a steamed clam.

"Is that really you? Lawsamercy! Beth! You look gorgeous! Oh no! I spilled my drink!"

It was all Beth needed to hear to put some loft under her wings.

The bartender quickly handed her a dish towel, scooped her glass away, and said, "I'll replace that for you. Don't worry."

Beth reached for some paper napkins, handed them to Cecily, smiled, and said, "Here. Do you really think so?"

"Yes ma'am! You look unbelievable! Turn around! Are you wearing mascara?"

"Yep!"

"Mascara too! Mercy! What next?"

Beth did a little spin in the narrow space where she stood. Laughing with delight at the great success of Beth's makeover, Cecily shook her head and clapped her hands.

"Eyeliner?"

"Yep!"

"Amazing! I knew it! I just knew there was a swan in there!"

"Thanks! Well, I owe it all to you! I never would have done this."

"I know. Now, you thirsty?"

"I guess I just might be."

"Jimmy darlin'? Can we have a glass of white wine for my friend?"

Jimmy was grinning all over his freckled face and he couldn't give Beth her drink fast enough.

"On the house," he said. "Any friend of Cecily is a friend of mine."

"Gosh, thanks!"

During the period of time it took to down two glasses of wine, a Diet Coke, and two appetizers, Beth checked her cell phone for missed calls at least ten times. Cecily's suspicions were confirmed.

"So, no phone call, huh?"

"Who? Who didn't call?"

"I'm figuring either it's Hollywood or Max Mitchell?"

"Um . . ."

"Okay, so it's not Hollywood. Want to tell me what's up?"

"I am wildly aggravated and mildly depressed."

"Okay . . . why?"

"Oh, crap. I hate men. That's all."

"Yeah. Love stinks. That's a song I think."

"J. Giles. Bunch of old dudes. My mom loves them. Anyway, men stink too."

"Not all of 'em. Just the ones I like."

Beth looked up at Cecily. She found it hard to believe that Cecily had anything but a perfect life. And as that thought floated through her mind, another one was arriving. Somehow she always wound up telling Cecily every self-possessed little detail of her life and rarely had she ever asked anything about Cecily's personal life. Once again, Beth came up short in her own eyes. She was a twit, an unfortunate but fitting term.

"Know what?"

"What?" Cecily said.

"This growing up thing is a very imperfect adventure."

Cecily sat back and took a long look at Beth. Then she smiled that knowing smile, the one for which the Singletons were so well known.

"It's a process, honey bunny. A long process that I expect continues till we go the way of all flesh, like my grandmomma used to say. Even though it hurts sometimes, don't be rushing through. You'll miss the good stuff. You know what I mean?"

"I guess. Sometimes I feel like I'm in control of my life and sometimes I wonder what in the world is wrong with me. You know? Here's my big worry. Did you ever fall in love and get blown out of the box?"

"Are you kidding? That's the only kind of relationship I've ever had. It's my own fault, of course. I mean, I seem to collect all these hurt birds that I think I can fix. I make terrible choices."

"You think love is a choice?"

"I don't *think* it. I *know* it. Look, at some point you say yes or no, right?"

"I guess so, but that's not a very romantic point of view, is it?"

"I'm just saying, until you meet the right guy? Say no. When Mr. Fabulous comes along, you'll know. At least that's what my momma always said. And my grand-momma."

"You mean like you know in your gut that you're going to spend the rest of your life with someone and you're imagining what your kids will look like and you know this is it? And when you're with him you can't breathe, and when you're not, you're possessed by when you'll be with him again?"

"Oh, lawsamercy. I thought you had sworn off this stuff."

"Me too. Guess not."

"Run away, girl. Like they say in that first-grade reading book? Run, run, run! You're too young!"

"I don't think I can run. I don't want to. Please don't tell anyone."

Cecily just shook her head and looked at Beth with an expression you might give someone on death row.

7

Goose Bumps

Maggiepie2@marthagene.net
Susan, I'm sending Mike to the island to check on Beth. He's older than her and more mature. He'll tell us if she's up to no good. Quit worrying. xx

Susanthepen@writenow.net
Old woman, your son is hopelessly immature and will probably throw a kegger. Beth has to work, you know, and she's not there to play hostess to your kids and their friends. But I love you. xx

Maggiepie2@marthagene.net
Ungrateful wretch! He'll entertain in my half of the house. I'll tell him not to be a slob, but I doubt if it will do any good. Boys. xx

It was around four in the afternoon when Monsignor Ben Michaels arrived at the Island Gamble. He knocked politely at the kitchen door and Beth invited him inside. It had been some time since Beth had seen the inside of a church, much less fulfilled her obligations as a Catholic. But like true love and deep hatred, guilt had a life span too. Beth blushed deeply and to his credit, the good monsignor made no indication that he noticed the blood rising in her cheeks. After all, guilty consciences were a large part of his business.

"Can I offer you a cold drink, Father?" Beth said.

"Ice water would be nice. Thank you. I'm beginning to wonder if this summer is ever going to end." He removed a white handkerchief from his pocket to wipe the moisture from his brow.

"Yeah, me too. It's been brutal."

The moment was a little awkward for them as they were nearly strangers to each other, but his appearance worked to put her at ease. His thick white hair and pronounced paunch were the perfect complement to the crinkles of age that laced his kind blue eyes.

Beth opened the refrigerator and took out two small bottles of water, offering one to him. He took it and Beth had a sudden flash of her Aunt Maggie knowing that she had given a priest a bottle to drink from as though he was an ordinary person and not a representative of the Vatican. She would kill me dead, she thought.

"Would you like a glass?"

"No, no. This is just fine. Now let's see. I think I remember your face from when you were a young girl," he said. "Weren't you at Midnight Mass on the millennium?"

"Wow! You have some memory!"

Father Michaels chuckled and twisted off the cap of the bottle, taking a long drink. Beth did the same.

"Nothing like plain cold water," he said. "Well, to be honest, I'm just guessing. The odds are that you were there because your family took up three entire pews! That was some night, wasn't it?"

"Yes. Yes, it sure was." Beth remembered all that allegedly had happened with the statue of the Blessed Virgin Mary and how the old people were fainting and calling out, claiming to see the plaster come to life. She and the rest of her family had

not seen anything out of the ordinary happen that night, but the sudden and cloying
smell of roses had nearly choked them all.
There had been no denying that the condensed fragrance of roses was there and
definitely real. In her opinion, the entire in-
cident had been too weird to dwell on and
Beth had not thought about it in years. "I
remember now."

"Yes, well, I think about it from time to
time too. After that night we had television
crews and all kinds of media folks coming
around looking for a story and I just sent
them on their way. Had to lock up the
church! Can you imagine such a thing? I
mean, I can't say everything didn't happen
as the parishioners said, but I can't say
that it did either."

"It was all very strange. I remember that
we all loved the bells and how all of us
went to the beach to watch the fireworks.
It was really exciting. Holy moly. What a
night, right?"

"Yes. Yes, indeed it was a holy moly
night. Shall we sit for a moment?"

"Oh! Yes, of course! Where are my manners? Let's go into the living room. This
way."

Beth prayed silently that her Aunt Maggie did not really have hidden cameras.

Father Michaels followed Beth to the ocean side of the house where the constant swirling of the ceiling fans cooled the room. It was a much more desirable place to sit than the kitchen, which baked in the afternoon sun. So as they found their place in the living room, Beth wondered for a moment, given the business at hand, if Livvie was hiding behind the silver of the old mirror, watching them.

"Wonderful house," Father Michaels said, and settled in an armchair. "Wonderful house."

"Thanks. It's been in our family like practically forever."

"Yes, I know. I used to come here for dinner when your grandmother was alive. I was just ordained and newly assigned to this parish. She was a good woman. You know, you resemble her a little."

"Well, thanks. She died when I was little so I don't remember too much about her except that she fed all the stray cats in the neighborhood."

"Including me! She sure made the best

okra soup I've ever eaten to this day. She really did."

"I don't have a clue how to make that or red rice or a lot of things my mom cooks. I'm pretty much a salad person."

"And where are your Aunt Maggie and Uncle Grant? Did I hear they went off to California?"

"Yes, they did, and my mother is in France. She's teaching at the American University for a year. I'm watching the store, so to speak."

"I see. Well, I'm sure they appreciate it. Although, I have to say, it doesn't seem like a terrible sacrifice to be here."

Beth wasn't about to start throwing dirt on her family by telling the family priest that she was living in bondage so she just smiled.

"So your family is all gone for how long?"

"A year. I mean, they might come home for Christmas or something. No one seems to have thought about that yet."

"I see. Well, wouldn't that be wonderful if they did? I'm sure they will if they can."

"I hope so. It would be weird to not be with my family on the holidays."

Father Michaels, sensing Beth was looking at many lonely nights, decided to
change the subject. The moment had arrived to get to the heart of his visit.

"Now tell me, Beth, was there was something that happened that made you pick
up the phone and call? I mean, are you
nervous staying here alone?"

"Annoyed, maybe. Nervous, no. I practically grew up here too."

"Annoyed? Why?"

Beth searched his face trying to decide
if she should tell him the truth. If she did,
how could she tell the story without sounding like a wall-licking lunatic?

"How open-minded are you, Father?"

"Well, I've been a priest in the Lowcountry of South Carolina all my adult life.
Strange Brew is the name of the game
around here, you know."

"I'll say."

"I mean, sometimes I think that perhaps
I have heard it all. And, to put your mind at
ease, I've heard many stories about this
house too, you know. So, just tell me what's
bothering you."

"Okay. Okay. Um, the other night . . ."

For some peculiar reason about which

Beth was unsure, she told him about the slamming noises and the messy state of her grandmother's bedroom but she did not tell him anything about the mirror. He listened quietly and intently and when Beth was finished he spoke.

"I believe you."

"You do?"

"Yes, I do. I have a theory about these things that would probably give the world of science a great big belly laugh."

"A theory? I'd sure love to hear it."

"Well, in a nutshell, it goes like this: Some people live happily and die happily. They have strong faith and believe that when their time comes, they are going home to God. So off they go to heaven. Others, well, their lives are marked with frustrations and heartbreaks they couldn't reconcile while they were alive. But since you can't take heartbreak and frustration through the pearly gates, they have to leave it here. What you are witnessing in your grandmother's bedroom isn't your grandmother—"

"It's her frustration?"

"Yes, I think maybe it is. Or her anger and any other unresolved business that was very deep in her heart."

"Bizarre."

"Yes. Bizarre. And I can't guarantee that blessing her bedroom will rid the house of this, uh, *phenomenon,* but it might. So, what do you say we give it a go? And while we're at it, why don't we do a general blessing for the entire house?"

"Can't hurt."

"My thought exactly."

When Father Ben Michaels left later, Beth had a story to include in a book someday. She had stood with him and recited a number of prayers while he squirted holy water across the room from a little plastic flask with a cross on it. If she hadn't been so disturbed by all the noises and the continuous disorder of the room, she thought she probably would have dissolved into a pile of snickers during the ceremony. The whole ritual just seemed like voodoo. Once again, she kicked herself, realizing that it was grossly immature of her to mentally mock religious practices condoned by her church. In fact, she had high hopes that between his prayers and Cecily's salt, something would work to give her some peace and quiet. Maybe his theory was right; she didn't know. If nothing else, it had been a relief to tell the story to someone and not to be treated like she was delusional.

The bill! She should have given him something! But she had not given him a donation for the church because she didn't think of it until he was already gone. Besides, she didn't have any cash in the house, didn't use checks, and it seemed inappropriate to ask him if he would like to take a ride to the ATM machine at Dunleavy's Pub. But she did feel that she was obliged to make some material gesture to thank him. Maybe she would buy him a nice card and maybe drop it off at the rectory with some cookies? No, she'd ask Cecily. Cecily would know what to do.

"Make him cookies," Cecily said. "I don't think he would be expecting a donation from you, baby."

"You're right. For once my youth is working in my favor."

"How's the scary room?"

"Neat as a pin. Who knows? Maybe it will hold, for a while anyway."

"Prayer is a mighty powerful potion."

"Whatever. We'll see. So, my cousin is coming Friday and I'm just wondering about that. Am I supposed to go out and buy like a ton of food for them? I'm sort of on a budget."

"Not in my book. I'd buy a coffee cake and some orange juice. They're probably going to go out for lunch and dinner, don't you think?"

"I'm totally clueless for this running a bed-and-breakfast thing. So listen, Cecily, do me a favor, okay?"

"Sure."

"If you talk to my Aunt Maggie, please don't mention that I had the priest over to perform an eviction, okay?"

"An *eviction*. Listen to you! Why would she care?"

"To tell you the truth, if it worked, I think she'll miss the hullabaloo. You know, like all this peculiar stuff gives the house some, I don't know . . ."

"Distinction? Cachet?"

"Yeah, something like that. Maybe. I don't know."

"Your secret is safe with me, but if she comes home and finds that room all tidy, somebody's gonna have some explaining to do, you know."

"I can't even believe we're having this weird conversation."

"Right. Let's talk about other things like Mr. Heartthrob. Did he call?"

"No."

Silence.

"He's a dog."

"You're telling me? Anyway, I start work at my other job tomorrow night, so that's a good diversion. And tomorrow I was planning to ride up the coast to see what I could see."

"Well, make sure you stop at Litchfield. Between Georgetown and Myrtle Beach there's nothing but development all over the place."

"What's up at Litchfield?"

"Lunch, you silly girl. You have to eat, don't you?"

The next morning, Beth and Lola were on Highway 17 North, driving with a mission. And a plan of sorts. She was going to take pictures. Lots of them. She was going to talk to the locals. Where there was a construction site, she would stop and ask questions. She would learn the questions she should be asking everywhere and take notes like a madwoman. When she returned to the island, she would take the bold step of calling Max on the pretense of following up with some details. Then she would write her draft, polish it, hand it in, and begin her other job.

She got the whole way to Georgetown and realized she had not seen one single site worthy of her pitch and she didn't even have a map. She drove on. When she got as far as Litchfield-by-the-Sea, she pulled into the BI-LO shopping center. There was a tiny bookstore right there called Litchfield Books. They would have a map, she thought. She parked and went inside.

There was an elegant woman behind the counter with long, thick strawberry blonde hair that was surely the envy of every woman she met. She looked up from her paperwork and smiled at Beth when the bell on the door tinkled as she entered.

"Hi," she said, "can I help you find something?"

"Yeah, gosh, a map. I need a map. Thanks."

"Sure. Now do you need a map of the state? The county? A local map? A map of Thailand?"

"I *wish* I needed a map of Thailand!" Beth smiled and relaxed. "No, I guess I need a map of the local area."

"What are you looking to find? I mean, around here everything is either on or off Highway 17. Save your money. I can just tell you where to go."

"Oh dear. Well, here's the thing. I have an assignment for a weekly newspaper in Charleston to write about the changing face of the beach towns. You know, shopping malls and condo communities? I'm supposed to go along the coast and ask people if they like the changes, hate the changes, don't care about the changes. I mean, right now I don't know why I ever thought this was such a good idea."

The woman looked at Beth and remembered being Beth's age, just starting out in the world, really too young and inexperienced to do much of anything besides sound like she just dropped in from Mars and had no clue where to begin or how to do her job. Her heart softened.

"You poor thing. I'm Vicki Crafton," she said. "Have you had lunch?"

"Hi, I'm Beth Hayes. *Island Eye News.* My dog's in the car."

Vicki took this to mean that Beth had not had lunch and that she felt uncomfortable leaving her dog in the car alone, especially in the heat of the day.

"Well? Does your dog bite?"

"My dog? Goodness no! She wouldn't bite a bug! She's a mini Yorkie. "

"A Yorkie! A little tiger! Oh, I love them! Bring her in and let's get you something to eat. I'm famished. A lot of people come in here around lunchtime, so if you hang out for a while, you'll hear lots of stories. My dog's in the back office. They can have a playdate."

"Cool. I'll be right back."

"Hey! Let me ask you something."

"Sure!"

"Is your mother Susan Hayes? The 'Geechee Girl Remembers' columnist?"

"That's her."

"Well, the nuts don't fall very far from the tree, do they? Ha!"

"No ma'am, they don't!"

Beth hurried outside to get Lola. Beth was so proud of Susan. Wait till I tell her! she thought.

Lola was thrilled to have a walk across the parking lot and she yanked Beth toward the grassy area on the side of the store.

"Okay! Okay! Got it!"

When Lola's business was completed, Beth picked her up, pushed open the door of the bookstore, and there stood Vicki with her dog.

"Oh my goodness! He's so cute! What is he?"

"Soft-coated Wheaton terrier. His name is Mac and he loves everyone and everything. Say hello, Mac."

Mac. Sounds like Max, she thought. Was there a conspiracy for the world to remind her of Max everywhere she looked? Mac, who had been sitting politely, stood up, looked up at Vicki, made a soft woof sound, and wagged his tail vigorously.

"Your dog talks!"

All five pounds of Lola and the forty-two pounds that was Mac went around in circles, sniffing each other. Then Mac ran off to the back office with Lola on his heels.

"That's where the toy basket is. Dog heaven. And my husband Tom is back there in case they cook up any nonsense. Anyway, speaking of cook, I'm gonna faint from hunger. Want to split a chef salad or a sandwich? I'll send someone over to the BI-LO to pick something up. The portions are huge. I've got drinks here."

"Sounds great."

"I'll go get it," another lady said.

"That's Carol. She's been with us forever."

"Turkey on white bread with mayo and lettuce? Hey, Carol. I'm Beth."

"Sounds perfect," Vicki said.

Over the next hour and a half, Beth nibbled while she interviewed the customers, employees, and owners of Litchfield Books and took their pictures; it seemed as though everyone had a story to tell. People railed against Lowe's, which wanted to open up a superstore that was almost four times the square footage allowed by the town. When that plan failed, it was considered a people's victory. They moaned the loss of Hard Rock Park, saying it was just too expensive in the current economy, but who could have known the markets would implode? Everyone agreed they'd had a fantastic roller-coaster, the best one they had ever been on. There was hope that they would reopen. And then there was the bickering about beach renourishment that was so desperately needed because of unpredictable erosion that threatened the stability of all the beach homes. Plenty of politicking went on as each little municipality fought for its share of the budget of the Army Corps of Engineers. And last there were the Bikers.

The population that made up the world of motorcycles was a curious one. First, there were the people who owned the big Harleys. They ran the gamut from professors to investment bankers. That group just liked the feel of the wind in their hair and the roar of their engines. They would come to the Myrtle Beach area as a group and frankly, despite the noise of their bikes and some moderate rowdiness, they were very good for business. But unfortunately, there was another caste, distinctly different from the white-collar-turned-macho-for-the-weekend group. These guys were belligerent thugs who did drugs, got roaring drunk, and were out of order at all hours of the day and night. They were continuous guests of the county and state, brought up on charges of public lewdness and breaking every law on the books regarding civil behavior. One group brought money to the merchants and the other brought fear. And none of them wore helmets. It was very hard to support one group and not the other without appearing to discriminate. The police force of Myrtle Beach was always overworked when the rough characters came to town, struggling to maintain order and to keep the noise down.

Beth listened to their stories, and as each one drifted from the store and back to their life, Beth saw that stopping there to buy a map had turned out to be a very lucky fluke. And, most important, she decided she had plenty of anecdotal information to produce a reasonably interesting article. She hoped.

"Gosh, thanks for all your help," Beth said. "This was amazing. Really!"

"Glad to help," Vicki said, and handed her a business card. "Just call me if you forgot something. Oh, and Beth?"

"Yeah?"

"Call me when you win that Pulitzer."

"Oh yeah, that . . . right!"

On the drive back to Sullivans Island, Beth's mind spun one gilded fantasy after another. She envisioned Barbara Farlie's face, giddy as her eyes passed over the

pearls Beth intended to write. She imagined that she heard whispers of recognition when she went out into the world and
she could see herself nodding modestly in
appreciation. Her stories would be picked
up and syndicated as her mother's had
been, and they would be featured together
on the cover of some respected magazine
as the greatest mother-daughter journalist
team of the year, maybe ever. Max Mitchell would read her work and be so astounded by her maturity and intellectual
prowess that he would be reduced to a
stammering flibbergibbit, begging for her
affection. Those expectations were beyond ridiculous and she was well aware,
but it was fun to dream.

After throwing together a draft and
changing her clothes, just by the skin of
her teeth, she made it to her other job on
time. Drew was there at the podium answering the phone and taking reservations. Robert was going over the dinner
specials with Billy Condon, the chef, and
Alan was setting up the bar, doing inventory of the liquor, wine, mixers, and gar-
nishes. Beth gave everyone a little wave
and greetings were exchanged.

Hey! Welcome aboard! Good luck! What did you do to your hair? Gee, it looks great! Whew! Sure am glad you showed up! It's been crazy here! Put your bag in here with mine. . . .

Beth put her handbag away, and as quickly as she could, she went to Drew's side to immerse herself in learning the un-appreciated art of taking and organizing dinner reservations.

"This part of the job makes my left arm hurt," Drew said. "Did you cut your hair?"

"Yeah."

"Nice. Okay, here's the deal. A table for two usually stays an hour and fifteen at a minimum, but if they order dessert, that's another twenty. Table of four, that's closer to two hours, especially if they have cock-tails at the table and then wine, but you have to allow for two and a half hours. Tables of over four start the horror show. Two hours for sure, sometimes closer to three, especially for parties of eight or more. This is the layout of the dining rooms. See how I have the tables marked off by number? So, why don't you answer the phone the next time it rings and let's see how it goes?"

Beth had barely digested what he had said and in the next breath she was to answer the phone?

"Um, what if I goof this up? I mean, what if I take too many tables for seven-thirty or something?"

"We'll deal with it." The phone rang and then rang again, lighting up two lines. "Go ahead. I gotta go talk to Billy about the tuna ceviche. Some customer called saying they got sick from it, that there must have been some shellfish in the marinade."

"They probably just want a free dinner," Beth said to Drew's back as he walked away.

Drew stopped in his tracks and spun around to face Beth.

"I knew I liked you," he said. "The world is filled with liars, you know."

"Got it," Beth said, and answered the phone. In her most adult voice she said, "Thank you for calling Atlanticville Restaurant. Please hold. Thank you." She pressed the second line. "Thank you for calling Atlanticville. This is Beth speaking, how may I help you? For tonight? How many? And at what time?"

"She's a natural," Drew said to Robert, who nodded in agreement.

"A table for eight at six? Sure, we can do that. And the name please?"

As if she had been a hostess all of her life, Beth repeated those same words over and over until the tables for that night were completely committed not once but twice.

"We can offer you a table for four on the porch at around nine-thirty? No? Well, if you'd like to give me your number, I can call you if we have a cancellation?"

"How's it going?" Robert said, passing her by with a tray of appetizers for a table of four.

"Is it always like this?"

"Pretty much. Well, especially on the weekends."

Beth answered the ringing phone again and again, apologizing, disappointing people, declining large parties, politely suggesting other evenings, and taking reservations for Friday, Saturday, and the following week as well.

The way the restaurant worked reminded Beth of a synchronized drill team. Or perhaps a dance company. Everyone had a part and the execution of it was a panorama of beauty to watch. Trays floated by, lifted high over heads, people ducked or stepped aside, candles were lit and re-lit, menus collected, distributed, re-collected, and stacked. Customers were greeted with grace and a smile and whisked to their table, seated, handed menus and wine lists, and on and on it went. Until that table of eight at six never materialized. And those other two tables of four lingered well past what would have been a reasonable time. They had been brought their checks, the bills had been paid, and their tables had been cleared down to the votive candles. They even declined the drinks at the bar that Drew offered hoping to pry them away from their tables. Three tables held hostage by customers in a restaurant of diminutive proportion made a difference.

"Where's the table of eight for six o'clock?" Drew asked.

"I don't know," Beth said. "They never showed."

"Didn't you take a phone number?"

"Yeah, of course, but I must have written it down wrong."

"Great," Drew muttered under his breath.

"I'm so sorry, Drew!"

"It's okay. And these other two tables have been here so long I could charge them rent."

"For real," Beth said.

The porch was packed, the dining rooms were packed, and the waiting area was bulging with bodies. It was clear, even to Beth, that they would never be able to serve them all. The kitchen closed at ten and all of those patrons, standing three deep around the bar, were waiting in vain.

Beth thought that Drew looked especially harried and said, "What can I do to help? I mean, I'm not taking any more reservations, that's for sure. For tonight, anyway."

"Did you say you could bartend?"

"Sort of."

"Well, sort of is good enough for now. Get out there and give Lidia a hand, okay?"

"Yes sir!"

Beth's exuberance was endless and just for a moment Drew remembered his own youth and the fires that had smoldered within him. Drew was barely thirty-five yet Beth suddenly made him feel every one of his years. What if his life was half over? Was he losing his edge? Did he seem that old to her? The thought of actual old age and the certainty of death made him shiver. But his dread was fleeting because as soon as someone nodded in his direction to gain his attention, he automatically resumed his professional posture and went back to work, forgetting about the Grim Reaper and all the geriatric insults that were sure to come.

"Need a hand?" Beth said to Lidia, who was filling drink orders as fast as humanly possible, plopping them on trays and shoving them toward the waitstaff. Despite the advancing hour and the whirl of the ceiling fans, the temperature on the porch had to have been over ninety degrees. Lidia's upper lip and décolleté glistened with moisture.

"Yeah, thanks. Take this over to table sixteen in the corner. They've been waiting forever."

"You got a corkscrew?"

"Don't need it. It's a New Zealand wine. A lot of the winemakers there quit using corks."

"Oh! Boy, what I don't know could fill a library!"

"You and me, honey!"

Beth picked up the tray with the wine bottle and two glasses and made her way slowly through the crowd. All at once, her heart lurched against her ribs. There at the table in the corner sat Max Mitchell and a startlingly attractive woman with blond hair, a narrow chin, too much lipstick, and an insignificant and bony cleavage. The woman, who appeared to be about ten years older than Max, was obviously dressed for a highly anticipated wardrobe malfunction. One tug on the breezy ribbons of her flowered camisole and all would be revealed. Her fluttering eyes were fixated on Max's face. She smiled knowingly, nodding her head as he spoke, as though every word that spilled from his lips was ex cathedra. Beth noticed things that others did not, and while that simple act of practiced noticing had boosted the academic regard for her writing, it had not added one fig of value to her personal life.

"Great," she whispered under her breath, assessing the scene before her. "Great."

Inside of just a few seconds, Beth was suddenly and unfortunately overwhelmed with massive feelings of inadequacy. She blushed, broke a mortifying sweat on the back of her neck, and feared that if she said even one word, just one word, she would stammer like an idiot. Beth's immediate thought was to slip the bottle into the cooler next to them without Max realizing it was her and then to scurry away to the ladies' room to adjust her breathing and to press a cold towel to her temples and neck, call Cecily, rant, and beg for advice. Not possible. She had to go through the wine delivery ritual.

"Thanks," Max said, and then looked up to see her. "Beth? Is that you?"

"Yep. Hi, Max. Are y'all waiting for a table?" She twisted off the cap of the bottle. "Gotta love those New Zealand wines. No cork!"

She poured a measure in a glass and put it in front of him.

"I didn't know you worked here! What happened to your hair?"

Somehow, by the grace of all the gods in the Lowcountry air, Beth found the presence of mind to turn the awkward moment into something humorous. She turned her face to Max's dinner companion.

"Men," she said in the most nonchalant

manner she possessed in her Never-Let-Them-See-You-Sweat bag of tricks. Then she turned back to Max. "Really, Max. It's just hair."

Max, feeling slightly cornered and off his game, made another sensitive remark. "But I thought you were a journalist!"

"I am a journalist, Max. I'm just doing this gig for the fun of it. Can I get y'all anything else?" Beth's mouth went dry and she could hear her tongue clacking against the roof of her mouth.

By then, Max's dinner companion was showing signs of annoyance, rapping her fingernails on the table.

"A table might be good. We did come here to eat, after all," she said, and not very politely.

Beth noticed the absence of a wedding band on her hand, but an expensive wristwatch and, lo, a veritable minefield of sun damage and wrinkles around her eyes. She decided the old dame was well north of forty. She could have been fifty! Why was Max entertaining someone so old? It made no sense to Beth, whose heart still pounded despite her every attempt to calm herself.

"I'll check on that right away."

Instead of returning to the bar to help Lidia, Beth rushed inside to Drew, reprimanding herself every step of the way. Why should she help Max get a table? Max had not introduced her to his date. Max had not stood up like a gentleman would when he realized it was her. In fact, Max had been a jerk. Still, she was going to use her influence on his behalf, if possible. She wanted him to think she could make things happen.

Drew was flipping through the reservation book, brows knitted, completely focused. The dining room was so noisy she didn't have to whisper.

"Um, I've got a situation, boss."

"Oh? What's up? I finally got those two tables to move."

"Well, that's good. Um, there's this guy outside? Um, with a woman?"

"Someone you know?"

"Uh, yeah. Sorta."

Drew looked at Beth directly in her face and saw her panic, or if not panic, he could see that she was very flustered.

"Does he have a reservation?"

"I don't think so."

"So . . . what do you want me to do?"

"Oh, hell . . ."

"Where is he?"

"Oh, crap. Corner of the porch. Sixteen."

"Go wash your face. It's all like blotchy or something. I'll take care of him. By the way, I need you for Sunday brunch."

"No problem."

In that moment, as he swooped into action to heal and vanquish Beth's embarrassment, Beth adored Drew. Work on Sunday? She would scrub the floors if he wanted her to. Without knowing any of the details, he had understood. And later that night when she tried to sleep, every bone in her body exhausted from work and stress, all she could see were the faces of Max Mitchell and that old woman, grinning at each other. She felt like a complete and utter fool.

8

New Shoes

Maggiepie2@marthagene.net
  Susan, not to panic, but there are two girls and two boys in our house this weekend. Should I ask Cecily to object on our behalf?

Susanthepen@writenow.org
  As you wish, but remember they are all over twenty-one and you'll sound like an old woman, old woman! Didn't you ever have a sex life? Love ya! xx

Maggiepie2@marthagene.net
  Ladies do not discuss. xx

It was Friday morning. The first sliver of daylight had barely appeared on the horizon. Before Beth opened her eyes, she knew instinctively it was just sunrise. She was damp with perspiration, tangled in her

sheets, wide awake, and thoroughly annoyed. Her legs throbbed from standing
on the hard floors all night at Atlanticville.
Her feet ached and her heels were rubbed
raw from wearing real shoes. Beth had so
much anxiety she thought her head might
literally explode. Her cousin was arriving
that afternoon with his entourage and there
was not one crumb of food in the house.
Max had not called in the middle of the
night to apologize for his frosty behavior.
He had not called at all, just for the record,
and now it was almost a week since their
dinner quasi date. Well, she said to herself, Max was an ass and that was that.

"I'm totally over him," she said to the
darkness, feeling sick inside.

She was not over him. Not one bit.

Who had her cousin Mike said he was
bringing with him? What time was he rolling into town? Who cared? She had her
own agenda. And not one but two jobs for
Pete's sake, whoever Pete was. She
needed to polish her article and turn it in
to the *Island Eye News*. In addition, she
had to work again at the restaurant that
night. And Saturday night and now Sunday for the brunch shift. And another thing,

if he had any pride at all, Max should regret having been seen with that old hot mess of his, she thought. The question was how in the world would she make him realize that he should regret it? It was too early to call Cecily or anyone except her mother in France, where it was noon. But she would not call her mother to discuss Max because she felt her mother would never understand the depth of her feelings or even the reason for her discontent. Her mother would tell her to snap out of it.

Cecily was the answer, not her mother. If she had learned only one single thing from Livvie Singleton's granddaughter, she was certain that Cecily would have an idea on how to make Max Mitchell squirm. Lucky in love or not, Cecily was more experienced.

She decided to walk Lola and transform her own frustrations into a plan, and most important, she needed to shake off her funk. By the time the rest of the world began their day, Beth would be one step ahead. Hopefully.

She pulled on a pair of shorts, an old T-shirt from an Alison Krauss concert, her flip-flops, and crossed the dunes, stopping halfway down the sandy steps. The sun's ascent was unfolding slightly east of Breach Inlet and its slow rise was so dramatic that Beth caught her breath and jerked Lola's leash. She would have sworn on a Bible that that side of the world looked as if it might actually burst into flames.

Despite the promise of another sizzling day, at that hour the fine white sand was soothing and cool as it passed through her flip-flops. By noon, that very same sand would gather enough heat to scorch the calluses of the carelessly unshod, who would race and holler bloody murder across the many island paths that led to the shore. That thought brought the curl of a smile.

The incoming tide was laced with ripples so quiet you could have said that it was sneaking its way ashore. Scores of miniature birds dug in earnest for their breakfast around the water's edges, scampering away as the next wave threatened to wash away their tiny world. Beth marveled at the predictability of it all, that the tide would change every six hours and that the sun would rise again each morning. It gave her courage or fortitude or some measure of peace. She wasn't sure why, but she felt reassured knowing life went on and, like the old people always said, things always seemed better in the morning. And they did.

The beach was empty except for a few people and their dogs in the distance near Station 22. On another day she might have jogged down the beach to join them. But that Friday morning she was just ambling along, thinking about her lot and taking in her little dog's fascination with her new surroundings. She unhooked her leash and Lola took off running. Lola sniffed every lump of seaweed at the high-water mark and chased the fat seagulls who watched Lola with keen-eyed suspicion. As one or another moved toward Lola, she barked energetically and they would waddle away. This made Beth smile too.

As soon as she felt it was a decent hour, she could call Cecily. If nothing else, Cecily would make her laugh and it would feel good to unburden her heart.

What would Cecily advise her to do? She would probably begin by telling Beth that she had no business chasing after a man of Max's age, that the older woman she saw him with could have been there for another reason in spite of her clothing or lack thereof. But once she realized that Beth was really and truly dead serious about gaining Max's affection, how to make it happen would take center stage. Cecily loved a challenge. Beth hoped Cecily had some secrets to share with her—a Gullah perfume or a root tea that would bring him around. No matter how loudly Cecily denied her success with men, Cecily surely had *something* that worked because her dance card always had a waiting list. Wherever she went, men seemed to fall all over themselves to get her attention.

Perhaps she should call her Aunt Sophie too, just for a second opinion, she thought. Sophie was cool and even more experienced and she might be able to enlighten her in the ways of older men. The excuse for a chat with her Aunt Sophie sounded like a great idea.

What would Sophie do if she fell in love with an older man like Max, say some old coot around fifty? Or, heaven forbid, sixty? She thought about it for a few moments and decided that first Sophie would manage to show up where said old coot was

going to be—perched on a barstool or dining alone in a restaurant. Sophie would
look totally gorgeous, which was easy
enough for her, and second, she would
completely ignore him, pretending the old
fart was merely a gaseous fume. Her eyes
would pass over his once or twice without
recognition. Genius! With an ego the size
of Max's? Being ignored would drive him
right out of his skull. And before the waiter
could deliver the champagne he would
surely send over to her, Sophie would turn
slowly but deliberately on her kitten heels
and depart without a wink or a nod. Sophie's version of Max would be left
stranded, choking on his newly found massive infatuation with her. Maybe something
like that would work for her too. She was a
little insecure about her ability to pull off
that scenario, but surely there was a ploy
that would be worth a try.

"Ooooh! This is all so stupid!" Beth cried
aloud to the salty muses in the morning
air, half expecting a reply. "What am I doing wasting all this energy? Ridiculous!"

She clapped her hands and called out
to Lola, who ran back to her, sticky and
sandy.

"Look at you! We need to shampoo your hair, miss! Turning into an island girl, are we? Chasing seagulls and rolling around on smelly things! Come on! That's no way for a lady to behave."

Beth showered herself and Lola and was towel-drying her little dog, who hated being groomed. Lola was a dog after all. She heard someone downstairs, opening and closing cabinets in the kitchen.

"Who's there?" she called out.

"Just your caterer, ma'am!" It was the chipper voice of Cecily. "I figured that between running the road up to Pawleys yesterday and then your first day at Atlanticville, you probably didn't have time to pick up groceries."

Beth hurried down the stairs to greet her.

"You're right! You are too sweet! Thanks!"

"Well, I was going for myself anyway so it's no big deal . . ."

"Still! Thanks! You want some coffee?"

"Why not?"

Beth pressed the start button on the coffeemaker and the water began to drip, sending the rich smells of ground beans from Colombia swirling into the air.

"Too bad coffee never tastes as good

as it smells," Beth said, peering into the refrigerator. "Holy crap! What did you do? Rob the freaking Pig?"

Piggly Wiggly was the name of the family's favorite grocery store chain and one was conveniently located in Mount Pleasant in a small shopping center.

"Nah, I just got a few things."

"Yeah, like two of each for the Ark?"

"Yeah, I'm stocking the Ark. So what's going on with you?"

"Well, I got up early. Couldn't sleep. Took Lola to the beach and she got so sandy I had to give her a bath, which she hates. Whined the whole time, which I ignored. Anyway, my legs are killing me, my brain's about to pop, my cousin's coming—"

"You gonna waste the whole morning telling me nothing or are you gonna tell me what got you up so early in the first place?"

There was a pregnant pause and in the next moment Beth blurted out the truth.

"It's Max. Who else? He came into the restaurant last night with this woman, who was older than him, and I mean by a lot. He acted so stupid when he saw me that I wanted to die. I mean, I kept my cool but it was clear he thought there was absolutely no reason for me to think anything was strange about seeing him with someone else."

"What happened?"

"Nothing. I mean, I had to bring some wine to his table and when he realized who I was—the haircut and contacts, I guess—he didn't stand up or introduce me to his date and I just felt awkward and stupid standing there. It doesn't sound like much, I know. I mean, if you'd been there you'd know what I mean."

The coffeemaker's alarm pinged, the signal that the coffee was ready to pour.

"Sit down," Cecily said, pointing to a chair at the kitchen table. "You take sugar in your coffee? Milk?"

"Just sugar. I'll fix it. Thanks."

Cecily placed a steaming mug before Beth and pushed the sugar bowl toward her. She watched as Beth added three teaspoons to her coffee and slowly stirred it. As she sat opposite her, she noted that Beth's complexion was growing ruddier by the moment and that her sighs were deep and prolonged.

"Oh Lord. You got it bad. That's a lot of sugar 'eah?"

"Yep. I guess."

"Well, you want my opinion, right?"

Beth nodded her head.

"He's oblivious, honey. First, he has no clue that he upset you last night. It's the Max Mitchell Show. He's not worried about how you're feeling. His only concern is how you make *him* feel. And I don't mean you in particular. I mean for him—and I might be wrong about this but probably not—women are interchangeable. I suspect there is a long line of bodies behind him and in front of him. I don't want to see you in that pileup. You know what I mean?"

"You're probably right but I can't get him out of my mind. I mean—"

"How good-looking is this guy?"

"Movie star."

"And how old is he again?"

"Like thirty-seven or something."

"What's a thirty-seven-year-old movie star man want with a young thing like you? Sex, that's what."

"Well, I do have a life, you know."

"Right. Worse than that, what does a young thing like you want with an old guy like him?"

Beth tried to change the subject. "I have to finish my piece for the *Island Eye News* and I'm thinking I need to call him and go take his picture to run it with the article."

"Humph."

"What do you mean *humph*?"

"I mean, I'd see hell freeze first. But that's me."

"Well, it's a legitimate excuse and it's just business anyway."

"I'd take a picture of a baboon in a red dress and use it before I'd go running to him."

"Really?"

"Yes ma'am! Really."

"Shoot."

"Look, I gotta get moving before this whole day gets away from me. You got any mail for me?"

"Yeah, I threw out all the catalogs and junk mail and piled everything else in the basket on the counter over there."

Cecily got up, poured the rest of her coffee down the drain, and put her mug in the dishwasher. She picked up the mail from the basket and thumbed through it.

"Well, praise the Lord! I was waiting for this bill!" She stuffed the mail in her bag and went to the door. "Listen to me, shugah-plum, whatever you have to do to forget this guy, do it. He just smells like trouble to me. Too much work."

"Right. When hell freezes."

"That's my girl! I'll see you later this afternoon. Gotta water my babies."

Beth watched Cecily back out of the yard, and as quickly as she noted the time was well past eight, she dialed Max as fast as her fingers could press the numbers on her cell phone. He did not pick up, her call went to voice mail, and her spirits sank again. Maybe he's in the shower, she thought, and left what she hoped was an easygoing voice mail.

"Hi, Max. It's Beth Hayes and I was wondering if there was a good time today for me to swing by and take a few pictures of you and the site for the paper. Please call me back when you have a moment. Thanks! Have a great day!"

She closed her cell phone and decided to call her Aunt Sophie. She got her voice mail as well.

"Hey, Aunt Sophie! It's your niece Beth calling from the center of the universe here on sunny Sullivans Island, missing you and wishing you were here. Everything's fine but, uh, when you have a minute or two, I sure would like your advice on something. Everything's okay with the house so don't panic. Just gimme a call? Thanks! Love you!"

She was sure her aunt would return her call but what if Max didn't? There was nothing left to do except wait. Meanwhile she would give her article another editorial swipe and wait for her cousin to arrive. So she edited and waited and waited. The phone did not ring at all and it was now almost noon. Max was ignoring her and she was becoming upset about it. After delivering an angry tirade to the empty house, one loud enough to rattle the walls and make her throat raw but hopefully not so loud to wake the dead, she calmed down and decided to go take the pictures anyway. Maybe he had left his cell in his car or maybe it fell in water and he had not replaced it yet. There could be any number of reasons why he had not called her that had nothing to do with him ignoring her.

She decided that just in case he was romantically involved with the old bag of bones she had seen with him, she would wear a tank top. A skimpy one. But under a shirt. A shirt that she would leave more than partially unbuttoned. That should get his attention. So feeling like something of a vixen, she dressed accordingly, drove down the island, parked her car, and reapplied her lip gloss. She did not know why but for some inexplicable reason men were fascinated by glossy lips. Beth giggled thinking that perhaps it was because they could see their own reflection like Narcissus. She got out and started shooting the scores of workmen with a long lens, and after ten or more shots, her focus landed on the profile of Max Mitchell about thirty feet away. His hand flew up over his face when he realized what was happening.

"Whoa! Beth! No pictures!"

Beth thought that he was kidding and began to laugh.

"No pictures? For real? Are you running from the IRS or something?"

He began walking toward her.

"Yeah, right. Gosh, it's great to see you! Sorry I didn't call you back yet. This place has been crazy all morning."

His words relieved her. She had to agree

that it was indeed chaotic with all the hammers and drills. Max hugged her so abruptly that it caused her to drop her camera.

"Oh no!" she wailed. The camera, which had been an expensive gift from her mother, now had a cracked lens. "Ah, gee whiz, Max."

"Oh God, I'm sorry. Here, let me see it."

Beth got a sudden rush of goose bumps. For some reason Beth could not define, she thought that perhaps Max might have deliberately caused her to drop the camera. She simply said, "Don't worry about it. I have other lenses."

"Oh, okay. Well, good. So, you're back on the journalist beat today, I see?"

"Yeah, I gotta turn this in, so I'd better get going. Did you enjoy your dinner last night?" She couldn't help it; the words just rolled off her tongue.

"What? Oh yeah, I did. It was really good. And thanks for getting us a table."

"No problem. Your date said she was starving and it sure looked like she was." What is the matter with me, she thought, what am I doing?

"Ooooh! Meow, Miss Hayes."

"Meow yourself. Just how old was she anyway? Like fifty?"

Max chuckled at Beth's jealousy. Things were working out exactly as he had hoped they would. "She happens to be an investor of mine. And she's divorced and lonely so I try to bring a little joy into her life from time to time."

Beth arched her eyebrow just as her mother did and said, "I'll bet you do."

"My my, Beth. I am sure you have the wrong idea. It was just a business dinner."

But the way he smiled and by the way his eyes looked at her, she knew he was playing with her.

"Right. I saw the way she was fawning over you. Please."

"Beth! You shock me! You must think I'm some sort of a cad. What can I do to change your low opinion of me?"

"I just know how men are, that's all." Beth realized that sounded juvenile and naïve but there was no taking back the words.

"Why don't we have dinner tonight?"

"I can't. I have to work. But thanks."

"Tomorrow?"

"Gotta work."

"Well, can I stop by this weekend?"

"I have a houseful of company." Beth said this and realized she was enjoying telling him no.

"Wow, like when are you supposed to have any fun?"

"Sunday night through Thursday morning, I guess."

"Then I want to take you out Sunday night through Thursday morning."

What a rascal! "Why don't we start with Sunday night? And then we'll see." Beth smiled and silently congratulated herself for handling him so well. "My company should be gone by then."

"Sounds good. So who's coming to town?"

"My cousin Mike, the investment banker from Atlanta, and his girlfriend and some guy they want me to meet."

"Really? Maybe your cousin wants to invest in this project. There's still room."

Beth was a little surprised that he had not commented on the fact that a potential rival was staying under her roof, only that he was looking for money.

"I'll tell him," she said, and gathered her things preparing to walk away. "See ya!"

"Hey, Beth?"

Beth turned around to face him.

"You behave yourself, you hear me?"

Those words pleased her to no end. "Please. I'm practically a nun."

She stopped by the offices of the *Island Eye News* and was greeted by Barbara Farlie herself.

"Well, look who's here!" she said. "What'd you do? Cut your hair?"

"Yeah, I cut my hair and ditched my glasses."

"Humph! Looks good. Got something for me?"

Beth fumbled around with her bag and camera and pulled the manila envelope from her bag. "Yes ma'am. I sure do! And I've got some pictures on the memory stick in this camera but I haven't looked at them yet."

"Well, why don't you download them on Katie's computer. She's not here today. Gone off to God knows where. Kids today. Don't want to work."

"Speak for Katie but not for me. I happen to love work."

Barbara looked up at her and said, "I knew I liked you for some reason and I guess that's it. Now let's see if you can write. Want some water?"

"Yeah, that would be great."

"Well, help yourself. There's the fridge."

Barbara Farlie took Beth's article, went into her own office, and closed the door. Thinking that it meant that she wanted to read Beth's article in private made Beth nervous. She took a seat at Katie's desk, booted up her computer, slipped the memory stick into the USB port, and began to go through the pictures. She had some nice ones of the people she spoke to in Litchfield, and the ones of the site formerly known as Bert's were crisp and clear as well. And Max? In every single picture and from every single angle, he looked edible.

"Ah, the wonders of the digital world!"

Farlie's door opened and Beth spun around in her chair to face her. Barbara Farlie had a grin on her face as wide as her facial muscles could stretch. It was clear from her watery eyes that she had been laughing.

"What's funny?" Beth said.

"You are. My glory, I haven't read something so impassioned since I was involved in an antiwar rally back in my college days!

Whew! We'll run it the next issue. What else have you got?"

"The pictures?"

"No, honey, I mean another article for me. What else do you want to write?"

"Gee, I hadn't even thought about that."

"Figures. Well, leave the pictures up. Identify the bodies for me and then you go on home and think about it. And leave me your receipts. Come by next Thursday and you can pick up your check."

"So you liked it?"

Barbara shook her head and smiled with all the wisdom of her years.

"Yes. I liked it. Very much, in fact."

"Really?"

"Yes, really. And you know, you can email your work in too."

"Geez, why didn't I think of that? Thanks!"

"It's okay. So, have a nice weekend."

"You too! And, thanks again!"

Beth didn't know which pictures the paper would use or if the article would be buried somewhere but she was feeling very good then. She had accomplished something of real worth. When the paper came out she would send her mother a copy, and her aunts. And perhaps her old professors too, she thought. It was sort of amazing to Beth that someone would pay her money to express her opinion or that they would trust her to gather facts.

She was feeling like a bona fide success story when she pulled into the yard at home and spotted the Georgia tags on her cousin's SUV. She got out and bounded up the steps, two at a time.

"Mike? You here?"

Lola, incarcerated in her crate for a while, began yelping at the sound of Beth's voice.

Mike, whose head was in the refrigerator, looked up to see her. "Hey, cuz! Whoa! What happened to you?"

"Well, you sweet thing! I'll just take that as a compliment!"

She gave Mike a hug. Now Lola yelped and banged against the side of her crate so much so that it moved.

"For real! You look like a babe! Well, I mean—"

"Shut up, jerk. Momma's coming, baby." She released Lola and held her in her arms, attaching her leash. "So, where are your friends?"

"Phoebe! Woody! Come meet my cousin!" Mike yelled for them so loudly that Beth jumped, startled. "They're on the porch taking in the view. That ocean's making a lot of noise."

"I know. It's high tide."

"Right. You live here. Where should we put our stuff?"

"Anywhere downstairs. I am assuming that Phoebe will be staying with you?"

"If it's okay with you," Mike said.

"Listen, Romeo, I'm not getting in the middle of this. I don't care what you do in the dark."

"It would be extremely odd if you did."

Mike wiggled his eyebrows and Beth giggled.

"Perv! I'm gonna go walk my dog."

Passing through the living room on the way to the porch, she could see Mike's friends leaning against the rails. Woody looked benign enough, tall and lanky, knit shirt and khaki shorts. But even from a distance she knew that Phoebe was of the ilk with whom Beth would never have associated unless they were stranded on a desert island, and even that would have taken some time to get a conversation going. She was an overly cheery, petite blonde who probably traded on her looks to get through life.

"It's gonna be a long weekend," she whispered to Lola. "Let's go be nice." She walked out onto the porch and they turned to greet her with curious expressions. "Hey! I'm Beth! Welcome to Sullivans Island!"

"I thought Beth had really crazy red hair and glasses," Phoebe said. "Doesn't she?"

"I did." Beth sighed. "I changed things."

"Oh," the little moron said.

"I'm Woody," he said, extending his hand and smiling. "It's really nice to meet you. Thanks for having us."

"Glad to, but you know, this is Mike's house too. I'm just going to take my dog out and I'll be right back."

"Oh! She's so cuuuuute! Is she a girl? Come here, precious! What's her name?"

Lola recoiled, burying herself in Beth's neck. Lola was a dog of discriminating taste when it came to humans. Basically, she was a one-human dog. Phoebe probably had a big fat Persian cat named Marilyn who sat on a white satin cushion. With tassels. And a diamond collar.

"She's got a pink leash, Phebes. Of course she's a girl!" Woody said.

"Lola," Beth said. "Lola and I will be back in two minutes." Beth cut her eyes at Woody, who crossed his arms and shook his head as if to say that he agreed that Phebes was a little thick between the ears.

"Cute!" Phoebe said. "Y'all hurry back! Mike's making margaritas!"

"Lola's trying to quit," Beth said over her shoulder, knowing she had probably left Phoebe in a state of confusion but that Woody got the joke.

Poor Mike, she thought as she walked Lola across the yard. It was hard to understand why he always went after that certain type. They were sweet and pretty but never very smart. What was he afraid of?

Beth was of the opinion that there was nothing on the earth sexier than a guy with great brains and a good sense of humor. Looks were a secondary consideration. But then that wasn't exactly her current situation because Max was way off her normal list of choices. They were having dinner on Sunday! Just the thought of being across the table from him gave her a thrill.

Beth wondered if Woody thought she was his date for the weekend because he had looked at her in the way men do when they want to let you know that they're available and that you appeal to them. What kind of expectations did he have? Maybe he was just friendly. She hoped that was it, because he surely wasn't her type. Too skinny. Besides, she had Max. No, she didn't have Max. She had her fixation on Max and her fantasies of Max but she did not have Max. Maybe Sunday would change that.

Back in the house, the blender was working overtime and Phoebe was cooking some kind of taco chip/canned chili/salsa combination in the microwave that smelled like burned dog food. Mike poured the first round of cocktails and offered one to Beth.

"Thanks, but I have to work tonight so it's probably best if I hold back."

Woody, who was seated at the table glued to his BlackBerry, checking email, looked up and stood when he heard Beth's voice.

"Right!" Mike said. "So, how's the job going?"

"Sit! Sit!" Beth said, making note of his good manners. Someone had raised him right. "Jobs? I've got two for some stupid reason. Um, the job at Atlanticville is really a little insane. And it's tiring. You know, cranky patrons waiting for a table. I'm on my feet all night. This heat doesn't help anybody's mood."

"What's Atlanticville?" Phoebe said, taking a sip of her drink. "Oooh! This is so good!"

"It's a restaurant down the island," Mike said. "Hey! Can we get a table for tomorrow night?"

"Party of three? Of course you can!"

"What's your other job?" Woody said.

"Writing for the local newspaper," Beth said. Woody wasn't bad-looking at all, really, she thought. "I just wrote an article for them."

"About what?" Phoebe said.

"On the gentrification of funky old beach communities between here and Myrtle Beach."

Gentrification was a pretty big word for Phoebe, who wrinkled her brow.

"Would you like some of this?" Phoebe said, offering the platter of guaranteed gastrointestinitis to each of them. She had added chopped jalapeños, mayonnaise, and sweet pickles to the top. Only Beth, the wiser one of the lot, refrained.

Mike pushed a glob into his mouth, struggled to swallow, and smiled at Phoebe. Woody snickered at Mike and was more judicious, pulling plain chips from the bottom of the gooey mass. Mike reached for another wad.

"Think you're hungry, Mike?" Beth said. He must have a cast-iron stomach, she thought.

"Mmm, mmm," he said. "My girl Phoebe is the cocktail party queen. Aren't you, sugar?"

"I like to make up different kinds of finger foods," she said, and actually batted her eyelashes at everyone.

"I like to cook too," Beth said, lying for no good reason and thinking, What can I cook? She would have to learn to make something besides cereal and sandwiches. At some point. "Well, actually, I like to eat. More than I like to cook, that is."

It was after three o'clock before she knew it. Woody, Phoebe, and Mike had gone off to the beach for a swim and Beth was alone in the house. She had put Mike in the newly un-haunted bedroom, explaining privately that ever since Cecily and the priest had done their best, the room had been dead quiet, no pun intended. It was the best bedroom in the house as it was large, had its own bathroom and the best ventilation. Knowing its history all of his life, Mike was initially suspicious. But then Mike had said, No problem, if the room starts going nuts, Phoebe's gonna be all over me. Beth looked at him with a straight face and pretended to be holding back vomit.

"You need to get a man in your life," he said. "It'll make your coat shiny."

"Very funny. But in fact, I am seeing someone."

"Really? Well, that's good. Hey, what do you think of Woody?"

"He's nice enough. What's his story?"

"He works for Uncle Henry the slave driver, and he's the guy in charge of your trust account."

"Really?"

"Yeah, one of the reasons he wanted to come was to meet you. So see? It's just business."

"Good."

What did that mean? Did Mike think she was unworthy of someone like Woody? Nah, she decided. He probably just never gave her social life one iota of thought. And Beth did present herself as serious. Sort of. Besides, she knew that Woody found her to be attractive.

She dressed for work, straightened her hair, and left them a note.

If you all want to come by the restaurant, I'll buy y'all some drinks! Otherwise, I'll see you around eleven. xx Beth

Somewhere around nine-thirty that night, Beth spotted Max at the bar. He was alone. The second seating was well under way so she was able to slip out to the porch to say hello. Max was looking very good and his face brightened when he saw her.

"Well, hi there!" he said. "You've been one very busy girl tonight!"

"No lie! I didn't even see you come in!"

"Can you sit for a minute? Can I buy you a glass of wine?"

"Oh, I wish I could but my boss would probably object."

"Well, you look awfully nice. What time are you getting out of here?"

Beth felt a poke in her shoulder and turned to see Mike, Woody, and Phoebe standing there.

"Somebody said the drinks were on the house in this joint," Mike said.

"Well, hey y'all! Max, this is my cousin Mike from Atlanta and his friends Phoebe and Woody . . ."

They shook hands and began chatting away about Atlanta and all the spots they knew in common as Beth ordered two beers for the guys and a Cosmopolitan for Phoebe, asking Lidia to put it on her tab.

"I have to go back to work," Beth said. "Drew is giving me the hairy eyeball."

"Okay, we'll see you later on," Woody said.

Max was busy talking about his development project to Mike, who was listening and asking questions. Phoebe asked for directions to the little girls' room and Beth showed her where it was. Throughout the remainder of that night's work, between answering phones and seating customers, Beth kept an eye on them from the podium where she stood most of the time. Every time she looked out to the porch she could see Woody watching her, just kind of quietly observing her. In a nice way. He would smile, a little sheepish for being caught, but it was all very aboveboard and polite. Max, on the other hand, was hanging on Mike and flirting with Phoebe, wagging his finger at her and making comments to her behind his hand. Beth felt uncomfortable with Max's behavior because she didn't understand why he was being so chummy, too familiar with her cousin and his friends. Maybe the cause was too much alcohol. Yes, that was probably it. And the next time Beth looked out at the bar area, they were all gone.

"Lidia? Where did my cousin go?"

"He said to tell you either they'd be right back or he would see you at home later. They were going off with that guy Max to look at his construction site. You want to settle your tab? I can keep it open if you want."

"Yeah, leave it open. They might come back."

They did not return, and when Beth got home Max's car was there in her yard. He couldn't wait for her or come back to the restaurant to say what they were doing? She quickly checked her cell phone. There were no messages from him or from anyone. It was pretty late. She was ready to drop in the bed and sleep until noon, but when she went up the steps and into the kitchen, she saw that it could be hours before she could close her eyes. She didn't like what she found. The sink was filled with dirty dishes, food was all over the counters, the garbage can was overflowing, and Lola was whining her little head off from her crate. She could hear them all out on the porch, laughing and having a great old time.

She opened the crate, attached Lola's leash, and said, "Don't ever let your family visit too often, miss. They'll just walk all over your welcome mat."

She walked Lola on the street side of the house to avoid seeing them. The truth was that though the house really belonged to the whole family, she felt pretty territorial about it. Who did they think was going to clean up their huge mess? Her? She was livid. And just what was Max doing hanging around with them late into the night like old friends? Well, maybe it wasn't so late, but it irked the devil out of her anyway. She felt abused and overlooked.

When she got back inside, there stood Woody at the sink, rinsing dishes and loading the dishwasher.

"Hi," she said. "You don't have to do that."

She meant nothing of the kind and intuitively Woody knew that she was annoyed.

"Sorry about the mess. Uh, I guess things got a little out of control."

It was difficult for her to be angry with him, seeing him there cleaning her kitchen and apologizing.

"I guess y'all cooked, huh?"

"Yeah, Phoebe wanted lasagna and salad and garlic bread and a pie—man, that girl can eat!"

"And make a mess. Is there a single pot that she didn't use? Wow. Looks like a bomb went off in here."

It was easy to lay the blame at Phoebe's feet because she didn't like her anyway.

"I'm afraid we all had a hand in this disaster. Don't worry. I'll clean it all up."

Good grief, he's so nice, Beth thought.

"Tell you what," she said, "I'm gonna go put on some shorts and I'll come back and give you a hand."

"That'd be great," he said. "We can shoot the breeze—something we haven't really done yet."

Beth gave him a thumbs-up and started for the front steps. Lola skittered behind her, joyously, just so happy to have her back in her line of sight.

Out of the darkness of the porch came Mike.

"I'm hitting tha sack. N don't let anyboda wake me up tomorrow. I'm sleeping late."

"You're bombed."

"Yeah." He smiled and pointed his finger at her. "BTW, we need more scotch so you might wanna make a node a that."

"Don't tell me you drained Simon's twenty-five-year-old single malt."

"Yup. Was it that old? Hell, thas older tha Phebes!"

"Go to bed, Mike."

Before going upstairs to change, she stepped out onto the dark porch. In the pale light there was Phoebe climbing into the hammock with Max. Before she could stop herself, she spoke.

"Can I get y'all anything else? The bar's closing."

"Oh!" came the voices of the guilty.

Her mother would have been proud of her, she thought. Probably. But Beth was on the verge of bursting into tears.

9

Cheap Talk

Maggiepie2@marthagene.net
Susan, haven't heard a thing from the island. You?

Susanthepen@writenow.org
Mag, probably time to let them grow up? But you might email Cecily? Just a tiny query? On second thought, don't. Let's leave them alone. xx

"Our friends did not show well tonight," Woody said when she told him about stumbling on Phoebe and Max. "I'm sorry."

"It's okay. Not your fault."

Beth was in the kitchen with him, cleaning up and trying to pull herself together. She was so upset she doubted she would sleep a single wink that night. Max made an awkward, hasty departure, saying he would call her in the morning. Phoebe simply disappeared to her room without a word. Beth was left to wonder, Why weren't they ashamed? There had been no apologies. Didn't anyone have a conscience anymore? A sense of propriety? Beth had not said anything else to Phoebe or Max but the few words spoken on the porch, but she nearly talked the ears off the sides of Woody's sainted head.

"What a couple of idiots!" she said. "Can you believe them? And Mike is as drunk as forty goats!"

"Stupid," he said. Woody tried to improve her mood by injecting humorous anecdotal stories into their cleaning streak.

"Completely!"

"So listen to this. I had a date with this woman last year and I took her to this new slick restaurant in Atlanta, right?"

"And?"

"Well, she tells me she's getting sick so I took her home. Stomach flu, she thinks. About an hour later I go to this bar on the other side of town."

"Yeah?"

"She's in there raising hell and knocking back dirty martinis with some jerk."

"You're kidding."

"Nope. I just went over to her and said, I'm glad to see you're feeing better."

"She must have died."

"No, unfortunately, she did not die. But I think what you said to Phoebe and Max was pretty good."

"Thanks."

"It's hard to be clever on your feet. Well done. I'm gonna take out the trash."

"Thanks." Beth turned on the dishwasher and the hum of it sounded like a lullaby and it began to put her at ease.

When Woody returned, he could tell the storm was passing.

"I hate men," she said, blowing her nose. "How old are you?"

"Not old enough to hate, I hope."

"Oh, not you, Woody! I don't hate you."

"I'll be thirty in January. Would you like a glass of wine? A small reward for restoring order to the battlefield?"

"Sure. Thanks."

He took two goblets from the drainboard, dried them, and poured. He handed Beth hers.

"Thanks. And sluts. I hate sluts too."

"What? Well, I certainly don't. I mean,

you know, they have their place in society."

Woody smiled at Beth and she smiled back, then she shook her head.

"Woody! You wound me!"

"Wound?"

"Yeah, wound." She covered her heart with her hand and leaned against the stove. It was obvious that Beth was kidding him. "Men are dogs, Woody. Dogs. Bacon-eating, sniffing, prowling, low-down dirty damn dogs. Well, I say, here's to having a little virtue!"

"What a waste of a toast. And, not all men are dogs. And one more thing, while we're on the topic of righteousness, not all women are so virtuous either."

"You're right, you're right, you're right."

"Thank you. Now, come on. Let's go out on the porch and enjoy a few minutes of the night. I'll bring the vino."

"Okay. Why not?"

Beth looked around to see Lola curled up and fast asleep in her crate.

"She's not used to being around a lot of people. Wears her out."

"She's a cute little dog."

"Thanks."

She followed Woody outside. They settled in rocking chairs and were quiet for a few minutes.

"The scene of the crime," she said. "Stinks."

"A lot of stuff stinks. Too much, in fact. Listen, Beth. I've known Phoebe for a while. She gets real friendly when she's had too much to drink. She's harmless, really."

"Harmless, my big fat butt. What's Max's excuse?"

"Your butt's not fat. As for Max? My momma's crazy sister used to say, Well, he's got one, doesn't he?"

This made Beth burst into giggles. And she blushed to know Woody had gauged the proportions of her derriere.

"Groooss," she said, drawing the word out long.

"Boys *are* gross. And when girls get all liquored up, sometimes their panties have a way of falling off and nobody seems to recollect how it happened."

"Headwinds. A big old wind flushes up their skirt, and boom! Britches go flying!"

"A windfall!" Woody laughed at his own

joke, leaned forward, slapped his knee, and Beth looked at him like he was certifiably insane. "What? You don't get it? Windfall?"

"No, I get it. I get it fine. Dr. Cornball has arrived." Beth shook her head and smirked at him. "Great."

"Who's corny?"

"Um, you? My stepfather, Simon. He's always making these ridiculously silly jokes. My mother spends a lot of time rolling her eyes."

"I've been told by many women—*many women*—that my quick and easy wit is a sign that they should not be intimidated by my superior intelligence."

"Oh, please. What'd you do? Graduate from Harvard at the top of your class?"

"Uh, yeah. Actually, I did."

"Graduate school?"

"Yeah. Undergraduate too."

"Well, bully for you, Einstein. I'll take another glass of wine if you're pouring."

She asked herself how many times she could be mortified in one day? Apparently there was no quota and she didn't need to touch her cheek to know that her face was in flames.

Woody was chuckling to himself because this wasn't the first time he had inadvertently flashed his résumé and had the same reaction. He wasn't a braggart but he did have a lot of pride in his accomplishments.

"Don't you find it reassuring that your personal banker isn't a dumbass?"

"Very." Actually, she thought, I do.

"You went to school in Boston, didn't you?"

"Yeah, BC."

"Well, Boston College is no slacker school."

"Well, I'm weird. I mean, I like to study."

"Me too. Otherwise I wouldn't have done as well, I guess."

"Me either. Well, all I've done so far is graduate. I'm supposed to be packing for Iowa, but noooooo!"

"Yeah, I heard about that from Mike. So, what happened?"

"I was hand-selected by the Family Committee of Elders as most likely not to destroy the house."

"Good thing they didn't leave it with Mike. He's been pounding down the booze ever since we got here."

"Yeah, I noticed. He blew through Simon's twenty-five-year-old single malt and that's gonna torch his wallet to replace it."

"That's not good."

"I wonder if he does that all the time. Drinks like that, I mean."

"Only lately he sort of does. At least when I'm with him."

"That's not good either."

"No, it's not. Another kind of woman wouldn't put up with it."

"Maybe that explains why he chooses idiots. Do we think someone like Phoebe would ever object to him getting wasted?"

"Not in a million years. She wouldn't object to anything. Gosh, I love this porch."

"Me too. Best room in the house."

"So listen, can I ask you a personal question?"

"Sure."

"Just how involved are you with that guy Max?"

Beth was silent then as the porch slowly began to transform itself into the confessional again. Dark porches had a way of doing that. Salt air floating by on slow breezes made you brain-drunk, longing to be understood. Justified.

"Well, I guess the honest answer is that I am not as involved as I would like to be. I mean, I think I could see myself with this guy forever and that is a very weird thing for me to say."

Beth could almost feel Woody's regret that she had answered in those words. He had posed the question because he wanted to know the answer for his own heart. But Woody was the consummate gentleman and she had no fear that he would act or speak inappropriately. In fact, she had rarely encountered someone quite so well mannered as he was.

"I see," he said. "Well, that is a mystery."

"Why? What's mysterious about it? Don't you think, I mean aside from their nonsense tonight . . . don't you think he's fabulous?"

Woody laughed a little and said, "Well, I'm not sure I'd call him fabulous. But I do think he is an interesting man."

Interesting man was a careful choice of words to her. It could have meant a thousand things. *Isn't it interesting that Beth's intended boyfriend is such a philanderer, snaking her cousin's girlfriend right under everyone's nose?*

"So what is that supposed to mean?"

"Well, he's a smart guy, that's for sure. Maybe a little long in the tooth, but whatever."

"He's only thirty-seven."

"Hey, I'm minding my own business on that one. I have to say that little development project he's got going is a great idea. But I think he's underfunded because he sure did pitch us hard to invest."

"With money from Uncle Henry's firm?"

"With money from anywhere."

"Excuse me, but if Max wants my cousin to be his partner, he shouldn't be coming on to his girlfriend, right?"

"Absolutely. But in his mind actually, one thing has nothing to do with the other. And remember, they all had too much to drink."

"What do you mean *in his mind*?"

"Just that. Certain guys think that way."

"I love the way men can compartmentalize."

"Yeah, keep it simple is my motto."

They were quiet then. He could sense Beth's incredulousness at his opinion on the lines of separation between business and horsing around with a blowsy broad.

She thought that he had implied a cocktail binge could excuse certain behaviors. He *had* implied that. But what he really meant—and this was the more bothersome thing for Beth—was that no one really cared about one another in that unholy triumvirate—not Mike, Phoebe, or Max. It was just about blowing off steam, having fun, getting crazy, and throwing around sexual innuendo until their sassy repartee was exhausted. Therefore, it all didn't mean a thing.

That opinion didn't settle well with Beth. She had concluded during her Boston years that that wasn't how she wanted to approach relationships. She was more serious about her intentions and how others viewed her as well. Someday, she would write about the Phoebes of the world and how all that cavorting around like a cheap hussy would get you nothing of substance in the end. But, she thought, maybe I'm being too prim, too straight. Maybe I'm the one who doesn't know how to have fun, like my old librarian from grammar school. Mrs. Willard with the hairy mole on her chin still gave her the shivers when her face came to mind.

"Woody?"

"Yeah?"

"Okay, think about this before you answer. Am I a cardigan kind of girl or am I a conga line kind of girl?"

Woody started to laugh and Beth giggled too.

"Come on, I'm serious. I know it's a stupid question but I want you to tell me what you think!"

"Um, well, I've only known you for a few hours, you know, so it's hard to say with real conviction. But I would say that you seem to know when to be which one, more than a dead ringer for either one in particular. Did I say that right?"

"I'm not sure."

"What I mean, Miss Hayes, is you don't just conga with anyone and you know when it's time to suit up."

"Oh. Well, that's okay, I guess."

"To put it in the context of a serious relationship, I wouldn't want to wake up one morning and find myself married to a woman who couldn't behave herself half of the time."

"Who would?"

"Too much work. I mean, life's not a game for me."

"Me either."

"So what do you want, Beth? I mean, where do you see yourself, say, at thirty?"

"Married. Published, I hope. Maybe a baby on the way. Deliriously happy? I don't know. What about you?"

"Yeah, I used to think I'd be in a serious relationship, maybe engaged, well on the way to my first million. But here I am on the doorstep of thirty and none of that is happening yet. I mean, I've got a decent portfolio of my own but my stuff is so conservative I'm looking at very slow growth. But man, the markets are so terrible these days. Scary stuff."

"Yeah. That's what you hear all over the news. So what do you think is gonna be?"

"If I knew that, I'd have my own firm."

"Well, there you have it, sports fans. Life is uncertain."

"And when times are uncertain, I think you are supposed to hunker down and not do anything stupid."

"Is that what they taught you at the Harvard B School?"

"No, Miss Hayes, I learned that from my old man."

"And what does your dad do for a living? Run the stock exchange?"

"He's a farmer."

"Wow. Cool. And your mom?"

"She teaches school. And she helps my dad. And in the interest of full disclosure, I have two older brothers who run the farm with my dad."

"God, farming sounds so romantic to me. You know, you just get away from the world and make things grow—"

Woody sat forward in his chair with a burst of laughter.

"Are you serious? Tell you what, someday I'll take you out to the farm and you can see for yourself how romantic it is to get up at four in the morning to feed and milk the cows when it's twenty below outside."

He's taking me someplace? What does that mean? Nothing, she thought, it's just talk.

"Holy cow, no pun intended."

"Who's corny?"

"Okay, okay. But twenty below? I can't imagine. You're probably right. So where do they live? Alaska?"

"Nope. Iowa."

"Iowa? Ah, the elusive Iowa! Well, maybe when I finally get there I'll meet you at your family home and we'll all have a big old glass of fresh milk together."

"You know what? You'd better watch out. It's stuff like that that gets you hooked on farming."

"I'll bet." She realized she could spend the rest of the night talking to Woody. He was filled with all sorts of stories and surprises and he was kind. When she looked at her watch she saw it was almost two in the morning. "It's late. Rats."

"Yeah, I gotta turn in so I can get up tomorrow and get drunk with Mike and Phoebe."

"How stupid." Beth got up and straightened her rocker back in its line just as her Aunt Maggie would have done. Then she took Woody's and did the same.

"You're telling me? Here, wait. I should've done that. I'll turn off the lights."

"I'll help." When they reached the kitchen she said, "I have to check the stove twice."

"What?"

"Family ritual. Listen, Woody? Thanks for all your help tonight."

"It was nothing. Sorry about the mess."

"No big deal."

They said good night reluctantly and if asked they would have said that the reluctance was because neither of them was particularly sleepy. The truth was that the conversation between them had come so easily and they had actually enjoyed themselves. No games. No preening. Just friendly banter as they got to know each other a little.

Beth took Lola upstairs to sleep in her room, and as she was washing her face she wondered about Woody and his family. What exactly was it about people from the Midwest that was so appealing? The Midwest was so different from the South, or at least it seemed so to her. People from Ohio and Indiana seemed more reserved, more prudent. More stoic. While she thought that Woody would have told her anything she wanted to know about himself, he was not the kind of guy who fought for center stage to tell the world how amazing he was. Not one little iota. He was honest, or at least he seemed to be, and he was dignified. Whoever gets him will be a lucky girl, she thought, because he's gonna make a great husband.

Morning came quickly and Beth was in the kitchen pouring a cup of coffee when her Aunt Sophie called.

"Hey, girl! How's my favorite niece I've been missing? And don't tell anybody I said you're my fave but you know you are."

"Hey, Aunt Sophie!"

"God, my life is so crazy. I'm so sorry I haven't called you!"

"Oh, don't worry about that! It's so good to hear your voice!"

"I called the house number last night and no one answered. Y'all gotta get voice mail someday."

"Well, you know it's the same phone number that we've had since forever. Aunt Maggie hates newfangled changes and I guess she thinks it has historic value or something."

"Maggie thinks everything has value, which is one of her redeeming qualities, if you think about it. It's also why that kitchen has nineteen billion mugs that don't match, right?"

"Yep. Actually, there's an old answering

machine in the pantry. I'm going to hook that up right now."

"Good idea. So what's going on, sugar?"

"Well, let's see. I cut my hair and colored it back to normal."

"Well, good. Do you like it?"

"Yeah, I do. It's healthier-looking. And I got contact lenses, so I can actually see. And, I got two jobs, and lemme see what else."

"Two jobs?"

"Yeah, both part-time. Not a burden and they keep me busy. Oh, and Mike is here from Atlanta with some girl he's seeing and also this guy who works for Uncle Henry's bank and manages my trust fund."

"Really? Well, ahem! Are we having a double-date house party?"

"Yeah, right. Well, Mike is having his little honeymoon, but I am locked in my room upstairs with Lola. And if you breathe that, I'll get killed by the Morals Police."

"I'm saying nothing! So is everything okay?"

"Yeah, I just had a question about the opposite sex, but now I'm not so sure if I need the advice at all."

"Oh, tell me anyway. There's nothing like a little romance to get the juices flowing."

Beth told Sophie all about falling for Max. She told her about their incredible dinner and then about seeing him with the other woman at the very place she worked. But when the time came to talk about the prior night, she went very light on the details of his flirtation with Phoebe.

"Anyway, we're having dinner tomorrow night and I'm just wondering how to make him, you know, like me. And I should tell you, he's older."

"Age doesn't matter. Men are all the same. Wait. How much older?"

"Maybe like thirty-seven?"

"Yikes. Still, that's your business. Aren't you over twenty-one?"

"Last time I checked."

"Okay, then here's what you do. Look great and get him to talk."

"What do you mean? Talk about what?"

"About himself. I guarantee you that's his favorite topic. But here's the trick."

"What?"

"Challenge what he says. Like if he starts talking about why he's single, point out that men who marry before age fifty live ten years longer."

"Is that really true?"

"Yes ma'am! It was in some big study a few years back. But between us they can do a study to prove anything, right?"

"Probably."

"No, I'm telling you. Studies are skewed all the time."

"Speaking of . . . how did the studies go on your vitamin business?"

"The studies went fine but—and this is for no one's ears but yours—my crazy twin is losing her mind."

"What do you mean?"

"Well, we have been trying them out ourselves, right?"

"Yeah, I guess."

"Well, they seem to agree with Allison, except that they make her a little weirded-out. I mean, in ways you don't want to know. But I don't like them because they make my heart race. She says that Geoffrey is adjusting the formula. And, he had better do it PDQ because this stuff goes on the market pronto. I can just see it now. Thousands of people get deathly ill, go to the hospital, and bang, we're out of business and in court for the rest of our lives."

"Don't worry, Aunt Sophie. Aunt Allison is like, sorry, but she's a crank. But she's not going to endanger the public."

"Let's hope not. Anyway, back to your hunk of burning love?"

"Yeah, oh Lord. Max."

"Listen to me, sweetie. Blow out your hair. Put on some perfume and makeup. Wear something that shows what you've got, but not so provocatively so that you look like a tramp . . ."

"Aunt Sophie!"

"Just kidding. I'm telling you, let him talk about himself. Now, tell me, have you heard from your mother?"

"Yeah. Like twice a day. Email. You know her. She's too cheap to call. Anyway, she's having a really great time."

"Well, I hope so. It was the only dream she ever had, that is, besides having you."

"Oh, that is so sweet, isn't it? Mom's like fiftysomething and living her dreams."

"Yeah, it sure is. Okay, now if you need me, call me. Call me anyway to let me know how this hot date goes, okay?"

Beth promised that she would, and just as she hung up, Phoebe and Mike came slowly into the kitchen, looking bleary-eyed and frayed around the edges.

"Morning, cuz. We got any coffee?"

"In the pot. Milk's on the counter. Where's Woody?"

"In the shower."

"Oh. How'd y'all sleep?"

"He slept like a log, but not me, honey. I was up all night," Phoebe said.

"Why? Were you sick?"

Phoebe looked at Mike and then back to Beth.

"Just tell her," Mike said.

"Well, this is kind of screwed up, but did anyone ever say that this house is haunted?"

"Gosh, no!" Beth lied. "What happened?"

"Somebody was breathing in my ear. Every time I fell asleep, somebody would whisper in my ear and I would wake up. Then I would drift off again, and two minutes later, I swear someone was breathing in my ear. As long as I stayed awake it didn't happen, but the minute I would drift off into a dream, here came the daggum breathing on me again!"

"Well, maybe you should sleep in the hammock tonight," Beth said, unsmiling, looking Phoebe straight in the eye.

"Why would Phoebe want to sleep in the hammock?" Mike said.

"Why don't you ask her? I gotta go walk my dog. And Phoebe, it would be really nice if you lay waste to the kitchen again, clean up after yourself. Woody and I washed y'all's dishes for an hour last night."

"Oh Lord. I was just wondering what happened to all that mess. The last thing that I remember, I was gonna come in here and clean up. Then I woke up in bed about a thousand times. And then I just forgot. I know what! Let's make blueberry pancakes!"

Beth caught Mike's eye and rolled her own at him as if to say, You've got a real genius there, cousin.

"Let's not," Beth mumbled.

Mike sighed. "Why don't we go out for breakfast, Phebes? Then no one has to clean up anything."

"Now that sounds like a plan," Beth said, and scooped up Lola under her arm.

"Sorry," Mike said, and then under his breath he mumbled to Phoebe, *She sounds just like my mother.*

"Don't call me *she*. *She* is the cat's mother," Beth said to Mike as she passed him.

"See you later, Maggie," Mike said, smirking. "Unless you want to come with us? I was thinking maybe the Sea Biscuit on the Isle of Palms?"

"Up yours," Beth said quietly, giving Mike the finger.

"She's such a lady," Mike called out, making sure Beth wouldn't miss his wise-crack. "A simple no thank you would do, you know!"

"Up yours sideways!" Beth called back, having the final remark, passing through the living room. She opened the front door and crossed the front porch to take Lola toward the beach. "Come on, miss. Let's go chase a seagull."

It was about nine-thirty and too late to take Lola out on the beach for a long walk. All the dogs had to be off the beach by ten so that people wouldn't be terrorized by them, not that any dogs ever truly terror-ized a human on the beaches of Sullivans Island. But there were occasions when large wet dogs, Labs and goldens in par-ticular, would shake off their water and sand right next to a stranger with a napping infant. Or these same lovable mutts were known to occasionally pilfer a sandwich from someone's picnic. And sometimes they would commandeer a Frisbee game by jumping in the middle, grabbing the Frisbee out of the air, and taking off down the beach just lickety-split!

So, okay, Beth thought, maybe there *was* a reason for the stringent dog laws. Not that Lola was interested in any of those pursuits, but if she had been caught on the beach at the wrong hour, it would be difficult to explain to the Canine Cops that Lola was different from all other animals. On the planet. Ever.

By the time Beth returned the house was empty and she passed the rest of the day quietly, answering emails from her mother and catching up with her friends on Facebook. That night Beth went to work and there was no sign of Mike, Woody, or Phoebe. When she returned home, still no one was there. Had they left for Atlanta? Beth checked her grandmother's room and saw that Phoebe and Mike's things were there, in piles all over the room. No, they had simply passed like proverbial ships in the night. She took a book out to the porch to read for a few minutes and thought about what Phoebe had reported that morning about the breathing and whispering in her ear. Maybe her grandmother was on her side, telling Phoebe to get her skank butt out of their house. It was a happy thought. Around midnight, she heard their car pull into the yard, music blaring.

Oh great, Beth thought, the neighbors are probably on the phone with Aunt Maggie right now and any minute the phone's going to ring. It's going to be Aunt Maggie saying she knew this would happen and why did she trust her with the family's reputation? Was anything broken? Had the police been called in to settle the problem?

Well, if that happens, Beth thought, I'll just tell her she needs to talk to her crazy-ass son and his love machine, not to me. I haven't done a damn thing to compromise anything. Not that I wouldn't like to if I had the chance, she thought.

Beth was working herself into quite a little snit when the music suddenly stopped. She heard the kitchen door slam and from there the noise became more reasonable. She could hear them talking but she was far enough away that she could not make out their words. A few minutes later, they were all on the porch with her, beers in hand. Woody, as expected, was obviously the most sober among them.

"Hey," Beth said, not getting up from her rocker. "Where'd y'all go?"

"We went downtown. Mike wanted to give Phebes a trip down memory lane."

"Yep!" Phoebe said. "We cocktailed all over Charleston."

Thinking that was obvious and that her Sunday departure couldn't arrive fast enough, she said, "Gee, did they check your ID?"

"How did you know that? Y'all! How did she know that?"

Because you should add expert in *juvenile behavior* to your résumé, Beth thought. "So, big shot, where'd you take them?"

"Oh, my cynical little cousin! I can see the wheels turning in your precious head!"

"Meaning what?"

"That you're worried I dragged them into the dives I used to frequent, but no, I did not. I took them to the rooftop bar of the Vendue Inn for a little sunset viewing, and *then* we went to the dives."

"Like Big John's?"

"Excuse me, Paris Hilton, but the halls of Big John's are hallowed," Mike said with a laugh.

"Did we go there?" said Phoebe, obviously confused and nodding off in her chair.

"Yeah," said Woody, "that's where you ate the pickled egg."

"Oh. Right."

"Then we went to AC's, the Silver Dollar, and Beer Works."

"And the Blind Tiger," said Woody.

"Well, you did get the grand tour," Beth said. "Did y'all eat dinner?"

"Eat? Dinner? Man! I knew we forgot something. Is there anything in the fridge?"

Mike was not as bombed as he had been the night before, although the prior night they had set the bar pretty high. Maybe he was just noisy, partially intoxicated, and in love with loud music. But Beth didn't want to feel responsible for them being hungover the next morning because they had not eaten. She did feel a little guilty, but only slightly so, about slipping the verbal knife between Phoebe's ribs earlier in the day. Clearly, she thought, Relais & Châteaux was not stopping by to present me with the Hostess of the Year award.

"Would you like me to make some scrambled eggs and toast?"

"Ah, geez, Beth. We don't want you to mess up the kitchen, do we, y'all?"

Beth could see Woody smiling at her. He said, "Well, for me, I could always go for some scrambled eggs. You cook and I'll clean and we won't let them anywhere near us."

"Deal."

They were all fed, and as expected, drowsy from a full stomach, the hour, and the alcohol. Mike and Phoebe held Woody and Beth to their word and did not help at all. They simply rose, said thank you, and moseyed down the hall. But this time, Beth didn't care. She liked the idea of having Woody's company for a little while. He was terrifically pleasant to be around. In the parlance of her peers, Woody had his merde together.

They were leaving after morning coffee, and as they loaded the car, Beth sighed in relief. Woody saw her face and said that he would bet that she was glad to see them go, wasn't she?

That was when Beth realized that she liked Woody a lot, but still, only as a friend. Without a second thought that he might misinterpret her words, she said, "Woody? You can come and visit me and Lola anytime you'd like. You don't even have to come with Mike."

"Well, thank you."

"Okay, y'all drive safely and call me to let me know you're not dead in a ditch."

"We will," Woody said.

"Don't work too hard!" Mike called to her.

Beth just waved to them from behind the screen door. Her mind was already traveling to her dinner that night with Max. He had called to say that he would pick her up at seven. She thought that she might like to go somewhere to watch the sunset with him too. It surely sounded like the perfect way to start the night, but first she had to work.

One hundred and forty-odd brunches and who knew how many Bloody Marys and mimosas later, Beth was back at home getting dressed for her date.

"So, miss, Mom's got a hot date tonight. Should I wear this or this?"

Beth was holding up two dresses for

Lola to consider. Lola just made a noise that sounded like *ark ark* and walked around in circles on Beth's bed. Finally, she plopped down and looked at Beth as if to say, How the hell should I know? I'm a dog, not Anna Wintour.

"Okay, you're right. I'll wear the white one."

10

Tabasco Night

Maggiepie2@marthagene.net
Susan, Just, FYI, don't get mad but Beth spent a bunch of money on contact lenses and a professional hair rescue. Cecily says she looks terrific. xx

Susanthepen@writenow.org
Well, good! She has two jobs, doesn't she? Why would I get mad about that?

Maggiepie2@marthagene.net
Because you ain't spent a hundred dollars on your own hair all your life?

Susanthepen@writenow.org
Unlike some people! xx

Beth styled her hair in long fat ringlets held back with combs. It took some effort to keep them from frizzing out because of the humidity but she managed with the help of long clips, pinning them up until the last moment. Then she sprayed herself with a sample of cologne she found in the bottom of her makeup bag. She wished that night had already arrived so the heat of the day would have been on the wane. In addition, there was something peculiar about dressing for a date that would begin in broad daylight. But she relaxed knowing the cool air of night and the right atmosphere would all come soon enough.

At the last minute she was uncertain about wearing white. It seemed too young and virginal, not at all the image she wanted to convey. She put the dress on and looked at herself in the large living room mirror from as many angles as she could. It was the newest and most flattering dress in her closet, and so in the end she decided to wear it after all. Maybe darker lipstick and more mascara would make up the difference. So she worked on her makeup a little more and thought to herself that she had done all within her power to make herself attractive. If he didn't think she was, well then, perhaps he was not so smart after all. She turned on the stereo and streams of "At Last" sung by Etta James drifted through the rooms. Although it was written and recorded long before Beth or even her mother was born, it still sounded contemporary. And very seductive.

Unlike their first dinner date, where Max arrived late to find her on the floor with a bloody lip and half strangled in stereo wires, on that particular evening Max was prompt and Beth was vertical. This time he would find her in the kitchen, folding the last of the laundry from her company and replacing a dish towel neatly on the rack. As she tried to make the old funky kitchen look like a magazine layout, she laughed to realize she had a strain of the Maggie Gene. Mike may have been right. Truly, she was becoming more and more persnickety about the tidiness of the house just like Maggie.

She heard his car and went to the screen door, opening it. It delighted her to see him coming up the back steps with a fistful of flowers for her. They were obviously from the grocery store but what did it matter? The florists were closed on Sundays, he had gone to some effort and she had to give him credit for that.

"Wow, look at you!" he said, standing back appraising her. "You look like a vision of . . . I don't know . . . who's the artist that painted that gorgeous woman rising from the sea in a clamshell?"

"Botticelli. A family favorite. Yeah, actually people tell me that all the time." Beth giggled and took the flowers. "Thanks. Gosh, they're so pretty!"

"Can I have a squeeze or something?"

"Uh, sure!"

She hugged him lightly in a fraternal way but somewhere in that moment more than fraternal feelings passed between them. Well, for Beth especially, whose head was swirling in the ethers of what it would feel like to sleep with him. Just as quickly she chided herself for considering giving the mattress a shake just because he showed up with five dollars' worth of flowers and threw her an Art History 101 compliment. Nonetheless, she was warmer all over, not so sure about how he was feeling, but since he couldn't read her lascivious thoughts, the night was off to a good start.

"Would you like to come in?"

"Sure. Why not? Did your cousin and his friends go back to Atlanta?"

"Yep. They left this morning." Beth searched the cabinets under the sink and counters for a container.

"I really liked your cousin Mike. And that Woody is a real straight-up guy too. Very smart."

"And Phoebe?"

Max sighed and looked at her in all innocence.

"Beth? The woods are crawling with Phoebes. And just so you know, she's the one who pushed me into the hammock. I know that it must have looked bizarre to you, but believe me, not my type."

What she had seen with her own eyes didn't line up with his explanation but she decided to let it go. What was the point of making an issue? She didn't own him.

"I wouldn't think so. It's okay."

Finding a dusty relic from the last time someone had flowers delivered, she rinsed it, filled it with cold water, and placed the flowers inside, fluffing them around as though she was trying to make them comfortable in their sudden chill.

"Is it really okay?"

"Of course!"

"Good."

"Would you like a glass of wine or something?"

"If you want one, or we could just get going."

She put the vase on the kitchen table and took a step back to admire it, buying herself a second or two to decide on whether to stay for a while or to depart. Flowers or no flowers, Lola was in her crate, eyeballing them from below her eyebrows, showing zero enthusiasm for Beth's visitor. Beth noted that but then thought perhaps Lola was just worn out from the heat.

To stay or to go? Part of the decision was based in vanity. In that weather and at that time of day, Beth's hair had about a thirty-minute window of perfection before it would begin to droop. Individual strands would soon lift up to resemble a frothy halo. Should he see her curls in the sunset from the widow's walk with a glass of wine? Or should she save that for later? She decided. Save the hair. Hie thee coif to the restaurant. Surely, wherever he planned to take her had to be air-conditioned.

"I think we should go, and if we're not

out too late I can show you the island in three hundred and sixty degrees, later when it's dark. All the stars come out around ten."

"You mean the widow's walk, right?"

"Yep."

"Awesome. You know, I saw the widow's walk the first time I came here and I wondered if you all ever went up there."

"Used to. When my mom was a kid it was her favorite hiding place. Later on when Aunt Maggie married my Uncle Grant he enlarged it a little, putting that enclosure on. It's a great place to watch a storm."

"I'll bet."

"We used to play there when we were little. I haven't been up there in years. So, where's dinner?"

"I was thinking Shem Creek. There's a sunset bar on top of Jackson Hole, and then we can either eat there or walk over to the Water's Edge. They've got the best wine list."

"Whatever you want to do is fine with me. Wait one sec. I have to get my bag. And lock the front door. Twice."

"Twice?"

"Family tradition."

"Got it. All family's are a little crazy."

"Ours especially."

Beth passed through the living room and gave the big mirror a glance. Nothing. Good, she thought.

"How about you just keep your opinions to yourself tonight, Livvie?"

"You talking to someone?" Max called out.

"Yeah. No," she called back. He'd never believe what goes on in this house, she thought. *I'm* not even so sure. "Okay, so, I'm ready to go."

When they arrived at the restaurant they were greeted by the owner, Brad Jackson.

"Hey, how're y'all doing tonight? Can I put your name on the list for a table?"

"No, I think we're just gonna watch the sunset, maybe have a glass of wine," Max said.

"Sounds good! Nice to have y'all! Just watch your step there."

Beth and Max climbed the stairs and made their way through the crowd to the bar. Beth could feel her hair start to rise.

"What's it gonna be?" said the bartender.

"Two Pinot Grigios?" Max said, not looking at Beth for an okay signal.

"Fine," Beth said. What if I wanted something else? she thought, but said nothing.

Beth noticed that the bartender, a pretty blond woman around the same age as her mother, had an exquisite diamond ring and wedding band on her left hand. Why would someone with a doorknocker on her hand be tending bar? She put the glasses in front of them and said, "Here we go. So, where are y'all from?"

"Atlanta," said Max. "You?"

"Old Village. Moved back here a few years ago. Got married."

"What does your husband do?" said Beth, determined not to be left out of the conversation.

"Oh, I'm sorry! I'm Linda Jackson. My husband Brad and I own the place. Our regular bartender is on vacation." Linda shook Max's hand and he grimaced in pain.

"Wow," Max said.

"Oh, sorry! I gotta keep working on that handshake thing. Brad says I shake hands like a trucker! How about you all? Is this your daughter?"

"What?" Max said, as though she had asked if he had raging syphilis. "No! Are you kidding? I'm single!"

Beth saw her question and his answer as providential.

"Oh, shoot! Whoops!" Linda said. "Well, it's a big mistake not to get married, Max."

"And just why is that?" he asked, amused by her emphatic statement.

"Well, they did this study? At the NIH or someplace? Anyway, the study said that men who marry before fifty live ten years longer than those who don't. So basically, you're cutting your life short if you stay single. That's all. Go ahead. Kill yourself. Stay single."

"I guess she told you, huh?" Beth said. "I heard about the same article. She's right."

"Excuse me for a minute," Linda said with a laugh, and stepped away to serve another customer.

Beth was embarrassed that Linda assumed Max was her father, but if they were from a third-world country he technically could have been. Gross, she thought.

Max was seriously and thoroughly annoyed at Linda's question too because what did that make him? A dirty old man? Max had never been too old for *anything* in his entire life! And since he arrived at her door that evening he had been thinking of Beth as a morsel, his own personal Lolita. I have intentions for tonight and this Linda person is blowing it for me, he thought.

He cleared his throat. "Why don't we step over to the railing where we have a better view?" Max said.

"Sure," Beth said, just as happy to leave Linda's watchful eye as he was.

The deck was bulging with humanity as it usually was and it was difficult to turn around without bumping into someone's elbow and sloshing their drink from their glass. The music was a little loud and the other people were laughing and carrying on, feeling more festive than Beth or Max at the moment.

Beth looked out over the water and took in everything from the old shrimp boats tied up to the nearby pilings to the deepening colors on the horizon as the sun began its fiery descent. Was he really too old for her? she wondered. How would she know if she didn't at least give the whole thing with him a try? But my mother would flip out, she thought. But maybe not. Wasn't history loaded with couples who had age differences? Weren't there other reasons why the outside world would have thought they had no business being together? Of course there were. But should she care? Didn't Edgar Allan Poe marry his thirteen-year-old cousin? Okay, she thought, that's disgusting. We're not that bad. What about Miss December, Demi Moore, and Mr. May, Ashton Kutcher? I'll bet she's glad she went to the gym, she thought. And weren't John and Cindy McCain like eighteen years apart? Yes, they were. So, she decided, if it all seems okay to me, then I shouldn't worry about what other people think. Screw 'em, she thought. I'm crazy about Max.

"What are you so deep in thought about?" Max asked.

"You're gonna die if I tell you. I was wondering what it would be like to sleep with you. I mean, well, yep, that's what I was thinking, to be brutally honest."

Max's eyebrows took a jump for his scalp and he could not conceal his satisfaction as he flashed every tooth in his head in a grin as wide as a big-mouth bass.

"I was hoping you'd come around to that."

"Well, I did. Does that terrify you?"

"No, no. Not one bit. Uh, but I think decorum dictates that I have to feed you first."

"So you can work up your nerve?"

"Don't worry about me working up anything."

"Woo hoo!"

"But I have to say, you little tease, I'm starving."

"Who's a tease?"

She wanted to continue taunting him and say something like, Well, you'd better eat protein so you'll have your strength. Or to say any number of other provocative things about oysters and spinach that passed through her mind, but she didn't want to trivialize the moment. When they finally reached the bedroom she wanted him to take whatever transpired between them as dead serious.

So in an effort to seem cool, calm, and collected she said, "I guess I could go for a crab cake." Then she worried. Would fish give her bad breath? Holy mackerel, you have to worry about everything, she thought. She would drench it with lemon juice.

Dinner began as a hurried affair with liberal dispensing of cocktails and wine. As the evening went on and now that Beth had dropped the bait, she wasn't so sure if she had the chutzpah to reel in the big fish. It didn't matter because it was similar to accepting a diamond and promising life-long fidelity. Once you put the ring on your finger, you were as good as married. Sort of. But Max could sense Beth's uncertainty. He was not interested in dragging her into a cave and having his way with her like some Neanderthal. So he began to take some distance to put her nerves at ease.

"We should order some dessert, don't you think? I mean, what's the rush?"

Beth took this to mean that perhaps his interest had faded. Instead of being relieved of her promise to deliver the goods, she was suddenly inspired to work harder to strengthen his interest, which was exactly what Max knew would happen.

But Beth was not as naïve as he imagined. She could play cat and mouse with the best of them.

Looking directly into his eyes, she said, "Sure, why not? Let's get something gooey. We could walk it off on the beach. If you want. It's low tide."

He looked directly back into her eyes and challenged, "That sounds just like what the doctor ordered."

So after a decadent dessert of Mimi's double milk chocolate pound cake with semisweet chocolate frosting and fresh grated coconut, drizzled with hot chocolate sauce, garnished with slivers of strawberries and kiwi, all nestled in a puddle of a lemon-lime coulis and sprinkled with powdered sugar, they had coffee. With a shot of whiskey. Beth fed Max with her fork and he made sounds that would embarrass the clergy of any denomination, even though they both knew the sound effects were, in part, only for entertainment. Max couldn't wait to get the check. Beth couldn't wait for it to be paid.

They parked at her house, Beth took

Lola for a short visit to the yard while Max washed his hands. The night was clear and the sky was strewn with the glitter of endless stars. When she returned, he had opened the second bottle of wine of the evening that he had simply taken from the refrigerator, making himself at home. She really didn't want anything else to drink but Beth knew the mischief was about to begin. She began to tingle with excitement.

"Want to go up top or do you want to take a walk?" she said.

"I think let's go up and have a look. It's such a clear night."

They climbed the spiral staircase to the top of the house and stood in the open air looking up and all around. She was feeling a little dizzy, but between the stairs and all she'd eaten for dinner, it was no surprise.

Beth's hair was windswept in the opposite direction of wherever she faced, giving Max every opportunity to study her in profile. He was amazed by the tautness of her skin and how she had yet to earn a single wrinkle. Her complexion was smooth and pale in stark contrast with her dark hair, and her unusually blue eyes were framed by thick dark lashes. He would not have said she was a classic beauty but that she was a beautiful young woman who had not yet grown into her looks. Soon she would be stunning and her face was the kind that would improve with years. Even as an observer he had to admit it because his vanity had him in a choke hold. His own looks were post-peak and he knew it.

Max had always considered himself to be a handsome devil because the world had always assured him that he was. But he realized the days were at hand where he would have to rely on fastidious grooming, the contents of his wallet, and some measure of gallantry to take him where he wanted to go in the future. Beth's youth might be an asset to him. Certainly her cousin's position as an investor could be a lifesaver if he played his cards right.

"That's the Big Dipper," he said.

She was about to say, No duh, genius, but caught herself and said instead, "And that's Orion's Belt." She felt very full and wished she had excused herself before climbing up to the top of the house.

"And that is the full extent of my astronomy knowledge. Except for that really bright star over there that looks like it's going to come down here and eat us alive. Maybe it's aliens."

Beth giggled and said, "Oh, good grief, Max! No! Bright stars like that aren't necessarily closer. We might be looking at a planet or an old star."

"How do you know that?"

"Because while you were pouring over architectural drawings, I was in a classroom learning this stuff."

"So, what else do you know?" Max moved closer to her and pushed her hair away from her face.

"Um, Vega? Well, it's the second-brightest star in the northern celestial hemisphere and it comes out first."

Max stood closer to her, pushed her hair away again, and narrowed his eyes, staring into hers.

"Uh, what are you doing?" she said.

She knew that this was the moment he was going to kiss her and all at once she felt a pressing need to release some air from her digestive tract in an unladylike burp. She hoped it would be silent and, heaven knows, odorless, so she turned away. Unfortunately, just as he reached for her lower back to pull her closer to him, she felt an invisible hand push her face back toward his. Here came Mimi's milk chocolate pound cake and all the trimmings for a return visit. It spewed all over Max's shirt, down her white dress. Between coughing and, well, the unfortunate continuation of the unforgettable events of the moment, Beth began to wail in earnest.

"Oh, shit! Shit! Shit!"

"Good God!" Max held out his arms from his side, shook them, and looked down at his shirt in disgust. "I don't guess you want a glass of wine, huh?"

Beth coughed and coughed and sent the last of the lemon-lime coulis moving like a lava flow down the tin roof toward the front yard as she prayed it would rain overnight. She felt immensely better once the episode was over. When she turned to face him she nearly died.

"OH! MY! GOD! It's all over you! Oh no! I'm so sorry!"

"Me too! Jesus, look at my shirt! Can't wear this one tomorrow. I'm gonna go in and clean up."

"Oh, Max! This is terrible! I am so sorry!"

"Beth, no one ever throws up on their date on purpose. I know that."

With that he turned his back to her and went down the steps. Beth paused for a moment, considering flinging herself over the railings to end it all. For a split second it seemed like a more desirable solution to the situation. But then, for some inexplicable reason, she started to laugh. How horrible! Who would believe this? Here she was, with the love of her future life, ready to throw the man down and show him what youthful vigor was all about, and she had thrown up all over him instead! It was rich! The stuff of novels! No it wasn't. It was a travesty. How would she face him ever again? Oh God, she thought, it's over. Well? Maybe not. She would face him in the way her mother had taught her to conduct herself in times of severe adversity. She would use her sense of humor. Humor was a powerful tool. If that failed, she would claim a food allergy, which she actually had from time to time. And if that failed to move his heart, she would remind the coldhearted son of a dirty mongrel that dessert had been his idea in the first place. And, who or what had turned her face back toward Max at that critical moment?

She called out from the front door toward the bathroom, where she could hear the water running.

"I'll be right back! Gonna change my clothes!"

He didn't answer but she hoped that he had heard her and she rushed up the stairs. She carefully removed her dress and threw it in the bathtub. The dress was a total disaster and she would never wear it again. Ever. Then she soaked a washcloth in cold water and washed the remnants of her makeup from her face. Quickly she brushed her teeth, and while she rinsed with mouthwash, she watched her face in the mirror as it began to grow hives. Big red ugly hives began to appear in frightening numbers across her chest and down her arms. She began to itch and all she would do was think about screaming the F word to the rafters. She dug around in the medicine cabinet for Benadryl and found a pack of it, downing two pills as fast as she could.

"Here I am in my underwear, covered in hives, after vomming all over Max. Some femme fatale I am."

"You okay?" he called up the stairs.

"I'm not dead yet!" she called back in an English accent in a reference to Monty Python's Black Knight, wondering if he got the joke. "I'll be right down."

She threw on a pair of shorts and a halter top, knowing she looked like a fright, and then she threw a linen shirt over the halter to conceal her hives. And she grabbed a clean knit shirt for him from her Uncle Grant's chest of drawers.

"Good grief," she said to the mirror in her bedroom. "Happy Halloween."

She found him in a rocking chair on the porch, feet up on the banisters, listening to the ocean. The light was very dim, coming only from the lighthouse and from the few houses nearby. A blessing.

"Clean shirt?"

"Oh, thanks." There was no trace of gratitude in his voice. Max stood up, yanked his soaking wet shirt over his head, and threw it in a wad to the floor. He unbuttoned the other one and put it on. Even though she could sense his general dissatisfaction,

Beth had a chance to assess his abs, which even in her delicate but recovered state looked very good to her.

"I brought you a glass of water," he said, pointing to the glass on the table. "You feeling better? Just what the heck happened to you?"

"Oh, just lucky, I guess. Thanks."

"You call that luck?"

"Seriously, listen, I have a sometime shellfish allergy. I think it was the crab cake."

"The crab cake? Then why did you order it?"

Beth was a little taken back by his tone. "Because I love them. And they hardly ever make me sick. But I think that combined with that crazy dessert—"

"Which was a really stupid idea . . ."

"May I remind you that it was your idea to have dessert in the first place?"

The conversation was not traveling in a good direction and she was sinking into a hole of insecurity, thinking that she was small and insignificant, stupid, and that ultimately she would be forgotten. Worse, their schoolyard banter was hardly worthy of a pair of belligerent fifth graders.

"Maybe. Whatever. Look, I gotta get up early."

"Okay," she said.

"Okay then." He stood and looked at her, unsmiling. "Too bad. Tonight could've been the start of a great love affair."

"Yeah," she said, suppressing a sigh, feeling more forlorn than ever. "Well, there's always tomorrow."

"That's right." He pinched her chin and awarded her the smallest of smiles, a piteous thing. "I'll call you this week."

She knew he would never call. She watched him back out of the yard knowing that whatever chance she had thought existed for a romance with Max was finished. He had been grossed out at a new level. After about ten more minutes of solemn despair for the wild night that never was and reliving the shattered dream of his affection for her, she began to feel annoyed at how callous and unsympathetic he had been. But later, when she tried to sleep, all she could do was think of him and how close she had been to having him. Even if only for one night.

But the next evening brought a pleasant surprise for Beth. Around seven o'clock, just as the day was turning into night, she looked out into the yard and there was Max, getting out of his car with a paper bag brimming with groceries. She stood on her side of the screen door like a mannequin, listening to him talk.

"You feeling better? I brought the stuff to make chicken soup. It cures everything. It's the only thing I know how to make beside hamburgers and steaks. Can I come in?"

He did care after all, and Beth could feel her heart beating in her ears from the excitement of seeing him.

"Of course! Come in! But I'm fine! I don't need soup. I mean, if you want to make soup, that's great, but I'm fine really. I feel perfect! Seriously! Honestly! I don't want you to go to any—"

"Beth?"

"Yes?"

"Just thank the nice man and pour him a glass of wine."

"Thanks, Max. Would you like a glass of wine?"

"That would be good. Thank you. Now, where's your biggest pot?"

"I'll find it."

"Great."

Beth watched Max in awe as he began to cook. She could hardly believe that he was cooking for her.

"You seem surprised to see me," he said with a grin.

"Well, yeah, I thought I'd never see you again."

"Oh, come on now. What's a little disaster between friends?"

"I was worried."

He chopped up the white part of three leeks, soaking and rinsing them twice. Then he cleaned and chopped carrots and celery. He juggled them, to her delight tossing them over his shoulder into the pot, and then added the leeks along with a whole chicken cut into eight pieces. He covered the entire contents with water, threw in a handful of parsley, a generous toss of salt, a bay leaf, and put it on the stove, raising the heat to high.

"That's all there is to it?" Beth said.

"Pretty much. Once it boils, you skim it and then let it simmer for an hour and a half. By the way, it's all organic. What's on PPV? Want to watch a movie?"

"Sure."

Beth was completely mesmerized by Max. The fact that he was there was a sign from God, she hoped. Everything about him seemed so comfortable, as though they had known each other for years. He had come in acting like he was perfectly at home, and yes, as though she came with the place and therefore he owned her too. Even the manner in which he clicked his way through the four hundred or so channels was done with a kind of proprietary masculine finesse as though the show he wanted to watch was hiding, lurking behind a number on the screen. Any second he, the hunter, would capture it and bring it in to entertain them, like a circus animal. Max was in charge. Beth loved it.

They settled on a rerun of *Law & Order: SVU* and Max was so drawn in by the episode that he seemed to hardly know where he was, except that he pulled Beth next to him and put his arm around her shoulder, giving her a squeeze now and then. Beth was so happy she could hardly breathe. She didn't move one inch in any direction, afraid that if she changed positions in the slightest, he might move away. She thought when she went to sleep that night that at least she would be able to remember what it felt like to have his arm around her.

"I talked to your cousin Mike today," he said during a commercial.

"Oh yeah? What's up with him?"

"He's pitching your Uncle Henry to invest in my deal, but it's probably a long shot."

"Why's that?"

"Well, the economy and all. But if he comes through it will make all the difference. Anyway, this project is just a model. I'd like to duplicate something like this all up and down the Atlantic coast. He'll quadruple his money in no time."

"Really?"

"Oh yeah. Definitely."

"So how come your other partner dropped out?"

"Said he wasn't liquid enough. Who knows? People are nuts."

Beth assumed that liquidity meant that the guy was overinvested. She remembered the term from her economics classes.

"Oh, so how much money are you looking for?"

"Oh, wait now, you shouldn't be bothered with those kinds of things."

In spite of her resolve to stay put, she sat up straight.

"Hold the phone, Mr. Mitchell. Are you saying something sexist like this is man's business?"

"No, of course not—"

"Yes you are!"

"No I'm not. I just don't want to put you in the middle. I mean, I don't want what business I do with your cousin or your uncle to influence our relationship one way or the other," Max said.

"Well, that's stupid."

"Really? Why?"

"Because I hate secrets, that's why."

"Ah, and you see, I think secrets add to the mystery of life. Why don't we check on that soup?" he said.

By the time they were seated at the table, it was dark. Beth lit the candles in the clear glass hurricanes that seemed to live in perpetuity on the dining room table and put on some music. All the doors and windows were open and the salty damp smells of the beach at night were all around them. The ocean seemed so close that if you closed your eyes you might have thought you were having dinner among the dunes, sheltered from the elements by huge mounds of sand instead of four walls. A chicken soup dinner just didn't get any sexier than this, Beth thought.

They tore the baguette into pieces and put them in a sweet grass basket, resting inside a folded linen napkin. Beth put together a salad from what she could find, dressing it with a simple mixture of olive oil, salt, and lemon juice. Max added a handful of thin soup noodles to cook while he removed the chicken meat from the bones and returned it to the broth. To them dinner looked like something from a professional kitchen.

"We should take a picture of this," Beth said. "It all looks amazing, especially your soup."

"And I was just thinking the same thing about your salad. And you."

Gone was all the sarcasm of the night before. This Max, Beth thought, is the one I like so very much. The nice one. The thoughtful one. The one who wanted to take care of her, who told her to forget the dishes and took her by the hand to the sofa. And then to her grandmother's bedroom. And later to the guest room where Woody had slept. And finally to her bedroom . . .

11

Afterglow

Susanthepen@writenow.org
Maggie, I know this is stupid, but I had the most awful nightmare last night. I dreamed Beth was trying to dig her way out of a hole and it was like not night or day but something like the middle of the night on a full moon and it was raining. She was stuck in this big hole and couldn't get out and back in the house. What to do? Should I call Cecily?

Maggiepie2@marthagene.net
If that was my kid, I'd call my kid. Call Beth! You'll feel better! xx

Midmorning on Tuesday, her bedroom door creaked open inch by inch, like a haunted house in an amusement park, and there stood Cecily. Unfortunately for

Beth, she was discovered without a stitch of clothes and barely covered by a sheet.

"Mmm, mmm, mmm," Cecily said. "Did I miss the party or what?"

Beth sat up with a jolt. "Oh gosh! What time is it? Where's Lola? Where're my clothes?"

"It's nine-fifteen on Tuesday and this is planet Earth. Don't worry. I walked my furry little niece. She's in the kitchen, having breakfast."

"Breakfast?"

"Um-hmm. I made her some toast. But honey chile? Your clothes are flung all over the living room, your grandmomma's room, and the steps. For a minute I thought she came back to kick up a little dirt, but when I saw your panties on the—"

"Oh no! I gotta get up. Did he leave?"

"Who?"

"Max! Who else?"

"Well, well, well. So, what do you know? Yeah, he's gone."

"He had to go to work. Right. Work." The world began to come into focus for her. "Okay, thanks for waking me up. I'll be down in the kitchen in ten minutes."

Cecily closed the door slowly and quietly, and as Beth caught her expression, there was no estimating the effort Cecily was exerting to hold back some mighty laughter. Beth didn't blame her. She was so busted, but strangely, Beth didn't care one whit. Now if her Aunt Maggie had burst in with steaming hot biscuits on a breakfast tray with a bud vase, Beth would have leapt from the window stark naked and hid in the oleanders. If her mother had knocked briskly and then opened the door without waiting for a response, which was her habit, Beth would've had to pick her up from her dead faint on the floor and call EMS, and then put on a robe. But it was Cecily and Cecily could deal with truth.

Beth decided a hot shower was most definitely in order and turned on the water. She looked at her face in the mirror. Her lips were a little swollen and her mouth tasted pretty funky but these things were no surprise.

"I think we broke all the records," she whispered to no one but herself. "I'm a very bad girl. Very." Adding, "Why am I whispering?"

She had never felt better in her entire life and her Catholic guilt was nowhere to be found. She stood under the hot water for a full ten minutes reliving the night, and then she scrubbed from one end of herself to the other. While she toweled off and went through her normal routine of applying various products she still couldn't stop thinking about Max. What a night! What a glorious night! He had raised her up to the maximum thrill via undisclosed locations! And she thought she had certainly fed his flame very well. Remembering the sounds he made and the things he said to her last night caused some gyrations, tingles, and tiny tsunamis in various muscle groups. She would never forget how it was. Making love to a man was very different from making love to a boy. Boys thought every movement beyond straight missionary was a personal victory for them, but men went for broke very differently. If she never slept with Max again, at least she would have the memory. And a new benchmark.

"So?" Cecily said when Beth came into the kitchen. Cecily was putting their dirty dishes from last night into the dishwasher.

"So what? You don't have to do that! I'll do it!"

"Whatever. Would you like to tell me what happened here last night?"

"No. Absolutely not. But basically Max thought I was sick so he came over and made me chicken soup." Beth poured herself a mug of coffee and pulled out a plastic container from a cabinet to store the rest of the soup, which she hoped wouldn't give her salmonella from sitting on the stove all night.

"And why did he think you were sick?"

"Because I threw up Sunday night from shellfish."

"Gross."

"You have no idea."

"How bad?"

"Bad. I hurled all over him." Beth's eyes twinkled in laughter.

"Lord have mercy!" Cecily covered her mouth with her hands in revulsion and laughter. "How can you laugh?"

"Gallows humor. I gave him a clean shirt from Uncle Grant's stash."

"He'll never miss it. He left a ton of stuff here. Well, heavenly days! How was the soup?"

"Like a miracle drug."

They were giggling, shaking their heads at each other and pointing fingers.

"Girl? Your momma would beat your behind!"

"Girl? My momma ain't here! You had breakfast? I could eat a horse!"

"Nah, I'm good. I had some yogurt. What does your week look like, I'm afraid to ask?"

"My week? Who cares? I'm in love, Cecily. Totally and completely in love. I swear, I'm gonna marry this man and have his babies."

Cecily gasped and her eyes grew large.

"*Come on! What?* Just *what* are you saying? Oh no. How in the world could you possibly know this?"

"All kidding aside? Because I feel it here," Beth said. Her hand over her heart and her dewy eyes left no doubt about her sincerity or conviction. "Aren't you the one who said when you meet *the one,* you'll know? Well, he's the one! I knew it! Didn't I tell you?"

"Yeah, but honey, I've met *the one* about twenty-five times and been wrong about twenty-five times. Maybe more, with all the back-and-forth fool I put up with."

"Come on! I'm serious!"

"I know. So am I! Oh me. Look, Beth, just because he's, well, really sexy and can make a mean pot of soup doesn't mean he'd make a good husband. Or a good father. You don't even know who he is! Don't go giving your heart away like this. It's too precious! And it's too soon!"

Beth snapped the lid on the plastic tub and opened the refrigerator door, looking for an empty spot.

"I really have to throw out some stuff," she said, and jammed the container in between the milk, the juice, and all the beer Mike and his friends had left behind. She closed the door and leaned against it, folding her arms across her chest. "Look, Cecily. You know I appreciate your advice and all, but I'm telling you, Max Mitchell is the man I've been dreaming about since I was just a little girl. He's gorgeous, he's brilliant, he's tenderhearted, and I don't know what else I could want in a man. I mean, he's perfect. Um, really perfect. I look at him and the rest of the world just fades away. Gone! Poof! Nothing else matters."

"Then you'd better get busy finding out absolutely everything about him that you possibly can. That *till death do us part* thing can be a very long time. Besides, I don't want to see you get hurt."

Beth knew that Cecily was right and she was loath to admit that all she knew about Max could fit in a thimble, if you didn't count how he was in bed. Anyway, she thought, how would I go about getting information about Max's history? One of those Internet companies who did background checks for a fee? She thought for a moment and then said to herself, Wait! Wasn't he trying to get her Uncle Henry to invest in his business? So wouldn't there be some kind of paperwork that Uncle Henry would have to look at to get the details of the deal—like a prospectus or something? Uncle Henry wouldn't give a nickel to anyone without knowing every single solitary rotten thing there was to know about them, probably down to their federal income tax returns, their driving record, and even their golf handicap. Brilliant! She would call him. No, she couldn't do that. That would be too strange and he would ask too many questions. She would call Mike. No, wait! Bad idea. He would blab it all over the world. She would call

Woody. Yes! Woody would keep his mouth shut and she really didn't want the news of her liaison with Max traveling the family wires. Not yet anyway.

"I gotta go," Cecily said. "I'm praying for this to be a case of severe infatuation. Love is fatal, you know."

"Listen to you! You're such a Debbie Downer today."

"For good reason."

As soon as Cecily was gone she finished cleaning the kitchen and dialed Woody's cell phone. He answered right away.

"Beth?"

"Yep! Hey! It's me."

"Wow! How nice to hear your voice! I had such a great time visiting with you. Sullivans Island is really awesome."

"Yeah! It was fun for me too! So y'all got back okay, I guess?"

"I was going to write you a note first thing this morning but I am so swamped here you wouldn't believe what's on my desk. Piles of stuff. Mike didn't call you yet?"

"No, the miserable dog didn't call me, but I figured that if you all got creamed in a wreck I would've seen it on CNN or something."

"Right. Well, we got back fine. Traffic was pretty intense as soon as we got close to the city, but that's normal. So what's going on?"

"What's going on? Uh, well, let's see. Well? I sort of need a small favor if it's not too big of a deal and isn't going to violate any major laws."

She told Woody that she wanted to know if Max had pitched her uncle to invest in his deal. And, would it be possible to find out something about his background? Woody was quiet for a moment, trying to understand why she was asking the question.

"Is that it?" Woody asked. "That's the whole favor?"

"That's it."

"Well, that's no big deal. I don't know what we'll discover but I can sure let you know if there's anything suspicious in his financial affairs. It would be highly unusual for him to disclose anything about his personal life beyond a basic résumé."

"Thanks, Woody. You're the best."

"No problem. Glad to help."

As soon as Beth hung up, and as if she could smell skunk in the international ethers, the house phone rang and it was Beth's mother, Susan.

"Bonjour, ma petite! Ça va?"

"Hey, Mom! I can't believe you called me! What's going on?"

"Well, if I eat one more pain au chocolat I'm going to explode!"

"Oh, sure! If I know you, you're washing them down with French wine!"

"By the magnum! Not really. Seriously, it's going great, but I miss you and I just had to hear your voice!"

"I miss you too! Hey! Are you coming home for Thanksgiving?"

"Well, you know they don't celebrate that over here, so it's not a holiday. I was actually planning to come home for Christmas."

"Excellent!"

"Anyway, I am calling you, and I know you're going to tell me you think I'm crazy—"

"Who me? Although I do have the safety of distance . . ."

"Smarty-pants! I had this dream last night that you were, well, it wasn't such a good dream. I just wanted to hear you tell me that you're okay."

"I am fine, Mom. Really truly. I'm fine."

"Really truly?"

"Yeah, really truly. Why? What did you dream?"

"That some crazy animal was chasing you. I don't know. It sounds stupid when you tell it, just like most dreams do."

"No animal here except Lola and she's practically human."

Beth could hear her mother's sigh of relief and she sighed too, realizing then how terribly she missed her. Beth had always been, in some cosmic way, a kind of extension of her mother. She was her own person to be sure, but there was no one else on earth and never would there be anyone else on earth that understood her heart as completely and with such compassion as her mother did. And she was the same for Susan. Beth could feel her eyes welling up with tears. I'm such a wreck lately, she thought, get a grip!

"I wish you were here with me, baby. There's so much to see and to do and to learn. Paris is just mind-boggling. But I miss the island and I miss my girl."

"Well, it's hot as hell here so you're not missing a thing. Big mosquitoes. Thunderstorms wild enough to scare the liver out of you. Nothing has changed."

"Please don't say the H word," Susan said in her Mother Superior voice. "Say *the bells of hell* or *heck* or something else like *hot as the devil.*"

"Yeah, okay." Susan giggled. "Gosh, you sound great! So is Simon coming to see you? How's he doing out there in Barbie-land?"

"Must you remind me about all the babes in California right while I am preparing to devour an entire wedge of melted Brie with stewed apricots? I guess he's fine. We talk for a minute or two every other day. I miss him a lot too. I think he's coming over for a long weekend. We're supposed to go to Provence."

"Gosh, that sounds nice."

"If it happens it will be! But that's a big trip to make for a long weekend. Every-one's so darn busy. Hey, how did your weekend with Mike and his friends go?"

"How did you know about that?"

"Email. Maggie's all teched up with a new laptop and she sends me prayer chain letters and advice every five minutes."

"I'll bet you love that! Next thing you

know she'll be on Facebook spying on everyone. Well, Mike's completely insane but we had a lot of fun."

"And his friends?"

"They were cool. He brought this girl who's dumb as a post, but then he likes his women like that."

"Should I ask the delicate question?"

Beth knew this was about sleeping arrangements.

"Not unless you want to know the answer. Mike is twenty-six, you know."

"Well, for God's sake, if your Aunt Maggie asks, lie like a cheap rug, okay?"

"No problem. Heaven forbid that any-one's adult children have a sex life."

"What is that supposed to mean?"

"Everybody except me, Mom. Don't worry! I'll wear white with a clean con-science!"

"Of course you will! Okay, I'd better get going. I love you, Doodle!"

"Love you too, Mom! Have fun!"

Beth sank to a kitchen chair and started feeling melancholy. She missed her mother and wished she was on the island with her. She would know what to do about Max and how to handle everything. But this was part of growing up, she told herself. It was normal and natural to have a life separate from your parents. To have to do things you didn't want to do. To make real sacrifices. To keep secrets from your mother so she wouldn't worry. Besides, there was nothing to worry about. She had met a wonderful man and he was crazy about her too. At least in the dark. But was he wonderful and did he really care about her, or was he (Dear God, please don't let this be true and I'll never ask you for another thing. Thank you, God. Amen) just fishing for her uncle's support?

All the while Beth sat there, deep in thought, and Lola was positioned right at her feet, mewing like a cat.

"Okay. Come on, Lola. Let's go for a stroll."

Lola's nearly undetectable tail twitched like crazy and she barked in approval knowing exactly what Beth proposed. Somehow, Beth thought, dogs knew exactly how to snap you out of a gloomy mood. All the more reason that everyone should have a dog. They were furry Prozac.

They began their walk by passing Fort

Moultrie. It had rained, sprinkled really, and the grass was cool and moist. Lola was so happy to have some time alone with Beth and to be outside again that she almost hopped along the path.

"I forgot my cell phone! Oh, so what? Right, Lola?"

Lola looked up at her as if to say, Please! Can we just have a little peace and quiet here?

It was a gorgeous day with huge white cumulus clouds moving along the brilliant blue sky and the sun was bursting through them in streams of light. Getting outside was good for Beth too. There were things she needed to do and walking Lola gave her a chance to clear her head and organize her thoughts. What was the next article she would write for the *Island Eye News*? She had no idea. What would people say about the one she had written? Probably nothing. What would Woody find out about Max from her Uncle Henry? She couldn't wait to hear. What was Max doing that minute? Was he thinking of her? She was certainly thinking about him.

She and Lola just ambled along, Beth stopping every few feet to allow Lola to indulge in what seemed like thousands of sniffs. Every time they passed a squirrel Lola almost broke her leash, attempting to go after it. She was bred to be a ratter, after all. But Beth would say, No, no, Lola, you can't waste your life chasing squirrels, and after saying that six or more times, she wondered if the same rule somehow applied to her.

She had her dream and that was to write. Not poetry, not historical fiction or historical anything. She wasn't drawn to mysteries or thrillers or children's books, although children's books were probably one of the most interesting categories to her. How wonderful it would be to pen a classic that children all over the world would remember as a cherished part of their childhood. When she was a little girl she had loved all the Madeline books, and the Amelia Bedelia and Amber Brown series and of course everything Judy Blume ever wrote. Later on she had devoured almost any book she could lay her hands on, lying on a sofa in their old house downtown or in a hammock at Aunt Maggie's. They were mostly old classics or *Reader's Digest* condensed novels whose pages were speckled with mildew from the pervasive damp. It didn't matter. She loved to read so much she even read cereal boxes.

For years books had been her world. It was no surprise, really. Her mother worked at the Charleston County Library, and she was always bringing her armloads of new reading material. And libraries were such a wonderful thing, she thought. The very idea that you could wander through thousands of books and just choose whatever you wanted to read. As a child she felt a great responsibility to take care of those borrowed books so that another child might find them in good condition. Later on, she began to leave her opinions of the books on notepaper, tucked in between the pages where only the most diligent of librarians might discover them. Sometimes her feelings about a story and how it was written were scathing, and sometimes she couldn't stop singing the praises of the heroine or hero and, on occasion, the author. Did that mean she might consider a life of literary criticism? She would find out when she got to Iowa, she told herself. But first, she wanted to try to write her own stories, stories of the ilk she liked to read and of which there were too few in the marketplace. So far, she had written zilch except for one article for the paper.

But maybe she would write about falling in love. It was certainly the most powerful thing that had ever happened to her. It changed her worldview in almost an instant. Love wasn't syrupy, like the cynics and the lonely said. She knew because she had been both and never even realized it. Love was nothing less than miraculous. For the first time in her life, she woke up looking forward to the day with unbridled happiness, instead of dreading all she had to do. Every day was going to be a priceless gift. There was everything to look forward to in her future. She felt like at long last, life was worth all the trouble.

How she would reconcile her love for Max and two years of graduate school a thousand miles away remained a mystery, but considering herself to be from that moment forward a believer in destiny, she knew that unfortunate geographic detail would work itself out too. Finally, she understood what it meant when her mother said, *If it's meant to be, then it will be.* Actually for the first time, she understood many things that had seemed like so much nonsense to her all her life. She was seriously connected at the heart with another person and it was all-consuming. She could barely have a thought without him in it in one way or another. For the rest of her life and she was sure of it, Max would inform everything she said, did, or wanted to do with her life. And for the tiniest second, she allowed herself to wonder what it would feel like to have his child in her womb. Wait a minute! Pregnant?

"Whoa, Lola! Your momma is putting the cart before the horse!"

That was one of many old maxims her mother would use when Beth was getting ahead of herself. And intellectually she knew that one insane night spent with Max in one, well, three beds, did not yet constitute a whole life together. But another part of her wished it did.

When she returned home there were two missed calls on her cell phone, one from Max and the other was from Woody. Naturally, she called Max first.

"Hello, gorgeous!" he said.

Beth's brain turned into mush for a moment until she found the spunk to say, "Excuse me, but you're the gorgeous one!"

"Let's not argue over this."

He chuckled and she sighed.

"Okay. We'll settle it another time. How's your day going?"

"Unbelievably busy. Want to have dinner?"

"Absolutely. A girl's gotta eat, right?"

Boy, that was a really stupid reply, she thought. How about, Love to, Max! Can't wait to see you again, Max! Or just, What a wonderful idea, Max! Would she ever learn to be just a little clever? Just a dollop of demure, please?

"Right, gotta feed the body. Pick you up at seven?"

"Sounds great."

They hung up and it took Beth several minutes to come out of her happy stupor and remember that she was to return Woody's call as well.

She dialed his number.

"Hey! It's Beth. Sorry I missed you."

"No problem. How are you?"

"Good. What's the scoop? Did you find out anything?"

"Yeah, the deal is that Henry isn't interested in investing. He says it's just not the kind of thing he does. Flat-out not interested."

"Oh."

"Yeah. I mean, for what it's worth, I told him I thought it was a terrific deal, that I had met Max, liked him, and thought it was, you know, even in this economy, a good place to put some money. He's much more interested in this bus company he's been looking at. It's been a going concern for decades and makes money year after year."

"Does he think that Max's project is too high-risk or something?"

"No, he didn't even say that. The whole thing is just outside of his comfort zone. He only puts the firm's money in a certain type of profile, one that he's really familiar with. You know, where he understands the upside and the downside and all the things that can go wrong. Actually, I understand that because I actually invest for myself in the same way but in other kinds of deals. I like telecommunications and he likes bus companies. What can I tell you?"

"Wow. Okay. So I'm assuming there was nothing else about Max that came up."

"Nope, just that it was a no-go. There was no reason to begin due diligence. But again, I think Henry is making a big mistake. I've been to lots of beach towns along the coast and they all need a little bit of gentrification here and there. Certainly they need more conveniences."

"Yeah, well, I'm sure Max is going to be disappointed."

"Listen, I think the deal's such a home run that he won't have a problem finding other investors. Does he have a broker working on it? He should if he doesn't."

"Gosh, how would I know? I'll ask him."

"Well, FYI, let Henry make the call to tell him. It would seriously annoy him if you told Max before he got around to it."

"Yeah. No, don't worry. I'm seeing Max tonight for dinner but I'm not getting involved with Uncle Henry's business. Not me, honey! He's got a well-known short fuse. I've seen him blow more than once."

"We all have. Not pretty."

"That's for sure. Well, listen, thanks anyway . . ."

Beth hung up thinking Max was not exactly going to be thrilled to hear this news. She didn't know how badly he needed the money, but it never felt good to have someone say that your life's work isn't worth their serious consideration. In the least case, it would be a disappointment for him. At that moment, Beth did not think there was much she could do except to remain very upbeat and tell him not to worry, that is, if he chose to discuss it with her. She imagined that over the coming years, when they were married, there would be many occasions when she would have to listen to him and sympathize with his business struggles. That was what a good wife did, number one, because you cared, and number two, if a man couldn't open up to his wife, he would find someone else who would be more than happy to listen to the messy details of his trials and tribulations. She was so relieved that she had the time to think this through and to recognize that this was actually a test of her worth as a partner to him. If he decided to confide in her. Well, if he doesn't want to tell me about it, I will just have to pry it out of him, she thought.

Then her mind turned momentarily to Woody. Gosh, she thought, he has such a nice voice. And he's so logical.

She still had the entire afternoon ahead of her and the thought of making dinner for Max presented itself. She could grill a steak, bake a potato, and make a salad and he would probably like that a lot. Or, she could spend the time writing in her journal or perhaps she would try one of her Aunt Sophie's workouts just for the fun of it. Of all her options, the workout appealed to her the most. Maybe a little exercise would be good for her spirits. She had not looked at one of them since the first or second one had come out when she was still in high school, and she snickered to recall how easy they were.

An hour later, she was soaked in perspiration and in awe of her aunts. They were in some kind of fantastic shape and had some seriously daunting stamina especially considering their age. Mightily impressed, she dialed Aunt Sophie's number, got her voice mail, and left her a message.

"Heeeey! Here is your niece, Beth the Slug, half dead from doing your cardio

DVD. Just thought I'd tell you that I am dripping in sweat and very inspired by my aunts to shape up! Love y'all! Glad I didn't drop dead! How old are y'all anyway?"

Beth hoped Aunt Sophie would get a laugh out of that and call her back to chew the fat.

Late that afternoon, after her second shower of the day, Beth blew out her hair and dressed for her dinner with Max. She had decided that a restaurant was a much better idea than cooking for him. At least for that night. She'd had so much to clean up from the weekend and then from the chicken soup dinner and the Chinese bedroom fire drill that was last night that she was completely over the thought of washing one more dish or folding one more sheet. Maybe I can convince him to take me to Station 22 Restaurant, she thought.

By seven-thirty that night, Beth and Max moved from the bar area and sat opposite each other in a booth in the back of the restaurant. They sipped on vodka and tonics, after Bridget the dazzlingly pretty bartender checked Beth's driver's license and gave Max a hairy eyeball for the obvious reason. They held hands across the table while he nibbled and she devoured the hot cheese bread, waiting for their appetizers to arrive. Beth had ordered a special salad and Max, mindful of passing along a shell-fish allergic reaction with even one kiss, ordered the duck quesadillas. They were both having steaks, medium rare.

As far as Beth was concerned there was not one other person there in the restaurant except them. But every other minute Max's eyes scanned the room. His inattention bothered her but it wasn't worth making an issue of it. She didn't want to be That Nag and she guessed he had spoken to her Uncle Henry, who probably dropped the no-money bomb.

"Uh, should we ask for more bread?" Max held up the empty basket for her to see.

On a sarcasm scale of one to ten, his tone of voice was a seven, but he was smiling, which was confusing to her.

"Oh goodness! I ate way more than my share, didn't I?"

"It's okay."

"Are you angry with me for some reason?"

"No, why?"

"You seem cranky."

406 DOROTHEA BENTON FRANK

"No, I just had a tough day, that's all."

"Sorry I woofed all the bread."

"Forget it. It's okay. You can afford it. You still have that girlish metabolism."

"Please. I worked out this afternoon to one of my aunt's videos and almost keeled."

"Really?"

"Yeah, really. I have to stay in shape, especially with you around."

Max's mood seemed to brighten then. "Yeah, you'd better. Your aunts have a phenomenal business, don't they?"

"Yeah. They're always on the go trying to catch up with themselves."

"I know what that's like."

"Right? Me too. So, tell me all about your tough day. What happened?"

"Don't make me relive it." He took a long sip of his drink, swirled the ice around to gather the rest of the liquid for one last swallow, and drained the glass. "Would you like another cocktail or do you want to order a bottle of wine?"

"Whatever you think is okay with me. I could just have a glass of something with my steak if you don't want to get a whole bottle."

"Let me look at the wine list again. Okay, here's a South American red that's supposed to be pretty good."

He gave the universal signal—one raised forefinger combined with a nod—to the manager, and because he caught her eye, she came right over to the table.

"What can I get for y'all?"

"We're thinking wine? How's this Argentinean Malbec?"

"Very popular. It's the chef's favorite. Personally, I like this California Merlot here. Lots of plum and blackberry." She pointed to the list. "It's only four dollars more but it's about twice as good, but that's just my opinion."

"Well, I think we should go with your opinion. Why not? We'll have the Merlot."

"Thanks. I'll get that for you right away."

"What's your name?"

"Jesse."

"Well, thanks, Jesse."

"You're welcome. The sommelier is off tonight." Before she walked away, she winked at Beth and Max.

"I love that. A manager of a busy place like this and she still has a sense of humor. Amazing," Max said.

"Because it takes a gigantic sense of humor to run a restaurant, lemme tell you."

"I'm sure you're right about that."

"So, Max? Are you going to tell me what's going on or what? Something is definitely wrong here. You seem like totally wigged-out."

"I'm okay."

"No you're not. You seem very distracted. You can tell me. C'mon."

Max sighed hard and cocked his head to one side.

"Well, for one thing, your uncle took a pass on my deal without even really looking at it."

"Oh no! He did? Gosh, that's awful! Did he say why?" Beth thought she said that convincingly enough, without giving any signal that she already knew the story.

"Oh, it's okay. It wasn't personal. He just doesn't do commercial real estate deals. You know, in the investment world, everyone has their areas of expertise and this just isn't his."

"I don't know what all Uncle Henry invests in."

"Well, he probably doesn't want any risk right now."

"Yeah, all you read in the papers is that this company is closing and that one is closing . . . it's bad."

"Yeah, but it's not fatal, you know? This is when people with faith in themselves can really rake it in."

"Yeah."

"I'm not offended or anything but it's a very big disappointment because I really thought it would be a no-brainer, especially for a man like him."

"Oh, gosh, that's not right. It just seems so stupid. I mean, the country is in like this huge flipping mess, disasters in the stock markets, and here's a sure thing, right?"

"Well, yeah. Exactly! It's absolutely a sure thing or I wouldn't have all my money riding on it. And the way I have this structured, it is a very good deal for investors. First, there's a rapid payback. Then there's a percentage of ownership and buyout at the end of five years."

"Really? How rapid is a rapid payback?"

"Six months at the most."

"Wow. That doesn't seem like such a big risk then, does it?"

"It's not. It's hardly a risk at all."

"And what's the percentage of ownership?"

"That depends on the level of commitment, right?"

"Right." Beth had no idea what the correlation might be between commitment and percentage of ownership but it made sense to her somehow. "So what would be a healthy commitment?"

"Anything more than a hundred thousand."

"Wow." That seemed like a fortune to her, but when she considered all that was going into the building, maybe it wasn't so much.

Their waiter put their appetizers in front of them and Beth ate hers as though she was starving. It seemed that Max had awakened all sorts of appetites in Beth, and watching her eat made him shake his head and smile.

"I never knew a salad could be so delicious!" she said. "Do you want a bite? This fried goat cheese is unbelievable."

"No thanks, I'm happy with this. Do you want a quesadilla? It's pretty good too."

"Sure!"

Max offered her a steaming forkful of

his food and Beth allowed him to feed it to her, her eyes never leaving his. Of course, he had given her too much for one mouthful, so with her hand over her mouth she had to go through some grimacing and interesting exercises in mastication to make it disappear.

"Good?" he asked.

She bobbed her head up and down, grinning with enthusiasm for the small bite of a tortilla stuffed with a few shreds of seasoned duck meat. She loved it so much when he fed her she would have believed it was manna.

"Oh yeah," she said emphatically. "I could eat a whole lot of that before I got sick of it."

"Let's not talk about getting sick, if it's okay with you?"

"Oh, shoot, I'm never going to live that down, am I?"

"Sorry, but probably not."

"Nice."

Although Max said *Sorry, but probably not* in a pleasant enough way and with a large grin, she didn't think it was such a nice thing to say. Truly, no gentleman and most of all no genteel son of the South should ever remind a lady of something so devastating and humiliating. It was best to let those kinds of demoralizing incidents go to their eternal rest as quickly as they could take flight.

That one uncertain moment left the possibility of romantic disingenuousness in Beth's heart, but Beth decided to erase it from her mind. He had been on the receiving end of some very bad news that day and he was understandably moody. Beth reassured herself that no man could make love with the tenderness and simultaneous wild abandon of Max Mitchell and not truly care about his partner. The very thought that he didn't feel great affection for her seemed absolutely absurd.

They worked their way through their steaks and then shared a piece of Station 22's trademark coconut cake and at long last Beth wanted no more to eat. The conversation had shifted away from Max's problems, and the more wine he consumed the more their thoughts traveled to the bedroom.

Throughout dinner Max would say things like *Remember last night?* And she would blush and say *I loved it.*

As he poured out the last of the wine, he looked around to see if anyone was listening and then whispered something naughty. *Just wait until I get you in bed later.*

Beth swallowed hard and whispered back to him, *Remember Mae West said, I'll try anything once, twice if I like it, and three times to make sure.*

Max ran his hand through his hair and said, "I think it's time for the check."

After a dinner of titillating innuendo, the rest of the evening did not play out as Beth had hoped and expected it would. It was only nine when they left the restaurant and returned to the Island Gamble. Max, who was cruising through all the channels on the television and drinking a bottle of water, seemed mildly uninterested in rushing to the bedroom, which surprised and disappointed her. But while she walked Lola, she told herself this might be another difference between guys her age and Max. Perhaps older men saw no reason to rush toward the inevitable. They would get to the bedroom before the night was over; she was certain of that. Or, she thought, since it was really too early to go to sleep for the night, maybe he didn't want to undress, fool around, get dressed, undress again to sleep with her, fool around some more, and then get up somewhere in the middle of the night, dress yet again, and slip out in the dark before she would know he was leaving. It would be too much dressing and undressing, and just as a practical matter, they should wait until ten-thirty or so. Or maybe he was worn out from the night before. Even she was still somewhat fatigued and he probably was too. She told herself not to pressure him to hop in the sack and then expect crazy energetic sex all night. Somewhere around her sixth or seventh rationalization of why he wasn't all over her she started feeling insulted. Exactly why *wasn't* he all over her?

By the time she went back in the house, gave Lola a treat, and put her back in her crate, she had worked herself into a respectably sized hissy fit.

He was half asleep watching an old movie. She stood between him and the television screen with her hands on her hips and said, "Max?"

"What? You're blocking the screen."

"Max! Do you want to screw or what?"

Max sat up straight, looked up at her, opened his eyes wide, burst out laughing, and said, "Did I hear you right?"

"Yes! Now just tell me! Yes or no!"

"What red-blooded male in his right mind would say no to that? Come with me!"

Max led her upstairs to her room and thus ensued the shortest time spent in a sexual act in recorded human history, including the infamous Masters and Johnson studies. While Max immediately fell into a deep sleep and snored and snorted like something from deep within the forest primeval, Beth, in a state of very specific dissatisfaction, told herself that Momma was right when she sang that old Supremes song from the sixties. *You can't hurry love.*

12

Bank on It

Susanthepen@writenow.org
Maggie, Had a dream about Livvie last night. We were shopping together, can't remember the details but she was awfully happy about something. I love when I dream about her.

Maggiepie2@marthagene.net
Susan? Think there's a connection between Beth and Cecily running around together and how we never could have done that with Livvie unless we were babies still in a carriage? Times have changed.

Susanthepen@writenow.org
I went shopping with her all the time. Where were you? With Lucius on the porch? xx

Beth spent the better part of the next morning wondering about two things. The lesser issue was this: Exactly how did Max pull off another David Copperfield and disappear from her bed in the middle of the night without her knowing it? She never even felt one hair rise from the mattress whenever it was that he got up to leave. And the other infinitely more important question was, How was she going to save Max from financial peril so that he would love her forever?

Truly? In her brief years, Beth had learned that *nothing* was forever. The blissful periods of her life had been so very fleeting and the dark ones slogged on through a tar pit, only seeming like they might last an eternity, but neither bliss or despair ever did. This new joy would surely pass, or maybe it wouldn't, if she could cement things. Her immediate mission was to seize the happiness that was her love for Max and ride that wave the whole way to the beach. In any case, these were excellent questions that women have pondered since the whole cosmic misunderstanding about the apple in the Garden and that stupid snake. To where do men disappear and how do we hang on to the good ones?

After she showered and dressed, she walked Lola, apologizing for tossing her bahunkus in her crate the previous night and just abandoning her to satisfy, or to attempt to satisfy, her own carnal needs. Lola was either in a forgiving mood, had no memory of the event, or was just happy to be outside taking in all the smells of the world, because Beth could detect nothing untoward in Lola's attitude. It was difficult to tell with dogs, even those believed to be partly human.

Later, while munching on a breakfast of low-fat blueberry yogurt, one half of a toasted dry English muffin, and coffee, she came to the conclusion that there was one man and only one man who could have a reasonable solution. Woody. And if not him, Aunt Sophie might be able to help her sort out the whole problem. It made her nervous because even in her state of almost utter delusion she knew there were serious dangers in enlisting their help. One involved getting the actual money, and the other public exposure. She didn't want her

whole family to know anything about Max
yet and Aunt Sophie might let it slip. And
she wasn't positive she could secure the
funds to help Max either. But she was feeling very desperate to seal her relationship
with Max. That was what mattered most.
But since she knew she could not do this
on her own, there was no other path but to
make a cautious move to seek advice and
help.

After she cleaned up the kitchen and
fed Lola, she ran upstairs and dialed
Woody's direct office number.

"This is Woody Morrison." His voice
sounded hassled and hurried.

"Hey! It's Beth! Is this a good time to
talk? You sound busy."

"Uh, no. This is fine. Let me just close
my door. Hold on, okay?"

She could hear the squeak of his chair
as it rolled away from his desk, then the
heels of his shoes echoing as he took a
few steps, and last the door closing with a
profound click, creating a hushed sound.

"Okay, I'm back. So what's going on?"

"Hon, you need to get yourself a rug
and a can of WD-40."

"You're telling me? We're renovating the whole floor because of a huge leak from one of the upper floors. Everything around here is almost gutted to the bricks. No curtains, no carpet, they even took my plants out. Jackhammers and buzz saws screaming all day long—you can hardly hear yourself think."

"Good grief!"

"It's *so* bad that your uncle and all of the other partners went fishing for two weeks in Jackson Hole."

"Wow. Major bummer. Did you know we have a restaurant here named Jackson Hole? I went there the other night. It's pretty good." Except for the crab cake, she thought.

"No kidding. Well, we'll have to go there. Anyway, what's going on?"

"Well, I'm not so sure where to start but I've been thinking and I need your help."

"Sure. Shoot."

"Well, I keep thinking about Max's development project. And you were right, it's a phenomenal deal. I can't see anything wrong with it."

"Yeah, I still don't know why Henry

passed. I mean, I know what he said about it being out of his normal scope, but I'm thinking maybe it wasn't a big enough investment to get him excited. Even so, I still think he made a huge mistake to let it go."

"Exactly. I read the papers and I see what's happening out there. There are so few opportunities to make any real money in a short period of time."

"Boy, is that the truth! Can somebody bring back the MasterCard IPO? Ah, the good old days."

Beth was completely uninformed about the MasterCard IPO. Most likely she had been buried in a library studying for a test or writing a paper.

"Then there's another thing that has been rattling around in my mind."

"What's that?"

"My own trust. It's not exactly earning what it has in the past."

"Is that so? Hold on, I'll pull it up on my screen. What's your Social Security number?"

Beth rattled if off to him and Woody typed it into his database.

"Okay, let's see what we have here."

"Humph. What you've got there is a bunch of stuff that is totally uninteresting to me, and the rest of it? I don't even know what it is, much less understand how it all works anyway."

"That's why you have me, Miss Hayes. Okay, okay. Here's the scoop. Last year you earned about ten percent. The same thing goes for the prior, uh, one, two—four years. This year you're going to be down by about thirty-five percent, but so is the rest of the world. Not too bad."

"Wait a second here. My earnings are off thirty-five percent and that's a good thing? Could you explain that to me?"

"Sure. First of all, there's this darn recession. There are some real pessimists out there who say that by year's end we're going to be in a hole like we haven't seen in decades. First, it was housing and then it was Detroit, right?"

"And? What's that got to do with me?"

"Well, it's like dominoes. A guy in the auto industry loses his job. Then he can't afford his mortgage, so he loses his house. On and on it goes. People aren't shopping, going to movies, restaurants, traveling—nobody's spending money."

"Trickle-down disaster. I know. I know. Bor-ing!"

"Exactly. But true. Retail chain stores, entertainment, hotels, et cetera . . . all those industries are impacted and the values of their stocks go down. Look, Beth, I don't think you have to worry. Your portfolio is half equities and half debt, which is the classic way to invest a trust like yours. And it's a good mix of different kinds of things. Foreign markets, domestic municipalities, and so on. So this year you earn a little less? It's not catastrophic. We'll make it up."

"But I have no say-so about any of this. Zero! Zilch! Nada! And it's *my* money. I could be going down the tubes and I can't do a thing to stop it."

"Are you saying you don't trust your broker?"

"No! Of course not!"

"Well, FYI, your uncle is the one who chose what to invest you in. I'm just watching the markets and keeping an eye on the account. If you want I can have him call you."

Beth could feel a frost descending into the conversation, and that was the last thing she wanted.

"Oh, Woody. I'm not blaming you for anything. In fact, I'm pretty sure I should be thanking you for something if I knew what you were talking about. I'm just frustrated. I see this perfectly wonderful opportunity to make a ton of money and I can't do it because I have no power over my own life."

"You mean Max's deal?"

"Yeah. And you agree with me, right?"

"Look, I didn't really dig into it to see any downside, but on the surface? Yeah, I already told you. I think it's a great chance to make some serious money. I wonder how much you have to spend to get in the game?"

"I'm not sure of all the details and it doesn't matter anyway. I can't do anything about it."

"Well, actually, you can."

"What do you mean?"

"You could actually borrow some money against your capital."

"You mean, like get a loan and use my trust like for collateral or something like that?"

"Exactly. In your case, you'd have to get

your mother to sign off on it. But, yeah, you'd go to the bank and get a loan."

"Really. Any old bank?"

"Well, I'd recommend using a well-known bank. Bigger banks make more loans. It would be less complicated and probably faster."

"Gosh." Beth was quiet for a few seconds and then she said, "So, Woody?"

"Yeah?"

"Can you help me figure this out?"

"Of course."

"What are you doing this weekend?"

"Why? Is this an invitation?"

"Yeah! Pack your calculator and a bathing suit, come spend the weekend, and help me figure this out. I have to work at night but we can hang out during the day?"

"That sounds like a great idea. I'll pay Max Mitchell a visit or two and get more details. We can discuss our entrepreneurial possibilities on that porch. God, I love that porch. When you get home Friday night we'll grab a glass of wine and make a plan."

"Oh, Woody, that would be wonderful. You are the best!"

"Thanks! Wait. If I wait till Friday to come I won't get to see the job site at work."

"So, can you come Thursday?"

"Much better idea. Not much doing here anyway with everyone gone. I'll take off early to beat the traffic and probably get there around six?"

"Great! If I'm not here I'll leave a key . . ."

He would find a key under the terracotta planter with the chipped ruffled lip containing an asparagus fern on the second-from-the-bottom step on the ocean side of the house. In case there were robbers lurking about, the obscure location would fool them all and save the family's generations of priceless treasures from being sold to pawnshops and traded in back alleys for drugs. (To date, this had never happened, but that didn't mean it could not. And there are no such alleys on Sullivans Island.)

"Easy enough. When I get there, I'll come down to the restaurant and eat at the bar."

"And be that Lonely Guy?" Beth found herself pulling on the phone cord and looking at the ceiling smiling and she wondered if she sounded like she was flirting.

She let go of the cord and stood up straight. After all, they were just friends and nothing more.

"Yeah, I'll try to look heartbroken and see what happens."

"You'll have the local talent drooling all over you, you know. I mean, Sullivans Island isn't Atlanta, but we have our own healthy quota of nympho-ho cougars on the prowl."

"One can always hope."

She knew he was smiling. "Ew. Dog." Beth giggled and they said goodbye.

Beth was upstairs in the second bedroom she was slowly converting to an office of sorts, which would never be photographed for an issue of *Architectural Digest,* that much was certain. The clutter alone would have made her Aunt Maggie twitch her way across the entire universe into eternity. But a few stacks of catalogs and opened bags of pretzels here and a pile of books, magazines, doggie accoutrements, and dirty laundry there didn't bother Beth, who was working away making a list of topics for possible pitches for the *Island Eye News.*

She thought she might write about the

scarcity of public parking and why that scarcity was a good thing. After all, she didn't want Sullivans Island or the Isle of Palms to become some horrible eyesore, with wildly overpopulated commercial areas. They would need more policemen to keep the peace, which would cause taxes to go up that would be a burden to older residents, and most important, it would destroy the serenity that made those islands so desirable in the first place. There was a growing lobby of merchants who wanted to grow their businesses but they couldn't serve their customers when there was no place for them to park. Beth saw them all as the enemy.

She continued to muse over the problems of the island lurching into the twenty-first century until Cecily came by the house to perform her weekly chores. She recognized the sound of Cecily's car as she pulled into the yard with its hum and then the solid thud of her car's door when she slammed it shut. There was something comforting about recognizing a familiar sound. Beth stood, began saving her work and closing down her computer.

Minutes later Cecily's voice called out. "Anybody home?"

"No! We've all gone to hell in a hand-basket!"

"Very funny! Hey! Want to hear some juicy, juicy stuff?"

"Who me? I'll be right there!"

Beth hurried down the stairs.

"Hey! I feel like I haven't seen you in a year or something!" She gave Cecily a light hug and a short triple pat on her shoulder blade.

"It's true!" Cecily returned the hug and the pats on Beth's back. "What are you up to? Although I'm almost afraid to ask."

"You should be! But wait! You were gonna give me a little dirt?"

"Oh, goodness! Yes! Okay, so last night I took myself to Rue de Jean downtown to meet this friend of mine who was late, late, late! And while I was waiting at the bar, this gorgeous man caught my eye. Next thing I know he says hello, my friend calls and cancels, I start talking to this guy and he starts trying to buy my love with sweet talk and champagne and—"

"Well, did he?"

"Now, what kind of a question is that?"

"I think he did!"

"Mmmm? You know it! His name is Niles, and lawsamercy, I think I might have to marry this one!"

"Cupid's in this Lowcountry air," Beth said with conviction. "I swear."

Over the next hour, they talked and laughed like old friends until Cecily pushed herself away from the table and reluctantly excused herself to do her work. It was not beyond their notice, although it was never mentioned between them, that Beth's grandmother and Cecily's grandmother could never have exchanged such a friendly hug in public or private, much less a conversation so personal in nature. They would have suffered a withering lecture from their peers and elders on the importance of knowing one's place in the world. If, heaven forbid, word of a friendship got around, they would have been branded as social pariahs. Liberals. Sympathizers of the wrong cause. Déclassé. Worse, and even more mysterious to Beth, was that their elders never would have understood why on earth they would *want* to be friends with each other. What was the point? They came from different worlds, after all, and their reference points for everything had nothing in common, did they? What possible useful intellectual exchange could there be? No, their different worlds were better kept separate, in the opinions of all those around them. Daily life was tidier that way, better and more reliably defined for everyone.

But this was not the case for Beth's mother. Susan was barely a teenager in 1963, coming of age herself, when the lines of demarcation started to blur. Generations of white supremacy, deep hatreds, morbid suspicions, and barriers of every kind began to dissolve. As all mothers do, Susan had told Beth countless stories of how it was when she was a child on the island, but her memories were vastly different from mothers who came from elsewhere in that many of them contained powerful images of segregation and the horrors of the civil rights movement which was happening all around them. And perhaps most important her grandmother's conflict over Susan's relationship with Livvie was never understood, much less valued as it should have been, or resolved.

No matter how many times Susan repeated the same stories, Beth could never quite grasp the conundrum that was her grandmother. M.C. turned her children over to Livvie's loving care like a litter of unwanted puppies and then tried to undermine the affection her children felt for Livvie through guilt and snide remarks. M.C. always wanted to know, how could her own flesh and blood love a housekeeper more than their own mother?

Perhaps it was her grandmother's own inability to cope with life that hindered her as a parent and the yet unchanged times opened the door for her to rationalize her resentments toward Livvie. M.C. was constantly startled by Livvie's innate intelligence as her parents had always said African Americans were not supposed to be so smart. She was intimidated by Livvie's straightforward manner. From where did a black woman gather the courage to be so outspoken? M.C.'s world, the shameful quagmire of her parents' manipulations and Big Hank's fury, was built of contradictions, insecurities, and ineptitude. Livvie's world was one of plain old-fashioned right and wrong.

Beth knew, as did her mother and all her aunts and uncles, that without the steadfastness of Livvie Singleton, they would never have become who they were. While Susan's mother was always scheming for a ploy to keep Susan home, Livvie was there to encourage Susan to reach for more, to hold her to a higher standard, to make her want to become all she could be. And Livvie did the same for every Hamilton child as though they were her own. Even today, as Beth thought about the haints that appeared to inhabit the Island Gamble from time to time, Livvie was still watching over them from the mirror, while her grandmother's alleged frustrations raged on, although that particular one had been reduced to a single episode of whispering in Phoebe's ear.

On her bad days, Beth would muse that perhaps that was exactly the sin her mother was committing by insisting Beth give up a year to house-sit. Perhaps those kinds of demands were genetic. Maybe her mother thought that Beth's wings were hers to clip. On better, happier days, Beth would tell herself that she was there not only to discover herself but also to discover the core meaning of the rest of the family and who they truly were. What did it mean to be a Hamilton?

Sometimes being a Hamilton meant keeping secrets, because Beth deliberately did not tell Cecily that Woody was coming for another visit or that she planned to find the money Max needed and lay it at his feet. Cecily would have broken out in a cold sweat and then collapsed to the floor in a coma.

On Cecily's departure, she called her Aunt Sophie and this time Aunt Sophie was raring to chat. She was driving from Coral Gables to Miami and moving slowly on the turnpike.

"Talk to me, sweetheart! I'm so stuck in traffic it's ridiculous."

"Well, first of all, did you get my message?"

"The one about you nearly dropping dead from doing my DVD workout? I laughed so hard! You think Al and I are a couple of old goats, don't you?"

"No, but whew! I could feel it the next day!"

"Well, that's how it's supposed to be, right?"

"Don't ask me. I haven't done that kind of exercise in ages! I guess I do wonder how you do it, though, to be honest."

"We can do it because we do it all the time. If I don't work out every day, it takes me maybe a week to get my stamina back. So how are you? How's that crazy island living going? And how's that man? What's his name?"

"Max. Max is good."

"Really? Great! So then, I gather things are going well?"

"Uh, yeah. We're becoming better friends every day."

Beth could hear her Aunt Sophie's sigh of relief and Beth's inner alarm pinged. For some reason that Beth could not explain, she knew that her aunt disapproved of Max. Sophie had never laid eyes on him or even heard his voice and she disapproved of him all the same. It was probably the age difference, which was understandable. Beth was very glad she'd had the presence of mind to refer to him as a friend and not the love of her life because it would have made the rest of her conversation all but impossible to have without becoming defensive.

"Well, that's good to hear. So there's no romance?"

"Good grief, Aunt Sophie!"

"I thought you were crazy about him. What happened?"

"Nothing. Nothing happened. What's a romance anyway?"

"I couldn't tell you, honey. My love life is a wasteland. Dry and dead like the Sahara. A nonexistent—"

"Oh, please. That's because you live on an airplane."

"Yeah, maybe that's why. So what's going on?"

"I just wanted to run something by you, that's all."

"Tell your auntie who loves you so! Tell me every little detail."

"Well, this same guy Max is the one who's putting up a new building where Bert's was? And he . . ."

She explained Max's project and the investment plan that Woody came up with to her aunt as calmly and maturely as she possibly could, even offering Sophie the chance to get in on the deal if she wanted to. Sophie listened carefully and asked a

lot of questions and finally declined to invest, saying that her money was all tied up
in the expansion of her own business.

In the end she said, "Look, sweetheart,
I'm not going to tell you what to do. You're
your own woman and one helluva lot
smarter than I was at your age. But I will
tell you this. First, I don't think you have
enough facts. I'm glad you invited this
Woody fellow down for the weekend because this is what he does for a living and
he'll know where to look for problems. Second, I would strongly urge you to discuss
this with your mother. She's the trustee,
isn't she?"

"Yeah."

"So you can't do this without her anyway, right?"

"Well, no, but I wouldn't. Mom and I talk
about everything. I mean, Aunt Sophie,
come on! I am an adult for Pete's sake!"

"Well, okay then . . ."

Beth hung up the phone and stood there
for a moment just looking at it. She had
begun to weave her tangled web. She had
lied to her aunt about the level of intimacy
in her relationship and she was going to

borrow money against her trust one way or another if it was the last thing she ever did. But, she told herself, her intimate life was no one's business. She realized that telling Aunt Sophie what the actual situation was would make her aunt remind her that sleeping with the investment is a monumental conflict of interest. So, she had merely withheld a detail and what was the matter with that? Nothing. And, as to her intention to rob a bank if necessary? She was going to rely on Woody and take things one step at a time. So far, she had done nothing more than explore the possibilities.

Max was coming to dinner at seven. Beth was going to cook something divine for him. She was going to tell him that Woody was coming back to Sullivans Island for the express purpose of looking further into his deal. She was going to seduce Max like nobody's business and he was going to be hers forever. It seemed like a doable plan.

Her menu was simple as her culinary skills had yet to take seed much less blossom. Shrimp cocktail, grilled steaks, baked potatoes, salad. She was capable of that much and knew what she had to do. Simmons Seafood was her first stop. She drove up to the Isle of Palms, winding around the island until she reached the shopping center of Simmons's new location. In that same small strip mall was a salon and for a brief moment she wondered if she should stop in and see if someone had time to blow out her hair. If there was one thing that women of the Lowcountry knew, it was that if you had thick hair prone to a frizzfest, a professional blowout was your savior. Your hair would look and feel like hair, not a wad of steel wool or a handful of feathers.

"I'm going for it," she said to no one, parked the car, and marched herself up to the door of Anna's Cabana like she went there every day.

Then she stopped. This was the place where Beth, her mother, and her Aunt Maggie came to have their hair done the day her mother married Simon. She wondered if the owner, Anna, was there and would remember her. That entire event began to rerun in her head as though it had just happened a week ago. What a day that had been! Some guy . . . what was his name? Eugene! Yes, Eugene had done her hair while Maggie and her mother had their hair and nails done by Anna and some hilariously funny woman from Brooklyn. She remembered drinking smoothies and cappuccinos and that they had laughed and laughed until they were giddy. Her mother had been distracted and nervous but who wouldn't be? Getting married was very serious business.

Somehow they got from the salon back to the house, which Maggie had decorated with more tulle and flowers than Beth had ever seen. And then they dressed for her mother's wedding. She wondered, how many girls could say they remembered getting dressed for their mother's wedding? Probably a great deal more than wanted to remember.

Susan had worn a very simple long gown and a small pillbox hat with an attached veil. In the golden light of that afternoon she looked more like Jackie Kennedy than Jackie Kennedy. Maggie wore a black dress and a triple strand of a very good quality of fake pearls, and if asked, she would tell you that if you squinted, she looked just like Grace Kelly. Didn't she? Beth was resigned to the fact that her mother was in love. But in her heart she was miserable because this act marked the end of any possibility that her mother and father would reunite. She wanted her mother to be happy and she didn't care if she had the wildest affair of the century with Simon. But marriage? How, then, could her father ever return? But she kept her feelings to herself and smiled, playing the role of the perfect daughter, because they were all each other had. Until then. Now everything would change. Now there would be another man. Simon. Beth only wished there was a quiet place where she could go and weep.

They had asked her what she would like to wear and she remembered that she had said that honestly it didn't matter. Aunt Maggie, who of course was in charge of every detail of the day and night, wanted her to wear something that would photograph well but was practical. They settled on a very plain dark green velvet gown that was shortened later to cocktail length. She had worn that dress so many times it had a shine where the nap had worn away. Maggie had been right as she usually was.

Beth had walked up the aisle with a smile plastered across her face. And her mother had married Simon with an even larger smile plastered across hers. And her father was never coming back. Beth thought she would never be able to find peace about it. But after her father passed away, his funeral an event she could barely recall for some strange reason, Beth was glad her mother was no longer alone. After all, Beth told herself, her mother was entitled to her choices, and one day, Beth was going to go live her life. Eventually.

But on that blistering hot day years later, as she stood in front of Anna's Cabana, the *eventually* seemed like light-years again.

She pushed open the door of the salon and walked to the small reception desk.

The middle-aged, Botoxed-within-an-inch-of-her-life, surgically-enhanced-in-every-way blonde looked up. Even her teeth weren't real, or so it seemed. They looked like Chiclets.

"Hi! Can I help you?" she said.

"Um, yeah, maybe. I was just wondering if anyone was free to wash and blow out my hair?"

"Well, I'm not sure. Why don't you just have a seat and I'll find out?"

"Okay. Thanks."

Beth watched the receptionist move across the salon like a miniature leopard on a sprightly prowl. *Click, click, click!* She was fascinated by her body language and overall persona. Although she was easily old enough to be her mother, everything about her seemed childish to Beth. To begin with, her entire outfit, from her headband with the trailing long ties to her shiny strawberry red toenails, was a little bit too small and something Beth might have worn when she was fifteen—high platform sandals with multicolored straps? Except for her enormous diamond ring, Beth wondered, how much of her was real? And the way her hips seemed to swivel? She thought, who swivels their hips when they walk? Someone recovering from a long career in pole dancing? Perhaps, Beth thought, perhaps.

Here she came clicking her way toward her again. This time, she leaned forward and down and her prodigious breasts nearly popped her buttons. Beth gasped.

"Darlin'? Do you have five minutes to wait?"

"Yeah, sure."

"Do you want something to drink? You look flushed."

"No thanks. I'm good. It's just the heat."

"Yeah, it's as hot today as two rats getting it on in a wool sock. Right?"

Beth was unfamiliar with the expression and it took a moment to grasp its meaning. There was a momentary struggle to restrain a burst of giggles. Instead, Beth arched her eyebrow and said, "Yeah, it's pretty hot out there."

"Well, you make yourself at home and Anna's gonna take you in just a minute. Her two o'clock canceled. By the way, what's your name, hon? I need it for the ticket."

"Beth. Beth Hayes."

"Well, I'm Lucy and it's awful good to meet you."

"Thanks. You too."

Beth had never encountered anyone quite like Lucy and she was bewildered by all her energized razzle-dazzle. Lucy was indeed something to behold.

Soon she was shampooed, combed out, and seated in Anna's chair. Anna took a handful of her hair, held it up, and examined it.

"I know this hair," she said, and looked across her shoulders into Beth's reflection in the mirror. "Have I met you before?"

"Yes. My mom got remarried a few years ago and you did our hair for the wedding."

"Who's your momma?"

"Susan Hayes? I mean, Rifkin."

"I should've known. And Maggie is your aunt. I know those two! Love 'em! I was at the wedding with my then *boyfriend*. How're they getting along? That Aunt Maggie of yours is a bird now, 'eah? Part on the left or the right?"

"The left."

Beth giggled. She had never heard anyone call her aunt *a bird* but she knew exactly what she meant. Maggie had exotic plumage to be sure, but only in a good way.

"So, Aunt Maggie's in California . . ."

Beth told Anna probably a lot more than she wanted to know and Anna listened, nodding her head. Beth noticed that Anna was wearing a wedding band and a small but beautiful diamond.

"So, you're married now?" Beth asked.

"Yeah, I married a big cheese. Tied the knot two years ago."

"Yeah, he's a big cheese, all right," the stylist next to them said, and laughed.

"Go on and hush your mouth, Brigitte Miklaszewski! You know Arthur is! Beth?" Anna whispered. "My husband is a cheese sommelier. Big cheese is a little inside joke."

"Oh!" said Beth, who had no idea such a thing existed in the entire world.

"Yeah, I'm Madame Fromage, honey, and I wouldn't trade places with anybody!"

"Are you Beth Hayes?" said the woman in Brigitte's chair.

Beth nodded her head.

"I know your momma too! Love her! I'm Caroline Wimbley Levine."

Beth leaned across and shook her hand.

"Well, it's nice to meet you. Gosh! This is like old home week! Wait till I tell my mom!"

"Yeah, I know your mother and I met

you too when you were about sixteen? I came to your house with this guy I was seeing at the time. Are you already out of college?"

"I sure am," Beth said.

"My my. Where does the time go?"

"That was back when you were dating that guy, Jack Taylor? Remember him?" Anna said. "God, he was cute!"

"Cute, yeah, but no spark. You know what I mean?" Caroline said.

"Well, if there ain't no spark . . ." Brigitte said.

"He wound up with that Mimi what's her name who makes the pound cakes, didn't he?" Anna said.

"Yeah," Lucy said, putting a bottle of cold water in front of Beth. "And her sister, Linda? She married that hunk Brad who owns Jackson Hole on Shem Creek after his wife Loretta died when she got hit by that car? Nasty mess that was. I heard her head got squashed like a watermelon!"

"Lucy!" Caroline said. "Some of us have delicate constitutions!"

"Well, they closed the casket, so it must have been bad," Lucy said.

"Holy crap," Beth said.

And the blow dryers screamed on for the length of time it took Anna to transform Beth into a poster child for fabulous hair. Her mother would have said she was a Breck Girl.

"Wow," Beth said when Anna spun her chair around to observe the great difference in her appearance. "I needed this!"

Beth paid her bill and said goodbye to all of them a little reluctantly. It wouldn't be so bad to be middle-aged if you could be like them, she thought. They weren't even close to dead yet.

Beth got her shrimp, an Old Bay boiling bag of seasoning, and some cocktail sauce from Simmons and then drove across the connector bridge, racing for Whole Foods. Time was running short and she did not want to get caught in the rush-hour traffic that plagued Highway 17. Once she had purchased everything and was back in her car zipping across the causeway at the speed limit, she saw the red lights start to flash. She was going to be held captive by the bridge opening to let the tall-mast sailboats pass. She slowed down, rolled to a stop, and was the very first car behind the barrier, right on top of the bridge. Judging from the lineup of boats, she was going to be there for a few minutes at least. She turned off the engine and got out to have a look, standing right by the railings, unconcerned about her hair. The brilliant blue sparkling water against clear skies cut only by the vista of green marsh grass was spectacular at that time of day. Then there were the smells, plough mud and salt, the sweet heady fragrance of pittosporum and jasmine, thick and wild, enough to make you forget the world. And there was the seemingly orchestrated dance of the birds, seagulls, pelicans, and the occasional osprey, flying over the boats, squawking and gliding on the currents of breezes. One by one the boats passed under the bridge, waving hello to her, and as she waved back, Beth's head was filled with memories of doing this exact same thing so many times with her mother when she was a young girl. Why had she never done this with her father? It was so beautiful, too beautiful to describe. Her father would have loved it.

She had heard, maybe from Cecily or someone at Atlanticville, that there was a growing consensus to replace the charming old Ben Sawyer Bridge with one of those hideous flyover bridges made of poured concrete. The thought of it made her want to cry. There would be no more closings and excuses to get out of your car and wave at the boats below. Of course the bridge closings were supposed to happen at appointed times to lessen the inconvenience to motorists and they never did. It seemed as though the bridge tender, who was in charge of such things, opened the bridge when he felt like it and sometimes kept it open longer than necessary. This riled up the old islanders, who would turn up at a town meeting and complain. What if they had to get to a hospital? What if it was a matter of life and death? But the truth was everyone loved the old bridge and any attempt to replace it would be a cause for furious public outcry. Maybe, she thought, she should attend the next meeting of the Town Council and see what was going on about that. The longer she was on the island, the more impassioned she became to preserve every part of its original character. And, perhaps this could be another pitch for the *Island Eye News.* Why not?

By the time Max arrived with two bottles

of wine, one red and one white, thrilled that Beth was cooking dinner for him, Beth was feeling closer to his age, more mature. She was in love with a wonderful man, a wonderful man who was so successful, charming, sensual, and who looked in her eyes with such desire that it made her lose her balance and her breath. And her life had suddenly taken on new purpose. She was not only going to help him finance his dream but she would become the people's steward and public servant working against drastic change. She would take extremely prudent views on gentrification. Slowly, carefully, she would guide his decisions to fit the fabric of the island. She would applaud his choices in her writings and he would take pride in her support. And she would gain the esteem of all of her family members in doing so as well.

"What's different about you tonight?" He stood in the doorway to the kitchen staring at her while she loaded a tray, hoping she had remembered everything she needed to grill outside.

"What do you mean?"

"Let me take that for you," he said. "Maybe it's just that you smell so damn good."

"Well, thanks," she said. "I'll get the plates. We're having dinner on the porch." She handed him the tray, smiled at his beautiful face, and kissed him on his cheek. "Doesn't that sound like a good idea?"

"It sounds brilliant."

Taking a page from her Aunt Maggie's design obsession, Beth had decorated the small porch table with a crisp white linen cloth. Two oversized conch shells backed up to each other in its center and ivory columns of beeswax candles stood inside the spotless etched crystal hurricanes protecting the flame against any sudden gusts of night air. Starched white napkins were folded like bishop miters and the gleaming flatware was placed carefully at exact intervals. It looked modern but very inviting in its spare symmetry.

They had a sunset glass of wine on the widow's walk. He helped her start the grill. She fed him steamed shrimp with her fingers and he turned the steaks. Frank Sinatra crooned through the French doors, and all through dinner, which began right after dark, he told her how beautiful she was, kissing her or merely touching her shoulder or fingers at every opportunity.

Each time she looked in his eyes she realized exactly how right it was to be with him. It was where she belonged.

This! she thought, remembering her earlier conversation with her Aunt Sophie. This is romance.

13

Woody

Susanthepen@writenow.org
Maggie, I'm having pangs for Beth. And Simon and you. Like an old sentimental fool. I never thought I would miss y'all and the island so much. I don't think I'm gonna make it through this whole year. xx

Maggiepie2@marthagene.net
Susan, I miss you so bad I could spit, except that I would never spit. If you're really that homesick and it isn't for you over there with all those baguettes and berets, come home! There's no place on earth like our Sullivans Island, is there? xx

It was precisely six o'clock in the evening when Woody arrived at Beth's home on Sullivans Island. He located the hidden key and held it up to the fading sun. Its brass edge caught a flash of light, leaving him to think for an instant that the key possessed some powers of its own. He stood there for a moment, duffel thrown over his shoulder, looking up at the house. He wished he knew the history of its generations because he had never known a family so vivacious and irresistible as Beth's or a house like the Island Gamble. No one would have said that it was an architectural marvel but most people would have agreed that it had a personality, representing its locale and time well, but unique in that it seemed welcoming and forbidding at the same time. It was as though the house had eyes, was alive, and had its own opinions. It wanted to know about those who walked its rooms, whether a whole lifetime was spent there or just a brief visit. Was it alive? Something had certainly frightened Phoebe, he thought, but then Phoebe leaned toward the melodramatic.

Woody was not afraid of the house. In fact, his feelings were quite the opposite.

He had thought of little else all week except being on that porch with Beth and how he had never wanted to leave. So when Beth suggested he should return on a business excuse he had all but jumped at the opportunity. He began to ascend the steps, taking them one at a time. He crossed the porch, slipped the key in the lock, and opened the front door easily. He could feel the emptiness. No one was at home.

He dropped his belongings in the same room where he had stayed the previous weekend and went to the kitchen in search of something to drink. Beth's little dog Lola was fast asleep in her crate. Woody didn't want to wake her so he tiptoed across the floor to the refrigerator. Inside was an abundance of water bottles and little else beyond a half-empty container of two percent milk, a few eggs, and an unopened carton of orange juice. And the beer he and Mike had left behind. It appeared that Beth had not gone grocery shopping since they had left, but that was fine with him. He wasn't big on snacks anyway. The phone rang and he hesitated to answer it. After all, it would not be for him because if it was Beth calling she would have dialed his cell. He listened as the caller left a message on her answering machine, which was an artifact from the eighties.

Hi, Beth! It's your Aunt Sophie calling. I was just wondering how you're doing and wanted to say hello. And I wanted to know if you spoke to your mom about your investment idea and what she said. I wish I had the wiggle room to invest with you but every last centavo we've got is in the vitamin business right now, as you know. Anyway, they go on sale next week. Pretty exciting for us! I think I told you that we got a huge, but I mean HUGE, order from GNC and Whole Foods, and oh! Al and I got the cover of People *magazine for next week, and what else? Uh, I guess this message is long enough, right? Call me back! Love you!*

Well, that was nice, he thought. So her aunts Sophie and Allison were expanding their business into vitamins? Why not? People were desperate to live longer and feel better. Personally, he thought vitamins were a crock, but hey, if other people thought they felt better as a result? Go for it.

For some inexplicable reason, he felt like it was all right to make himself right at home and take a self-guided tour. After all, he had been in his car for hours. He opened a bottle of water and began to wander around to stretch his legs and see what there was to see.

There was nothing grand or mysterious downstairs, just a maze of bedrooms furnished with old chests of drawers, hooked rugs, end tables, and lamps. And the bathrooms, squeaky clean as they were, appeared to have been upgraded back in the 1950s. The spigots dripped, leaving a stain in the bathroom basins, and there was some evidence of corrosion on all the fixtures. But, as everyone knew, that was part of the joy of being a homeowner near the ocean. Salt ate its way through just about everything.

Someone had spent a lot of money on white enamel spray paint, he thought, and smiled to himself. This family was not frugal but they were clearly not throwing away anything that a coat of paint could rehabilitate. Everything reminded him of his own parents and how they lived. Organized, clean as a whistle, and money was spent with a sober regard for what it took to earn it.

Antique quilts decorated some walls, family photographs and poster art others. There was a charm in the way everything was arranged and the positions of the objects—alarm clocks, frames, pillows, and so forth—the way they were placed demonstrated thought and care, right down to the tomato-shaped pincushion on Beth's deceased grandmother's table next to her bedroom chair. Her sewing basket rested there on the floor. Woody thought that he might have believed she could arrive at any moment to darn a pair of socks. Everything was waiting, probably just as she had left it the day she went to sing with the angels. He wondered if that corner of the room was a sort of altar to Beth's grandmother's memory or if it had simply been too heart wrenching to put her things away. How long had she been dead? He found himself standing there in that room for a long while, wondering what kind of a woman she had been. He picked up what must have been her wedding picture. There she stood, looking out of the picture straight into his heart. Her very serious groom wore a World War II army uniform, and without motive his heart softened to both of them. He felt himself actually choke back tears. She looked so vulnerable and he appeared so resolute. Then, before he left the room, he borrowed the two pillows from the bed for his own. He liked to sleep with a lot of pillows and didn't think Beth would mind.

There was not a lot of extra anything to be found in the house except for family pictures and books. Every room had at least one hundred books whose topics ran the gamut. Mysteries, romance novels, political memoirs, historical naval battles, thrillers, biographies, and a slew of books on southern history, especially the Civil War.

Next, he found himself in the living room, examining the pictures in the silver-tone frames that stood in staggered rows on a large round table in the corner. The lives of all the family members were represented and he had to laugh when he realized he had come across one of his boss, Henry. There was Henry Hamilton with bony knees, dirty Keds, and a rusty bicycle at about the age of eight. Young Henry looked mean and cross, a real tough guy at forty-five pounds, as though he might hop out of the picture and deliver a sock to your jaw.

"Oh, man! This is priceless!"

After a good hearty laugh, he placed the photograph back on the table, exactly in its original spot. Then he examined his face in the large mirror. Should he shave for dinner? Probably a good idea, he thought as he rubbed his chin with the back of his hand, and decided to take a shower as well. It couldn't hurt. Woody was not particularly vain, the kind of guy who never missed a chance to preen in a mirror or to take a sly glance at his reflection in a store window, but this mirror made him want to turn and check himself out from all possible angles. For no good reason whatsoever, he placed his hand on the mirror, and to his surprise the mirror felt warm, as though it had a pulse.

"Must be the heat," he said aloud to the empty room.

A naughty thought crossed his mind that it might be interesting to look around Beth's room upstairs, but he hesitated, deciding that would definitely be an invasion of

Beth's privacy. Knowing Beth, she would know he had been there by a trace of his cologne.

It was six-thirty and his stomach began to rumble.

"Time for a feed," he said, trying to remember what was on the menu at Beth's restaurant, recalling the flash-fried tuna rolls had looked delicious.

His mouth began to water and he was thinking a cold beer would taste awfully good just then too. But rather than drink alone, he decided to dress for dinner. He hurried toward his room, turned on the shower to get the hot water going, and stripped down to his birthday suit. He foraged his duffel bag like a trained pig hunting truffles, digging for his dop kit and shaving cream. Dop kit? Check. Shaving cream? MIA. Although he was in his altogether, he dashed to the second bathroom to see, perchance, had some kind absentminded soul left a can of it behind? There was none. By that time his bathroom was steaming up and there was no other option but to race upstairs to see what could be found. Surely Beth had something he could use.

"I might wind up smelling like fruit cocktail, but so what?"

He took the steps two at a time with his natural attributes swinging in the breeze as he hurried along. Where was the bathroom? He opened several doors to no avail. Finally he opened the only door he had not tried and sighed in relief.

"Ah! Here it is!" he said, and flipped the light switch.

There was a small cabinet recessed in the wall loaded with personal hygiene products. After he moved around what seemed like more bottles and boxes than you could find on a whole shelf at a drugstore, his hand finally touched down on the cool aluminum of a pink canister of shaving cream. Why did women buy so many products? Did they use them? He decided it was best to lather up, replace the can, and hurry back to his shower. He shook the can vigorously and squirted a generous pale pink mound into the palm of his hand, applied it carefully in a Santa beard all over his face and neck. It smelled pretty good, he thought, not too bad after all. He put his glasses back on, rinsed his hands, dried them on the towel, and turned off the bathroom light. Just as he was making his way down the steps he heard a scream and looked up into the horrified face of Beth on the bottom step. On a curious note, Beth was wearing only her panties, bra, and a pair of red canvas embroidered espadrilles that tied around her ankles.

"AAAAAA! AAAAAA! AAAAA!" she shrieked, staring with eye-popping intensity exactly where decorum would dictate a lady should not.

Avert your eyes! her conscience screamed inside her head, and she fought back, thinking, Shut the hell up! Holy crap! Who? Freaking? Knew?

"Oh my God!" he screamed back.

"Woody! I thought you were in the shower!"

"I thought you were at work!"

"Some idiot spilled a glass of red wine all over . . . Oh my word. For God's sake, Woody!" Finally, she looked away and shielded her eyes. "Go get a towel!"

"Right! A towel!"

They both appeared to have had their feet nailed to the floor as neither of them made a move for the sake of modesty.

"Get a towel! Woody! Jesus H. Christ on a crutch from Lourdes! A towel!"

"I'm going!"

Her voice sounded annoyed but they knew better. They were thoroughly amused.

By the time he retrieved a towel and returned to the stairs, Beth had disappeared behind her bedroom door. He thought, if he was Beth he would be rolling on the floor, holding his sides and howling with laughter. That was exactly what he felt like doing. What were the odds that something like this could have happened? About a million to one, he decided. Woody flew to the downstairs bathroom without a single comment to her. For the duration of his toilette, Woody could not stop laughing to himself. How could he face her? What would he say? That he was a full-service banker? Oh no! Wait! He thought, What if this gets back to Henry? That humorless bastard? He'll cut my ass! But he had to admit, Beth's body was even more beautiful than he thought it might be.

As quickly as her mother's old Volvo could take her, Beth returned to the restaurant. She was wearing a navy T-shirt dress that was more or less too patriotic a combination with her espadrilles for her normal taste, but customer-proof from flying glasses of red wine. Understandably, she didn't want to run into Woody again at the house just then, so she grabbed the first clean thing in her closet that was presentable. All the way back to work, she was shaking from fits of nonstop giggles. It was the shock of it. Nothing like that had ever happened to her before and she thought it was absolutely hilarious. Woody had been completely embarrassed. Wait. Was he embarrassed? No. In retrospect, it didn't seem that he was embarrassed one little bit. Caught off guard, maybe. Wishing he hadn't looked so ridiculous with a gallon of shaving cream smeared all over his face, perhaps. But he had stood there like any other normal man, giving her the opportunity to behold and appraise the goods, and she had been caught as slack-jawed as an old bloodhound. Men were brazen things.

"Good thing you're back," Drew said, "We're going crazy tonight. Where did all these people come from?"

"They're evacuating Ohio again. I'll take the phones," Beth said.

"Must be. Deal. Thanks. No recession tonight!" Drew said, and went to welcome and placate the growing number of patrons gathered at the door and on the porch.

It wasn't long until Beth spotted Woody at the outside bar. He gave her a little wave and she waved back, shaking her head at him and smiling. He wasn't alone for long, though, because, just as Beth had predicted, three attractive women, slightly older than Woody, obviously out on the town for fun, surrounded him and began pummeling him with small talk and big flirtation. From her distance, it was hard for Beth to follow exactly what was happening, but whatever it was, she didn't like it, especially whatever it was that was going on between him and the little blonde with spiky layered hair. Perky, spiky-haired blondes irritated the daylights out of her.

They were having a very busy night, more so than usual, probably because they had lowered their prices to meet the challenges of the economic times. Beth seated some tables three times over the course of the evening. When the hullabaloo began to slow down, she went outside to check on Woody. The three women/

sirens had moved on to another victim but the little blonde still had her eye on Woody. Beth glared at her, thinking she'd like to slap her right across her face, and then just as quickly she told herself that she was being ridiculous. She walked up to him and gave him a hug, one that was close and long enough that the blond twit might think there was possibly something between them.

"So, here we are. Let's start over," she said. "Did you eat?"

"Yeah, I had the tuna roll and a bowl of gazpacho. It was really good. Listen, about what happened earlier."

"Nothing happened," she said, lying, sincerely hoping he couldn't detect all the confusion she was feeling. "I don't know what you're talking about."

"Okay. But anyway, I apologize."

"There's nothing to apologize for," she said. "So, how was your trip?"

Woody had turned away then, looking at the blonde, who was watching their every move. He gave the offending one a polite nod and Beth's thermostat took a ride on a rocket to the Pleiades. He looked back to Beth, whose jaw had gone into Sudden Onset Rigor Mortis.

"Are you all right?" He was genuinely mystified by the abrupt change in her mood. But, he told himself, women are re-nowned for mood swings.

"Who me? Of course! I'm fine. Why wouldn't I be?" What is the matter with me, she thought. "Uh, so listen, things are winding down so I think I'll be out of here in like, soon? Meet you on the porch back at the house?"

"Sounds great. Or, I can wait for you if you'd like. Follow you home so, you know, you don't get kidnapped by terrorists or something."

"Whatever," she said, and gave him a smile so small it could have been con-fused with something churlish. "Let me go see what's happening in there."

After going over her schedule for the remainder of the weekend, Drew told her it was fine to leave for the evening. Beth got her handbag and went back to the porch where Woody waited.

"I'm liberated. Want to go now or do you want to stay and have another drink?"

Woody smiled at her as though he was taking her in all at once—her size, her manner, her eyes, and he remembered every detail about her that he shouldn't have known.

"Woody? Did you hear me?"

"What? No! Of course I heard you! I was just thinking about the porch and wondering if the moon is up over the water. That's all."

Beth was somehow disappointed by those words because she had thought he was looking at her differently, sizing her up like men do when they are thinking about spreading their feathers, not that his feathers held the slightest interest for her. She told herself that she was just experiencing a flash of personal vanity that was without any meaning at all.

"Oh," she said. "Well, let's go see."

The house was waiting for them. As they opened the French doors in the living room across the ocean side of the house, the rush of air billowed the sheer curtains and instantly cooled the rooms. The tide was high enough to hear it as far back as the kitchen, and unlike any night that Beth could remember, this one seemed awash with every Lowcountry spell of seduction she had ever known.

What a waste, she thought, wishing Max were there.

"Can I get you a glass of wine?" Woody called out. "I picked up a bottle on my way here."

"Yeah, thanks! I'm gonna take Lola out and just change my clothes real fast. Okay?"

"Sure!"

"Hey! I meant to ask you. You didn't tell Mike anything about the deal with Max, did you?"

"No. I didn't even tell him I was coming here."

"Good. With his mouth it would be all over the news by now."

"Ah, come on, he's a good guy."

"Yeah, a good guy with a big mouth. He'd love to start something with my Aunt Maggie, who would freak out. *Dahlin'! You're ruining the sacred family reputation by shacking up!*" Beth gave her imitation of Maggie her best Scarlett O'Hara accent.

"Is that how your aunt talks?"

"Very funny."

"But you did that last weekend! We were all here!"

"You don't understand. It's different when he sleeps around."

"Ah, the old double standard."

"Exactly."

Beth scooped up her little dog from her crate and rushed her down the front steps to the yard, putting her gently on the grass. While Lola went in search of the perfect spot, Beth thought about her clothes. The dress she was wearing was so stupid but it was one of only five she owned. Although she never would have said so, she felt a little funny that Woody might think she was changing her clothes to save them for work, which she was. Admittedly, just weeks ago she had been a student, living in jeans and sweaters, flip-flops and T-shirts. She hated the fact that she had so few things to wear to work that made her look like a professional hostess. And prideful as she was, she would never ask Simon or her mother to help her buy a wardrobe that was work-appropriate be- cause surely she would spend more than she was earning and that just didn't make any sense to her. And anyway, who knew how long her job would last?

When Lola reappeared from her search and destroy mission under the lantana bush, Beth raced with her up the steps, into the house, and up to her room, passing Woody on the porch.

"Be right back!" she said.

"I'm not moving! Take your time!"

She hoped Woody would think she was changing into shorts because it was more comfortable to throw your feet up on the banisters and, um, modest. Yes, suddenly modesty was going to play a front and center role in her friendship with Woody. The last thing she wanted to do was give her banker friend the wrong idea. She was not at all like Phoebe. In fact, Woody knew that she was not available, so what was she really thinking?

She searched her closet for a clean shirt and a pair of shorts and settled on the same thing she had worn that day before she went to work.

On paper she was a wealthy young woman, but she surely couldn't afford to dress like one. That truth annoyed her and strengthened her determination to take control of her life, and that control included her assets. The terms of her diminishing trust account were so wrong, just so wrong. She wondered if her mother was paying attention to all the money she was losing. Did she even know? Thirty-five percent? In Beth's mind, that was a huge amount to lose. An enormous amount!

"Ah! There you are!" He stood when she came on the porch. "So, tell me, how was your day?"

She loved it that he stood up from his chair when she appeared.

"My day? Let's see. Around noon, I cured cancer—"

"Oh! My! All forms of it?"

"Yes, all forms."

He handed her a glass of red wine and looked at her with a lopsided grin. "Wow, congratulations. You *are* talented!"

"Thank you. And by six, I was wearing a glass of red wine instead of drinking one . . ."

"Ah yes, that unfortunate bit that we shall never speak of . . ."

"Thank you. Yes, that." Beth was smiling. She was so happy to be in Woody's company. He made everything seem so easy to deal with, even the most embarrassing situations.

He raised his glass in a toast. "Well, here's to the gym. Glad I kept my membership going."

"Oh. Shut. Up. I'm just glad you're here."

"Me too. Let's sit."

They pulled their rockers up to the banisters but found themselves still standing as they stared, watching to the east as the moon was full and on the rise over the ocean. The whole world was cast in its dusty blue glow as it quickly changed from orange to gold to a radiant white. It was gorgeous.

"Why does it seem so close tonight?" he asked.

"I don't know but it does. Doesn't it? Like you could pick it right out of the sky."

Woody was so caught up in the magic of the evening that he turned Beth around, put his hand behind her neck, and went in for the kiss that he hoped would steal her heart. Beth, to her complete astonishment, did not resist. In fact, she responded in a way that surprised her. She felt a crazy weakness in the pit of her stomach, like a fluttering. Even her wrists and shoulders felt funny. Old Woody had it going on like she never would have dreamed in a thousand years, and Beth could not think of another thing in that moment except that he tasted so good and that his mouth was the absolute perfect fit. He took her goblet and put his with hers on a small table just between the rockers and they picked up where they had left off. Now she was leaning against one of the columns and he was very close, close enough that neither of them could ever have said that there was any innocence about what they were doing and where they were headed. To be honest, she could count the change in his pockets with her thigh so one can only imagine what else she was learning. And he could feel where she was powerful and still sense her soft places too, which was taking him to another level of consciousness and at a rather sprightly clip, despite his feeble attempts of restraint.

Now, it is the height of poor taste to detail someone's intimate life, but let us just say that what transpired between Woody and Beth was just short of the shorts. It would be impossible to see clearly through all of the steam generated that night to say exactly who it was, but one of them finally came to their senses and called for a five-minute recess. There was a lot of stammering and lip biting on the part of Beth and a fairly gargantuan internal dose of *Shit! What am I doing with my client?* stemming from Woody's poorly represented conscience.

But neither of them had any regret. Neither of them. Not one speck. They said good night wondering in their minds what it would be like to really be with each other, sleep together, wake up together, and further, they laughed because they were so overcome by the sheer power of their attraction to each other that they didn't know what else to do but to laugh.

"Well, I hope you sleep okay," she said. "I know I won't."

"Are you sure you don't want to elope with me right here and now? I'll make an honest woman of you."

They both giggled and finally she said, "Oh, Woody. What are we doing here? This is crazy."

"No, Beth. It's not crazy at all. It's wonderful."

"Yeah, I guess it is."

She looked at him then, in the pale moonlight, in his tortoiseshell glasses, in his patrician profile, in his boyish lankiness, in his brilliant mind and perfect manners and his enormous heart, and something happened to slightly tarnish her feelings about Max.

"Is this a bad thing?"

"No, Woody, it's a complicated thing. You know that."

"Well, you go get some sleep and let's see how it looks in the morning."

"Good idea. Night."

He took a handful of her hair into his hand and smelled it.

"You have the most beautiful hair and I love the way it smells."

"Tomorrow, Woody," she said, easing away from him. "Let's see what we see."

Together they locked the doors, checked the stove twice, and turned off all the lights. She began to climb the steps to her room, and she could feel a pall in her heart. She knew that Max would never show her the same sensitivity or tenderness or consideration. He didn't have it in him. And so she had to decide what she really wanted. Were those things really so important to her? But to be fair, she thought, Max is who he is, and if she thought that who he was wasn't enough to carry her through marriage, raising a family, maybe moving to some other part of the planet, she knew she had better rethink her love for him. No, she decided, before she drifted off to sleep, she was deeply in love with Max, and in an all-encompassing way she knew she would never feel for anyone else. Even Woody Morrison, wonderful as he was.

Woody, back in his room, completely exhausted and overwrought by the tumult of his feelings for Beth, pulled off his trousers and shirt, went to the bathroom to wash his face and brush his teeth, hoping this time she was safely upstairs. When he returned to his room, the bed had been turned down and his duffel bag was parked neatly on the floor next to the chest of drawers. Maybe he had done these things himself, but for the life of him, he could not recall having done so. He shrugged it off to the late hour, his fatigue, and crawled in between the sheets, turning off his bedside lamp. It wasn't long before Woody fell into a swirl of dreams.

At some point during the night, Woody was partially roused from his sleep, and try as he might to sleep again, he could not. Eyes still closed, he turned over, feeling around with his foot for a cool place on the mattress, pulling the pillows around him to get comfortable again. He thought he heard someone breathing, someone who was in the room with him. The breathing was regular and he wondered if it was Beth. Given all the realities, he decided to remain still and see what happened. The breathing continued. The next thing he knew, the sun was coming up between the venetian blinds and no one was there. Carefully, he looked at the other side of the bed and he could tell the sheets were untouched, except by him. I probably dreamed it, he thought.

Beth was in the kitchen making coffee when Woody saw her for the first time that day. She was wearing a casual sundress and was barefoot, which for some reason seemed wildly appealing to him. He was wearing khakis and a knit shirt, with Top-Siders and no socks.

"Morning! You look nice!" she said. "How'd you sleep?"

"Okay. You?"

"Good. Thanks."

"Actually, I slept, but can I tell you something strange?"

"Who me? I minored in strange. You can tell me anything."

"Well, I woke up in the middle of the night and I would swear on a stack of Bibles that someone was in the room with me."

"Why do you say that?"

"Because I could hear breathing."

"It could have been your own breathing."

"Maybe. But maybe not."

"Sometimes I snore . . ."

"You snore?"

"Only if I have a bad cold or something. But sometimes I wake myself up, it's so loud."

"Really? Well, I'll make a note of that. And, FYI, I don't snore even when I have a cold."

"Really?"

"Yeah. And here's another thing, though somewhat less terrifying. When I went in to go to bed, my covers were turned down, like in a hotel? I mean, I swear on my unborn children, I didn't do it."

"Woody? Honey? You probably didn't. Same thing happened to me the first night I was here. Don't worry. The ghosts are tame. If they like you, that is. Do you want milk in your coffee? I forget."

"Yeah, a splash is fine. Are you telling me you think this house is haunted?"

"Absolutely no thinking required. Always was. Always will be. I even had the family priest take a crack at it." She handed him a steaming mug. "Drink this. You'll feel better."

"Thanks. A priest? You're kidding me, right?"

"Nope. He squirted holy water all over the place and said a bunch of prayers. It's been relatively quiet since then, except for the deal with Phoebe."

"And I thought it was some bull. So why do you think that happened?"

"Because my grandmother didn't like her kind and wanted her out of here."

Woody got the chills and rubbed his bare arms.

"Good call. So why did this happen to me?"

"Your guess is as good as mine. But I'll tell you what I think. I think they were giving you the once-over."

"They? The once-over?"

"Yeah. They. I think they wanted to see who you were."

"Oh. Well, I hope I passed the test."

"You must have, or else . . ."

"Or else what?"

"They would've thrown your stuff all over the place."

Woody took a long drink of his coffee and then placed his mug on the table in front of him. Beth stood by the stove looking at him and Woody stared back at her. It was a solid minute before he spoke.

"Beth?"

"Yes?"

"Do you realize we're talking about ghosts just like we could be discussing the weather?"

"Yes."

"Don't you think that's a little abnormal?"

"Define normal."

"I don't know. How about a serious conviction that we live in a three-dimensional world?"

"Oh, Woody. Get over it. A little *moo hoo ha ha* adds to the charm of being here. Do you want toast?"

"Nope, I'm good. I thought maybe I'd go down the island, buy a muffin or something, see if Max is around, you know, get my investigation under way early?"

"Great idea! Want me to go with you?"

"Nah. Let me nose around on my own first."

Woody put his mug in the sink and went toward the door to leave.

"Woody?"

He stopped and turned back to face her. "Yeah?"

"I didn't know you were a muffin man." Beth was overcome with giggles.

"I'll deal with you later, ma'am."

He held the screen door until it closed so the loud *thwack* of it wouldn't echo all over the neighborhood. To begin with, Woody just wasn't a noisy guy and he saw no sense in banging and slamming his way through life. So when he came upon Max's construction site and saw Max screaming into his cell phone, and heard all the deafening noise of the building in progress, it took him a few minutes to tune into it all.

He walked over to Max, who brightened up considerably at the sight of Woody, and almost immediately Max finished his phone call and reached out to shake Woody's hand.

"Hey! You're back!" Max said, like Woody was his long-lost brother. "What's going on?"

"Hey!" Woody said, and shook Max's hand soundly. "I came back to see what's going on with your deal and to see if there was still room for a couple of new investors."

Max could not believe his ears. A godsend! This was an incredible stroke of desperately needed luck! Just as quickly as he could, but with his usual well-honed aplomb, he steered Woody toward the trailer he had moved onto the property and set up as a temporary office.

They talked and talked, and before long Max had Woody believing that they did indeed share the same DNA. The camaraderie between them boggled Woody's mind; he was unaccustomed to making friends so easily. When they got to the delicate issue of how much was coming from whom, Woody held back, asking Max to explain the projected earnings and pay-out schedule one more time. Woody was finally satisfied.

He said, "I'm in for twenty-five thousand. And I think Beth's looking at a much higher number."

"Really?" Max said, hoping Woody could not read the massive relief in his face.

They agreed to have dinner at Atlanticville, each for reasons of their own.

"What time do you want to meet?" Woody asked.

"How's seven? That gives me a chance to go home and wash off the dust."

"Great, because I'm sure I will think of other questions to ask."

"Well, you make a list of them and I will try to answer them all as honestly as I can," Max said.

Atlanticville was a crazy house again that night, and Beth was like a chimney swift, never touching land, flitting from one place to another. Woody and Max were seated at a table near her podium, but she was so busy she seemed oblivious to them. However, their eyes never left her.

"She's a great girl," Max said, taking a sip of his wine.

"I think she's the most amazing girl I've ever met," Woody said.

"You do?"

"Yeah, I do."

Max sat up straight. This was a dramatic sea change in the world of Max Mitchell. He was no fool. He fully realized that the only reason he was going to gain thousands of dollars in his business account was because of Woody Morrison's ability to make that happen.

"This sounds serious," Max said.

"Yeah, well, I guess sooner or later I was going to ask you about, you know, how serious you are about her?"

"Well, I think she's a wonderful girl and obviously I have tremendous feelings for her."

"Are you in love with her? I mean, you know, like do you think there's a future for y'all?"

"That's a tough question."

Max sat back in his chair and took a long look at Woody. Woody was so young and honest and his heart was just all over his sleeve. Max had been that way once; he remembered feeling that kind of heart-palpitating passion. But it had been a long time, and for now, and most important, he didn't want a single thing to get in the way of finalizing this investment. Quite simply, he couldn't afford for anything to go wrong.

"Well, either you do or you don't, right?"

"Yeah, but up until this very moment I did not know that you were in love with Beth. I mean, if we're going to be partners we can't be fighting over the same woman."

"So, what do you suggest?"

"Well, Beth has some say-so in this, don't you think? I mean, has she declared her feelings for you?"

"No. Well, not in so many words. I know she cares about me and I know she likes me very much, but I think we all know she's insane over you, Max. Look, I just don't want to see her get hurt."

Max watched as Woody's pain spread over his face. Max knew Beth was not in love with Woody but he saw no reason to humiliate him.

"I don't either. Look, while we are beginning a great partnership here, we are also developing a conflict of interest. And I'm going to be back and forth to North Carolina a lot in the near future. Why don't you use that time to see what happens between you two?"

"So, you're saying that you're putting on the brakes with her?"

"No, just slowing down the freight train."

"Why would you do that for me?"

"Because we're going to be partners. Plain and simple. And listen, Woody, I'm kind of a lone wolf, you know? I got obliterated in love once and that was enough for me. Completely and totally obliterated. I don't ever want to feel that way again. So I'm not looking for a swing set in my yard here. She's young. You're young. You know what I mean?"

"I think I hear you loud and clear."

After dinner, Beth and Max walked out to the parking lot.

"I have a little surprise for you, Max."

"Yeah, what's that?"

"One hundred thousand dollars. It should be in your account by Monday afternoon, if it all goes right."

"Come here, you gorgeous creature!"

"Max!"

After kissing the neck and lips off Max in the parking lot for the whole world to see if they cared to witness her doomed expression of ill-placed affection, Beth drove home. Max announced that he was saying good night then, instead of going back to her house because he had to get up early and drive to Wrightsville Beach, where his next project was in its infancy. She understood but was disappointed.

"No, I get it. It's okay."

"We'll talk tomorrow, okay?"

When Beth got home she found Woody on the porch watching the tide roll in across the shore.

"Hey!" she said just as she spotted him in the half-light. He immediately stood up from his chair. "How was your dinner with Max?"

"Absolutely fantastic. The more I see him, the more I like him."

"See? I told you he was wonderful!"

"We're going to make up for all the money we lost last year and then some," Woody said. "I can't thank you enough for introducing me to Max. This is terrific."

"Didn't I tell you? Isn't he great?"

"Yeah. Hey! We hardly saw you all night!"

"I know. I'm sorry. Drew had me running around like a crazed rabbit!"

"You must be exhausted! Can I get you anything?"

"Oh no, thanks. I'm fine. I'll just go see about—"

"I walked Lola about half an hour ago when I came in."

"You did? Gosh! Thanks!"

"Glad to help. I like dogs."

"Lola's not a dog."

"Of course. I knew that."

"Good."

"So, you know we have to get your mother to sign a statement agreeing to allow you to borrow against your trust, right?"

"Yeah, so? No big deal. She'll do it. I'll write up all the particulars and fax it to her. She can sign it and fax it back. What else do we need?"

"A fax is a legal document. That should do it. If the bank has any questions, they can always call her, right?"

"Sure."

"Or they can call me. I'm your account

manager, remember? Are you sure your mother won't object?"

"Why would she? Anyway, listen, don't worry. I can handle my mother."

14

High Anxiety

Susanthepen@writenow.org
Maggie, Did you hear Soph and Al got the cover of People *for next week? Hot stuff, right? xx*

Maggiepie2@marthagene.net
Susan, those two aren't going to be happy until they spend the weekend in the White House. Especially Allison.

Susanthepen@writenow.org
Meow, Maggie. xx

"Woody?"

"Yeah?"

"What if Uncle Henry just happens to notice that one hundred thousand dollars is missing from my account?"

"What will he do? Well, first, he'll pull out the executive set of CUTCO knives some kid sold him when he or she was home for the summer from college. He'll then select the one with the serrated edge that you never have to sharpen. Then, after he hacks me into chunks and shovels me into a cooler, he'll drive my carcass down here and feed it to the sharks while he's sipping on a great Burgundy. But that won't happen."

"And why not?"

"Number one, your mother is going to sign off on the loan. Two, I have signing authority on your trust. And three, I don't know how to say this without sounding obnoxious, but your Uncle Henry is a very big dog and only handles portfolios of over a hundred million. Well, they used to be one hundred and now they're, well, less. Your trust is like an itty-bitty blip on his global radar, which is not to say he doesn't care."

"Oh. I feel much better. Thanks."

"No, I mean he'll never even see it. You'll have all the money back in your account plus another twenty percent before he knows it's gone."

"You're right."

"Look, he might get a little insulted that I made this investment without consulting him, but that's not a big deal. Believe me, in this economy? He's frying much bigger fish."

"For real. Like Orca."

"You got it."

"Okay. So. Then. Will you call me so I know you got back safely?"

"Of course! Listen, let me do the worrying here, okay?"

It was a gorgeous Sunday morning and Woody was headed back to Atlanta. He was in his car, motor running, and Beth was standing by his door, leaning in the window, shifting her weight from one foot to the other.

"Oh, Woody. I hope you're right. You know, I just want to be in charge of my own life."

"I agree. Now, go call your mom and get it over with. Let me know what she says. I'll be on my cell. And hey, thanks for a great weekend."

"Anytime. It was great to see you. Be careful!"

He backed out of the yard and waved to her before he pulled away. She waved back and then she sighed, long and hard, worrying.

She was uncertain of how to start the conversation with her mother. What were the words to say that would guarantee the right outcome? *Mom? I need to discuss something pretty serious with you?* No, sounds like my life might be hanging by a thread. *Mom? Do you know how much of my money Uncle Henry has lost since last September?* No, too accusatory. How about, *Hey Mom? Got a minute to chat?* She decided just to be natural and not to let her mother hear any stress in her voice one way or the other. She was determined to play it cool but she realized she needed to work up her nerve to pick up the phone.

She flipped on the television intending to channel-surf when she landed on QVC, which was her favorite station next to the one where they cleaned up nasty people's filthy houses. There was her Aunt Sophie in the television studio selling her new vitamins, along with a package of her DVDs and hand weights for a *One Time Only* price. The toll-free number was large on the bottom of the screen with their web site. The number of units sold continued to rise. An easy calculation in Beth's head told her that in less than thirty minutes her aunts had sold to over a thousand customers at seventy-five dollars each, which was charged on any credit card on the planet in three easy payments of twenty-five dollars, over ninety days, not including shipping and handling charges, and taxes where applicable. Whew! Beth thought. That was seventy-five thousand dollars and growing by the minute! Her aunts made a huge profit from the sales. No wonder they were so rich. Beth watched in fascination.

The screen then switched to a taped session of her Aunt Allison in a workout studio doing one of her exercise routines, demonstrating how easy it was to get in fabulous shape and have a body like hers. Beth was struck for the millionth time by how closely Sophie and Allison resembled each other. In fact, it was all but impossible for her to distinguish between them unless she held them down and found out who had the tattoo. She wondered why her Aunt Allison wasn't live in the studio helping Sophie hawk their new line of performance-enhancing, spike-your-metabolism, stamina-building pills that seemed to be useful for whatever ails you. But then she decided that even Allison, egomaniac that she was, would recognize that Sophie had the better personality when it came to being charming, engaging, and selling. But there was something off about Sophie's sales pitch. She sounded forced, as though she didn't believe what she was saying. Well, no one would ever convince Beth that her favorite relative was a snake oil salesman, and she sure was making money, hand over fist. But something still bothered Beth. She decided to play her aunt's message on the answering machine again to see if she could sense anything strange in the tone of her voice.

Beth stood in the kitchen and listened to the tape carefully and decided she might be letting her imagination run away with itself. Aunt Sophie sounded fine. She sounded strange on television but on the phone she seemed just like herself. Beth took a bottle of water from the refrigerator and looked at the kitchen clock on the wall. She had an hour before she had to be at work and now was the best time to call her mother in France. She dialed the number.

"Mom?"

"Beth? Is that you, sweetheart? Is everything all right?"

"Yeah, of course! Everything's great! I just wanted to hear your voice and run something by you. Gosh, I miss you!"

"I miss you too, baby! What's going on?"

"Oh, a bunch of things. I just saw my pretty aunties on QVC. I guess they are in the middle of launching their vitamins. And they have the cover of *People* magazine next week so you might want to look that up online. I'll save you a copy."

"Well, that's a very big deal! *People,* huh?"

"Yeah, hot stuff."

"I'll say. They're something else, those two. And what else? Have you seen Cecily very much?"

"Oh yeah, I see her all the time. She's the greatest."

"Yeah, she's a groovy chick."

Beth giggled and said, "Mom? Nobody says *groovy chick* anymore, not since Woodstock."

"Sure, give me a hard time! So, how's that job at the restaurant going, and the other one too?"

"Well, my first article comes out this week, so I'll send that to you, and the restaurant job? It's hard as hell!"

"Could you not say *hell,* please?"

"Okay. It's as hard as purgatory?"

"Much better. Thank you."

"Oh, Mom. Anyway, I wanted to tell you about this real estate investment opportunity I have that I am very interested in because my trust-fund portfolio is losing money all over the place."

"It is?"

"Yeah. The recession is eating it alive. I'm down like thirty-five percent."

"What? But Henry's supposed to be watching it for us!"

"Yeah, well, good old Uncle Henry is fly-fishing is Jackson Hole, Wyoming, while his offices get redecorated."

"He is? Good grief. Well, still, honey, I wouldn't dream of investing in anything without his advice. He's the family money maven. Anyway, tell me about it."

"Well, you know they knocked down Bert's, right?"

"I knew they were going to do that. I guess they figured it would cost more to fix it than to replace the building."

"Whatever. It's history. Anyway, the land was bought by this man from Atlanta who develops beach properties for commercial use."

Beth outlined the rest of the details to her mother, who listened and asked a lot of questions.

"And I imagine you want to break into your trust to invest in this?"

"No, not exactly. I just want to borrow some money against it. Only for ninety days."

"Look, Beth, here's my problem with this. Actually, I have more than one. First, your father was adamant that he didn't want you to touch your trust until you are thirty. I think he thought that by the time you were thirty you would understand that you never touch the principal."

"Oh, please. If there's anything left!"

"Hear me out. Second, when you talk about this fellow Max, it sounds to me like you are personally involved with him."

"We're just friends. I swear," Beth lied, and hated herself for it, but did her mother have ESP?

"Okay, but still. It sounds like you are

more than friends. Mother's intuition. How old is he anyway?"

"He's thirty-seven."

"Too old. Don't even think about it, you hear me?"

"Mom, honest to God—"

"Please don't—"

"Okay, honest to goodness."

"Better. Much better. And third, why would you want to invest in something your uncle declined? It doesn't make good sense to me. Does it?"

"Well, you're there and I'm here. If you were here and met him and saw the prospectus, you'd get out your checkbook. I'm just thinking this is a great short-term way to make up what I've lost and any idiot can see it's going to be awesome."

"Any idiot, huh? How much money are you talking about?"

"One hundred thousand," Beth said as nonchalantly as she could without swallowing her tongue like a whole tube of liverwurst.

Susan was quiet for a minute and Beth wondered if she had lost the connection.

"Mom? Are you there?"

"Yes, I'm here. Beth?"

"Yes?"

"Did Aunt Maggie leave anything behind in her medicine cabinet that interests you? You know, like happy pills for people on a major bummer?"

"Um, no."

"You're serious, aren't you?"

"Look, Mom, I'm dead serious. I even had my account manager down here to look at it and he's putting his own money in."

"How much?"

"I don't know. Probably about the same or a little more." Another lie.

"I see. Look, Beth, we're just not the kind of people who go around doing things like this. We're not risk takers. You and I are not rich."

"Really? Uncle Henry's not a risk taker?"

"He went to business school. He's trained to understand risk."

"My account manager graduated first in his class at Harvard Business School. And what about Aunt Sophie and Aunt Allison? They were only twenty-one when they opened their first studio. Who supported them? Where'd they get the money?"

"My stepfather gave it to them, God rest his soul."

"See? Look, I'm going to write out what I need for you to sign and I'll fax it over to you. You look at it and tell me what you think. If you decide you want to support me, just sign it and fax it back. Couldn't be easier."

"Beth, I just don't think this is the right time to be doing something like this. The world is too uncertain."

"Look, Mom. I know it's hard for you to think of me as anything but a little girl. You just don't realize that I am old enough to be married and have a family of my own."

And you don't *want* to realize that because it would make you feel like you're a thousand years old yourself and then you can't be eternally cool, she thought but did not say.

"In another culture, perhaps."

"Mom? You were my age when you got married."

"Times were different then."

"Okay, Mom. Listen, do what you want, but at some point you, Aunt Maggie, Uncle Henry—all of you are going to have to start treating me like an adult."

"Oh, Beth. Let me give this some thought, okay?"

"Okay. But I only have like a day to decide, so time matters, Mom."

"I hear you. Let me just take a walk around the block and I'll call you back."

"Hey, Mom?"

"Yeah?"

"I love you, and thanks."

"I love you too, Beth."

"And listen, Mom, this is a really good, solid opportunity. I swear."

Beth wondered if her mother was going to hang up the phone and call Maggie or Simon or Grant, or would she try to track down Henry in the backwoods of Wyoming? Or maybe she would just take a walk around the block as she said she was going to do. Beth tried to put it out of her mind so she took Lola out to the front yard. Lola was a great diversion. Beth sat on the bottom step and watched her dog run around for a few minutes. After she had scared away a few squirrels and some little black birds of a species unknown to Beth, Lola came and sat right at Beth's feet, panting from exertion.

"Does my baby want some water? Come on, miss, your momma's gonna take care of that right now."

Just as she changed the water in Lola's bowl and placed it on the floor, the phone rang. It was her mother.

"Okay, I've thought about it and here's what I think."

She had not opened with a blast of *No way, forget it, you're too young to do this, you're an idiot . . .* so Beth held her breath and waited for her to continue.

"I tried to think of what I would do in your situation if it was me making the investment, and I just think that one hundred thousand dollars is an insane amount of money to risk. To be honest, it makes me feel a little bit sick to my stomach. So, I'm thinking put in ten thousand and see if he lives up to his promises, and then invest in another deal with him for more money if it turns out that he's a straight-shooter. How does that sound?"

Beth's head was spinning with panic and her heart began to race. Ten thousand? That's all? She had already told Max she was going to give him ten times more than that! She would look like a fool! A complete and total fool! He would never believe a word that came out of her mouth again for the rest of her life! She might as well give him nothing if all she had to offer was this humiliating pittance! He would never see her as a full partner! Much less a wife! She was going to lose Max! Lose him! Forever!

She was just about to start screaming but something told her to calm down and just say, Okay, that sounds good, and thank you and you're probably right, which she managed to do. Just barely.

"Look, Beth, you said this guy is developing beach properties all up and down the coast, didn't you?"

"Yeah." Beth was so upset she could hardly stay focused on the conversation.

"So, if this one works out, you might want to do another. I think it's always a good rule of thumb to start slow and build, don't you? I mean, that's what Henry would say. I'm pretty sure about that."

"You're probably right. But it's not what I had hoped for."

"Well, life is like that, isn't it? I mean, Beth, ten thousand dollars is an enormous amount of money! Think about it! It's more than some people ever have to invest in anything besides their home, and for a girl of your age to have it to invest is a very incredible thing!"

"I guess."

"So, Doodle, you send me the paperwork and I'll sign whatever I have to sign and that's it! And, hey! Congratulations! This is your first independent investment! Woo hoo!"

"Thanks!" Beth tried to sound enthusiastic but her disappointment had shaken her so badly it was as though her life were over. In that moment she wanted to die.

"Well, honey, I just wanted to let you know that I think you're brilliant and I trust you and your judgment. And I love you. Here's the fax number."

Beth wrote it down and said goodbye to her mother, trying to sound upbeat. How was she going to tell Max? She would drop this bomb, he was going to walk away from her, and she would never see him again. Wait! she thought. Is Max only in this for the money? She had thought that before, but more and more she had become convinced that Max really cared about her for her and not just for her wallet. This was the obvious pitfall of mixing business and pleasure. She had to ignore her insecurity and proceed with confidence! She would just tell Max and he would understand. Wouldn't he? She would say, Max? Remember that one hundred thousand? Well, now it's ten. Yeah, right, that would impress him. Yeah, sure, that'll work with him. And that other ninety thousand would just have to come from someone else, like that wrinkly old woman she saw him with at Atlanticville. Holy shit! she thought. I can't let that happen. I just can't. He needs the money. I know he does!

He had never come right out and said he was desperate in so many words but she knew it, and if she was desperate, she told herself, it was only because she wanted to be the one who made life so easy for him. She wanted to clear his path, pave his way, pre-solve any and all problems he might ever have. He would want her with him for the rest of his life. She would be his lucky charm, his guardian angel, his savior. Now, that dream along with her heart and soul were blown into little bits of laughing dust, floating through all the rooms of the Island Gamble, mocking her, whispering terrible things about her. *She had to be a big shot, didn't she? Now what! Look at her! She's ridiculous! Everyone knows it!*

She sat down, elbows on the kitchen table, her head resting on the heels of her hands, and began to cry. Oh God! Why couldn't she ever have anything for herself? Why couldn't she make one decision on her own and have everyone else think that if *Beth said so* it must be all right? But nooooo! Not in this lifetime, she thought. Beth was so angry with her mother she didn't know what to do with herself. If she had been Henry at her age, fresh out of business school, they would've all jumped up and said, Oh, Henry's always been so smart and everything he touches turns to gold! He's Uncle Freaking Midas Touch! And her twin aunts? Well, there were two of them, a team, and who could argue that they understood what the whole world of fitness was about? All you had to do was look at them! But for Beth? Never. It had never been easy for her and it never would be.

At last, Beth began to pull herself together and she typed up the paper for her mother to sign.

It read, *I give my daughter, Elizabeth Hayes, permission to borrow against her trust account with Hamilton Investments, 2020 Peachtree Road, Atlanta, Georgia, up to ten thousand dollars.* There was a line drawn for her mother's signature under which it read *Susan Hamilton Hayes Rifkin*, and of course, it was dated for that day.

Beth printed the document and stared at the paper. Her mother had tried to understand the depth of Beth's plight, but plain and simple, she did not. But she had tried. Beth had to give her that much credit. And her mother also thought she had come up with a perfectly acceptable compromise. If this had been only a business deal it might have been reasonable. It wasn't that she didn't trust Beth's judgment, it was the amount of the investment that made Susan so nervous. But she did trust her judgment. She had said so in those exact words, had she not?

Big deal, Beth thought, convinced that no one in the world really understood her. Ten thousand.

Suddenly an idea was born in Beth's mind. She rewrote and reprinted the same document, only the second time she drew a line where the dollar amount was to go and printed it. Then, carefully, she wrote in the numerals of the dollar amount so that it read *10000*. It was a small space with no room to write out the amount as you would on an ordinary check.

She faxed it to her mother right away and thought out loud, "We'll just leave this one to fate."

Feeling less like a congenial hostess than she ever had, she managed to get to Atlanticville in a timely fashion. Work was a misery. It was hot, the restaurant was crowded, and she wound up clearing tables because two people called in sick. When one table complained that they had been waiting for their food for almost an hour, she was about a splinter away from telling them to go to hell and see how they liked the service there.

She hated her life more than ever and at least three times she fought back tears of anger and thought about just running away and chucking it all—the family, graduate school, and everything.

Alan and Robert pulled her aside twice to see if something was wrong.

"You sure you're okay?" they said.

"Yeah, just pissed about something un-related to this place. I'm okay."

"We can take you out tonight and get you drunk. How's that sound?" Robert said.

"I'm in," Alan said. "Come out with us! We're excellent company."

"We'll see. Y'all are the sweetest."

"*We'll see* sounds like a no, bubba," Alan said to Robert.

"Yeah, darn. Looks like it's just us again, trolling the bars all alone . . . It's very sad, Beth, very sad. Pitiful, really. Right, Alan?"

"Pitiful," Alan said, looking somber.

They were so adorable. Beth brightened a little and told herself she needed to do a better job of concealing her feelings. It wasn't professional to consider telling patrons where to get off or to mope around in a cloud of gloom.

By the time she returned from work, her mother's return fax was there. Beth exam-ined it and went over her plan again. She simply added a zero and faxed it off to Woody at his home with a cover sheet that just said *Got it!* fully expecting him to call her right away. If her scheme worked, fine. If it didn't, well, then she would plead insanity and let the firing squad commence. If Beth could not spend the rest of her life in the arms of Max Mitchell, she had all but decided with certainty that life wasn't worth living.

And speaking of Max, he had not called her all day. Weren't they supposed to have dinner that night? Yes, they were. Beth looked at her watch. It was already five o'clock. Where was he? She checked the message machine. Nothing. She checked her cell phone, and sure enough, she had missed his call. She dialed him back.

"Hey!" she said. "How's the greatest guy in the world?"

"Well, you're not going to like this."

"What?"

"I'm still in Wilmington. We break ground here in two weeks and the contractor doesn't have all the permits and it's just a big mess. But I should be back tomorrow night. I'm sorry."

She thought he was going to Wrightsville Beach, but she supposed she had heard him wrong.

"Oh, it's okay. I'm sort of tired and I have to work on this article for the paper."

"Which reminds me, whatever happened to the other one?"

"Oh, it comes out tomorrow."

"Cool. Well, that will be fun to see. And Woody went back to Atlanta, I assume?"

"Yeah, he left this morning."

"He's a great guy."

"Yeah. Smart like anything."

They talked for a few more minutes and finally said goodbye.

She called Woody and got his voice mail. She called Cecily and got her voice mail too.

"So, what am I supposed to do all night? Sit around and stew?" She was talking to herself, but this was not so unusual, especially given the tensions of the day. "Oh, shoot, I may as well work on my piece for the paper."

She went upstairs, got out a legal pad to take notes, and started rereading the letters to the editor in the *Moultrie News* and some other articles from the *Post and Courier* that she had been saving. Noise was the new cause du jour on Sullivans Island. It had long been a problem downtown in the French Quarter, on the Isle of

Palms beachfront, and, of course, on Folly Beach since the days of their amusement park and the pier. But Sullivans Island was a family-oriented island, and different in that it had never really curried the favor of pub crawlers.

Beth was unsure of her political stance on the topic. In some ways, she liked the liveliness of Dunleavy's Pub, Off the Hook, and Poe's Tavern. It made the island seem like a happening place and she didn't feel so isolated from the modern world. But through reading the stack of letters and articles and by talking to the guys at Atlanticville she was beginning to understand the problem. And, most especially, now that she was going to be an investor in the health of the area, it was even more important for her to fully grasp the issues.

A few residents who had purchased homes near the bars in the business district were complaining bitterly about the late-night noise. How stupid! she thought. If you wanted to live in a quiet spot, why on earth would you buy a house near a beach bar? Let's look at it another way, she thought. Should the complaints of a few dictate the rights of the many? Yes, in this case, because wasn't every resident entitled to peace?

The noise went farther than the backyards of the neighbors of the bar scene. There were some residents who had owned houses on the island for over fifty years and the voices from the partyers and their loud music carried over as far as Atlantic Avenue and as far back as Raven Drive.

When Beth was a little girl, Sullivans Island was a sleepy beach community. The wildest thing that happened at night might have been a stranded tourist with a flat tire. In recent years the popularity of the island's business district had grown dramatically. Now there were easily a thousand people who came and went from all the bars and restaurants on Friday and Saturday nights to meet friends and listen to music until two in the morning. And all that noise traveled across the island like pollen, hence the complaints. Happy voices calling out to one another sounded like a good thing unless you were trying to keep your children asleep in their beds. Shouldn't tax-paying residents have the pleasure of sleeping with their windows open, waiting to be lulled off to dreamland on the sounds of an incoming tide?

But here was the problem no one seemed overly concerned about. Yet. If someone was on the porch of a bar or in the parking lot of a restaurant in the wee hours of the morning, carrying on at the top of their lungs like a maniac, shouldn't the authorities call their sobriety into question? Locking up rowdy drunks was surely safer than letting them drive home and killing themselves or, worse, some innocent people in another car. But the island had no holding cell, did it? If the island turned their heads while people, as drunk as forty goats, got behind the wheel of their cars resulting in tragedies, one after another, wouldn't that be a liability for the island at some point? Certainly it would be for the bars that had overserved them. Beth had lots of questions that needed answers and she imagined she would have to go over to the police station on Monday and also place a call to the island attorney. But where was common sense in all of this? Once people were made aware that the island residents did not want to live like that, wouldn't visitors come to their senses and have a little regard for others? As of yet, no.

Beth was not the only one stewing in her juices waiting for a phone call. What if Woody looked hard at her fax and realized she had added that zero? It took all of her willpower to put it out of her mind.

Woody Morrison arrived at his home late Sunday night after watching a tennis match with some friends of his and checked his email. There in the basket of his fax machine was the letter of permission from Beth. It looked fine to him and he wondered what Beth had been through to get her mother to go along with their plan. One phone call and her mother said yes to a hundred thousand dollars? Amazing. Maybe Beth should go into a career in sales!

While undressing for bed, he began to feel some anxiety over the whole thing. He knew there was nothing legally wrong with what he was about to do, but he had never done anything like this without Henry's counsel. He was Henry's golden boy. The fact that Henry himself had judged the deal as unworthy of investment for whatever limp reason he claimed, Woody worried that it might seem disloyal for him to steer Henry's niece toward it. But they had Beth's mother's stamp of approval and that was all they needed. He would call his friend at HSBC first thing in the morning and get the transfers and loans settled. Despite the times, Woody's reputation and track record were platinum and he would get it all done by noon. He was sure of it. Besides, he was so dead in love with Beth Hayes that he would have done anything to prove it, especially now that Max had indicated he would clear the field for him. Woody hoped that all he needed was time for Beth to see how right they were for each other. The last thing he thought about as he pulled his covers over his shoulders was how much his parents would like Beth. They would love her. She was the quintessential girl next door.

On Monday morning, Beth picked up the *Island Eye News* wrapped up neatly in a plastic bag at the end of their driveway. She tore it open, very excited to read her first published article. Right there on the front page was a picture of Max Mitchell and he had never looked more handsome. The headline, clearly written by Barbara

Farlie, said *Meet Max Mitchell,* and a sub-title read *Developer Brings Island into 21st Century.*

Beth scanned her words and, beyond the headlines, Barbara Farlie had not changed a thing. Beth was thrilled!

"Wait till Max sees this! This is going to bring him so much business! This is wonderful! Holy crap! I'm a real journalist! I'm a paid professional!"

She dialed Max's cell phone but got his voice mail. He was probably out of range, she thought, and left him an excited message to look up the newspaper online because now he was famous!

The rest of the morning was spent talking back and forth to Woody and faxing signed forms between the banks. As predicted, the deal was done right around a late lunchtime. Woody and Beth were beside themselves with excitement.

"Did you talk to him?" Beth asked.

"Yeah, but only long enough to get the routing information for the transfer. It's raining like the dickens up there and his phone kept dying. But he's very happy about the money, that's for sure."

"Well, good. I wish he'd call me! I've

been trying to get him on the phone all morning."

"He'll call."

"I know he will. We're having dinner tonight."

"Really? Well, hoist a glass of champagne with my name on it. We're all partners now!"

"I know! Oh, Woody! This is the most thrilling thing I have ever done in my whole life!"

"You know what? Me too!"

Beth was still giddy when she realized it was four o'clock in the afternoon and still Max had not called. She called him again and this time he answered.

"So, hi! What's going on? Where've you been?"

"Hi. Busy. Crazy busy."

"Well, you got the money, right?" Max didn't sound right.

"Yep. Thanks. It makes all the difference."

"Are you going to make it back in time for dinner?"

"I don't think so, Beth."

Now Max sounded parental and his tone was filled with annoyance.

"Why not?"

"Look, I went online on my foreman's laptop and read that article. Remember I told you not to take my picture?"

"Oh, please, you look like a movie star!"

"Well, thanks, but I really hate having my picture taken and I thought you knew that."

"Yeah, well, it wasn't up to me. The editor in chief chose the pictures."

Was he angry with her over one insignificant photograph?

"I see."

"So that's it? A little thanks for the hundred thousand dollars and goodbye?"

"No. I'm sorry. Look, I've just had a really terrible day. Really terrible. I'll call you when I'm on the way back, okay? It will probably be tomorrow."

"So? No celebration dinner tonight?"

"Nope. I'll see you tomorrow night. I hope."

"Hey, I miss you!"

"I miss you too! Listen, what's your street address in case someone wants to send you flowers?"

She perked up at the promise of flowers from him and gave him the address just as fast as she could spit it out of her mouth. But the flowers would never arrive.

In the meantime, Cecily called Monday afternoon to say she wasn't coming over. She was fully occupied with Niles in the throes of their new love and he was wearing her out. Presumably and hopefully, she was doing the same to him.

"I need a facial and a nap," she said to Beth.

"A facial? Do you know I have never had a professional facial?"

"You don't need one, honey, with that peaches and cream skin of yours! Anyway, I'll see you tomorrow. Is everything okay?"

"Of course! Everything is great."

But everything was not great, and Monday night turned out to be one of the most unnerving nights of her life. Beth called Max every two hours until one in the morning and he never answered his phone. She prayed to God and begged for Max's safety, and when she couldn't shed another single tear, she took herself to bed. *Something* was terribly wrong.

Her first call to Max had been prompted by her spontaneous desire just to hear his voice and perhaps have a celebratory glass of something on the phone together. That seemed appropriate, all things considered. But he didn't answer. Was he out with someone else? Maybe his assistant architect or foreman? So she waited until nine and dialed his number again. This time all she wanted to do was apologize over his picture appearing on the front page of the paper. That had to be why he wasn't answering the phone. But why would a picture make him so angry? She just didn't understand. It didn't make sense. But she would apologize anyway and smooth things over. The third and fourth times she called him she was sure he was either in bed with another woman or in a hospital.

To add to her growing frustration, she couldn't call anyone to say she was concerned about his safety or her money because she had lied to almost everyone about the nature of her relationship with him. The only one who knew all the facts was Woody. If she had called Woody, he would surely have panicked to hear the escalating concern in her voice. The truth was, Beth was worried at a level that would have been impossible to conceal. And after what had transpired between Beth and Woody on the porch that night, she really didn't want him to see her in doubt over her feelings for Max or Max's integrity. Since then she had all but declared her choice. Based in part on Beth's faith in Max, they had signed away a fortune to him just that morning. She knew Woody cared about her and trusted her and those were the reasons why he had moved so quickly to make everything happen. What if she was wrong? What if she was wrong?

15

Bad News

Susanthepen@writenow.org
Maggie, Tell me I'm losing it and I won't disagree with you. I keep having these terrible dreams! Last night I dreamed Beth was standing on the edge of the ocean at Station 221/2. She was screaming and screaming over the noise of the ocean, which was churning the way it does when a hurricane is coming. I can't take this. Something is wrong. Am I losing it?

Maggiepie2@marthagene.net
Quit eating escargots. Snails never did agree with you. What you need is some Bluffton oysters and a good glass of cold white California agricultural product, like Henry would say. Funky food makes funky dreams. Try a little poulet ce soir. xx ooh la la!

It wasn't like Beth really slept that night, it was more like she tossed and turned, had a fitful nap for an hour, and then woke up to house noises. Yes, the house noises were back and they were the worst she had ever heard. All through the night, the clock chimed, floors creaked, the halls whispered, and occasionally something would slam, like a door or a drawer, or there would be a distinctive sound like the *thunk* of a dropped hammer that would reverberate through the rooms. She would have sworn she could smell the fragrance of Aramis, her father's favorite cologne. Finally, at six-thirty, she gave up her bed to the day and got up to face the morning. These were dark omens, and as familiar as the islanders were with signs and wonders, Beth didn't know what to make of it all. Rather, that is, she didn't want to know.

She pulled on a pair of shorts and a T-shirt and decided to walk Lola on the beach. She was so tired. Her eyes were swollen from crying, her hair was a sweaty rat's nest of mats and tangles. She had not looked this bad since the day after she had her wisdom teeth removed. She washed her face and looked at the dark circles under her eyes. There was nothing to be done about the way she felt and looked except to drink a lot of caffeine and hope that her youth would trump her over-whelming exhaustion.

She hooked Lola to her leash and crossed the dunes, leaving the house wide open, thinking it was well protected by all the dead crazies. Although the day had all the promise of a classic hot and humid summer day—blue skies without a cloud, birds atwitter by the score, rising sun—something terrible was in the air. She knew it just as she knew something was seri-ously wrong with Max. Where was he? Why had he not called her back? The si-lence from him was so deafening, she would have believed he was dead because she couldn't find him in her heart. It seri-ously frightened and unnerved her.

She wished she could reverse time and go back to the very first day she met him. What was the matter with her? Why had she been so anxious, so *hell-bent and de-termined* to impress him? Did this relation-ship happen all because of her own ambition to be recognized as an adult before the world would have offered a ceremony of some sort that opened that door for her? Perhaps. Perhaps it did. Why was she in such an infernal rush?

And exactly what was it about him that she found so irresistible? Why had she fallen so hard for him? He was gorgeous to look at for one thing. Everyone agreed on that. And he exuded confidence, taking charge of every situation. When she was with him, he made her feel alive all over and made her believe that everything was going to be wonderful. He didn't just look in her eyes like others did. He looked in her eyes with an intense kind of desire that she had never even known existed, as though he could read every thought in her head and knew everything about her that ever was or would be. She didn't just love him, she idolized him. She loved every whisker on his face and the way they grew and every single curly hair on his head. She loved the way he smiled and smelled and that sometimes he seemed slightly dangerous. If Max had been a drug, he would have been a controlled substance.

The beach was almost empty of people, except for a few old salts tossing tennis balls and Frisbees with their dogs. The tide was going out. Soon, locals and tourists would begin arriving with their children and chairs, umbrellas and coolers, toys and books. They would spend a great part of their day soaking up vitamin D and digging their toes in the wet sand near the edge of the water. Their little ones would build castles of sand and mud and dig moats all around them. When they got hungry, they would eat pimento cheese sandwiches and sandwiches made of pineapple and cream cheese, all on white bread, cut into perfect halves. Their mothers would wipe their faces, kiss their cheeks, and they would run back to play. In the afternoon, they would return home, caravans of families, rinse off under their outdoor showers, and sit on their porches and steps until they were dry enough to go inside without tracking sand and water from one room to another. Little ones, with golden arms and freckled noses, would take long naps under overhead fans, crooked in their beds but fast asleep on their backs like starfish. The adults would continue to read or start supper. Eventually they would all migrate to the porch for gin and tonics while their children played all the old games like swing the statue out in the yard on the grass that glistened with the dew of evening. Later still, all of them would disappear inside for suppers of rice and something else, but always rice.

That life, Beth realized, was the one she wanted. She had dreamed of having something like that with Max, but now, because he had not returned her calls, she feared that everything was in jeopardy. And what did that say exactly, the fact that she feared her whole future hung in the balance because of a few unreturned phone calls? Something way inside her heart knew she had given far too much and received far too little.

Without planning to walk such a distance, she saw she was near the crossover at Station 221/2, which was very close to the construction site. Maybe, she thought, I should go over there, and if Max is around, he can give me a ride home and tell me where he's been. Good idea, she thought.

So she crossed the dunes for the second time that morning, wishing she had pulled herself together a little better, but then, so what? He knew what she looked like when she wanted to look good. This was the beach, for heaven's sake, and it was barely eight o'clock in the morning. And she was a fourth-generation Geechee Girl, which required no explanation to the locals.

Once she got away from the sounds of the ocean, she expected to hear the construction crew shattering through the morning quiet with whirring band saws and whacking hammers, but she did not. And then she thought maybe they didn't start work until a little later and she might see a few guys sitting around eating donuts and drinking coffee from a thermos. But when she rounded the corner, there were no trucks, no noise—in fact, the entire site was deserted. This was strange, very strange. Beth knocked on the door of the darkened trailer and no one was inside. Everything was locked up. What was this? She had goose bumps all over her arms and legs.

Beth couldn't get home soon enough. She fast-walked, carrying Lola most of the way, with every conceivable excuse for the abandoned site running through her mind. Maybe someone died and they were taking the day off out of respect for the family of the deceased. Probably not. Maybe there was a terrible traffic jam on the Cooper River Bridge and they were just stuck, waiting there for a wreck to be cleared away. Maybe. Maybe the foreman had a heart attack and canceled work for the day. Slight chance of something like that, she told herself, but not very likely.

By the time she got back to the house, she was dripping in perspiration from the threat of panic, humidity, and the rising heat.

"I'm going to put this all out of my mind until I've had a shower and dressed for the day," she said to Lola, and filled Lola's dish with cool water.

Lola's ears were flat against her head as she could sense Beth's distress. Nonetheless, she lapped up an impressive amount of water and followed Beth wherever she went, sitting quietly outside the bathroom door while Beth tried to shampoo and scrub away all her trepidations and watch them disappear down the drain.

As she dressed, she decided to gather up her notes and pay a visit to Barbara Farlie, now that she had a new idea for a piece simmering away. Dropping in on Barbara was a good distraction from the

Max dilemma until she could gather more information. It was still early in the day and she felt sure that when she got back to the business district she would see all the workmen hammering away.

She parked her car in the parking lot of Station 22 Restaurant and walked across the street. In less than the hour it had taken her to go home, shower, and dress, the police had cordoned off Max's entire site with endless banners of yellow tape. Beth became dizzy and nauseated from the stunning surprise of that and for a second she thought she might actually pass out cold, but she took a deep breath, steadied herself, and hurried over to one of several police officers who were milling around.

"What's happened here?" she said. "What in the world?"

"Crime scene."

"What kind of crime?"

"Sorry, miss. We can't discuss it. There's an investigation under way."

"But I have a lot of money invested in this . . ."

"Oh yeah? I'd call a lawyer if I were you."

"A lawyer? Why?"

"Sorry, honey. I can't discuss it. As I said—"

But before he could finish his sentence, Beth had spun around and was rushing back to her car as fast as she could. Did he call her *honey*? She didn't even care.

Her head was throbbing and her eyes were burning with tears again.

"Oh dear God! What should I do? Please! God! Tell me what to do!"

As soon as she got home, she called Cecily, voice catching and hands trembling. Obviously she had to call Woody, but she didn't know what to say to him yet. Cecily would help her figure it out. She answered on the third ring.

"Cecily? Oh God! Cecily?"

"Beth? Is that you? What's wrong?"

"Oh, Cecily! I am . . . I'm in so much trouble! So much terrible trouble!"

"Girl? Are you pregnant? Beth? Are you pregnant?"

"No! No! God! That would be nothing! Do you hear me? Nothing! I wish that was all it was!"

"What then?"

"I can't . . . it's so . . ."

"I'll be right there! Don't go anywhere!

Don't do anything until I get there! I'm at Staples and I will be there in ten minutes. Do not worry, okay?"

"Worry? You have no idea!"

"We will get this all figured out in no time!"

"No! We won't!"

"Yes! Yes we will! Just go sit on the porch and put that little dog in your lap. No, turn on HGTV and see what those crazy real estate people are up to! You know? Watch *Property Virgins*!"

"Real estate? *Property Virgins?* That's the *last* thing on this earth I ever want to hear about again! Cecily! You don't understand! I might wind up in *jail*!"

Beth was crying hysterically, gasping for breath, and sniffing loudly. It was all Cecily could do to understand what she was wailing about. But she was certain that indeed something awful had happened to Beth, and before Cecily could figure it out, she was almost on the causeway. *Jail? Jail?* What in the world could she have possibly gotten herself into? She hadn't even been on the island that long! Then she remembered Max. Very quickly, she put two and two together. He was the guy Beth thought she was in love with and was going to marry! Oh! The poor girl! Sure enough, as she turned right on Middle Street, there was the scene of the crime.

She followed the twenty-five-mile-per-hour speed limit for a few blocks but then realized that every single last officer the island employed, probably including the dogcatcher, was at the site, and who was going to chase her down and give her a ticket? Cecily put her foot on the gas, and inside of two minutes she pulled into Beth's yard.

Suddenly the house looked old and everything about it was wrong. The shutters were hanging crooked on their hinges, the back steps sagged, and the roof looked dull. Even the landscaping seemed to be drooping.

"This must be very bad," Cecily said, getting out of her car. "Very, very bad."

She raced up the steps and burst into the house calling Beth's name. There was no answer. At last, after searching downstairs, she saw her through a window, holding on to a banister on the porch for support. Cecily could see Beth's shoulders convulsing and that she was sobbing. She grabbed a box of tissues and went to her. She threw one arm around Beth's waist and offered her the tissues.

"I'm a dead woman," Beth wailed, taking two and wiping her eyes. "You don't know!"

"No you're not. Now, blow your nose and let's go inside where the nonexistent-during-the-day neighbors can't hear us. You'll sit and figure out how to tell me the whole story while I make us some tea and listen."

Beth seemed rooted to the porch, unable to budge her feet.

"Come on now. Once you tell me everything it won't seem so bad."

"No, it's truly terrible. Telling it won't make it better."

"Come on, Beth. Every problem has a solution just like there's a lid for every pot. Let's go."

Beth moved so slowly and with such profound sadness, as though she were taking that final walk to the gallows, but she finally made it to the kitchen table, where she sank into a chair.

They were quiet for a few minutes until they could hear the heat coming up under the kettle. The water sizzled a little as droplets rose and splashed against the hot sides of the stainless steel. Cecily took out two mugs, the sugar bowl, the cream pitcher, and a lemon, put them all on the table, and sat.

"I don't know if you want lemon or milk, so we have both. Talk to me."

"Cecily? I don't know where to start."

But she did start, and soon, after three cups of tea each, Cecily knew as much as Beth did. The clock struck noon.

"That's it?"

"Yep. That's the whole sordid tale."

"Well, I must say, I am in awe of your cojones."

"Oh, thanks a lot. Do you understand that my mother is going to kill me?"

"Yes. She will. She's going to beat you bloody up one side and black and blue down the other. Unless we figure this out. Look, first, you have to call Woody. He has a right to know everything that you know, don't you think?"

"Yes. I know he does, but I can't face him. I can't face anyone. Not right now."

"Who am I? Nobody?"

"Of course not, please Cecily. I called you because you're the only one I trust not to go crazy and start yelling at me like an animal!"

Cecily reached across the table and put her hand over Beth's.

"You called me because you know in your heart that I am your true friend. No matter what. We've got the Livvie-Susan bond."

"Thanks be to God for that. Yes. Yes, you are my friend, and you know what? Besides Woody, you are my only friend."

Beth began to weep again. This time her tears were so large and fast and in such profusion that they ran together, splashing the table as they fell, forming tiny pools.

Cecily could actually feel Beth's suffering all through her own body, and not knowing what else to do, she got up and stood behind Beth, rubbing her back in circles with her hand, saying, *It's okay, it's all going to be okay.* She recognized that Beth's sobbing and the depth of her despair weren't normal even given the gravity of the situation. She had never seen anyone cry so hard. It seemed as though Beth was releasing a veritable lake of tears she had been holding back her whole life, letting them go all at once. The sounds of Beth's wounded heart continued to break Cecily's heart as well. She imagined her disappointment in Max was somehow tied into her disappointment over losing her father, and maybe some part of her felt she had lost her mother too when she married Simon. But mostly it seemed apparent to Cecily that no one had ever given this child a chance to grieve with someone sympathetic to listen. And she was still a child in many ways. So trusting. So naïve. So desperate to be the center of someone's world to the point that even a creep like Max could get the job by just showing up. He was no better than Rasputin.

Finally, after a while, Beth seemed to be slowing down, having worn herself out. Cecily walked back around the table to take her seat again, but as she passed the door, she saw a car pull up into the yard, blocking her own. It was a sedan.

"Hey, Beth? You know anybody who drives a black Plymouth?"

"No."

Two men in dark suits and sunglasses got out of their car and looked up at the house. They could've been the Blues Brothers, but they weren't.

"Well, we've got company. Go wash your face. Right now, Beth."

Beth jumped up and took a quick look out of the window over the sink.

"Maybe they have the wrong house."

"I doubt it, now scoot!"

Beth didn't have time to go upstairs, wash her face, and put on some makeup that would disguise her distress. If there was one thing she had inherited besides her blue eyes, it was the kind of complexion that got blotchy and swollen when she cried. For years she had struggled to save her tears for great calamities such as death, fear of death, and now she could add fear of prison to her list. Not to mention being completely ostracized by her family. Forever. And that was the paradox. Now that she needed her family more than she ever had, they were going to disown her. She was about to lose everything.

She slipped into the bathroom Woody had used and held a cold wet washcloth to her face, especially on her eyes. When she heard Cecily call out for her, she flushed the toilet to buy her another minute and finally reappeared in the kitchen, where the two men waited by the door.

"Are you Elizabeth Hayes?"

"Yes." Beth's voice was hushed because in that split second she realized they could be there to tell her anything. That her mother was dead, that Aunt Maggie, Simon, and Uncle Grant had been killed in a car crash or an earthquake. That Uncle Henry had run into a bear . . .

"I'm Agent Colson from the FBI and this is my partner, Agent Feron." They offered her their identification and it all seemed legitimate to Beth. "We'd just like to ask you a few questions. May we come in?"

They could have been showing her false identification and Beth would not have known it. Their presence was so intimidating, Beth was terrified.

"Sure," Beth said, shaken. "Would you like a cold drink? Tea? Ice water?"

Lola, who was cowering behind Beth, began to growl and bark, although it wasn't very threatening.

"Does the dog bite?" Feron said.

"Oh heavens no! I'm sorry. Lola! Get in your crate! She's just protecting me."

Lola scuttled into her crate and Beth latched the gate.

"Yeah, she's ferocious," Cecily said, and reached in the refrigerator, taking a bottle of water. Cecily was as cool and unruffled as she could be.

"I'm sorry," Beth said. "Cold drink?"

"No, we're fine, thank you. Is there somewhere we can talk to you for just a few minutes?"

"Y'all go on to the living room and I'll make myself busy in here," Cecily said.

Beth's face was almost white, and after the men left the room as she pointed the way, Cecily pulled Beth back.

"Listen to me," she said. "Remember Martha? Lying to a federal agent is a felony! Tell them everything you know, you hear me? I mean, everything!"

Beth bobbed her head, sighed for all the world, and said, "Can I have that bottle of water."

Cecily gave her the bottle she was holding and Beth left to join the agents.

"Please, sit down," she said to them, realizing they were waiting for her to invite them to do so. If nothing else, she had to say, FBI agents had manners.

They sat on two chairs opposite the sofa and took out small flip-top notepads and pens. Beth sat in the center of the sofa so that the three of them formed a triangle.

"What's this about?" Beth asked.

"Can you tell us how well you know a fellow by the name of Max Mitchell?"

Beth inhaled and exhaled hard.

"Very well. Too well."

"How so?"

"Meaning that I met him and wrote an article about him for our local paper."

"We read the article. That's what brought us here. To the island and to you."

"Really? Anyway, we went out some, a lot in fact, and I invested a fortune in his business."

The agents sat back, looking surprised. What did she mean by a fortune? She was just a young girl!

"How much is a fortune?"

Beth hesitated to say because she didn't want her stupidity to wind up in the news before she had the chance to come clean about it with her family. But she also knew that if she lied she could wind up in a prison washing clothes with convicted murderers and drug addicts.

"Can this be confidential?"

"Sure, Miss Hayes."

"I gave him one hundred thousand dollars."

Agent Feron whistled under his breath and glanced at Agent Colson, whose eyes opened wide as he inhaled deeply. They both made notes.

"My father left some money to me," she offered as an explanation.

"I see. Okay." Feron cleared his throat. "Can you tell us when was the last time you saw Mr. Mitchell?"

"Yes. It was last Friday. I'm pretty sure of that."

"And then he told you what? That he would see you again? When?"

"We were supposed to have dinner Sunday night but he was up in North Carolina—Wilmington or Wrightsville Beach, I'm not sure—and he couldn't get back."

"Did he say why?"

"Yes. That his next project was all bungled up with permits and so forth but we would have dinner on Monday night."

"And did you have dinner?"

"No. He never showed up and he never returned my calls. Is Max all right? He's not hurt, is he?"

"No. Not to our knowledge. Not at all."

"Well, what's happened? Why are you looking for him? This is serious, isn't it?"

"You may as well hear it from us, Miss Hayes. Max Mitchell, who goes by many other names, is a notorious scam artist. We've been after him for almost two years. Because of that picture in your local paper, our office in Columbia was able to make a match. I wish I could tell you that you'll get your money back but you probably won't. If he's still up to his old tricks, your money is long gone. Most likely it went to pay some of the bills on his last deal."

If either agent had merely exhaled in Beth's direction, she would have fallen off the sofa. She was literally dumbstruck.

The agents stood and took out their business cards, offering her one, which she took with shaking hands.

"If you see him or hear from him, we'd appreciate a call."

"Of course."

"Thanks for your time," they said. "We're sorry to bring you such bad news."

"I was in love with him. I'm such a fool."

"No, Miss Hayes. I disagree. You're not a fool. It's guys like him who are the fools," Agent Feron said. "First, he bamboozled you, and then he took you on a very expensive ride. Unless we find him first, you won't be his last victim."

"But why did he do this to me? I thought he really cared about me." Her voice quivered, more tears began to well up in her eyes and spill over, sliding down her cheeks. "I thought he loved me," she said in a whisper. "How could this be?"

The agents, thinking of their own daughters who happened to be about Beth's age, looked at each other, their eyes filled with empathy for Beth. This could've happened to anyone.

"I'm sure he did care about you," Agent Colson said.

"Yeah, he cared about you," Feron said. "It's just that he cares a lot more about himself."

Beth mustered her strength, got up to walk them to the door just as Cecily was

coming up the back steps and into the
house.

"This is about Max, isn't it?" she said.

"Yes ma'am. Have you seen him?"

"No, never, but can I ask you something?"

"Sure."

"Just how old is this guy?"

"Why, he's forty-five. Maybe forty-six.
We think."

Beth, who was standing by the door to
the dining room, slid down the wall, and
after weeks of making jokes and innuendo
about fainting, she passed out cold. A minute or so later when she came to, Cecily
was standing over her, fanning her with
the newspaper, and Lola was making
mewing sounds from her crate.

"Hey! Are you all right? Drink this."

"Thanks." Beth sipped some of the water
from the bottle she had never opened.
"What happened?"

"You fainted. Here, let me help you up."

The two FBI agents stepped in to help
Beth to her feet.

"It's just such a shock," she said.

"Are you sure you're all right? Can we
call an ambulance?"

"Oh no, I'm fine," Beth said.

"I'll keep an eye on her," Cecily said. "Thanks."

"Okay then. We'll be on our way. Just, if you hear from him—"

"Don't worry. Believe me. I'll call you," Beth said.

Beth stood at the sink, watching through the window, and Cecily, who had held the kitchen door for them, continued to stand there as well, as if both of them were in a trance.

Finally, when the car had disappeared from their view, Cecily spoke.

"Okay, Beth, it's time for you to come clean all around. Are there any other lies you're holding back?"

"No. I told you everything. I swear. But I have a question."

"What?"

"I know I committed fraud, but can I go to jail for it?"

"Well, I'm no Johnnie Cochran, but I think you can only be prosecuted if your mother decides to press charges. Or maybe your uncle. Do you think they'd do that?"

"I have no idea what they'll do. Turn me

over to the cops? But I know there's going to be a whole lot of yelling before this is over. I guess I should call Woody now, huh?"

"Just get it over with before the FBI shows up at his door. Or, worse, at his office."

"Oh God. I would rather die than go through this."

"No you wouldn't. We'll get through this. Dial his number."

Woody was thrilled to hear Beth's voice until he heard her say, "Woody? I have something to tell you and you're not going to like this. Max Mitchell has run off with our money and the FBI just left my house."

"That's impossible, right?"

"Nope. And Woody? There's more. Remember the letter of permission from my mother?"

"Don't tell me you faked her signature."

"No. Worse. I added a zero."

"WHAT?"

"I did, Woody. I am so sorry I deceived you. I am so sorry."

"Let me understand this again. Your mother only wanted you to take ten thousand and you changed the document to read *one hundred thousand* by adding a zero?"

"Yeah. It was what Max wanted and I thought that I had to get it for him . . . Oh, Woody! I don't know why I did it. It was so wrong! What am I going to do?"

"You're going to be in some very deep legal trouble, but I guess you already know that."

And just when Beth thought she didn't have a tear left to shed, she burst into tears again. The clock struck three.

"Oh, Woody! I am in so much trouble! What am I going to do? Oh my God! I could go to jail!"

"No! No, you're not going to jail! I'm getting in my car. I'll be there by eight o'clock."

"What good will *that* do us?"

"Oh, Beth. I don't know, but I can't stand to hear the fear and panic in your voice and I want to be there with you, so I'm coming. We will figure this out together. See you soon."

He disconnected the call and Beth stood there looking at the phone, mystified.

"Well, that was a short conversation! What did he say?"

"He's coming."

"Why?"

"Believe it or not, to help." Beth reached for another tissue and blew her nose for the umpteenth time. "He said he couldn't stand to hear the panic and dread in my voice and he wants to be here. He wants to help."

"I like this guy," Cecily said.

"He's wonderful, Cecily. He really is."

"Let me give you a hand to straighten up the house and get the room ready for him. Where do you want him to sleep?"

"I'll show you. Oh, Cecily! Thank you so much for being here! What would I do without you?"

"I can't imagine."

Over the next few hours, Cecily stayed to help Beth ready Woody's room and she made a trip to the Piggly Wiggly. To make the time go faster, she and Beth put a dinner together so that when Woody walked in the door, he could sit down to a roasted chicken, mashed potatoes, and a salad. And Cecily bought a pie from the Piggly Wiggly's bakery with a pint of vanilla ice cream.

"If you feed an angry man first, he is

less likely to knock your teeth out. And I'll stick around to be sure he doesn't," Cecily said, bringing the bags in.

"I'm sure you're right. Here, let me help you." She took two bags from Cecily and put them on the table. "You know what, Cecily? I was thinking while you were at the Pig, and I might have a temporary solution to keep me from getting that lethal injection."

"What! Well, for heaven's sake, tell me this second!" Cecily dropped the rest of her bags all at once on the kitchen counter.

"Well, it's a long shot, but it might work. You know my Aunt Sophie, right?"

"You're thinking she would give you one hundred and twenty-five thousand dollars?"

"No, just park it in my account for a while until we can see if we can get any of our money back from Max. I mean, we might get some of the money back."

"You're dreaming, I hate to say it, but you're dreaming."

"Wait! The FBI said it was *probably* gone but they didn't know that for a fact. At least they didn't say it like it was for sure."

"Now, tell me why your Aunt Sophie would do this for you?"

"Because she can. Look, she really loves me and she knows I've never done a sketchy thing in my whole life. And because she's told me like a thousand times that she wishes she had a daughter like me and if there's ever *anything* she can do for me, all I have to do is ask."

"Okay. Ask!"

"Boy, wouldn't it be wonderful if Woody walked in here and we could tell him we had this all set?"

"It would be a miracle."

Beth and Cecily set the table, organized dinner, and Beth picked up the phone and called her aunts' house. One of her aunts answered on the third ring.

"Aunt Sophie? It's me, Beth! How are you?"

"What? I'm very busy right now and I can't talk to you! And a storm is coming! I can see lightning! Call back tomorrow! Sorry!" And she hung up.

Beth put the phone back on the receiver and looked at Cecily.

"What happened?" Cecily said.

"She hung up on me."

"What?"

"She said she was busy, a storm was

coming, there was lightning . . . That's just about the most bizarre thing she's ever, ever done!"

"What? What are you saying?"

"Right. What's the matter with her?"

"Maybe she was having sex?"

"Oh, please! Don't you think I would've heard her moving around or something like heavy breathing?"

"I was kidding. Bad joke."

"Oh." Beth rolled her eyes at Cecily. "Well then, what's wrong with her? I mean, my Aunt Sophie has never been like that. She was downright rude. Very rude, in fact."

"Maybe it wasn't your Aunt Sophie."

"Maybe. But why would Aunt Allison act like that? I mean, come on! That's just in-sane."

"I don't know. Why don't you just wait a couple of hours and call back. Maybe she was having a fight with her boyfriend, what's his name?"

"Geoffrey with a *G*."

"That's a stupid name to hang on a man, isn't it?"

"Yeah. Maybe you're right. I'll call her back. Oh Lord! Cecily! What if she can't help us?"

"Then you're back to square one, facing the music."

"Oh God! Isn't there any way out of this?"

"I wish there was. I'm going to go and open the doors in the living room and get some air moving in the house."

The next thing Beth heard was Cecily screaming for her to come quickly. She found Cecily in front of the mirror pointing to it.

She said, "What do butterflies mean? Look at them! They're all over the mirror!"

There were no butterflies on the mirror, but there were hundreds of them inside the mirror.

"Oh no! It's my Aunt Sophie!"

"What do you mean?"

"My Aunt Sophie has a butterfly tattoo on her hip. Cecily! No one in the family knows it except me!"

"Wait a minute! Maybe this is a sign from Livvie that you are supposed to get the money from her. Maybe you should go down there and ask her in person?"

"No, Cecily. This is a sign that my Aunt Sophie is dead."

"Beth Hayes? Hush up your fool mouth right this instant! Haven't you had enough trouble for one day? You are way, way overreacting!"

"No I'm not! I know something is dreadfully wrong with my Aunt Sophie. I can feel it in my chest!"

"Don't say she's dead! That's a *terrible* thing to even think!"

"That's why my Aunt Allison was so freaked out on the phone."

"Stop!"

"I think Aunt Sophie is dead, Cecily! I think she's dead! Why else would there be butterflies in the mirror?"

"Let's calm down, okay? Let's think this through. Tell me why your Aunt Allison wouldn't tell you if something were wrong with your Aunt Sophie?"

"I don't know! Because she's hiding something? Why would she hide something like that?"

"You tell me. In the meanwhile I think we should stop talking about this until Woody gets here. Your brain is worn out from today. Dealing with Max and the FBI is enough. So just stop thinking about this and go say a prayer that she's fine. Take a shower and fix yourself up so you don't look like this when he gets here."

"What did you say?"

"You heard me. Go!"

Beth stared at Cecily for a minute that seemed to last an hour and then she shook her head.

"You're right. Listen to me. I'm losing it. Aunt Allison was probably jacked up on some of her wacko vitamins."

"See? There we go! That's a perfectly reasonable explanation, isn't it? Nobody's dead."

"Right. You're probably right. I think I'll go take a shower."

"Good idea."

An hour or so later, Woody had arrived and they were all seated at the table. For someone who professed not to have much of an appetite, Woody was making short order of the chicken and mashed pota-toes. Cecily picked at her food while Beth barely swallowed a bite. Her concerns about Sophie had multiplied.

"Tell me about your conversation with your aunt again?" he said.

Beth recounted the conversation verbatim.

He wrinkled his brow. "That's completely screwed up. And what's the deal with their vitamin business?"

Beth explained that they had just launched a new line of herbal vitamins.

"But with no FDA approval, right?"

"No. Not that I know of."

"And tell me this weird butterfly story again."

He listened, finally pushed back from the table, and said, "You know what? Go call your aunt again. Just because we took the shaft today in a very big way, that doesn't mean that something *didn't* happen to your Aunt Sophie. Two bad things can come down in one day. Happens all the time."

"Usually in bunches of three. He's right, you know," Cecily said. "But law! I hope he's wrong."

Beth dialed her aunts again and Cecily and Woody listened on extension telephones in other rooms.

"Hello?"

"Aunt Allison?"

"Who is this?"

"It's Beth. Your niece."

"What do you want?"

"I'd like to speak to my Aunt Sophie."

"She can't come to the phone."

"Oh. Is she at home?"

"She's sick. I gotta go."

Allison, no longer pretending to be Sophie on this phone call, hung up on Beth again.

Woody and Cecily came to the kitchen, where Beth was still holding the receiver in her hand.

Cecily spoke first. "I'll watch Lola and I'll clean up."

"Go pack a few things," Woody said. "We're driving to Coral Gables tonight."

"But it's like nine hours from here," Cecily said. "Wouldn't you rather leave early in the morning?"

"No. I'm afraid that Beth's right about her aunt, Cecily."

"I'll be right back," Beth said, and ran up the stairs.

"Maybe Sophie *is* sick or maybe there's a perfectly good explanation for her Aunt Allison's behavior. But if they were my aunts? I'd be on the road. Something is very wrong with Allison for sure, and maybe Sophie too."

"Gosh, I hope not."

"Well, we'll call you as soon as we know something."

In a few minutes, Beth was there with her bag. She picked up Lola and gave her a hug and a kiss on top of her head.

"Hey, Cecily? If my mother calls? Or Aunt Maggie?"

"I'll tell them you went to Atlanta for two days or something like that?"

"No," Woody said. "Tell them the truth. No more lies."

"Okay!"

Beth gave Cecily a hug and Cecily whispered in her ear.

"He's kind of squirrelly-looking, but I like him, Beth. A lot."

"For yourself?" she whispered back.

"No! For you!"

16

Dark Cloud, Silver Lining

Susanthepen@writenow.net
Maggie, you know what? I talked to Simon for a long time last night, as I'm sure you probably already heard. I have to get out of here. I love Paris and the museums and all the fabulous things there are to do, but I'm just too far away from y'all. I need some humidity, some sand in my shoes, and my family. Guess I'm just an old Geechee Girl and that's all there is to it. I'm thinking in two weeks? Can y'all come home to Sullivans Island when I do? xx

Maggiepie2@marthagene.net
Susan, well, you old sentimental fool! Darlin'? I was surprised you wanted to go to France in the first place—those people don't even speak English or know how to fry a decent piece of

flounder. You come on home and I'll get everyone there. Send us your flight times when you know, okay? xxx P.S. Sure do love my sister!

All the way to Florida, eighteen-wheelers zoomed by, causing their car to wobble and shake. The trucks were too many to count, and at times they were a dangerous menace, getting right up on Woody's bumper, flashing their high beams, scaring them out of their wits.

They stopped for coffee and gas only twice. Woody drove until he was bleary-eyed and then Beth took over so he could sleep for a few hours. When they weren't sleeping, or pumping gas, they were talking.

"It's inconceivable to me that a man could do something like Max did to us, well, to you, really."

"Listen, he biopsied your wallet for a cool twenty-five thousand. That's not nothing."

"*Biopsied my wallet.* Where did you learn a term like that?"

"My mother. She has about a million

funny little sayings that she says all the time. She says creative language makes people listen to you. You'll love her."

"I'll bet I will. But okay, back to Max, he biopsied my wallet, as you say, but I only got scammed. He wasn't playing with my emotions. So what are you thinking?"

"I'm over it."

"Are you?"

"Uh, *yeah*! Max Mitchell, or whatever his real name is, probably cost me my credibility for the rest of my life with my entire family, *if* they ever speak to me again. Which they probably won't. Unless they don't find out. *If* my Aunt Sophie is okay, which I am doubting more and more, and *if* she is willing to help us, and *if* the FBI gets him, and *if* he didn't already blow all the money—"

"Too many *if*s."

"You said it. So, knowing that, how could I still be—"

"In love with him?"

"Boy, Woody. Let me tell you something, if that's what love looks like, you can keep it. You know, looking back, there were probably a thousand signs that he was a skunk and I ignored them all."

"Really?"

"Oh yeah. He would do these things or say something really insensitive, things that no one should ever say to someone they cared about. But I just wrote it all off, excusing everything. I don't know what came over me."

"He seduced you, Beth, just like a pro. Plain and simple. I mean, here's this guy, a good-looking devil if I ever saw one, and he comes along flashing big smiles and flattering you and all that. Pretty text-book."

"Humph. Yeah, but his true colors were there all the time. I was the moron who chose to ignore them."

"Now, I want to hear this because as far as I know, you don't miss much. Not much at all."

"Oh yes I do. Okay, remember that night when Mike got very tipsy . . ."

"Mike was solid in the bag."

"I stand corrected. Anyway, I saw Max climbing in the hammock with Phoebe, who was also solid in the bag. And he denied it, I mean, he told me that I wasn't seeing what I was seeing! I saw him in the hammock pulling Phoebe in and he said,

No you didn't see that, and I just said, Oh, okay."

"Nice. It's like the old joke? A woman catches her husband in bed with some other woman and he says, *Are you going to believe your lying eyes, or are you going to believe what I tell you?*"

"Exactly! Yeah, and one night he came to Atlanticville before he knew I worked there?"

"Okay . . ."

"And, he was with this half-naked old dame who was hanging all over him. She had to be easily forty or more and he said it was just business."

"Maybe it was."

"Right. How about monkey business? Look, first of all, he told me he was just thirty-seven and it turns out he's forty-five or forty-six. And he was sleeping with that woman and I knew it and when he said no, I just believed him."

"Beth? You are a lovely young woman. You're free of guile, honest, and caring, and you have all those good qualities men love so much in women."

"Fat lot of good it ever did me, but thanks."

"In the end, virtue will serve you well. It's so unusual these days."

"Yeah, you pick up the papers and it seems like everyone is a lying crook."

"Just like Max, except on a larger scale. Anyway, Max was a professional liar, a hustler, a felon on the run from the law, and a user of the worst sort. The only thing you had in common with him is that you were both in love with the same person. Him."

"I feel like such an idiot."

"So do I."

"Okay, but I'm a flaming idiot."

"It's okay. And you're not."

"Yeah? Wait till my Uncle Henry hears about this, and wait till my mother gets her hands around my throat."

"That's another reason I came down here."

"Why? To watch a family execution?"

"No. To stand by you until this is over."

"Really? Don't you have to go back to work?" Woody has to be the nicest person I have ever known, she thought.

"Nope. Basically, I'm fired."

"What do you mean? Did you talk to Uncle Henry?"

"Nope. I fired myself. First, I'm taking some personal days. But when it hits the fan? Old Henry is gonna go wild. I mean, wild!"

"Oh Lord, Woody. I'm so busy fretting over my side of the sewer, I didn't think about yours. You're right. Uncle Henry will not be amused."

"Well, look. I've known Henry for a long time and I have never missed a step with him. I'm just going to tell him the truth— that you got completely blinded by the biggest rush into romance I have ever seen. That when I met Max, which he knows I did, I thought he was okay too. If he fooled me, he could have easily fooled you."

"Oh, thanks a lot."

"No, Beth, wait. What I meant was Henry and I are in the business of sizing up companies and the people who run them. When you do that all the time you develop a sixth sense for the business. You can smell a bad deal or an unscrupulous person from miles away. And I'm good at this or I wouldn't be working for your uncle. Believe me. So along comes Max. He seemed like a hardworking, gregarious altar boy to me. Right out of the Wholesome

Boys' Central Casting. He completely, completely, completely fooled me."

"I feel only slightly better. Don't you think Uncle Henry is going to think you paid a fair penalty when he finds out how much of your own money you lost?"

"I think his first loyalty is to you, as it should be, and when he finds out I let this loan go through without calling him? He's never going to want to see my face again. And I wouldn't blame him."

"You don't know that, Woody. You have to wait and see what happens, don't you think?"

"Sure. We'll see. I hope I remember how to milk cows. Is this our exit?"

Within half an hour, they pulled into her aunts' driveway. Their house was typical of the wealthy neighborhoods of Coral Ga-bles, built of stucco, lots of arches, painted a pastel pink. There was a courtyard with a pool and the property was artistically landscaped with palms, aloes, and other kinds of succulents that could stand up to the vicious heat. The interiors were open spaces with cool marble floors and tons of light. Beth had only been there twice but she loved the house because it was glamorous and modern and so different from how she had ever lived.

It was just past seven in the morning when Beth rang the doorbell.

"Wouldn't it be great if my Aunt Sophie just opened that door, made us pancakes, and took out her checkbook?"

"Beth? Neither one of us have that kind of luck lately."

The door opened and one of her aunts stood there, squinting in the blinding sunlight. Without her makeup and hair done, it was difficult for Beth to figure out which aunt it was. But Beth quickly decided it was Allison, peeping around the partially opened door with a very unwelcoming demeanor. It *was* Allison. Allison's eyes darted back and forth between them as though they were robbers or, worse, Jehovah's Witnesses. She didn't recognize Beth at all.

"Good morning, Aunt Allison."

"Beth? Is that you?"

"Yeah."

"What are you doing here? I didn't know you were coming. How did you get here?" Her voice was agitated and edgy.

"We drove. This is my friend Woody Morrison. Can we come in?"

Allison paused before she answered, which was very unsettling to Beth.

"Only for a minute. I have to go out. In fact, I'm late."

Beth and Woody looked at each other as if to say, We drove five hundred miles to stay for a minute? And, where's she going at this hour? And where's she going dressed like that? Allison looked like she had been up all night. Maybe longer.

"Her pupils are huge," Woody whispered to Beth.

Beth nodded her head in agreement. "She's definitely on something. I knew it."

They stepped inside and stood in the foyer waiting for Allison to invite them into the house for a cup of coffee or to offer some basic hospitality, but she did not. They felt like interlopers, awkward and uneasy.

"So, what can I do for you?" she asked.

What can I do for you? What a strange thing to say, Beth thought, like we're selling encyclopedias? Something is incredibly out of whack here.

"Is Aunt Sophie all right?"

"Sophie? Sophie? Is Sophie all right? What are you talking about?"

"Last night you told me she was sick. And I got very concerned."

"Why would you be concerned about Sophie? People get sick. Then they get well."

"Well, can I see her?"

"She's not here." Allison paused. "She went to the doctor."

Woody had yet to say a word but he was listening. He too knew something was dreadfully wrong. Beth's Aunt Allison was having some kind of psychotic episode. And she was lying. That much was clear.

"What doctor did she go to?" Beth said.

"Why do you want to know that?"

"Because I want to go there and see my aunt."

"Why are you so nosy? Hmm? Answer me that, little girl."

"I'm not nosy, Aunt Allison. I love you and I am very worried about both of you. Is there something wrong? Do you need help?"

"It's time for you to leave. I have things to do."

At that point, Beth was beginning to shake all over from nerves.

"Where's Geoffrey, Aunt Allison?"

"I wouldn't know, would I? The son of a bitch took all the money and left, didn't he?"

Okay, Beth thought, now we're getting somewhere. But talk about parallel lives?

"Who's Geoffrey?" Woody whispered to Beth.

"Her boyfriend who's some kind of pharmacologist who made up the vitamins."

"He's gonna get it too!" Allison said, her voice rising. "Oh yes! He'll get his! The long arm of the law is gonna crack his head!"

What did that mean? Woody and Beth exchanged suspicious looks, knowing they were in the presence of a demented mind.

"He's going to get it! But good!"

Beth felt sick in her heart to see her aunt this way. Where was her Aunt Sophie? She was either in some terrible peril or, God forbid, she *was* dead.

"Aunt Allison? Something is very wrong here."

"Well, it's none of your business. So run along now."

Beth, who had never been in a situation like this in all her life, was very unsure of what to do next. So she simply stood up to her aunt.

"No ma'am. I'm not leaving until I am certain beyond any doubt that my Aunt Sophie is alive."

"Is that so? Well, then go and have yourself a look around. I told you she's not here. And then I want you to go. You just can't come in here like this! Who do you think you are? Hillary Clinton? She was in the yard this morning but she left."

"Okay. Aunt Allison? I am your niece who loves you and is very worried about you. And I'm going to get you some help. Why don't you sit on the sofa and I'll make you some breakfast?"

To her complete astonishment, her aunt went directly to the living room and sat on the sofa, leaving the front door of the house wide open. Woody closed it and followed them to the living room. Allison was staring into space and muttering, having a silent conversation with someone who wasn't there. She was hallucinating. Beth had witnessed people hallucinating in college, but that was drug-induced. Had her aunt taken some sort of hallucinogenic?

Beth knelt in front of her and spoke to her very sweetly.

"Aunt Allison? Where's Aunt Sophie?"

"What? She's right where Geoffrey left her."

"And where's that?"

"I can't say. Why are you asking me so many questions?"

For the next few minutes, Beth tried to get her aunt to say where Sophie was but Allison was adamant. She was keeping her secret. She was becoming more and more paranoid and suddenly her temper flared.

Allison stood up abruptly and said, "You can't treat me like this! Nobody can! I have a contract!"

She ran to her bedroom, slammed the door behind her, and locked it.

Woody and Beth could hear her screaming from behind the door, screaming and screaming and screaming. She was throwing things, crashing them against the walls, and she was banging her fists.

"I'm calling 911," Beth said.

"You do that and I'll have a look around."

As impossible as it was for her to comprehend, Beth was making a 911 call, the first and hopefully only one she would ever make in her life. She knew she had to tell the operator that she was calling to report a missing person, perhaps a homicide, and to ask for help for her aunt who had lost her mind. Was that what she should say? Well, that was the truth, wasn't it?

"Yes, she's in her bedroom, screaming and screaming. No, I can't understand what she's saying. No, I don't know if she has a gun. No, I'm not sure if she's dangerous, but I do know something terrible has happened to my other aunt. Why? Because I just know it."

If I tell them about all the butterflies in the mirror at home, they're going to cart me off to a loony bin, she thought.

"Yes, she's Sophie Hamilton. And it's my aunt Allison Hamilton who's locked herself in her room and is . . . well, she's deranged. We need help right away. Thanks."

She gave them the address again, hung up the phone, and Woody, who had remained within earshot, took her hands in his.

"Now look, it's going to be okay," he said.

Beth, whose waterworks had discovered a bottomless well, burst into tears yet again.

"No, it's not going to be okay, Woody. It can't be okay. My mother is going to die when she hears all this. Oh God! I wish my mother were here."

"You know what? So do I. But let's just see what the police say and then we will decide what to do."

It didn't take more than a few minutes for the police to arrive and Woody answered the door. Woody and Beth explained who they were and why they were there. The officer in charge was Sergeant Michael Coker, a no-nonsense fellow with a crew cut and a square jaw. He was so muscular and solemn that he could have been an ex-Marine. He sent two of his men to search the house. Another officer, who was trained to deal with psychological trauma, was dispatched to convince Allison to open her door.

There was an ambulance standing by and squad cars continued to arrive. Beth and Woody sat at the dining room table with Sergeant Coker and answered his questions.

"I'm sorry to put you through this. You're

both very tired; I can see that. But I need to know why you think there might be foul play."

When Beth explained what her aunts did for a living, Sergeant Coker's eyes lit up.

"My wife uses those DVDs of theirs all the time. That music drives me nuts."

"Yeah, I'm not a fan either. And now they have this new vitamin business . . ."

"So you think that maybe your Aunt Sophie might have gotten really sick from them?"

"Yeah, maybe, because she was complaining about chest pain a couple of weeks ago. But until we find her, I don't know."

"Has your aunt ever taken off like this before?"

"Never. But Aunt Allison said that her boyfriend Geoffrey has disappeared, apparently with a lot of her money."

"Enough to make her get this hysterical? Do you know his last name?"

"No, sorry. I never met him. But I'm sure we can find out. He was her partner."

"Okay, that's good."

"She's not just hysterical, Sergeant," Woody said. "She's showing some real signs of psychosis."

"Are you a *doctor,* son?"

"No, I'm an investment banker."

"Oh, an investment banker. I see," Sergeant Coker said, and shook his head. "Well, when they get her out of her room, we'll take her in for a psych evaluation."

"She was hallucinating," Beth said.

"How do you know that? Are *you* a doctor?"

Sergeant Coker had little patience for two young kids, no matter how distressed they were, making a professional medical diagnosis when they didn't look like they were old enough to know beans about beans. High anxiety made perfectly rational people jump to conclusions. He had seen it a thousand times.

"No, I'm a journalist. But I know hallucinations when I see them. I saw enough kids tripping out on shrooms in college, talking to their imaginary bunnies or whatever. She was staring off into space and having a conversation with someone who wasn't there. And she told me Hillary Clinton was in the yard this morning."

"Hillary Clinton, huh? That's a good one."

"Hey, Sarge? Can I see you for a minute?"

Sergeant Coker got up and went out to the garage.

"Think they found something?" Beth said. "Should we go see?"

"I'll go," Woody said. "You just stay put."

Two minutes later the sergeant and Woody reappeared. Woody looked stunned and Sergeant Coker's face told it all. Beth's heart sank and she prepared herself for the worst.

Woody took her hand and Sergeant Coker said, "I'm sorry, Ms. Hayes. I think we've found your Aunt Sophie, and if it's her, she's gone."

"What? Where is she? Can I see her? Are you sure it's her?"

"You don't want to see her, Beth," Woody said.

"Yes I do!" She started to hyperventilate. "That's my aunt who I love so much! You don't know!"

"No. Not right now. Do you want some water?"

"No! I want to see my aunt! I want . . . Oh God! Please make all this stop!"

"Where are you going?"

"I'm going to get some air and a glass of water!"

"Sergeant Coker? I can tell you without question it's her because Allison is her identical twin."

"Okay, Mr. Morrison, you stay with Ms. Hayes. I gotta make some calls."

When he walked away Woody followed Beth to the kitchen, where she was looking for a glass. Beth said, "Okay, Woody? What happened? What happened to her?"

"I don't know. Are you okay?"

"Yeah. I'm okay. So, where was she?"

Woody was visibly shaken.

"Maybe I could use a glass of water too."

Beth poured him a glass and handed it to him. He drank it down to the bottom and refilled it himself. Then he took a deep breath and blurted it out.

"In the damn freezer. Someone stuck her in the damn freezer."

"The freezer? Oh my God! How horrible! Oh my God! Geoffrey! That lousy son of a bitch. He's worse than Max."

"But why would he do that?"

"I don't know. It's the most inhumane thing . . . My poor aunt!"

"Yeah, it's so wrong. I'm sure it's against a thousand laws. But no matter how or why she died, why didn't they just call for help?"

"Maybe because Geoffrey wouldn't let Allison blow the vitamin business and Sophie was dead anyway?"

"Maybe. But what if the vitamins *didn't* kill her? What if she just had a freak heart attack or something?"

"Like a stroke? Possible. I mean, they were pretty old to be doing all the aerobics and stuff they did. I guess they'll do an autopsy?"

"Probably."

"Oh my God, this is the worst day of my life!"

"It's up there for me too and I didn't even know her."

"Oh, Woody!"

She threw her arms around him and hugged him hard. Instead of crying they sighed and sighed, almost too exhausted mentally and physically to feel anything anymore.

The coroner was called and her aunts' house became a crime scene, with forensics experts arriving, taking pictures, searching the carpet for hair, and dusting for prints. And when her Aunt Sophie's body was removed to take to the morgue, Woody held Beth's face to his chest so she didn't have to see it happen.

Allison had been screaming for almost an hour. Then there would be silence. Then the screaming would begin again. Finally, she started screaming there were bugs all over her and the police became concerned. In the end, they had to break down Allison's door, and when they did she was arrested. She put up such a fight, kicking at the officers and threatening them, that they had no alternative but to wrestle her to the ground, handcuff her, and take her away. Beth and Woody couldn't believe their eyes as they watched Allison's humiliation.

"But she's ill," Beth said. "They shouldn't treat her like that."

"She's a threat, Beth. What can they do?" Woody just shook his head.

Of course, someone had called the local television stations and the newspapers. Allison Hamilton's departure was fully documented by the media.

"This is too much," Beth said. "Too much. My Aunt Maggie is going be furious to see our name all over the papers. I mean, why is the public so hungry for this kind of news? It's no one's business."

Her face was so incredulous that Woody knew in that moment Beth was unable to figure out what their next steps should be. His heart was filled with enormous sympathy for her. The events of the last few days were too much for almost anyone.

"Beth, this is a terrible tragedy. Terrible. And you're right. It's no one else's business. But because your aunts were pretty well known, it's gonna be all over the news in an hour. We'd better call your family before they see it on CNN. The entire news media is going to have a field day with this."

"You're right. Oh my God. Who should I call first?"

"Who are you the closest with?"

"My mom, but she's in France. Uncle Timmy? He can probably get here the fastest and he's a shrink. He'll know how to handle this."

"If he knows how to handle this, then he's got to be a card-carrying genius," Woody said. "If you want, I'll start tracking down Henry."

"That's probably a good idea. Oh dear God, Woody. I can't believe this is happening. I'm so tired I can hardly think straight. Oh, I'm so glad you're here."

"So am I, but don't worry, I promised I'd get you through this and I will."

"Dear heavenly Mother, Woody. How will I ever repay you?"

For the first time all week, they had a laugh.

"I don't think you can."

"For real. Oh Lord! Who's gonna tell Aunt Maggie?"

Woody looked at her not knowing at all how to answer her, assuming it would be the most difficult call to make.

"Okay, I'll do it. And you know what? We have to call Cecily."

Beth walked away from him and dialed her number first.

"Cecily? Hey, it's me."

"Finally!"

"I know. Sorry. It's been very hectic since we got here but it's a good thing we came."

"I am so glad to finally hear your voice! You've had me sick with worry! Is everything okay?"

"No. Everything is not okay. My Aunt Sophie's dead."

"What are you telling me?"

"Yep, and my Aunt Allison has truly gone off the deep end—"

"Sweet Jesus, my King! *Please* don't tell me this!"

Slowly, slowly, Beth brought her up to date and Cecily, who had burst into tears, causing Beth to cry again, finally said, "Is there going to be a funeral here or there?"

"I don't know. I don't know what's going to be. But as soon as I do, I'll call you."

"Well, if it's here, I'd better start getting organized . . . Oh, Beth, I am just so sorry."

Beth walked into the kitchen, where Woody was on the phone with Henry.

"Yes sir. I will. Okay then. We'll let you know."

"Did he freak?"

"Of course he freaked, but he calmed down. He's flying back to Atlanta right away. He wants to know the plans."

"We haven't got any plans. I'm calling Aunt Maggie." Beth took a deep breath and dialed her Aunt Maggie's cell. She answered right away. "Aunt Maggie? This is Beth."

"Is everything all right?"

"No ma'am. I have something terrible to tell you. It's Aunt Sophie, Aunt Maggie. She's dead."

"Beth? Child? What in the *world* are you talking about? *Please!* Tell me this *isn't* true! It *can't* be! She's so *young*! Where are you? Oh, dear Mother! Please no! How could this *be*?"

Maggie began sobbing so loudly that Beth stopped talking and then she began to cry again herself. But this time Beth wept quietly and listened to the sounds of her aunt's heart being torn apart.

"Darlin'? I'm so sorry that you had to make this call. You poor child. How did you find this out?"

"I'm in Coral Gables . . ."

Beth told Maggie all she knew, leaving out the entire swindle story about Max, and Maggie said, "Well, I don't give a tinker's dam what, we're bringing my little sisters home to Charleston. Poor Allison! That's her identical twin! Oh my God in heaven! How could this happen to us? Hasn't this family been through enough?"

"Yes ma'am, we have. I haven't called

Momma because I thought maybe you might want to do that?"

"I'll call her right away! What time is it in Paris?"

"Um, I don't know. Uh, nine hours ahead of you?"

"So, it's cocktail time? Well, I hope she's got her cell phone with her and that it's turned on. You know she leaves it off half the time, so I had to learn how to text and email and every kind of thing just to stay in touch with her."

"Yes ma'am." Beth thought her aunt wasn't making good sense then, but she decided she was probably in shock. It was, after all, the largest bomb dropped on the family since Beth's father's scandal and death. "I thought maybe I should call Uncle Timmy to see if he could come down here? Because he's the closest? And because of Aunt Allison's, um, condition? I don't know where Aunt Sophie's papers are or anything like that . . ."

"Oh! Beth! You can call Timmy if you want but I can get on a plane in the next hour and be there tonight. You know, honey, you've never been through anything like this and it might be helpful if you had someone with more experience to, you know . . ."

"Take over?"

"Yes. Exactly. You don't need all this confusion, do you?"

"No ma'am. I'm actually doing okay, all things considered. But I would love the help. Do you have Uncle Timmy's cell? I have you on speed dial, but I left his number on the island." Aunt Maggie is the true matriarch, Beth thought, and she was in awe of how Maggie just told it how it was. Beth was not insulted in the least.

"Sure, sweetheart, here it is."

Beth jotted down the number and said, "Thanks."

"Goodness gracious, Beth. You are such a wonderful girl. Your momma is so lucky to have you."

"Thanks, Aunt Maggie."

"And, I'm so proud of you too."

They hung up and Beth looked at the phone. Wait until they find out what I did to my trust fund. Then they won't think I'm so wonderful.

"Uncle Timmy?" She had called him next.

"I'm on the next plane, Beth. You just hold on, okay?"

That afternoon, Woody flipped on Allison's television to see where the markets had closed that day and there was a nice big picture of Max Mitchell being taken into custody.

"Beth! Come here! Look!"

Another Ponzi scheme smashed! Max Mitchell, forty-eight years of age, of Cleveland, Ohio, was arrested today in Asheville, North Carolina, on charges of interstate fraud, money laundering, and an elaborate Ponzi scam that centered around all sorts of real estate development deals—houses, shopping centers, condominiums, and more. The FBI said that Mr. Mitchell, also known as Lou D'Andrea, Billy Bogart, and Ed Hammer, had eluded them for two years. Working with several other men, his alleged scams stretched from Portland, Oregon, to Sullivans Island, South Carolina, and he has stolen nearly one and a half billion dollars in various scams. This will be an interesting case to follow in the coming weeks, don't you think, Andrea?

Andrea, the other TV journalist, said, "If I had a bad dog, I'd name him Ponzi!"

"Holy crap, Woody? We're gonna get subpoenaed, you know."

"I'll be glad to testify."

"Yep. Me too."

"When do you think we should confess?" Woody said.

"When we have to, and not a minute before."

"Good plan."

By late that night, they were able to move about the house again, and except for the wrecked bedroom door, everything was pretty much in order. The garage, however, was still off-limits until the police had the results of the autopsy. Maggie was there at the dining room table drinking a large glass of white wine and trying to initiate a plan. She had chosen an outfit for Sophie that she thought was appropriate for burial.

When she asked Beth what she thought about it, Beth said, "I can't look at it."

"Well, shugah, you have to be practical. I sure hope when my time comes that someone will care enough to make sure my hair gets done right and that my dress fits like it should."

"If I'm around, Aunt Maggie, I'll take care of it."

"Remember I want to wear pale blue."

"Okay."

"For the Blessed Mother."

"Yes ma'am."

Maggie had asked her son Mike to put out his feelers with Mary Ellen Way should they need extra bedrooms for a funeral. She had asked Susan to write the obituary for the newspapers, and it was assumed that Susan was already somewhere over the Atlantic, racing home to Beth, insisting on being with her as soon as she could.

No other news could have lifted Beth's spirits like knowing her mother was coming.

Since his arrival, Timmy had been at the morgue trying to understand what legal entanglements they had to deal with to have Sophie's body brought home to Charleston and how long it would take to have Allison brought to the Medical University of South Carolina for inpatient treatment if she needed it, and it appeared that she would.

Maggie assured them all that she was going to oversee Allison's care, but she was adamant it had to be in Charleston as she had no intention of ever leaving South Carolina again.

Henry had been calling and calling, arranging lawyers for Allison and gathering details about Allison and Sophie's business. Because Beth was able to tell them what her Aunt Allison said that morning, Henry was arranging an audit of Allison and Sophie's business and he planned to bring a civil suit against Geoffrey with a *G* on their behalf. He couldn't wait for the criminal investigation to get smoking. He fully expected the State of Florida to track Geoffrey with a *G*'s sorry ass down and fry it for sticking his sister in the freezer like a potpie.

"I don't give a shit what," Henry said over and over. "That was completely unforgivable."

17

Fault Lines

It took some time to get everything sorted out, but in a week plus a few days, Sophie's body was in residence at McAlister's Funeral Home in Mount Pleasant, South Carolina, being prepared for her funeral. The autopsy results showed that Sophie had indeed suffered a massive heart attack. There were no significant amounts of belladonna alkaloids or any other kind of herbs that could have brought on a myocardial infraction of that severity. Foul play was ruled out and Allison was exonerated of any charges related to homicide. Sticking her in the freezer, however, was still a problem.

The entire family was returning to Sullivans Island to lay Sophie to rest.

"I'm going to call George Durst tomorrow and make an appointment for a complete physical. In fact, we had all better get a good physical this year," Maggie said. "I mean, I haven't stopped taking my pulse all week! Okay, y'all. We've got potato salad with the ham for dinner, corn pudding, and red rice. Doesn't that sound yummy? And I picked up a pound cake from Mimi's today!"

Henry, Timmy, and Susan burst out laughing.

"She's trying to kill us," Henry said.

"I agree, Henry," Timmy said. "But to be specific, I'd say it's another manifestation in the vast array of her unconscious obsessions to be the only child. It's treatable."

"What?" Maggie said. "Oh. Fine. Well, how's a carrot stick instead?"

"I think we just ought to buy her a tiara," Susan said good-naturedly. "It's cheaper. Times are tough, you know."

As Beth expected and hoped, it seemed that when they all got together their amazing love for one another and their incredible wit could get them all through anything. But this was a tragedy of a magnitude they had never known. Nothing could bring back Sophie and it was doubtful that Allison would ever be herself again.

"I saw her today. It's horrible. She's had a complete psychotic breakdown," Timmy said. "Seeing her twin dead and then standing by while her boyfriend disposed of her body?" He shook his head. "It was too much for her mind. She just snapped."

"So what's the prognosis, Freud?" Henry said.

"Stabilize her with lots of drugs, give her intense therapy, and pray for her to come around. She might. She might not. She didn't even know me."

"Yikes. So, she's not coming to the funeral, I guess?" Beth asked.

"Uh, no. That wouldn't be a good idea," Timmy said.

"She's in the psych ward in lockdown, honey," Susan said, to give Beth a fuller picture. "Medicated up to her eyeballs."

"Holy crap," Beth said.

And for once Maggie agreed with Beth's choice of words. "Holy crap is right, Beth. I just wish the newspapers and television would stop talking about it. If I ever meet that insipid Nancy Grace in a dark alley, she's in big trouble with me."

The wake was to be that night between six and eight and afterward they expected a lot of people to come by the house. This was the time-honored island custom. The Bereavement Committee from Stella Maris Church had organized food for the next day after the funeral. But for that day, Maggie and Cecily had cooked and cooked. They were ready for a crowd.

All the spouses and their children were still arriving, and happily, Mary Ellen Way had thrown open the doors to her home once again.

"I read the obituary in this morning's *Post and Courier*. What a terrible shock. Your sister Sophie was an absolute darling," she said to Maggie when she called. "And Allison? Poor Allison! It's the very least I could do! I'm just so happy to help."

When Maggie repeated the conversation to the family, no one said a word about the fact that Mary Ellen Way could not bring herself to say that Allison was a darling too. Mary Ellen was a perfect lady from the top of her beautifully coiffed head to the tip of her pedicured toes, but she wasn't a liar or a phony. The stories of Allison's temperament had swept the Lowcountry long ago. What could they do except say *Thank you so much for your dear friendship and for the use of your house*? And that's exactly what they did.

Around three that afternoon, Mike and Bucky rolled in. They picked up Phillip and Blake and Timmy's boys, Luke and Mark, and took them down to the other house to settle in and to dress for the wake, which meant neckties, blazers, and no matter how much they objected, Maggie insisted, they had to wear socks.

Teensy, taking the news in stride, had flown in earlier in the day and was downtown at Bob Ellis Shoes, checking out the sales. Mary Jo's girls were on the porch, rocking and trying to stay wrinkle- and perspiration-free. Mary Jo, genuinely distraught from the news, was having a nap. And lastly, Simon and Grant were on their way to the island from the airport.

After Simon arrived and had a gooey

reunion with Susan and Grant had a meeting and update from Maggie, dinner was ready.

"We have to be there by five-thirty, so everyone had better come get a plate of food," Susan said.

They ate everything in sight and Cecily helped them clean up after their meal. Before they wanted to know it, it was time to leave. All the parents rode in their cars with their own children, giving them strict instructions on how to behave. But in each car was a sibling of Sophie's, struggling with all their might to maintain their own composure. Cecily had thoughtfully placed a box of tissues, breath mints, and some bottled water in each car, and later on, after she had gathered up the pictures of Sophie from all over the house, she would meet them there.

Cecily was deeply worried and had almost grabbed Beth by her shoulders to give her a good shake the day she returned from Coral Gables with Woody. Didn't Beth know that Max Mitchell was all over the news! The jig was up! Had Beth told her mother and had Woody told Henry the truth?

"No," Beth said, and picked up Lola, who was licking her all over her face and wiggling with frantic excitement to have her back. "It wasn't the right time."

"Well, what do you think the right time looks like? When your momma waves the bank statement in your face? And Woody? You don't think Mr. Henry Hamilton is gonna miss one hundred thousand dollars? Honey, he's still got his First Communion money! Have you both taken leave of your natural minds like Allison? Shoot! Y'all are cracked, that's what!"

"Unless they bring it up? I think we should try to get through the funeral," Woody said. "That combined with Allison's condition and that fellow Geoffrey still on the run, well, that seems like enough to digest for the moment, don't you think?"

"You're both overwrought. You listen to me. I've been knowing Henry Hamilton all my life, and if you don't give him a heads-up? He's gone chop yours off!" Cecily ran her finger across her throat and made a sound that sounded like *keeeek*.

"She's right, Woody."

That had been several days ago, but

still they could not find the right moment to come clean. Woody returned to Atlanta, promising to come back for the funeral, and Beth, very happy to know he was coming back, did not say a word about Max Mitchell to anyone else. The only people who knew Beth had an interest in investing with him were her mother and possibly her Uncle Henry. And if they weren't bringing it up, neither was she. But she felt completely terrible about everything. When she wasn't thinking about her aunts Sophie and Allison, she was thinking about Max, angry at him one minute and baffled the next by what he had done.

Everyone took her serious mood to be a hangover from the shock of being the first responder to the Sophie and Allison fiasco. Each of them had something to say to Beth about how grateful they were that she had sensed the need to act immediately, and wasn't Woody a wonderful man to take her the whole way to South Florida? Beth wanted to say, There was nothing like a haunted house with a big spooky mirror to help your instincts, but she didn't. At some point she would have her turn to

speak, but not just yet. The older generation had arrived and assumed control of
everything, including most conversations.

In the parking lot of the funeral home,
they all got out of their cars and waited for
one another. The air was heavy with the
smells of musk, a combination of wet earth,
woodsmoke, and pine straw. It always
smelled like that in certain parts of Mount
Pleasant, especially on the land where
McAlister's stood. Because they had lost
so many family members and friends, they
had come to associate that particular scent
with funerals. That and the stench of carnations reminded them of death. They
never sent one another carnations.

No one wanted to be the first person to
go inside and absolutely no one wanted to
see Sophie in a casket. But they linked
their arms with their spouses and threw an
arm around the shoulders of their children
and went in the door all the same.

They were greeted by the funeral director, who asked them if they would like to
go inside the chapel. As they stepped inside the enormous double parlor, flowers
filled the end of the room and lined the
walls. Gorgeous floral arrangements were

everywhere, enough for three funerals. The director directed his comments to Henry, who had the most hair and the most expensive suit.

"We have closed the casket, Mr. Hamilton. The deceased was embalmed in Florida, but unfortunately their heat added to the fact that she wasn't found for three days before they put her in the freezer, led to tremendous swelling. I'm afraid things didn't work out as well as one might have hoped. We did our best, of course, but I don't think it would be wise to open it, especially if there are children expected tonight."

"I knew that was going to happen," Grant said. "She's a floater, am I right?"

"Yes, that is correct." Then the director lowered his voice. "A dry floater. We even used the trocar, and as I said, we tried our very best . . ."

"What's a floater?" Henry asked.

"You don't want to know," Simon said. "We're talking swelling, discoloration . . . all sorts of nasties. Hey, pssst."

"What?" Henry said.

"I'll bet this little dude squats to pee," Simon whispered behind his hand.

Henry suppressed a laugh and nodded his head in agreement.

"Wait a minute," Maggie said. "Are you saying we don't get to see our sister to tell her goodbye?"

"That's up to y'all," the diminutive director with the shiny bald head and pursed lips said, "but I would think in this situation it would be best to remember how she looked in life."

"Cecily's bringing pictures," Beth said.

"Ah geez. Is she like really gross?" Susan asked in an uncharacteristically timid voice.

"Susan!" Maggie said.

"Yeah, for Pete's sake, Susan," Simon said, and pinched her butt.

Susan slapped his hand away and blushed. Beth witnessed their brief interaction and felt like gagging. Truly, her mother and stepfather acted like horny teenagers, and it was embarrassing. And sometimes Simon was an ass, but everyone dealt with grief in their own way. Some wept. Others like Simon made ridiculous comments and gestures because they couldn't deal with the finality and pain of death or the pain they witnessed in others. Typical doctor, Beth thought.

"You go look, Grant, and then you tell me if it's going to be too traumatic for me, okay?" Everyone looked at Maggie and she said to the funeral director, "My husband's a doctor."

"I'll go with you, pal," Simon said, and they approached the casket on the other end of the large room with the funeral director hot on their heels.

"Steel yourself, gentlemen. This is going to be difficult."

Grant gave a signal for him to raise the lid of the casket and in two seconds flat he signaled for him to lower it.

"Thank you," Grant said.

"You're welcome." The director looked away from them and walked back toward the rest of the family.

"I sure could've lived without that," Simon whispered to Grant.

"No shit, bubba."

"Grant? Well?" Maggie said. "Should we all have a look?"

"No. Definitely not. You'll be scarred for life. Is there any whiskey in our car?"

"Of course not," Maggie said, unhappy about Grant's call.

"I have a rather brilliant white Bordeaux in the cooler in the back of our car," Henry said. "Does anyone have a corkscrew?"

"Swiss Army knife?" Simon pulled it from his pocket. "I love these things. So practical."

Grant, Simon, Henry, and Timmy made their way out of the door, stopping only to avail themselves of the plastic cups from a chute attached to the side of a Poland Springs watercooler.

"They'll be back," Susan said, looking at the peculiar expression on Maggie's face. "What? You're not going to go up there and look, are you?"

"I was merely considering my options, that's all. I just don't like this. That's all. We've never had a funeral with a closed casket, that's all."

"You said *that's all* three times. You're really thinking of doing this?"

"A closed casket sends a certain message, don't you think?"

"Maggie, I love you like crazy but this wake isn't meant to impress anyone. It's to mourn Sophie's death."

"I know that, but I just don't want people to talk. You know what I'm talking about?"

"Then you'd better plan a wide-scale massacre of all the media in Charleston County, okay? That horse left the barn a long time ago."

"I'm going to ask Grant again if he was really serious."

"I'm coming," Susan said.

"I'm staying," Beth said, and moved toward her cousins Bucky and Mike.

Susan and Maggie pushed open the heavy glass door and went from the extreme refrigeration of the chapel to the Lowcountry sauna of early evening.

"Why are funeral homes always so cold?" Maggie asked.

"Probably for some reason we don't need to know tonight," Susan said.

Their husbands were clustered in the parking lot, behind Henry's SUV, engaged in an emergency tailgate wine tasting.

"Would you like a little?" Henry said. "There's plenty. I brought a case. You know, self-defense against swill?"

"Pompous ass," Timmy said.

"Sure!" Maggie said. "Thanks."

"Susan? Up yours, Timmy."

"Why not? Thanks," Susan said.

Together, they raised their cups toward the fading sky overhead.

"To Sophie!" Henry said. "We love you, girl! Wherever you are!"

"To Sophie!" they all said.

"So Grant?" Maggie said quietly.

"Yeah, honey," he said.

"She looks bad?"

"Maggie, that funeral director, dweeb that he might be, is right. She doesn't even look like herself."

"Okay," Maggie said, and choked up.

"Hey, you okay?" Susan said.

"I don't know why this is bothering me so much. I should let it go, right?" Maggie said.

"Yeah, baby," Grant said in the tenderest voice anyone had ever heard him use. "Let it go." He put his arm around her and gave her a squeeze.

They looked up to see Cecily pulling up next to their cars.

"I'll go help her," Maggie said.

"Me too," Susan said.

"How's it going?" Cecily asked when she got out of her car. "I've got a trunkful."

"Do we need the men to help?" Maggie asked.

"No, I think we can handle it."

"Did you lock up the house good? You know, that's when the robbers come. Momma always said they read the obituaries and then watch the house," Maggie said. "Y'all! It's true!"

"Momma was a paranoid," Susan said.

"I locked it from top to bottom. Don't you worry about that. I don't want anybody stealing my deviled eggs."

They carried in the boxes of framed photographs of Sophie and placed them all around the room.

"She was so pretty," Maggie said.

"Yes, she was. I hope all these pictures make you feel a little better," Susan said.

"I can't imagine what could make me feel better on a night like this," Maggie said.

Susan and Maggie looked in each other's eyes, brimming with tears, and hugged each other hard.

"Hey, we still have us, right?" Susan said.

"Thank the good Lord too."

But there *was* something that made them all feel better that night—the hundreds of people who stopped by the funeral home to offer their condolences. Most of them had a Sophie story to tell, many of them were old classmates, a few of them were old boyfriends.

I took her to our senior prom. Boy, she sure could dance. I'm so sorry for your loss. She was the sweetest girl I knew. Our whole family is praying for you. Once when we were in the tenth grade, she did my biology project for me! She was just so nice to everyone, you know? She made us all feel so good. Sophie's DVDs are the reason I can wear this dress! Golly, she had a great figure, didn't she?

On and on it went, people signing the guest book, hugging the family, checking their own flowers they sent to be sure they got their money's worth, promising to come by the house for a drink, and all of them asking if there was anything they could do. Only a very few asked about Allison, as the news was so painful and they thought the family probably had enough adjusting to do. The facts would eventually emerge.

Mostly they said, "We'll pray for her every day." What else *could* they do?

Beth's boss, Drew Harris, showed up and hugged Beth.

"The other guys wanted to come but they had to work," he said.

"That's okay," Beth said.

"Well, here's a card they all signed for you," Drew said.

"Oh, gosh, thanks so much!"

"And if you need to take the week off, I get it," he said.

Beth stood on her tiptoes and kissed his cheek. "Thanks, Drew."

And at last, Beth spotted Woody in the crowd. He came to her side immediately and took her hand.

"How's it going?" he asked.

"Gosh. I'm so glad you're here. It's okay. About as terrible as you would expect."

"I'm staying with Mike and the other guys at the Way house. I'm not too far away if you need me."

He smiled at her and she smiled at him and it occurred to both of them that they had something very special going on.

Later that night, seventy-five or so people came by just to mark the event with a little shot of O Be Joyful, which was the family euphemism for liquor, or for a glass of wine. They came to readjust their own equilibrium. There was something jarring about the death of a relatively young person that shocked everyone and left them off-balance. And by visiting the family in their time of need, especially one they had known since the sandbox, they could have a private moment to shake their heads together and ponder their own mortality.

When the last guest had gone, the family, including Woody, gathered on the dark porch to regroup.

"A lot of people practiced their Corporal Works of Mercy tonight," Maggie said after everyone had found a place to sit or perch.

"What's that?" Simon said. "What kind of work of mercy?"

"You know, feed the sick, starve the fever . . ." Henry said.

"Good grief! When's the last time you went to church?" Maggie said. "You'd better look out for lightning tomorrow!"

"Try feed the hungry, give drink to the thirsty . . ." Susan said.

"We sure did that tonight," Timmy said.

"I've got ten bucks for whoever knows them all," Henry said.

Maggie and Susan recited in stereo, "Shelter the homeless, visit the sick, clothe

the naked, comfort the imprisoned, and bury the dead."

"You two scare me. No, really!" Henry said. "Is this really what you do for fun? Sit around and memorize the Baltimore Catechism or something?"

"You're a philistine, Henry," Susan said. "That will be ten dollars, please."

"Five of that is mine," Maggie said.

They were doing what they always did when they got together, just as their parents and grandparents had done before them. They were ending their day in conversation together on the porch of the Island Gamble, having a nightcap, sipping a cup of decaf or a glass of water, the purpose of which was to make sure everyone could go to bed with their hearts unburdened. Beth was the one who still carried a heavy load, but this still wasn't the time to talk about it.

"What a night," Henry said. "Awful."

"It's more like we lost two siblings instead of one," Timmy said.

"It's the truth, isn't it?" Maggie said. "Somebody's going to have to look after Allison and I guess that should be me."

"I think we'll all help, honey. I've about

had it with California anyway," Grant said.

"Me too," Simon said. "I can do what I'm doing anywhere. I could wrap it up in a few weeks. I can help with Allison too."

"Well, that's good," Susan said, "because as Simon and Maggie know, I resigned my job in Paris. I'm already back."

"What? Mom! That's so great!" Beth went over to her mother, pulled her up from her chair, and hugged her. "This is the best news ever!"

"I think so, but hey! Now you can go on to grad school!"

"Whoa! Not so sure about that. I'm thinking I want to be here with you."

"Wow! Susan!" Timmy said. "This is news! Your lifelong dream out the window? Why'd you do this?"

"Long story. I'll tell you all about it tomorrow. I guess I'm just feeling like there's been enough change around here and with us, and I don't know. Life's flying by. I think you ought to be in a place that means something to you, you know? Not just running around the world for what? I want to try and hang on to as much sameness as I can. Does that make sense?"

"It makes perfect sense," Maggie said. "What are you going to do with yourself?"

"Oh, didn't I tell you? I'm buying the *Island Eye News.* The publisher is moving to Oak Island."

"Good grief! Am I getting fired?" Beth said.

"No, miss. It means I get to keep a closer eye on you!" Susan said.

"Y'all want to know what I hate about California? It doesn't matter if you drive north or south, the water's still on the wrong side of the road," Maggie said.

"Excellent insight," Timmy said.

"And the Pacific is a lot different from the Atlantic," Simon said. "It's scary."

"Powerful bodies of water can be enormously unnerving," Timmy said.

"I hate change," Beth said.

"You do?" Susan said.

"Yeah, if I didn't learn anything else this summer, I learned this. When the world's like this, I mean the economy and all, it doesn't take money to make you feel rich. It takes purpose. You have to know who you are and go do what you're supposed to be doing. You only learn that—I mean fully learn that—from people who love you.

I think you can be like, I don't know, even sixty and you can still learn. Your family shapes you when you're really young and then holds you together when trouble comes along. Like look at all of us? We lose Aunt Sophie, which is totally breaking my heart I loved her so much . . ."

"And she loved you too, Beth, just like she would've loved her own daughter," Susan said.

"Yeah, I know, anyway, at the end of the day, there's nothing more important in the whole world than your family."

Everyone was quiet for a few minutes and then Maggie spoke.

"*Somebody* grew up when we weren't looking! Honey, if you learned that, there's not much else you need to know."

"Gimme a high-five, girl!" Simon said, and leaned over to slap her hand.

Then there began a succession of high-fives from everyone there, the cousins, the aunts, down to the last person, except Henry, who said, "Beth? Are you saying that your family is more important than money?"

"Yes sir. A lot more important."

"Good to know."

At first, Beth wondered what he meant, and then she realized it had to do with her trust account. He knew. Well, she thought, I have said my piece, and if he disowns me, he disowns me, and I will figure that out with my mom. And Woody. There's a solution to almost everything and other things you just have to accept.

Grant, who rarely said much when Maggie's entire family was there, said, "Well, if there's a speck of good news in all of this, at least Allison doesn't have a homicide charge hanging over her."

"It would be really good news if she knew *anything* was hanging over her," Timmy said.

"She's that bad, huh?" Grant said.

"Yeah, she's that bad," Timmy said.

"I'll look in on her," Grant said. "I think I've got an old friend at MUSC who's pretty experienced with psychosis. I'll call him after the funeral tomorrow."

"Um, Maggie? Not that I would have any objection whatsoever," Susan asked, "but are we talking about all of us living here in the house together?"

"No, darlin', I found a little house on the Internet that's downtown on Rutledge

Avenue. It's close enough to walk to the hospital. I want to be downtown to be near Allison."

"*Little* house?" Grant said. "Maggie, that is *not* a little house!"

"But it's got so much personality! And possibility. Anyway, in this recession there are bargains all over the place. And we still have to go see it, darlin'."

"I think someone in this family ought to buy a house in someplace like I'on, where it's all new, everything works, and the house doesn't give you any sass," Beth said.

"Oh, sweetheart! Did the house give you a hard time?" Susan said.

"Let's just say it will be refreshing to have some company with flesh and blood, okay? Let's just start there."

"I'm afraid I need to turn in," Woody said. "So, I'm going to say good night."

"Hey, Woody," Henry said, and stood to shake his hand, "thanks for the trip to Florida. If it wasn't for you and Beth, our sister might still be in the Sub-Zero and the other one might be thrashing about. Y'all saved the day."

"It was just a hunch," Woody said. "Glad I could help."

"Those guts and hunches are worth a lot to us, Woody," Henry said, prolonging his handshake. "We'll see you tomorrow."

Beth walked Woody to his car when he was leaving.

"Henry was giving me some very funny looks," he said. "He knows."

"Hell yeah, he knows. I think he's having a hard time hating our guts," she said.

"Florida may have saved us."

"Your mouth, God's ears, right?"

"Yeah."

He unlocked his car and it beeped loudly. Then he stood there for a moment just looking at her.

"What?"

"Nothing," he said.

"Yeah, sure," she said, smiling.

"Whatever," he said.

In that exchange, a romance was born that would possibly, maybe, might lead to something more serious or not. But they were willing to give it a try after certain details were ironed out which had yet to be discussed, namely, Max Mitchell. And their deceit.

"Get some sleep," he said.

Despite the sorrow of the family, the sun

rose the next morning with the promise of a beautiful South Carolina day. The weather did not match their mood.

They were unusually quiet as they went about the business of breakfast, and dressing and gathering into their cars to return to the funeral home. There they would transfer to limousines and form a procession behind the hearse that held the remains of Sophie Hamilton.

They were solemn as the funeral director ushered them into each car, and in a moment of kindness, Susan asked Woody to ride with them. Simon, Henry, and Teensy were in the car as well. As they pulled away from the curb, Susan spoke.

"Beth? There is no good time to talk about this, but since Uncle Henry is going back to Atlanta tomorrow, we might as well do this now."

Beth was caught off guard, but actually she knew the hammer was coming so she took a deep breath. She looked at Woody, who nodded, letting her know he was ready to defend her.

"My trust account, right?"

"Yes."

"Momma, I am so sorry, you have no idea."

"I am assuming you thought you had legitimate reasons, am I right?"

"Of course. But can we talk about the details when we get home?"

"It doesn't matter now, Beth. Things are as they are. How could you deceive us like that?"

"I was in love with him."

"Love? Beth, this was a very serious breach of trust between us, you know."

"Oh, Momma? But what can I do now?"

"Nothing, except work hard to regain our trust, Beth."

"Mrs. Rifkin?" Woody said.

Susan was so unaccustomed to being referred to as anything except Susan that she was startled.

"Max Mitchell was the most impressive charlatan I have ever met. He had me completely fooled and I am pretty good at assessing risk."

"You're the finest judge of character I have ever met, young man, which is why I am not firing you. But if anything like this ever happens again, you find me and tell me what's happening, okay? I don't care where I am on the planet," Henry said.

"Yes sir. Thank you, sir."

"Beth?" Henry said. "Your Aunt Sophie had a will and I am the executor of her estate."

"She did?"

"Yes. A sizable one, but then you know she was a *very* wealthy woman. She even had more money than I do, it seems."

"Oh, get on with it, Henry," Susan said. "The contest is over."

"Well, Beth, your Aunt Sophie had enough assets to bail you out of your hole and still leave an additional two hundred and fifty thousand dollars to you and all her other nieces and nephews."

"Oh! My goodness! Is this a good thing? I mean, who's going to pay for Aunt Allison's care?"

"Well, that's a very good question, and it's especially nice that this is your first concern. The ability to maintain their business is completely truncated by this tragedy. Allison and Sophie had excellent health care, as you would expect. But we don't know how long Allison will be hospitalized. So there are many unknowns about how to place a value on what they own, and many questions remain about how or why we should dispose of certain parts of it. There are all the studios, their house, their art collection, and Sophie's personal effects, which she also wanted you to have."

"Gosh."

Beth didn't know what to think. It was obviously complicated and beyond the experience of her years.

"What are you thinking, Beth?"

"I'm thinking that I'd rather have my Aunt Sophie back than all the money in the world."

"And that is precisely why we are not going to kill you, sweetheart. You made a very dumb mistake, and someday, like first thing tomorrow, you can tell me why. But today, it doesn't matter. We are all together again and eventually everything's going to be all right."

The funeral procession crossed the Ben Sawyer Bridge and Beth could not help but notice again that the colors were brighter and the edges of every house and leaf and the wings of all the birds were sharper and more clear than they were in

Mount Pleasant, and not because her tears had washed her eyes clean. The island was putting on her Sunday best to honor one of its daughters, Sophie Hamilton. And also because the island wanted Beth and every single one of her family, indeed every single other resident and visitor, to appreciate it for all that it was and, perhaps more important, what it was not. The island was not slick and shiny, nor subject to the fads of the day. No. It truly was the land of their ancestors where their spirits still walked. Sullivans Island welcomed them and watched over them all with a mindful eye and a loving heart, one as real, as grand, and as all-encompassing as your imagination could ever be.

EPILOGUE

The day after the funeral, the family began to disperse. Timmy and his family to Charlotte, Henry and his to Atlanta. Only Maggie, Grant, Simon, and Woody remained.

Woody was reluctant to leave Beth, worried about how she would fare explaining herself to her mother and the others, but by five-thirty in the afternoon they said their goodbyes.

"You'll come back, I hope?" Beth said, her hands resting on the side of his opened car window.

He reached over and covered her hand with his. "Of course I will. As fast as I can.

In fact—and I never thought I'd say this—
I'm sort of afraid to leave."

"Afraid? Why?"

"I don't know. I might miss something?
In any case, this place has some kind of
a magnetic pull on you."

"Oh, just a little one, about the size of
the moon."

"Maybe it's not just the place . . ."

Beth smiled at him. Life would never
be the same again for either of them.

"Oh, Woody, what would I have done
without you?"

"Let's hope we don't have to worry about
that for at least a hundred years or so."

"Woody!"

"What?"

Beth sighed hard, smiled wide, arched
her eyebrow, and said, "I'm thinking that
sounds like an excellent plan, Mr. Morrison."

"Good, Miss Hayes. I'll call you tonight."

"Drive safely, for Pete's sake, will you? I
don't think we could bear any more drama."

"Don't worry."

He blew her a kiss and she blew one
back to him.

Beth stood watching him back away

from her house while Cecily watched from the kitchen window with Susan.

"He's a really wonderful guy," Cecily said.

"Yeah, I mean, given all the dynamics and the circumstances of the last ten days, he surely behaved like a thoroughbred, didn't he? Amazing."

"Yes. Yes, he did."

"I hope she doesn't rush into anything with him."

"I don't think we have to worry about her rushing into anything with anyone ever again."

"Yeah. Just the geographic separation will help slow the pace of things."

Maggie had wandered into the room with the morning paper.

"What are y'all talking about? What'd I miss?"

"We're just talking about Woody and what a fine young man he is."

"Honey? That boy's a dreamboat, and if Beth has a brain in her head, she's not letting him get away."

"I don't think she will," Cecily said.

"Yeah. That fish is on the hook," Susan said, and arched her eyebrow at them.

"Y'all wanna see something? Look 'eah."

Maggie spread the newspaper across the kitchen table to show them a picture of Max Mitchell. Then she sat a framed photograph of Beth's deceased father Tom right next to it.

"Y'all see what I see?"

"Great jumping Jehosophat! He's . . . he's the spitting image of Tom! Max could be his little brother!"

"My goodness!" Cecily said. "Let me see that again?"

"Timmy pointed it out to me. Sorry to say, I can't take the credit."

"What did he say?" Susan asked.

"Just what you'd think Uncle Sigmund would say. Honey? That crook Max was nothing but a substitute daddy for her. But Timmy did say that somebody had better help her see that or it could play itself out over and over again. And heaven knows *we* don't need *that*!"

Cecily looked at Susan and said, "Lawsa. Well, if that's true, there's no one who can have that conversation with her except you."

"There are quite a few things we need to talk about. I'll add this to the list."

"Ssssh! She's coming," Cecily said.

Beth opened the screen door and came into the kitchen, where her mother, her aunt, and her friend stood in silence. She knew they had been talking about her.

"What's going on?" Beth said. "Has the jury reached a verdict?"

"Darlin'? Don't be so cynical," Maggie said. "It causes wrinkles. And you know we love you. Nobody's judging you. Now, I don't think I would've done the same—"

"Maggie! You old woman! Can't you remember what it was like to fall head over heels in love?"

"It's been a while, I'll admit."

"I can," Cecily said. "I've met a man. His name is Niles. Isn't that the most beautiful name in the world? I can't stop thinking about him morning, noon, and night. It's like love put a spell on me. No, not a regular spell, but a cunja spell! Niles! I'm about to lose my mind. I'm not kidding, y'all. I mean, when I wake up his name is on my lips. Just last night when he brought me home, I ran and got my pillowcase and rubbed it on his neck. I know he thought I was crazy, but I wanted to smell him all night. And he just laughed when I told him why and he said no one had ever done that before. I'm going to marry him and he knows it."

Maggie stared at her, dumbfounded. She had never heard Cecily talk about her private life beyond remembering Livvie. Susan and Beth burst into giggles and threw their arms around Cecily, saying, *You'd better watch yourself! Be careful! You'd better find out all about him! What does he do for a living? Is he a good kisser? No more details, please! Who are his people?* But the three of them went on, giggling like silly schoolgirls, while Maggie stood on the sidelines, still paralyzed in amazement. Cecily had a deeply important romance in full swing and she never suspected it at all. But then why would she?

"How does he know?" Maggie said

"Because we just know it. Isn't that crazy?"

"Don't ask me," Beth said. "I'm no longer qualified to judge anything when it comes to love."

"Oh yeah?" Cecily said, laughing. "What about Woody?"

"Woody? He's completely different!"

"That's the first sign that you're falling, shugah," Maggie said. "And you could do a whole lot worse than Woody."

"I *have* done a whole lot worse than Woody, y'all might recall?" She hooked her thumb in the direction of the newspaper. "What's Daddy's picture doing here?"

"Doodle? Why don't you come take a walk with me on the beach? It's low tide and the beach is almost empty."

"Why not? Should I bring Lola?"

"Sure. It's almost six."

"I'll go throw on some shorts," Beth said, and picked up her father's picture to take it back to her room.

She ran to her room to change, smelling lemons as she passed by the living room and just a trace of her father's cologne when she reached the hallway outside her door.

"So bizarre," she said.

Beth's bedroom was neat and tidy, and when she replaced the frame where it lived on her bedside table, the room seemed complete. She changed, pulled her hair up into a messy bun, and raced down the steps.

"I'm out here with the baby!" Susan called from the porch. "Ready, miss?"

"Yep, let's go."

"Y'all get back before too long, okay?" Maggie called out. "Cecily and I are frying fish and Grant likes his dinner before eight!"

"Okay!"

They crossed the dunes together. Beth knew her mother was going to give her a lecture about Max Mitchell and that was fine with her. But she felt sick in her heart knowing that the second part of that lecture was going to be about trust.

They walked for a while in relative silence, mentioning Lola's remarkable sense of smell and how beautiful their beach was to them.

"Some people prefer Hawaii," Susan said.

"Well, it's supposed to be incredible," Beth said. "But that's a long way to go for a swim, isn't it?"

"I think so. This beach is plenty for me."

"Me too."

Silence again and Beth could feel her mother's disappointment swelling. Apparently she was having trouble deciding where to begin. Beth thought then that she would help her by bringing it up herself.

"I know you are very upset with me, Mom, and I don't blame you."

"That's putting it mildly, Beth."

"I'm sure. What can I do?"

"You can start by helping me understand what in the world was going on in your mind."

Susan stopped and handed Lola's leash to Beth, and even though it was done politely, it was as though she was renouncing some of her affection for her dog too.

"My head? To be perfectly honest, Mom, it was more about my heart. I met Max and it was like, *boom!* That was it. I was out of my mind in love with him from square one. If he had asked me to jump off a building, I probably would have believed that he had my best interest at heart."

Susan searched Beth's face and she knew that her young daughter, her beautiful daughter, the person she cherished above all others, was being completely honest with her.

"Good grief. How in the world did this happen to you? I mean, you've never stolen a thing in your life and along comes this guy, Max. Inside of just a few weeks, you commit fraud? Do you see why I am having a problem understanding this?"

"Yeah, of course. Mom. *I'm* having a problem understanding this. I'm so ashamed of myself I could die."

"Well, don't die. We've had enough of that to last us for another decade at least."

"That's for sure."

"Look, Beth, your Uncle Timmy has this crazy idea that might not be so crazy after all."

"What?"

"Well, I don't know if you noticed this or not, but there is a really frightening resemblance between your father and Max. They could be brothers! Uncle Timmy thinks that in some way you might have fallen into this whole mess because of it. When I heard that—"

"Who did he tell this to?"

"Aunt Maggie."

"Oh great."

"Don't worry about her right now. What I'm trying to say is that it left me to wonder that if Timmy's right, how much grieving is still going on in your heart? And if you're still grieving for your father, why don't I know this? I mean, I am closer to you than anyone I have ever known. Why wouldn't you tell me?"

"Mom? Did you ever get over the death of your father?"

They were stopped then, facing each other in the strong breeze that was coming in from the east.

"That's an interesting question, because Tom was the complete opposite of my father. I think I came to accept both deaths, over time. My father's death was a terrible shock to the family, you know. And, we *knew* Tom was dying, so it was very different. But my mother didn't. She cried every single day for the rest of her life."

"Even though she got married again?"

"Yep."

"Well, that explains all the havoc in her old room, I guess. But still, you had three sisters, two brothers, and Livvie to help you handle it. Who did I have?"

"You had me and Aunt Maggie and our whole family."

"No, I really didn't. Everyone thought that Daddy got the punishment he deserved and y'all were divorced by then. Remember?"

"Of course I remember. But even if they thought it, no one ever said that in front of you. No one."

"Maybe. Look, your ex-husband was dying. It was my father who was dying."

"And you think no one gave you the support you needed."

"That's right, Mom. You all hung me out to dry."

"Oh my God, Beth. It might have seemed like we did. But I certainly *never* meant to make you feel that way. You should know that."

"I do know that, but it's really hard to get past the things like there's not a picture of him in the house except the one I have."

"I didn't want to make Simon feel awkward, honey."

"Whatever. And no one ever talks about him except to say something terrible."

"Look, Beth, he was their brother-in-law who ran around on me and that's the truth. It would be completely weird and crazy for the family to go around singing his praises."

"But he was my father. Look, I think about Daddy every single day and I pray for him every single night. I feel like I'm all alone in remembering him."

"Oh, Beth. I think about him all the time! I was dead in love with him! Without him there would be no you!"

"True. Guess what? I can smell his cologne all the time."

"You can?"

"Yeah. Especially upstairs."

"He's just checking on you."

"I guess. And every time I hear somebody say something terrible about him, like Aunt Allison did before you left for Paris? I want to run away and cry my eyes out. I mean, who's going to walk me down the aisle, that is, if I ever lose my mind and decide to get married?"

"Simon will. Or anyone you want . . ."

"Not the same, Mom. Where was he when I graduated from high school and college, and where is he on Thanksgiving and Christmas? Or my birthday? Do you understand that there's a hole in my life that no one can fill? Ever?"

"Yes, because I felt the same way when my father died."

"I guess you probably did. I don't know.

Maybe there's a part of me that fell for Max because he seemed like he would make me whole and protect me. Absolutely. But I'm just saying that no one should expect me to just get over it or to ever understand why Daddy preferred to spend his last days with Karen instead of us."

"Beth. He didn't reject *you*. He rejected *me*. He loved you with every bit of his heart."

"No he didn't."

"Yes he did! He left you every dime he ever earned. He didn't leave Karen the extra buttons from his shirts! And remember, when he was sick, he turned to us. Because he trusted us. He trusted *us* to take care of him."

"But he didn't want to spend his final days with us."

"No, he didn't want to spend his final days with *me,* and listen, he told me that he didn't want you to see him so sick. He thought he was protecting you from seeing something terrible. Parents like to do that, you know."

"He did?"

"Yes, he did."

"You never told me that!"

"I didn't? Well, wouldn't you assume that by now anyway?"

"No! I was just a kid!"

"Sometimes I think you're like already forty."

"I guess I have mature moments and really stupid ones, as you know."

"That has very little to do with chronological age."

"You're right. Well, listen, maybe he was a lousy husband to you, but I have lots of memories of him being a great father to me."

"Beth, you seem to have a short memory on the details. I always supported your relationship with him. I can't help what other people say."

"You're right and I know that. Anyway, I did a really, really stupid thing by giving Max all that money. I know that. And I guess some of this is tied up in a daddy thing. But one thing is for sure, nothing like that will ever happen again. I learned my lesson."

"I sure hope so."

"I just want to know how I can make things right between us again, Mom. Please! What can I do to make you trust me again?"

"Beth, I completely forgive you for what you did and I think I understand the why of it better now. But that still doesn't justify forging a document and committing fraud."

"I know."

"Trust? Let's be serious, Beth. That's just going to take some time. What else can I say? You did a terrible thing! It was criminal! You have to take responsibility for that. It's just going to take time for me to believe in you completely. I mean, I know that someday I will, but right now I feel very betrayed."

"So what can I do to speed up the process?"

"You know the old saying, Beth. Actions speak louder than words, right?"

"Yes ma'am."

"And you know what? I'm sorry that I didn't do a better job for you to help you deal with your daddy's death. From here on out, anytime you want to talk about him, I'm ready to listen."

"Lousy grief counseling doesn't justify fraud. I still can't believe that I did this."

"Me either. So, what about Iowa?"

"Maybe someday, but not for now. I think that now I need to be around you so I can get my head back on straight. I want Uncle Henry to keep all my money from Aunt Sophie and not let me near it."

"That's a good idea, Beth. Anyway, I don't think it's all that great to be alone."

"Right? Or that healthy. What about Paris?"

"Well, it's still in France and it appears that now I have a newspaper to run. And guess what?"

"What?"

"Maggie wants to write a column on food, another one on decorating with found objects, and another one on advice."

"Holy crap! It shouldn't surprise me at all."

"Who's more qualified to do it?"

"No one!"

"You can cover the community news, the calendars, and if you're very, very good, I'll let you handle the police blotter."

"My favorite! I love to read that, see what kind of varmints are around. You know what, Mom?"

"What?"

"I already miss Aunt Sophie something terrible."

"I know you do. So do I."

"Do you think she'll come back to the house?"

"Who can say? But if I know her? She will if she can."

"Maybe Livvie can help her."

When they got home, it was in the cool of the evening. They knocked the sand out of their shoes, put Lola in her crate, and found a place at the table. They had a delicious dinner of flounder, salad, and whatever was left over from Sophie's funeral lunch.

"Too bad this fried chicken only comes around when someone dies," Maggie said. "This is the best crust I've ever had in my whole life!"

"Ask the church ladies for the recipe for the paper," Susan said.

"Great idea!"

"Hey, Mom?"

"What, Doodle?"

The fact that her mother called her *Doodle* relieved her and gave her hope that she had advanced an inch or so, back inside the château's walls.

"You know what would be really nice?"

"What?"

"If we gave Cecily free advertising for

her business. I mean, right? After all she does for us?"

"Why not? Great idea!"

"Now you're thinking like a Hamilton," Maggie said. "Tell me, do you think Woody's coming back soon?"

"Oh yeah," Beth said.

"You sound mighty confident about that," Simon said.

"I put sand in his shoes," Beth said.

"And once you've got Sullivans Island sand in your shoes?" Grant said.

"Your heart will ache to return," Beth said, finishing the old saying.

"Strange but true," Simon said.

Later, when Cecily left, Grant and Simon decided to go down to Dunleavy's to check the temperature of the beer. Beth was upstairs working on an article about Max Mitchell's ponzi scheme. Susan and Maggie drifted out to the porch. They sat for a while, rehashing Susan's talk with Beth, Sophie's funeral, and all the things that had happened in the few weeks that had passed since Susan had left for Paris. About an hour went by and soon they heard Beth's footsteps coming down the stairs. She stopped at the screen door.

"Y'all want anything? I'm going to the kitchen to get a Coke."

"No, we're good, sweetheart."

"Thanks, Doodle."

A few seconds later they heard her screaming for them.

"Mom! Aunt Maggie! Come quickly! Hurry!"

Susan and Maggie jumped up from their rockers and found Beth in the living room, staring into the mirror.

"Look!"

On the other side of the glass, there stood Livvie in a housedress and an apron. She reached into her pocket and pulled out a handful of something and threw it into the air around her. Hundreds of butterflies, of every color there is in the world, swirled and fluttered all over the inside of the mirror, from top to bottom.

"Merciful Mother of God!" Maggie cried out. "Livvie! What does it mean?"

"It's Aunt Sophie," Beth said. "She's all right."

"My goodness!" Susan said.

"What do butterflies have to do with Sophie?" Maggie said.

"Uh . . ." Beth said, and told her Sophie's secret.

"You couldn't pay me to get a tattoo," Maggie said. "Nasty."

"We know that," Susan said with a laugh. "Would you just *look* at this?"

"Livvie!" Beth said. "Is everything all right?"

Livvie just smiled, nodded her head, and faded away. They stood there until the last butterfly had disappeared.

"This house drives me insane," Beth said.

"Don't say that," Maggie said. "You know insanity runs in the family."

"I think it's cool," Susan said.

Maggie cut her eyes at Susan in a suspicious look and Beth faced her mother with her eyebrow finally in a perfect arch.

"Okay," Susan added, "sometimes it's cool. Not all the time . . ."

Maggie, Grant, and Simon returned to California, making all the preparations to return to the Lowcountry. To their great sorrow, Allison's condition remained unchanged but there were new drugs in the works, drugs that Grant and Simon told them all might be of great help in bringing Allison around.

With them gone for a while, Beth and her mother had the time to cocoon and compare notes. The Island Gamble was calmer and you could hear the walls sigh from time to time, relieved to have its family searching for resolutions. The slamming and the thumps were gone. Beth and Susan were grateful for the peace. It had been years since Susan had examined the great heartaches of her life, and once Beth started talking about hers, it was all she could do to stop for a breath. Over and over, they would remark to each other that the pain of losing their fathers at a young age was almost unbearable; they had grown up to love the wrong men, had their hearts broken, and their confidence shaken to the core. But with each passing day and on the turn of each tide, they found new strength and faith in each other, something that could not be bought with all the riches of the world. Night after night, in the arms of the Island Gamble, over the sounds of the sea and the smells of salt and jasmine, they laughed and cried, healing each other with compassion, and in that journey, rediscovered the most important asset they shared, the love they had for each other, for every family member, and always for Sullivans Island.

ACKNOWLEDGMENTS

Everywhere I go, people tell me their stories about Sullivans Island. Perhaps they spent their childhoods there, vacationed there, fell in love there, or raised their own children there. Maybe they had only one meal there, or took a walk on the beach. It doesn't matter how brief the experience may have been, their eyes light up with the glow of a perfect memory, and I want to thank them first, most especially Reavis Davis of Sullivans Island for her wonderful memories and Kay White of Columbia for her terrific stories from Pell Pozaro. I cannot begin to tell you how much I enjoyed reading them. They brought back my childhood so vividly I could almost smell the plough mud! Many thanks.

Important things happen on Sullivans Island, lives are changed forever by events you never forget. And you may say that all islands are like that, or that people's lives are changed by events that happen anywhere and the location is immaterial. Anyone who's been to Sullivans Island is snickering right about now because we who know the island know better. It's a magical place, a tiny enchanted sandbar. So if you've told me your story, you might find a slice of it in these pages and I thank you for sharing so generously.

To my agent and great friend Larry Kirshbaum, the grandest of all gentlemen in New York, huge love and thanks for his excellent counsel, friendship, and patience. And to Susanna Einstein of LJK Literary Management, many thanks for your friendship, and for obvious reasons I'd like to borrow your name from time to time, if that's okay with you.

To my editor, Carrie Feron, whose patience alone is going to jettison her through the pearly gates straight to the throne next to the Blessed Mother—no time soon please—and whose vision and excellent editorial work is why this story hangs together and whose good humor has been the savior of us all, I bow and scrape. And to Lola, her precious pooch, thanks for being Beth's dog too!

And to the über Jedis at William Morrow and Avon: Brian Murray, Michael Morrison, Liate Stehlik, Adrienne DiPietro, Tessa Woodward, Lynn Grady, Tavia Kowalchuk, Seale Ballenger, Ben Bruton, Virginia Stanley, Bobby Brinson, Jamie Brickhouse, Rachel Bressler, Michael Brennan, Carl Lennertz, Carla Parker, Michael Morris, Michael Spradlin, Brian Grogan, and my new friends in California, Gabe Barillas and Deb Murphy (many thanks for your incredible hospitality), thank you one and all for your wonderful, generous support—love and kisses to you!

To Pamela Redmond Satran, Mary Jane Clark, Debbie Galant, Deborah Davis, Benilde Little, Christina Baker Kline, and Liza Dawson, my New Jersey faves, huge thanks for your friendship and wit.

To Jack Alterman for this gorgeous cover of our beloved island on which this story unfolds, and for my author photo too.

To my dear friend Buzzy Porter, thanks for being so great at every turn and for everything you do. See ya this summer at Chick-fil-A!

Oh, Debbie Zammit? We're still alive! I'm sending you tons of love and megatons of thanks for keeping me on track, for your meticulous scrutiny, for your crazy humor, and most of all for the tuna salad. I love ya, Miss Deb, for everything!

To Ann Del Mastro, Mary Allen, George Zur, and Kevin Sherry—the Franks adore you all and deeply appreciate all you do to keep our wheels turning.

To Penn Sicre, my friend of so many years it's almost unbelievable, many thanks for your faith.

I curtsy to my cousin Charles "Comar" Blanchard of Mount Pleasant, South Carolina, for about a million reasons and he knows them all better than I do!

To the real people who appear as characters in these pages—Mary Ellen Way, Drew Harris, Billy Condon, Robert Klotz, Alan Palmer, Jessie Jacobs, Bridget Welch, Mike Coker, Hailey Nagel from the very cool Allure Salon in Charleston, Chief Dan Howard, Judge Steve Steinert, Barbara Farlie, Brigitte Miklaszewski, Dr. George Durst, Vicki Crafton, her fabulous husband Tom Warner and their precious dog Mac—if your character acts out of character, the fault is mine, not yours, or you could tell the curious that you were just acting. In any case, I hope you all get a kick out of seeing your names in print. I send you all much love and thanks!

To three of the finest gentlemen to whom Sullivans Island has ever played home: Marshall Stith and Larry Dodds, and Everett Presson, many thanks for your advice, for your unfailing friendship, and for helping to fill in the blanks. Love y'all forever!

And to the booksellers across the land— and I mean every last one of them— especially Patti Morrison, Larry Morey, Rachel Carnes, and every single sainted soul from Barnes & Noble in Mount Pleasant, South Carolina; Tom Warner and Vicki Crafton of Litchfield Books in Pawleys Island, South Carolina; Jennifer McCurry of Waldenbooks in Charleston; Margot Sage-El of Watchung Booksellers in Montclair, New Jersey; Frazer Dobson and Sally Brewster of Park Road Books in Charlotte, North Carolina; and Jacquie Lee of Books-A-Million—how can I ever thank you for the many ways you have changed my life and my family's life for the better. I owe you so much and I thank you profusely for it all.

And to the ones who suffer most when it's deadline time or the muse won't speak, my wonderful husband, Peter, and our glorious children, Victoria and William, I love you with all my heart, and at the end of the day you are who matters most in my life.

Finally, to my readers, to whom I owe the greatest debt. I send you so many sincere thanks for reading my stories, sending along so many nice emails, and for coming out to book signings in all kinds of weather, especially when there are so many demands on your time. You're the reason I continue to write, and I hope someday you'll all come to Sullivans Island and get some of that magical sand in your shoes!

I love you all!